SHADOWS OVER THE SUN

SHADOWS OVER THE SUN

Elizabeth Darrell

This first world edition published in Great Britain 2004 by
SEVERN HOUSE PUBLISHERS LTD of
9–15 High Street, Sutton, Surrey SM1 1DF.
This first world edition published in the USA 2005 by
SEVERN HOUSE PUBLISHERS INC of
595 Madison Avenue, New York, N.Y. 10022.

British Library Cataloguing in Publication Data

Darrell, Elizabeth, 1931-
    Shadows over the sun
    1. Missing persons - Investigation - Singapore - Fiction
    2. Singapore - Fiction
    3. Suspense fiction
    I. Title
    823.9'14 [F]

    ISBN 0-7278-6170-0

Typeset by Palimpsest Book Production Ltd.,
Polmont, Stirlingshire, Scotland.
Printed and bound in Great Britain by
MPG Books Ltd., Bodmin, Cornwall.

Acknowledgements

I am deeply indebted to Dr Gordon Turnbull FRCP, FRCpsych, who, during his long years of service with the Royal Air Force, debriefed British Gulf War prisoners and the Beirut hostages, and is recognized as a leading authority on all aspects of military trauma.

My warm thanks are due to a great team of Army Air Corps men at the Army School of Aviation, who were responsible for my brief flirtation with Apache and Lynx helicopters.

Also to Group Captain C. B. Le Bas, former RAF Defence Adviser to the British High Commission, Singapore, who generously gave his time providing me with an insight to his work.

And to Chris Apperley, retired supervisor diver with the Cheshire Constabulary, who told me many tales of what can be found in the murky depths!

One

Hereford, December 2001

Forbes Nesbitt had a strong aversion to men who were high achievers. The one he had come to SAS Headquarters to meet was that and more. Nesbitt's own military service had been brief and undistinguished; his career in Intelligence had been longer but no more exciting. Opportunities to shine had eluded him and he was today being used as no more than a bloody errand boy. An errand boy of fifty-five waiting in the office of a renowned colonel for the arrival of a 29-year-old military whizz-kid.

According to his Army record, Nick Hawkwood had romped through Sandhurst collecting awards for shooting, war studies and sport. On the Army Air Corps pilots' course he had been rated outstanding. Two years in Northern Ireland during the height of the bitterness, two with the Sultan of Oman's army, two on attachment to the RAF with service in Bosnia and eighteen months as commander of this Special Forces flight had given Hawkwood every opportunity to build his reputation as one of the Army's top helicopter heroes. The reason for Nesbitt's visit would earn the bastard further kudos. Small wonder this wait was testing his patience.

Colonel Franklin remained urbane over tea and biscuits. 'Christmas grows more expensive every year, don't you find? My boys want the latest computer gismos, and as for the girl . . .'

A rap on the door heralded a tall blond captain in flying gear. He looked worried as his glance rested on a civilian visitor, then on the Colonel. 'Message said you wanted to see me urgently, sir, so I've come straight from the debrief.'

Chris Franklin smiled reassuringly. 'It's nothing of a personal nature, Nick. The urgency arises because Mr Nesbitt has to get back to London tonight, and driving conditions are worsening.'

'They are for flying. I've just grounded everyone for twenty-four.' His calm green gaze rested on Nesbitt. 'The snow's bad over Hereford and Gloucester, but you should have a relatively easy run after that. From the air the major roads looked passable.' He stood waiting for his CO to explain his summons.

Franklin remained behind his desk, cup and saucer in hand. 'Mr Nesbitt is with the Firm.' He used the familiar term for the Secret Intelligence Service. 'He has something to discuss with you.'

Hawkwood looked surprised but offered his hand. He had a strong grip and a smile that would weaken even geriatric female knees. 'Sorry to have kept you hanging around. Had a refuelling problem in addition to the deteriorating weather.' He drew forward a chair and sat without invitation.

Nesbitt was further irritated. It was all so damn casual compared with his own service days. Franklin even offered the man a cup of tea. The social nicety gave Nesbitt the opportunity to assess Hawkwood visually. Self-assured to the point of arrogance; built like the athlete his record claimed him to be. Not particularly good looking, he nevertheless had that 'Action Man' charisma women went for wholesale. Clear, intelligent eyes, clipped speech and nervous energy all supported the written plaudits Nesbitt envied. Hawkwood would surely make General at an early age – if he lived that long. The daredevil streak that gained him laurels could just as easily bring his destruction. Yet it was that very quality that had singled him out for this exacting mission.

Realizing Franklin had finally given him the floor, Nesbitt addressed the pilot. 'Three days from now one of our covert agents will be at a pre-arranged rendezvous. He will have someone with him. They have to be picked up under cover of darkness and to precise timing. The passenger is of highly nervous disposition, so any delay or miscalculation will ruin the operation. Our agent has taken enormous risks to bring this off and if the passenger takes fright there'll be no more hope of lifting him.' He added with unconscious pomposity, 'The mission carries a top security tag.'

'So the identity of the passengers can't be revealed,' said Hawkwood with professional understanding.

Nesbitt nodded sagely giving the impression that he was in on the secret, not simply an errand boy.

'And the location?'

'Iraq.'

Hawkwood frowned. 'There'll be a back-up aircraft?'

Franklin intervened. 'Another crew will be on standby, but you'll go in alone, Nick.'

The pilot reacted strongly. '*I* can't take it on. I'm scheduled to fly to the States.'

'You'll only be away five days. Back here in time for turkey and Christmas pud before you join the Apache programme on the twenty-eighth.' As Hawkwood made to protest further the Colonel forestalled him. 'You've been adjudged the best man for this high-profile mission. I back that decision.'

'But—'

'I'll leave you to choose your co-pilot and standby crew. You'll all fly out from RAF Benson tomorrow,' Franklin said decisively.

Nesbitt felt a stab of satisfaction to see Hawkwood so effectively silenced. He knew the young pilot had been selected as the first to be taught how to handle the formidable American attack helicopter about to be taken into service by the British. He was now discovering the penalties of being a military smart-arse.

Drawing a sealed envelope from his briefcase, Nesbitt handed it to the Colonel. Only he and the two pilots he would brief would know the location and timing for the lifting of someone who must surely be someone connected to Hussein.

After the briefing, the documents would be shredded. The standby crew would be told only on a need-to-know basis.

There was a short discussion on the coded messages to be used if the mission was aborted by the covert agent, or by SIS in London, and those to be transmitted by Hawkwood on successful completion of the pick-up. Then Nesbitt closed his briefcase and stood.

'My part in this is over. The rest is up to you.'

'We haven't touched on the codeword if *I* have to abort,' Hawkwood pointed out brusquely.

It gave Nesbitt further satisfaction to say, 'That's not considered an option. This mission is too vital.' He shook hands with Franklin. 'Thank you for the tea. Now I have to face a treacherous drive back to London.'

In his car he gave no thought to a hazardous, low-level night flight across hostile territory to an exact rendezvous to pick up persons unknown. If men yearned to be heroes they must accept the dangers. His only concern was a slow, uncomfortable drive over icy roads back to a carping wife who never allowed him to forget he was a nonentity.

The heaving deck of an aircraft carrier had never been Nick Hawkwood's preferred launch pad. Especially not tonight, when everything was washed by luminous moonlight. There would be little that was covert about this mission. At whatever height they flew they would be visible from afar. At less than a hundred feet even dozy camels would know they were there. The only plus was the precise timing of the extraction. Fast in and fast out! He and Andy Lisle had worked together on the details; checked then re-checked. They knew the successful pilot was the one who took off knowing that if anything went wrong it would not be due to personal carelessness.

The LSRV was in a small wadi two hundred miles south of Baghdad; the pick-up timed for 02.30 *exactly*. At the briefing this condition had become self-explanatory. The wadi was near – too damned near for the pilots' liking – a well-defined desert road and within range of a known rocket site.

No place to hang around in. Nick had vigorously questioned the choice of RV to be told it had to be there, or forget the whole thing.

The SIS were being secretive in the extreme over this mission. Chris Franklin and the crews involved reckoned the man being brought out must be one of Saddam's top military henchmen. So the risk factor was offset by the excitement of maybe lifting an Iraqi top gun from beneath Saddam's nose.

Once he knew this would not prevent his starting the Apache programme – something he dearly wanted and saw as the ultimate accolade – Nick recognized the kudos a successful result would add to his service record. This was a big one. No room for a screw-up.

Four pilots and two gunners had flown out from RAF Benson thirty-six hours ago. They had slept well and were all hyped-up. The stand-by crew were highly envious and disappointed that nothing had occurred to call them into action. One claimed he had made wax figures of Nick and Co., and stuck pins in them while muttering curses. They had laughed and promised him the option of sticking pins in the hush-hush passengers they brought back.

There had been no instruction from SIS London, or from their agent on the ground, to abort the mission, so Nick had made his usual check with the ground crew that the Lynx was fully serviced, armed and fitted with an additional fuel tank in place of the rear row of seats. It caused no resentment. They all knew Nick's habit of making doubly sure of every aspect before leaving the ground. He was reputed to be an ultra-safe pilot who treated aircraft with respect and invariably returned intact.

Now it was zero hour. Nick crossed to the helicopter beside Andy and Tim Chance, their gunner. They had flown together on many covert missions; knew each other's temperament and manner of operating. They were a first-class crew, and Andy was due to take over command of the SF flight from Nick.

A chilly wind whistled over the deck, where static aircraft looked ghostly, silvered by the moonlight. They were the only crew operating from the ship that night. The grey deck and the infinity of glittering sea beyond induced a sense of unreality in the small hours and Nick wished there was not such brilliant moonlight. Clear but subdued would have been better.

They got underway dead on time; Andy piloting and Nick as aircraft commander in the left-hand seat. Shortly after leaving their floating base he told Tim to test his guns. There was a short staccato burst. All was well.

'Should be the only firing you'll do tonight,' said Nick.

'Shame! I'd have brought a book to read if you'd told me earlier.'

'Sing some carols instead,' invited Andy. 'It's nearly Christmas.'

They soon reached land. Because it was so difficult to judge height over water, particularly when moonlight shimmered the surface, they had flown at two hundred and fifty feet. Now they descended to one hundred and embarked on the first leg of their planned route that would take them over isolated terrain the whole way. Night-vision goggles turned the ground flashing past below into a black and green landscape. With no visual aids over desert their navigation had to be absolutely spot-on. The up side was the absence of hills, and overhead wires which only occurred beside roads; the downside, that the desert floor at night is as deceptive as water, so they had to keep a constant check on their height. Travelling as fast as they were they were kept very busy.

Conversation was spasmodic and mostly concerned what they would do during their Christmas leave. Tim was bothered by sand stirred up by the rotors and billowing in through his open door. It made him cough, so he did not say a lot.

'There's the road we have to cross,' said Nick, spotting the straight line to his right.

'Got it,' affirmed Andy. 'Can't see traffic moving on it, can you?'

'Not a thing. How about you, Tim?'

'No headlights far as I can see,' came his hoarse reply.

'If there's a bedouin camel train we'll give them a hell of a fright in the next few minutes. Keep your eyes peeled for wires, although the chart doesn't show any,' said Nick.

They crossed the road and raced on into the darkness. No wires.

'We're now within range of that rocket launcher,' Nick pointed out calmly. 'Let's hope they're asleep now. Ten minutes to go, guys.'

'We might have to climb suddenly if the ground lining the wadi turns out to be higher than fifty,' Andy said. 'Give us a shout if you see anything, Tim.'

'Sure.' He was leaning from his open door sweeping the terrain from side to side, knowing he had a wider vista than the pilots had from the cockpit windows.

Five minutes later they were flying through the dried-out river bed towards the rendezvous landing site. Nick checked the time.

'Right on the button, guys. Let's hope they've allowed us enough room to land, and on level ground. This place looks pretty bumpy so far.' It was not ideal. They might have to hover.

'Three to go,' Nick announced. 'Bring back speed in one, Andy. Right,' he said shortly, 'two to go.'

Their forward thrust slowed; they descended to seventy-five feet. Nick now studied the ground even more closely. Within ninety seconds there should be a pinpoint of light flashing the letter G three times.

'See anything, Tim?'

'Nope.'

They overflew the grid reference they had been given. No light. Nick rapidly checked his navigation. This had to be the spot. It was in the wadi. There was not another within twenty-five miles. He knew they couldn't have made such a serious error.

'Hang around a bit?' asked Andy.

'Have to. Go down to twenty-five. If they're unable to signal we'll have a better chance of spotting them.'

Andy began systematically lapping north and south of the RV at rooftop height while Nick and Tim strained their eyes through the goggles. So close to the ground it should be possible to see two men who were eager to be found. Nothing!

Nick then had to make a swift decision. They would shortly reach their fuel limit and have to turn for home. He had not received the codeword to abort, so the passengers must be down there somewhere. He and Andy had worked on this together; run through it several times. They could not have ballsed-up. He *knew* they hadn't. So the agent who had selected the RV had either given the wrong grid reference or he had gone to the wrong place tonight.

Frowning, Nick checked the time once more. The aircraft and its crew were his prime responsibility. If they didn't turn back now they would not have enough fuel to reach the ship. He had no option.

'Head for home, Andy. It's a no-go,' he said heavily.

'Pity,' the young pilot returned, gaining height and circling to get on course to re-cross the road and run for the coast.

Into the silence Tim said, 'If they *are* out there somewhere they'll hear us getting further and further away. Glad I'm not in their shoes. Bloody shitty place to be stranded in!'

Nick's spirits had dropped dramatically. He was sure Andy's had. A failed mission was always a huge anticlimax, and this had been such a high-profile one. If the men were out there waiting, there was no way of proving they had not been at the RV. This abort could put a question mark against his and Andy's proficiency. If disaster subsequently befell the two prospective passengers, the question mark would become a very *black* mark.

Nick stared absently ahead as Andy packed on the speed and the Lynx began to judder. He had been adjudged the best man for this task and had failed to pull it off. There had been no last-minute signal of cancellation so those men must be waiting to be lifted. But even without a fuel restriction it would be almost impossible to locate them in the desert blackness. They could be miles out in their calculations.

The more likely explanation – and the most convenient as far as he and the other two were concerned – was that the pair had been intercepted en route, leaving them no means of signalling. Nick had a codeword to send indicating a successful extraction. When he had asked for one to signal mission aborted he had been told it was not an option; it was too vital. When he failed to send the word CYCLOPS it would be obvious the mission had gone down. The first time, and it had to be something as big as this. His heart had become leaden.

Ten minutes later a shrill noise filled the cockpit. Three lights began flashing on the control panel and the end of the engine-control lever above Nick glowed red. It he didn't already know the worst, the illuminated fire button left him in no doubt.

'Fire in left-hand engine,' he said, reaching up to retard the lever. 'ECL to ground idle.'

Andy glanced upwards swiftly. 'Confirm ECL to ground idle.'

Nick twisted round for signs of the fire. Could be a control-panel malfunction instead. The confines of the armour-plated seat and the restricted vision through his goggles hindered a visual check.

'Tim, what's the situation?' he demanded of the gunner, who could see more clearly from his door.

'Not looking good,' came the crisp response. 'Flames increasing.'

'Bugger it!' As Nick shut off the fuel, booster pump and crossfeed he recited his actions. Andy confirmed. Then he activated the extinguisher.

'Situation, Tim?' he asked again.

'Outside flames doused. Hasn't touched the core.'

They now had a serious problem, but Nick was too occupied for it deeply to unsettle him. He jabbed the extinguisher once more and prayed. This was the decider.

'Tim?'

'Negative, Boss. It's got a firm hold and spreading.'

Nick glanced across at his friend. 'Put us down PDQ. We'll grab our gear, get out and run like hell.'

Orange light from the flames lit the darkness beside Nick's door. He could already feel the heat penetrating the cabin and thought of the huge fuel tank back there with Tim. If that overheated . . . !

It was only a short drop to the ground, but it seemed to take an age to reach it. As Nick took from his life jacket the personal locator that would signal their position to military security beacons across the world, he reflected that the stand-by crew would after all get the excitement they craved coming out to rescue them. The pins in wax figures had worked. A failed mission *and* an engine fire! It was Sod's Law . . . and Tim was right. This was a bloody shitty place to be stranded in.

Andy set the Lynx on her skids in a forward run over the desert floor. The orange glare was suddenly dimmed by flying sand; the view through the forward cockpit windows was obliterated. They juddered and bumped through pitch darkness until, with a violent lurch and screaming metal, the heli-copter nose-dived, then cartwheeled over to crash on its right side.

Semi-stunned, fighting to breathe as sand filled his nostrils, Nick automatically thumped his harness lock to release himself. He was now lying horizontally in a small compart-ment darkened by smoke and a wall of sand that pressed against the windows.

'Andy, you OK?' he croaked, concerned for the man who now lay directly beneath Nick's seat.

No reply. Not even a groan. Nick struggled to peer over the armour-plated shoulder protector into the obscurity below. As his eyes grew used to the feeble light he saw that Andy's head was lolling at an unnatural angle; his face indistin-guishable from the heavy metal goggles which had been driven into it.

'Oh God,' Nick breathed. 'I'll never get him out in time.'

Further movement brought pain and a rush of wetness on his legs. Cautiously feeling his thighs, he found both were bleeding badly. He also had difficulty bending his right arm. Neither seemed important against his urgency to get out before the Lynx exploded. Yet he couldn't leave Andy. And Tim! *He had forgotten Tim.* With a ferocious effort he managed to swivel in his narrow seat to look into the cabin lit by the fire.

Christ, oh dear Christ! The fuel tank had broken from its securing clips and crushed the gunner against the row of metal seats their passengers were to have occupied. Tim's eyes were staring sightlessly; his mouth was open and spilling blood.

That fuel tank and the billowing flame-streaked smoke outside galvanized Nick. They were dead. Andy and Tim were dead. He could do nothing for them! The reek of escaping fuel, the heat and roar of the fire brought a flood of adrenalin to set Nick fighting his way upward to thrust the door open with strength born of fear.

He fell to the ground to discover he was in a crater of soft sand, which had caused them to flip over. 'Sod's Law,' he repeated on a sob of effort as he tried to claw his way up a shifting slope. They had hit the one hazard in an ocean of firm ground!

The pain in his legs and arm was augmented by the pain in his chest brought on by frantic exertion. If the Lynx blew before he was on firm ground and could run, he wouldn't stand a chance. It was sure to go up any minute. Taking Andy and Tim with it. Christ, oh dear Christ!

He eventually dragged himself over the rim of the great hollow and struggled to stand. He could manage only an ape-like shamble into the wilderness faintly illuminated for around twenty yards ahead. Wilderness! But he had his survival gear, and they would already have picked up the signal from his locator. Just sit it out until they came for him.

11

There was a roar, and some red-hot force hit him in the back to send him hurtling into blackness.

His wife brought the wheelchair round and he transferred to it from the car with practised ease. 'I'll stroll in the grounds for a while to stretch my legs,' she said. 'Then I'll go to the coffee bar for some breakfast. I'll wait for you there.'

He watched her walk away, too het up to say anything. He had so much to thank her for he had long ago run out of adequate words. As he went up the ramp he recalled his rage on first encountering steps he could no longer negotiate. He had raged at everything, even at Lucy. Time and her loving acceptance of a disabled husband had deadened it. Until yesterday's visit by a colourless member of the Ministry of Defence.

A nurse directed him to Major Higham's room, asking with curiosity at this early morning visit, 'Is he expecting you, Mr Hawkwood?'

'Yes.'

The Army psychiatrist was in his early forties, tall and lean with spaniel-like eyes behind rimless glasses. He shook Jon's hand firmly. 'You've had a long drive in icy conditions. Can I offer you tea or coffee?'

'Just facts,' he returned brusquely.

Higham nodded and sat again behind his desk. 'The facts are these. In time, physical strength and vigour can be regained following a period of ill-treatment and deprivation. Mental damage is a more complex problem. That's my concern.' He studied Jon. 'How much do you know of the affair?'

'Until one of our father's former syndicate colleagues unearthed news that a British Army helicopter had crashed in Iraq, and an ambitious git from a tabloid splashed across a front page that only two bodies were in the wreckage, and asked: What has happened to Nick Hawkwood? I believed he was in the US.'

'So you have little contact with your brother?'

'No. We're frequently in touch, but since he took command of the SF Flight it's been spasmodic. He never knows what'll come up; can't guarantee he'll be free. He was to have spent Christmas with us, but we weren't suprised when he didn't turn up. It's happened before. He was due in the States on the twenty-eighth. We assumed he'd e-mail from there when he had time. He'd warned us the course would be intensive. He couldn't wait to get started.' He struggled to control the tremor in his voice. 'Instead, he was going through hell. What did those devils do to him?'

'As a former officer you'll have been told what to expect if captured by a ruthless enemy. I haven't yet seen Nick, but the report by doctors who examined him before he was flown home suggests very brutal treatment. Torture, starvation, the withholding of even the basics of life. Degradation designed to break the strongest will. It usually does. The mental cost will only be apparent when Nick feels able to speak to me of his ordeal.'

'I'll speak to you of mine,' Jon said with mounting bitterness. 'My home has been under siege by newshounds; my wife and kids have been photographed in the seclusion of our garden. I've had to close my bookshop. Details of my Army service have been published, with emphasis on how I ended in a wheelchair. Our father's sordid history has been resurrected. They even tracked down Mother at what was sickeningly referred to as "Hernando's Hideaway"! Worst of all, I've been agonizing over what Nick was going through.'

Higham nodded his understanding.

Jon continued: 'I knew Nick must have been on a covert operation – the media pretty well hinted as much – yet the MoD claimed the pilots had made a navigational error and strayed into Iraqi airspace. It was a political hotcake. The ragheads were accusing us of landing subversive squads in their country, so instead of trying to get Nick back our government embarked on diplomatic fence-mending. Handshakes, tea and biscuits, and painted smiles all round.'

'They *were* negotiating for his release, until it became

obvious the Iraqi military were not holding him. Didn't know where he was, in fact,' said Higham quietly.

'So the smooth bastard who called on me yesterday said. If they'd sent in the SAS right away, Nick would have been saved days of suffering.'

'You spent long enough in the Army to understand the difficulties, particularly in a country where fanatical groups abound. It took time to discover who was holding him, and where.'

Jon stared at him, trying to hold down his explosive anger. After a short silence Higham resumed. 'Some people eventually recover from the trauma of torture, others never do. It depends on the personality of the victim, and on the nature of the punishment. One thing is certain: they never return to being the person they were before it happened. I'm sure your own experience has given you insight to that.'

Jon recalled his own days in this hospital trying to get his mind around the word 'paralysed'. His body had adjusted; his mind still fought it.

His parents had been through a messy divorce; Lucy was pregnant and fearful of a second miscarriage. Preoccupied, he had forgotten the rules and entered a burnt-out house where he heard kids screaming. It had been booby-trapped. He had been blown back on the road: the children were killed. He had blamed himself, not the Serbs. Nick had eventually talked sense into him, but the exuberent Jonathan Edward Hawkwood had gone for ever.

He glanced across at Higham. 'There are barely eleven months between Nick and me, so we've always been close. Our father worked for an international news agency as their Middle East correspondent. We were sent to public school over here but spent holidays with our parents. We got to know that part of the world quite well and grew up reasonably bilingual. Also somewhat self-centred, I guess, because we didn't twig that our talented parent had become an alcoholic until we were in our teens.

'We discussed it, Nick and I, but he said there was nothing

we could do after Father told us hard drinking went with the job. He said if we had to go to some of the barbaric, pestilent areas he frequented we'd understand.

'We were both keen on an Army career. Nick was accepted as a schoolboy recruit for the Army Air Corps. I didn't settle on a choice until I was at Sandhurst. Nick was already there with the senior intake. They'd dubbed him The Hawk due to his keen eye and his habit of swooping down on the unsuspecting enemy during war games. Soon after I arrived I was named The Owl.' The tightness around his mouth softened a little in reflection. 'I was a clever sod who came alive at night. Pubs, girls, high jinks.

'Nick was commissioned into the AAC; I opted for the Sappers. He took to the skies like a bird; claimed he was born to fly. The complexities of engineering delighted me. We romped through those first years. When I married, Nick continued his merry bachelor life.

'Then things went wrong. Seriously wrong. When Father was pissed, he began airing his views too freely in public. Arab friends were offended and officials removed him from their list of favoured media correspondents. Denied the means of getting hold of the breaking news, he hit the bottle with a vengeance. He grew aggressive and volatile, alientating even his colleagues. When the agency booted him out, Mother left him.

'He followed her back to England and made such a bloody nuisance of himself she eventually promised to stick by him, if he agreed to dry out in a clinic. She was facing deep financial problems, so Nick and I had to bail her out. It was mostly Nick, because I was married with a baby on the way. When Perez appeared on the scene, she broke her promise and sued for divorce. Father walked out of the clinic and caused no end of trouble for her and the Mexican. I won't give the murky details – you probably read them in the tabloids – but he was arrested several times for causing a breach of the peace.

'I did what I could – Nick was by then in Oman – but

Mother and Perez left for Mexico before the divorce was even finalized.' He frowned at memories of that difficult time. 'I believe he still loved her, and losing her on top of professional rejection was more than Father could take. Rage, bitterness, a sense of total betrayal, call it what you will, somehow inspired some of the best journalism he had ever produced. He wrote a searing series of articles for the *Sunday Telegraph* laying bare some damning facts about religious and social practices he had witnessed in the Middle East, and been forced by diplomatic pressure to suppress. I guess he felt he had nothing left to lose and was willing to publish and be damned.'

He fixed Higham with a resigned gaze. 'You'll know from reading recent slush accounts, he was *damned*. By the Arab world. They issued a death sentence against him.'

'I did read that, yes.'

'He was given police protection for a while until they realized he was virtually drinking himself to death, anyway. He's presently in a nursing home suffering from liver failure and mental deterioration. A brilliant journalist who's become a pathetic bundle of lost potential.'

Fresh anger surged through him. 'If Nick doesn't search out the brainless moron who announced to the world that the missing pilot was the son of Miles Hawkwood, I will. It was tantamount to condemning *him* to a death sentence.'

'In fact, your father's sins may have saved Nick's life,' came Higham's quiet response. 'Instead of a swift execution it seems they decided to exact the greatest misery first, which allowed time for a rescue.'

It did little to appease Jon's rage. 'After he'd been in their hands for almost a month! Nick got me through the initial stages of my legacy of Bosnia, then he suffered a personal blow no one could help him to overcome. Command of the SF Flight provided the risks and excitement he needed right then. When he was selected to pioneer the Army's new helicopter gunship squadron he claimed he was sitting on top of the world. Now you're telling me those bastards—'

'I'm telling you his ordeal will have wrought changes in him. To what extent will only become apparent as time passes. You demanded facts. I've given you the few I have so far.'

'And I've given you a whole lot more, so that you'll know what he was like before this . . . this atrocity. I spoke in confidence.'

'Of course. His military record is being sent. I'll learn more from that.' He got to his feet and came around the desk. 'As you know, this hospital deals with military trauma, physical injury and the subsequent rehabilitation of patients. War wounds and military accidents we take in our stride, but damage through torture makes us very hot under the collar. Trust us to do all we can for Nick.' He opened the door. 'He's in a side room in Intensive Care. Turn left at the end of the corridor, then take the next right and the second left. I'll be on duty until fifteen hundred should you want to ask me anything after you've seen him.'

The tyres of the wheelchair squeaked on the polished floor as Jon raced along the corridor, his powerful arms thrusting rhythmically. Doing the ton, he called it. Something he had done on a Ducati pre-Bosnia.

The sister in Intensive Care was expecting him. She offered tea, which he again declined.

'You've had a long journey in wintry weather, Mr Hawkwood. It might have been better to wait a day or two. Your brother will be kept sedated for some time.'

'I guessed as much, but I needed to see him.'

'Of course. It's a difficult time for you.'

'Not half as difficult as it's been for him.'

She frowned. 'Only myself and two nurses will have access to his room. Did Major Higham explain that we're keeping very quiet about this? We can't have the hospital overrun by newsmen, or have cameras flashing through the windows.'

Jon was furious. 'My brother has been through a private hell; are you suggesting I'm a moron who'd put him through a public one?'

17

'I'm simply outlining the hospital's stance,' she said frostily, and walked away.

He entered the side room and closed the door, raging inwardly once more. Yesterday, a quiet, colourless man had entered the antique bookshop he and Lucy now ran and, quietly and colourlessly, told them a horror story. They had shut the shop, gone home and stayed by the telephone until they received the call telling them Nick was safely back in England, and on his way to this hospital. That had come at 4 a.m. It was now eight thirty and the sense of shock still ruled him.

The face on the pillow could have been a death mask. Yellowed skin stretched tightly over the skull; the closed eyes were sunk deep in dark sockets. The infant blond beard was matted and discoloured. There was no resemblance to Nicholas Gareth Hawkwood. The bedclothes were kept from the body by a frame that suggested a white coffin. Machines monitored the sluggish pumping of his heart; blood dripped intravenously beside the bed. Despite the antiseptic state of the room Jon could detect a sickly smell emanating from the man lying so deathly still.

Rage overwhelmed him. He bowed his head in his hands. The Hawk and the Owl. Dear God, what had become of them both?

Two

Nick woke to the sound of his screams. His skin was running with the sweat of terror. Yet there was brilliant light; something they had denied him.

The screaming continued as he lay silently taking in the sights of antique pine furniture, cream walls, honey-coloured carpet, and patterned curtains moving in the warm breeze from the open window. The screams were being created by the lungs of Jon and Lucy's youngest in the adjacent room. And Nick was only unable to move because the damp sheet had become tightly wrapped around him.

He rolled free and sat on the edge of the bed, staring at blood red smears on pale cloth. Bandages on wounded men. On his brother! As his heart continued to race, an urgent need to vomit sent him to the bathroom, where he heaved and retched until exhausted. Then he took a long shower. By the time he had towelled off and dressed, the bloody bandages had become cream curtains splashed with poppies.

Down in the kitchen young Andrew was still screaming, jangling Nick's raw nerves. Lucy looked stressed as she set the table for breakfast, holding the baby on her hip and scolding Abigail for shaking Coco Pops everywhere but in her bowl.

'Sorry, Nick. Babe's in a foul mood. Nothing'll shut him up until he's so exhausted he'll fall asleep.' As she turned away to the dresser, Andrew's kicking foot caught the carton of milk and knocked it over. 'Oh, *sod* it!' she cried.

'Monday morning at the Hawkwood residence,' announced Jon as he manoeuvred his chair through the arch that replaced

19

a door. 'It gets worse as the week progresses, Nick.'

Abigail upended the carton, now containing no more than a dribble. 'I want some milk,' she wailed.

'Go to the fridge and get it,' commanded her father. 'We're not here to wait on you, madam.'

'There isn't any more,' said Lucy tautly. 'I was going to do a big shop this morning. There would have been enough for breakfast if Andrew hadn't . . .' She flashed a harassed look at Nick. 'Sorry about this. It's the last thing you need after . . .'

'They'll have milk at the village shop,' he said swiftly. 'I'll nip along there for some.'

'Jon'll go.'

'*I'll* go!'

Lucy angled a speaking look at Jon. He ignored it and told Abigail to spoon the cereal back into the packet.

As Nick took the path around the side of the house he heard Jon say, 'Can't you shut that kid up? He's been at it all night.'

'Don't you think I would if I could? I can hear him, too, you know, and I had less sleep than you. I spent half the night walking up and down trying to keep him from disturbing Nick.'

The village street was empty apart from an early riser mowing his front lawn before the sun got to it, and a Heinz varieties dog scratching itself beside the war memorial. Nick passed the shop and stood leaning on a gate leading to the water meadows. When he left hospital, Jon had insisted he stay with them rather than return to his basic flat in Hereford. As Pete Higham had thought it a good enough initial plan, Nick had agreed. Two days and he already knew it was a mistake.

Jon's anger and bitterness over his own disability had revived, and he was taking it out on Lucy. The easy, slightly flirtatious relationship she had maintained with Nick was at an end. Lucy couldn't handle the situation; didn't know whether to talk about it or pretend nothing had happened.

As for himself and Jon, they were treading warily around each other, unable to find their old rapport. But the children were Nick's main problem. That boy was constantly distressed. He thrust away the insidious voices that suggested why.

Nick knew he must leave, yet the prospect of being alone in his flat was suprisingly daunting. Three months in hospital had put him back on his feet, reasonably fit. He would eventually be able to push himself to the limits again.

He stared at the green serenity of the water meadows, heartbeat heightened once more. Mental recovery was the big problem. Higham had assured him he was experiencing the usual reactions to severe trauma and that time would enable him to conquer them. Nick knew he had always been impatient, demanding extremes of himself. Yet he was presently in the grip of a force he found difficult to fight. He was free, but *they* still dominated him. Until he regained complete control there would be no peace, no hope. No future?

Another pilot had embarked on the Apache programme. He would spearhead the new high-tech squadron. Command of the SF Flight had also passed to someone else. The SAS men Nick had flown to and from covert missions had saved his life, but he was of no further use to them. Of no use to the Army until he killed off the demons assailing him.

He had a date to see Higham in three weeks. 'You've done very well here, but it's a different ball game out there, Nick,' the man had warned. 'I need to keep an eye on how you're coping. Don't push yourself too hard. You'll get there quicker if you take things slowly. And as soon as you feel able to talk about it, give me a call.'

'Talk about what?' he had asked aggressively.

'That one thing they did to you that you can't yet acknowledge and confront. It's essential that you do to establish closure. You'll know when you're ready, and you'll need help to get through it. Ring me here, or on my mobile right away. Any time.'

He never would. He could not think about it, much less

put it into words. It had never happened. Yet it now set him walking fast to the corner shop where he bought two cartons of milk, two six-packs and a large box of chocolates.

He was too late with the milk. Lucy was setting off for the local nursery with Abigail. Inside the cottage Andrew was in his high chair, still screaming. Jon was frying eggs and bacon; the kettle was whistling in vain. It was all reassuringly normal. The hovering terror slunk away.

The baby finally fell asleep an hour later while Jon and Nick stacked the dishwasher and Lucy loaded the washing machine. Then Lucy shooed the brothers out to the garden while she cleared up the Coco Pops on the floor. The flower beds had been converted to lawn after Jon was disabled, but planters and hanging baskets provided some colour and a man came weekly to mow the grass.

'I think I'll have the whole place paved,' Jon said, gazing across the lush lawn. 'Expensive, but I'd save a gardener's wages over the years and I could come out here when it's wet and not get the bloody wheels stuck in the mud. God, isn't it quiet now he's stopped yelling! Lucy accepts it; says he's one of *those* babies, but it drives me bonkers. I didn't want another, but she said Abby needed a brother or sister.' He pulled a face. 'All those couples crazy to conceive who wait for years, and we do it first time. Never knew my sperm was so potent. Gave me no time to talk Lucy out of it. Why the hell are women so eager to surround themselves with the noisy, smelly little brats?'

Nick said quietly, 'I'd like to get a train to Hereford. Today.'

There was a brief silence. 'I guessed you were thinking of going. I should talk to you like a Dutch uncle, as you did to me. But I guess it wouldn't do any good. Nick, Hereford's a bloody crappy idea.'

'I won't stay more than a night or two.'

'And then?'

'I don't know. Head off somewhere. A place I've never been to. Avoiding trouble spots.'

'Difficult.'

He frowned. 'There must be a paradise somewhere waiting to be discovered. Sunshine, bars, girls galore.'

'That's never been your style. It doesn't work, anyway, getting away from it all. It goes with you. I know, I tried it.' Nick sat carefully in a garden chair and gazed at the pastel patio stones beneath his shoes. 'There's visible proof of what happened to you. It does go everywhere with you. You're not the man you used to be; never will be again. But you have a wife who adores you as you are now. You've kids and a nice home. You have the shop and a new interest in antique books.' He glanced over at his brother. 'You've heard of those weirdos who abandon life and spend months in some wilderness hoping to "discover" themselves. I have to find Nick Hawkwood again. Until I do—'

Jon gripped his arm. 'Give it time. You always were an impatient devil.'

'You two look ready for some fresh coffee,' said Lucy, arriving to put a tray on the pine table. 'I take it those chocs are for me, Nick. You really know how to treat a girl.'

Jon said too heartily, 'He's decided to leave us and go in search of a paradise where he can treat a few to a damn sight more than a box of chocs.'

Lucy giggled nervously. 'In his condition?'

Nick rounded on her. 'What condition is that? They didn't cut off my dick, just ran an electric current through it. Perked it up no end.'

Lucy's hand stilled in the act of handing him some coffee, and she paled. 'I didn't mean . . .' She slammed the mug down and ran indoors.

Jon reacted swiftly. 'Christ, Nick, she gets enough grief from me. That wasn't necessary.'

'Yes, it was. She's treating me like a freak. I'm still a normal man.'

'Try acting like one, you bastard!'

'*You* bloody insisted I come here,' he raged. 'An attempt to repay me for what I did for you after Bosnia, is it? I can stand on my own feet without any sodding help from you.'

'Go ahead,' Jon yelled. 'It's not your feet but your mind that needs sorting.'

Nick had to push aside a stack of mail to enter his flat that was merely a pied-à-terre. It smelled stale and neglected. He threw open windows, then unpacked the few things he'd bought in the local store. He would not be here long. He made black coffee and drank it, staring blindly at neighbouring rooftops, seeing multiple images of men in wheelchairs. He had not attempted to mend the rift with Jon. Jon had let him go without a word.

Nick knew he'd been out of line with Lucy, but she had attached jump leads to an underlying fear. It was as if she had known and was mocking him. He had had to accept that impotency was a result of extreme shock to the human system, but despite Higham's calm prediction that it was a temporary condition Nick felt humiliatingly emasculated. Until he could achieve that elusive erection they had control over even that.

He showered and dressed in old jeans and a sweatshirt. The mail was mostly junk. Many Christmas cards. He had expected to be away no more than five days. Bank statements showed he was remarkably well in credit. Forced economy!

The tape on the answer machine was full; light flashing. His hand hovered over the replay button. Seasonal greetings, probably. What had they done to him on Christmas Day? How had he spent New Year's Eve? He'd been blindfolded. No way of telling night from day.

He punched the replay button. Voices would drive away the demons.

Caroline: Hi, Nick. If you happen to be around on Saturday you can take me to a wild party at Lisa's new apartment. Give me a call.

Fran: You bastard, you let me down again! That's

	once too often. Find someone else to screw. Yourself preferably.
Garage:	Your car's ready for collection, Captain Hawkwood. Managed to get hold of a spare sooner than we thought.
Martins:	Mr Hawkwood, the set of lingerie you ordered is now in. (Christmas present for Fran.)
Waterstone's:	The books you ordered are ready for collection. We'll be open until eight on the twenty-third.
Gina:	Hi, lover boy. Happy New Year. I'm back from the Big Apple. How about you and me having some fun?

'In my condition?' he murmured thickly, shaken by this evidence that life had continued without him while he had been . . .

The rest of the messages went unheard as nausea rose as bile in his throat and he travelled to that place he had never seen but knew intimately. Then his heart lurched and he gave a small cry, but it was only the shrill ring of the telephone that had shocked his system. The insistent bell eventually drove him to reach out and pick up the receiver with a shaking hand. 'Hawkwood.'

A vigorous baritone assaulted his ear. 'Hawk, I've sat up until one a.m. to call you. If you were at all civilized I could have e-mailed and gone to my bed.'

Through his confusion Nick recognized the voice of his former squadron boss, James Wellnut. '*Cracker?* Where is it one a.m.?'

'Singapore. I'm our new Defence Adviser. Been out here six weeks. Total contrast to anything else I've done.'

Nick struggled to make sense of it. 'How d'you get my number?'

'Had occasion to speak to Chris Franklin. He told me you were at Jon's place. E-mailed him. You'd just departed. He

25

gave me your number; said to give you time to arrive there.'

James had organized Nick's transfer to the SF Flight when life had turned sour. His familiar voice was now a steadying influence. 'How d'you wangle a job like that?'

'No wangle.' He sounded huffy. 'Pure merit, lad. Brought promotion.'

'Hope you left the squadron in good order.' Nick swallowed the hint of nausea. 'It's good to hear from you, Cracker.'

'And you.' A slight pause. 'Chris said you're on leave after a bit of a beating.'

'That's right.'

'So come out and join us. Joyce'll love it. Always had a bit of a thing about you. Worried the guts out of me for a while, but it was only a passing fancy.'

Nick smiled. Joyce Wellnut was the most level-headed woman he had ever known. She wouldn't recognize a passing fancy if she had one.

'Did I hear you say you're on your way?' James prompted.

'That's right,' he repeated, as relief flooded him. Singapore would surely be as near to paradise as he could get.

'Fix a civilized bloke like Chris to e-mail me your ETA.' Then, more warmly, 'Make it asap, Hawk.'

'Will do,' he replied thickly.

Singapore, May 2002

The overnight flight was difficult. There was a sense of captivity Nick had never before felt within an aircraft cabin. The seat belt was particularly hard to cope with. He released it the minute the signs went off and ignored advice to remain belted in case of turbulence. Aerobatics he could cope with: restraint brought the fringes of panic.

In the past he had used long-haul flights to catch up on sleep, or to fit in some serious reading. Now he fought drowsiness and annoyed other passengers by pacing the aisles restlessly. After a mere two hours the drive to escape confinement really got to him. If this had not been a non-stop flight he would have left the 747 wherever it first touched down.

After dinner and a film, when passengers had settled for sleep in the dimmed cabin, Nick was still pacing. The senior flight attendant invited him into the galley and offered a tranquillizer.

'Nervous of flying?' she asked with a smile.

'Only when I'm being shot at.' Her eyes widened. 'I'm an Army pilot on leave.'

Her smile grew warmer. 'Ah, bad back-seat driver! Listening to the throb of the engines, monitoring every turn and the rate of climb. I have pilots as passengers quite often. They tend to get jittery once we start the descent.'

Nick was happy for her to think all that of him. She was easy on the eye and interested in him. He knew the signs. But he had no urge to respond. All he wanted was conversation to keep his mind occupied, and the excuse to stay on his feet. However, she needed to rest during the quiet hours before breakfast and the pre-landing activity, so when it became obvious this passenger simply wanted to talk she pressed the pill and a glass of water in his hands and suggested he return to his seat.

He lay back in the shadowed cabin thinking about James Wellnut. A man who played as hard as he worked, an above-average amateur artist and bathroom baritone, he had been a popular commander. It was inevitable that his name would become first Walnut, then Cracker. All aircrew had nicknames. Grown-up boys!

His thoughts wandered. Those early years had been a high-adrenalin period. Sandhurst, flying training, Northern Ireland, Oman, a joint-services Rapid Reaction squadron in Bosnia and at home, headed by James. Fast cars; fast girls. Courting danger and thrills up mountains or beneath the ocean. The honour of representing the Army in international events.

A series of disasters had ended his golden days. With the SAS Special Forces flight the Hawk had found the perfect outlet for his new aggression. Yet it had been a simple pick-up, not a glory boys operation that had led to his capture that night.

He had regained consciousness to find he was naked on the floor of some foul-smelling cell, wrists and ankles manacled, eyes covered with thick adhesive tape. It had taken him a while to make sense of it – he was still suffering the effects of blast from the explosion – but when he did, fear gripped him. He must be in the hands of Iraqi secret police. No hope of negotiations to free him; the government would deny any suggestion of covert infiltration by the British Army. He would die slowly and agonizingly. Better to have been killed in the crash like his friends.

They had begun with vicious beatings and electric-shock sessions, the first to cause physical damage and the other to inflict maximum agony. By the time they had accepted that their prisoner truly did not know the identity of those he had been sent to pick up, Nick had gone beyond the limit of human endurance. Then, through his daze of anguish and despair, he had overheard them excitedly discussing the news that they had in their hands the son of a man who had written infamous lies about their people. It was then the real horror had begun.

His heart began to pound. Sweat broke on his body. Conditions he had been fighting for several weeks. Must continue to fight or lose out completely. Gripping the arms of his seat, Nick concentrated his thoughts on a teddy bear in the arms of a sleeping child across the aisle. The toy was symbolic of innocence, gentleness and loving trust. The bear gazed back with friendly brown eyes. You're a sham, thought the traumatized soldier. There's no innocence or gentleness in this life. As for loving trust, it's a myth. Wise up, Edward!

Hands suddenly seized him and he cried out. 'Sorry, sir, didn't mean to startle you,' said the concerned woman bending over him. 'We've begun our descent into Singapore, so please fasten your seat belt. You slept through breakfast, but I could bring you some coffee.'

Nick struggled upright. 'Yes.'

Passengers were casting wary looks his way, but he was more worried by the belt. He left it undone until the attendant returned to fasten it for him. The long approach to Changi caused him no problem as a back-seat pilot, but the moment the aircraft was down and trundling to a bay he unclipped the belt and gazed thankfully at the wonderful world outside.

He was the first on his feet to take his bag from the overhead locker. As he prepared to make a dash for the door, his neighbour who had been humped beneath a blanket for the whole flight said, 'Next time go by sea, chum.'

The terminal was cool and spacious, with lush greenery and fountains to soothe weary travellers. Nick was soothed by the space and freedom to move; hardly noticed the plants and pools. His bag bearing a priority tag appeared swiftly. Then he was through Customs to find his hosts waiting.

James said nothing. His expressive dark eyes and the crushing grip of his handshake conveyed more than words. One battle-hardened serviceman greeting another. Joyce, in simple green cotton, kissed Nick's cheek.

'Long time no see, Nick. So glad you decided to come.'

Nick breathed in relief. No fuss, no exaggerated nonchalance. These two accepted him as a friend they had not seen for a few years, that's all. The search for Nick Hawkwood would be easier in their company.

The house used by the High Commission's Defence Adviser was a large, airy building of colonial origin, with louvred shutters in place of glass at the windows. Nick's spirits rose at the sense of freedom in rooms open to the day outside, and at the decor of yellow, pale grey and white. He craved light and space. They were here in abundance.

The Wellnut children had already been driven to school, and James almost immediately departed for his office. 'Duty calls, I'm afraid,' he apologized. 'I'll leave you in Joyce's hands. We don't stand on ceremony here, Nick, unless it's an official junket. Then my dear wife pulls out all the stops.

Be warned! It's certain to happen several times while you're here.'

Joyce led Nick to a rear bedroom. Left him to unpack and shower, promising breakfast whenever he was ready. A fan circled overhead, pleasantly ruffling his hair as he took fresh clothes from his bag, and the sound of birdsong in trees visible through the open window began to dispel the tension induced by the flight.

In shorts and a thin shirt he ate a hearty breakfast sitting at a table in what Joyce described as their unofficial dining room.

'We have a table that seats twenty in the next room, but we only use it for entertaining. I'll show you over the house later, Nick. It's rather grand. James said we're living above our station,' she said with a smile. 'I think he might miss flying – the excitement and larks of squadron life – after a while. But I'm loving it. So are the children. They get to see more of their father than ever before, and I have a husband safely on the ground with no likelihood of being sent to a trouble spot at a moment's notice. It makes a welcome change.'

Joyce's calm voice and the open aspect of the room further lulled Nick, so that he hardly noticed that she asked him no questions. The maid brought a fresh pot of coffee and they sat for a further half hour while Joyce revealed that James was painting again, that Gina was taking ballet lessons, five-year-old Robin was obsessed by dinosaurs and Emma, her daughter by an earlier marriage, had just entered the dreaded teens.

She made a face. 'A few squalls ahead, no doubt, but Singapore is keeping her well occupied just now. Heavens, is that the time! I'm afraid I'll have to love you and leave you. Lunch date with a ghastly woman who runs a children's charity the Brits support with purse and person. Why are worthwhile charities so often run by obnoxious females?'

'Because nice ones like you are no match for them.'

She laughed and got to her feet. 'Make yourself at home. I'll be back as soon as I can escape her clutches.'

Fifteen minutes later Nick watched her drive away through the palms and frangipani trees bordering the approach to the house, then he settled on a comfortable settee to read the *Straits Times*.

When Joyce returned at two thirty she found her guest sound asleep and pages of the newspaper flapping around the floor in the downdraught from the ceiling fan. Although the men didn't speak about it, service wives were all aware of what their husbands could suffer if captured by a ruthless enemy. James had hinted at extreme measures when they had discussed inviting Nick to join them. Her hand rested lightly on his shoulder as she studied the lines of strain and pain on his face.

'Poor lad!'

The children were used to socializing with a wide range of people and accepted their guest with natural friendliness. Emma was a different proposition. Thirteen, well-developed and clearly into sexual awareness, she greeted Nick dramatically, eyes widening as she gazed at him, colour tinting her cheeks. When he made the fatal mistake of reminding her she had been a noisy little brat of ten when he last saw her, the blush deepened.

'I was a mere child. I'm surprised you even noticed me.'

Throughout dinner her exaggerated sighs and languid poses were to make sure he now did. They failed. When Joyce retired early, leaving the men to talk, Nick was offered a nightcap.

'Whisky, thanks.'

James poured two and brought them over. 'I suppose I'd better come clean about why I asked you out here.'

Nick took a comforting gulp of whisky. 'So why?'

'I need a leg man.'

'As opposed to a tit man? I appreciate both.'

'Leg man as in undercover agent.'

'As in *what*?'

'There's something odd going on and official stonewalling strengthens my suspicions.'

'About?'

'The untimely death of the guy I replaced at short notice.'

'Foul play being hushed up by the authorities?'

'No, but I can smell a rat. You'll get the whiff when you hear the details.'

'The heat's addled your wits,' Nick declared. 'Who was your predecessor?'

'Group Captain Philip Dunne DFC. Harrier pilot who distinguished himself in the Falklands bash.'

Intrigued because James was not the fanciful type, Nick said, 'Give me the full briefing.'

'Ha, knew you'd be up for it!'

'Wrong. I'm not up for anything that isn't self-indulgent.'

'Balls! You're the original Action Man, Hawk. I'm offering you a slice of it.'

When James called him Hawk it usually heralded blackmail. Do-an-old-pal-a-favour kind of blackmail. 'Fill me in on Dunne's death.'

'Sailing accident. Presumed drowned.'

'So no body?'

'You've got it.'

'The tides and currents around these islands must be tricky. Fifty-fifty chance of a body never being recovered, surely.'

'I've learned Dunne was a good swimmer. Not in your class, but well able to stay afloat in an emergency until rescued.'

'What about the boat?'

'No sign.'

'Emergency flares?'

'No one saw any. Nor was there a Mayday call on ship-to-shore. Suspicious, don't you think?'

Nick remained silent.

'I've checked on the weather that day. Strongish wind, chance of some isolated storms. Nothing Dunne couldn't have handled. And there was no storm in the vicinity of his logged course. I've also checked shipping movements. Nothing went through that was big enough to create a gigantic wash in that area. So what happened to Dunne and his crewman?'

'There was another man with him?'

'Jimmy Yang, a young Chinese lawyer saving to buy his own boat and crewing for anyone to gain experience. His body has also never been recovered.'

'What was the official finding?'

'Presumed lost at sea.'

'Sounds about right.'

'There's more. Several weeks before Dunne disappeared his wife went home because her mother had been given three months to live. Their daughter, an only child, is up at Oxford. She always stayed with her grandparent in the vacs, and it was she who rang her parents with the bad news. Against the old lady's wishes, apparently. Alison Dunne was on the first flight home.'

'And?'

James raised his eyebrows. 'Party gossip has revealed that Dunne breathed a hefty sigh of relief.'

'He was having it off with an almond-eyed beauty on the side?'

'No. Lack of interest in that direction, according to those close to him. Our Philip was wedded to the Air Force; happiest in male company and passionate about rugged pastimes.'

Nick considered that. 'So why apply for a diplomatic attachment? Guy like him would prefer to stay with his squadron.'

'My thought exactly, but listen to this. Alison Dunne is the granddaughter of Sir Charles Fanshawe, one-time governor of Hong Kong and still very influential in the Foreign and Commonwealth Office. Dunne came here highly recommended by the old boy, so the story goes.'

'Do you do any actual work between all this informative socializing?'

'Fingers to the bone,' James assured him.

Nick drank slowly while he mulled over what he had been told. 'A man of Dunne's type wouldn't be dictated to by his wife, so he was either put under severe pressure by Fanshawe to take the job, or the Air Force suggested he cool his heels out here while some dust settled.'

'The latter's unlikely,' James reasoned. 'Any officer who'd blotted his copybook would never be appointed to advise and confer on bilateral defence plans, much less liaise with heads of industry on possible arms sales.'

'OK, Fanshawe discovered something that would blight the life of his granddaughter if it ever came to light. He pulled strings and Dunne was forced to toe the line. He would resent it like hell and possibly take it out on his wife. Not the ideal set-up for the job you've now got, but I haven't yet heard anything to support your suspicions.' He held out his glass and waggled it. 'As you know, I'm no sailor – prefer to be in the water rather than on it – but I know freak waves occur, and storms can be so localized they're not recorded.'

James went to the sideboard to pour drinks as Nick continued his reasoning. 'Small craft can be overturned by unprecedented activity by large marine creatures. It's happened. And, let's face it, there are nutters at the helm same as behind the wheel of a car. Nautical hit-and-run maniacs. That could account for the lack of SOS signals. Sorry, James, you'll have to give me more than the lack of a body and hints of murky goings-on in Dunne's past before I'll take you seriously.'

'That was just the background stuff.' He handed a full glass to Nick. 'The usual routine didn't apply in my case. I came out here ahead of Joyce and the kids. No handover period, so I was dropped in at the deep end.' He sat, cradling the cut crystal in his hands. 'Cranford Fielding – he's our Head of Mission. You'll meet him tomorrow – put me up until the Dunnes' stuff had been cleared from this house. Sir Charles sent out one of his squeaky-clean junior officials with Alison to help her through the stressful business. I met her briefly. Expressed condolences; offered any help. The usual. She didn't take up my offer. Seemed very aloof.'

'Not surprised. Two bereavements in as many months.'

'No! The mother *wasn't* dying. The squeaky-clean individual mumbled something about a misdiagnosis alarming the undergrad daughter unnecessarily. But wouldn't you think the Dunnes would have contacted the consultant for full details of the old lady's condition before Alison legged it home that same night? It wasn't as if death was imminent: she was given three months.'

Nick shrugged. 'So Mrs Dunne's the panicky type.'

'Or she wanted to leave Singapore in a hurry. Problems here. The whole thing could have been a ruse to explain her absence.'

'You're suggesting this woman is up to her neck in something nefarious because a consultant made an error in diagnosis? Read the British tabloids. It's happening on a regular basis.'

James seemed untouched by this reasoning. 'I put in a box any personal items of Dunne's that I found in the office and sent it round to the house. There wasn't much. A couple of watercolours, a presentation silver model of a Harrier inscribed as a farewell gift from his squadron, a mobile phone, an electric razor, spare civilian and uniform clothes.' He put his glass on the small table and leaned forward. 'But last week I came across a file containing a few sheets of paper covered with cryptic notes in Dunne's hand. They made no sense to me, so I showed them to my PA, Davina. She knew nothing about the file; said it must concern Philip's personal affairs.'

'So you passed it to his widow.'

'Actually, no. If it concerned his private affairs he was involved in something he shouldn't have been. I've deciphered some of it after a great deal of study. He recorded shipping movements over the past six months, highlighting some with red and others with blue. There are a number of grid references I've been unable to make anything significant of, and groups of letters some of which could indicate companies engaged in the manufacture of defence equipment. They certainly match up.'

Nick's interest stirred. 'You think Dunne was engaged in undercover sales of arms?'

'I think a question mark hangs over his death in the light of this file.'

'You've told Fielding all this?'

'He doesn't believe in making waves. Dismissed my theory with a single word. *Tosh!*'

'The official stonewalling you mentioned?'

'Not only him. The staff here will say only that Dunne was a daredevil who enjoyed taking risks. Even Euan Goss, my assistant, who knew Dunne better than most, supports the theory of an unexpected hazard causing a tragic accident.'

'Then why can't you?'

'Because those notes of Dunne's don't tie in with records of legit sales to the Singapore Armed Forces. And if I'm right about the initials, some of the companies are on our black list.'

'Then leave well alone. Dunne's dead, so bin the lot.'

'I can't. If a man dabbles in deep water he must deal with tricky people. They don't bin things; they find a replacement to continue the dealing. Even if Dunne's death was accidental; I'm his successor. Isn't it likely they'll consider I'm in line to take over from him? I have Joyce and the kids to think about. Whatever pressure was brought to bear on Dunne might be applied to me.'

'Then you must tackle Fielding again. Refuse to be brushed off. Outline your suspicions and fears for the safety of your family.'

'Trouble is, I've nothing concrete. A few papers covered in notes that could mean a number of things; a hunch that Alison Dunne used a phoney emergency to leave here in a hurry and an uncomfortable doubt over how her husband met his death. A pedantic, play-it-by-the-book, near to retirement diplomat will never accept that.'

Nick acknowledged the point. 'Hasn't anyone ever

commented on the uncharacteristic move by a man like Dunne in applying for this post?'

'Not in my hearing. Why focus on that?'

'It should be possible to get details of Sir Charles Fanshawe's past activities, some hint of why he might have pushed Dunne into it,' he said, ignoring James's question. 'The Falklands hero presumably had a spotless service record, so what shadows are there in his private life? Not a closet gay, was he?'

James shook his head. 'He made no secret of his violent opposition to admitting homosexuals to the armed forces. Same with women, apparently. OK to employ girls in the cookhouse or offices, but nowhere else. The sight of women in an officers' mess turned him purple in the face. As for letting them loose with a gun . . .'

'Sentiments shared by most of us, if we're honest. So he probably treated his wife as the little woman.'

'Curiously enough, social gossip suggests she was a self-assured and highly cultured supportive partner during the twelve months they were here. They were a popular pair. Mind you, what went on between them out of the public eye no one knows.'

'Except the servants. They don't miss a thing, as a rule. Do they go with the house?'

'We took over the two who served the Dunnes, adding a Filipino maid for the extra work of three children.'

'Have you gleaned anything from them that throws any light?'

'That's what a leg man does.'

Nick regarded his companion seriously for some moments, then said, 'OK, let's look at another angle. Philip Dunne, hero and red-blooded male, reaches a rank bringing heavy staff responsibilities that put an end to fun and games with lusty aircrew. In the Mess he's expected to set an example; he's no longer one of the lads. They all gather at one end of the bar; he's all alone at the other end.'

'If he's sensible he goes home to his wife at the end of the working day.'

'It's not the macho life he used to love. Seeing young guys doing what he still longs to do is more than he can accept. But what's the alternative? A desk job at some headquarters. He's over the hill . . .'

'Thanks,' interceded James dryly.

'. . . he's had his days of glory in a fast jet. Now he's jaded and disillusioned, yet if he leaves the Air Force what kind of job is likely to give him the ration of kicks he needs? He broods; takes it out on his wife. Alison confides in Grandpa and Sir Charles comes up with a suggestion. Dunne likes it. He wouldn't be tormented by the sight of guys half his age demonstrating their youth and virility in the air; he'd be kingpin of the defence scene with a hectic social life and enough meetings with hopeful industrialists to satisfy his love of male get-togethers. His prejudices are apparently sexist, not racist, so he welcomes the opportunity to enjoy the multicultural aspect of Singapore – to say nothing of escaping the British weather for three years. He lets the old boy twist arms on his behalf.

'Alison Dunne, like Joyce, welcomes having her husband tied to one place, unlikely to be sent to a war zone. Teenage daughter is out of their hair at university, hubby's temper improves, the marriage begins to revive in the new relaxing atmosphere. A year passes very pleasantly and successfully. She has nice friends and fresh interests: he expends his surplus energy sailing and, quite probably, enjoying aerobatics with the local flying club.

'Suddenly, the idyll is shattered. Daughter phones in floods of tears. Grannie is dying! Alison is overwhelmed with guilt. While she's been enjoying herself on the far side of the world her widowed mother has been facing pain and fear alone, never mentioning her suffering in letters. Alison's to her have been full of the fun she's having. No thought for the poor old lady.

'Dunne tries to reason with his wife, but she's distraught. She *has* to fly home immediately. After four or five hours of tears and recriminations, he's thankful to put her on the midnight plane. It's very peaceful without her. The pros outweigh the cons. Everyone sympathizes. He receives a deluge of offers to combat his loneliness, but he's free of husbandly duties, so spends more time sailing, et cetera. Then he gets a call from his wife advising him she's returning at the end of the week. The diagnosis was a mistake. Ma's back to her bridge sessions, her line-dancing class and her fund-raising coffee mornings.

'Sensing the end of an enjoyable period of freedom Dunne embarks on an orgy of physical pastimes, ending with a day's sailing when conditions aren't ideal. Enjoying risk-taking, he ignores his better judgement and the rules of navigation. *Wham!* He hits a freak storm. He sails into commercial shipping lanes and is unknowingly mown down by a large vessel. He chases a surprising pod of whales and closes with them. Whichever . . . RIP Philip Dunne.'

The short silence was broken by the continuous shrill of cicadas and the rasping of bullfrogs in the surrounding grounds. 'OK, so it's quite plausible as far as it goes, but how do you explain the stuff in that file?'

Nick sighed heavily. 'I flew in just this morning; I haven't seen the bloody file. If the PA working with Dunne over the past year can't fathom it . . . You don't need a leg man. A shredder or simple waste bin will answer.'

James rose. 'It's late, and you're jet-lagged. We've an invitation to a cocktail party tomorrow. Fielding will be there. You can keep your eyes and ears open, try a few casual questions. Sort of thing that might arouse curiosity if I asked them.'

'*No*, Cracker!'

'I know for a fact Jimmy Yang's sister has been invited. She's stunning. You'll really go for her.'

Nick got to his feet reluctantly. He was not yet ready for bed. Sleep too often brought nightmares. 'Don't know Jimmy Yang.'

'Dunne's ill-fated crewman. I told you about that. You can start your sleuthing with his sister.'

'You haven't got some crazy notion *she's* involved?'

James walked beside him towards the bedrooms. 'I haven't yet told you Dunne mentions "check on lapis lazuli".' His hand dropped on Nick's shoulder. 'Fleur Yang is a jewellery designer working with precious stones. Curious coincidence, don't you think? You'll enjoy following that lead, I promise you. She's hot stuff!'

While Nick showered he reflected that it had been an unreal kind of day. Being with the Wellnuts brought reminders of the past; reminders of a sunshine period followed by a violent storm that had knocked him totally off balance. He had not bargained for that. To offset it was the advantage of being in an unfamiliar, peaceful country, staying in a delightful open-air style of house. He had three weeks in which to get to grips with full recovery. Pete Higham warned it would be a hit-and-miss affair, but he had underestimated his patient. There would be no 'miss' factor where he was concerned. Nick was confident this break in Singapore was the 'hit'.

As he walked naked from the bathroom someone tapped on his door. James with more nonsense about rogue arms sales!

'Leave it until morning,' he called firmly.

The knocking continued. Nick swore, wrapped a small towel loosely around his waist and yanked open the door. Emma stood there in brief-legged pyjamas, her swelling breasts clearly visible through the thin cotton. Flushed and wide-eyed she took in his near naked state and the scars on his thighs.

'I know what happened to you. I heard James telling Mum. They don't realize how easy it is to hear things in the next room when there's no glass in the windows. How *can* they carry on as though you're an ordinary guest? Of course, James has always been *fearfully* macho, but I can't *believe* the way Mum's behaving. Laughing, telling stupid gossip, going on and on about the old days.' Her eyes rolled dramatically. 'It must be *awful* for you.'

Nick stared silently. More unreality!

'I've been waiting up so I could tell you *I* understand. *I* know what you must be going through. I'm here for you, Nick, whenever you need someone. Any time of the day or night. Please remember that.'

She turned to walk away in the manner of St Joan after inspiring her troops, having in a moment destroyed the serenity Joyce's laughter and talk of the old days had created.

It was another bad night. Sleep brought the usual vile images. He was a spectator to his own suffering; he could actually see that cell, see *them*. They were taunting his naked self chained to the wall. Then he was in that other place where they had either beat him senseless, or wired him up and switched on the current. He heard himself screaming; insisting he did not know the answer they wanted. They said they would get his sot of a father and force the facts from him. Or from his crippled brother. He was pleading with them, begging them to stop because no one knew the answer. Then they dragged him to the edge of a bottomless hole and began to push him in it.

He awoke bathed in sweat, heart racing. In the bathroom his stomach rejected the dinner he had eaten, leaving him exhausted and unable to face the rest of the airless tropical night without help. He went downstairs to fetch a bottle of Scotch from the sideboard.

Three

Collins Air Charters must be a highly profitable business, Nick thought, as he studied the interior of their hosts' home. He guessed Ferdy Collins left it to his Chinese wife to enhance the rooms with Eastern charm. They were oddly matched: a tall, wiry Australian pilot and a professor of psychology. When James introduced Nick, Ferdy invited a professional discussion later in the evening.

'Perhaps Captain Hawkwood does not wish to talk of flying,' scolded Kim Collins. 'He is on leave.'

Nick demurred. 'I'm sure you've discovered to your cost that we men who cavort around the sky will talk about it at any opportunity.'

'A rarity, indeed! A man who openly admits to an obsession with the kingdom of the clouds,' she teased gently. 'There are several pilots here tonight, but I hope you will also enjoy the company of our other guests. They are all interesting in their own fields.'

She was right. Those present were all professional people; a mix of cultures representing administration, commerce, science and the arts. Nick very soon realized the past four months had blunted his expertise at social mingling, so he found the first half hour heavy going. In particular his short conversation with the High Commissioner.

Cranford Fielding fitted James's description exactly. A play-it-by-the-book man; someone who carefully considered every step before taking it. He was probably perfect for the post; highly unexcitable, methodical with a good sound background in diplomacy. He certainly looked the part. Broad

42

shoulders, erect bearing, immaculate suit, pleasant smile and a firm handshake: a worthy representative of Her Majesty's government. Nick disliked the man within the first few moments.

'Of course, you won't gain a comprehensive impression of this country in a mere few weeks,' Fielding told him expansively. 'It's complex. Fascinating, but diversely orientated. One has to spend some years here before one even begins to get the feel of the place.' His pleasant smile appeared on cue. 'By then, it's time to leave. The big drawback with this job. Always on the move. Still, that's nearing an end. Pipe and slippers time. Comes to us all eventually. But we've had a good run for our money, haven't we, Barbara?'

'Absolutely,' his correctly gowned wife agreed. 'But you can forget the pipe and slippers. We have a country cottage to decorate, a large garden to tame, and six grandchildren to get to know more intimately than we do now. Don't even *think* of resting on your laurels, my dear.' She smiled at Nick. 'He thinks I'm joking, but I'm not. Oh, I have to have a word with Moira Singh. She's on the orphanage committee with me. Come to dinner with James and Joyce. We can have a proper chat. I'll arrange something.'

'An impossibly busy woman,' Fielding said, watching his wife thread her way between the guests.

Before he knew it, Nick embarked on the task he had told James he would not take on. 'She must have been a great help to Mrs Dunne after her husband's tragic death. James said the poor woman had to fly back here after dashing home in the belief that her mother had terminal cancer. Very traumatic time for her, followed by the shock of Dunne's fatal voyage. Difficult for any woman to cope with, especially when her husband's body can't be decently buried.' Nick pressed on despite the other man's expression of distaste. 'It's strange that the bodies of Dunne and his crewman have never been washed up, and no signs of a wreck have been found.'

'Not in the least,' said Fielding coolly. 'The waters around

Singapore and the outer islands are congested and tricky. A
man has to know what he's doing at the helm of any vessel.
Amateurs should stay on dry land.' He looked over Nick's
shoulder. 'Excuse me, I'm being beckoned by Paul Morceau.
Barbara will arrange a dinner date with Joyce.'

He walked away, leaving Nick to reflect that James would
be hitting his head against a wall attempting to pursue his
theory with Cranford Fielding. Apart from the man's reluctance to cause waves, he clearly had not shared the general
liking for Philip Dunne. He had also used the standard cocktail excuse of needing to speak to someone on the far side
of the room to walk away from a subject he had not wanted
to discuss. Nick grew intrigued. Was James really on to
something irregular here?

'You look rather lonely there in your corner. May I join
you? Or perhaps you prefer to be alone with your deep
thoughts.'

She was the most strikingly beautiful creature Nick had
ever seen; creature rather than woman because everything
about her had an alien quality that did not equate with the
kind of girls he went around with.

'I'm in the corner because I don't know any of these people,
and I'm hopeless at circulating.'

The smile that touched her claret-tinted lips was also in
her lilting voice. 'It's quite easy. Just move from group to
group, nodding now and then. There is no need to say
anything. They will think what an intelligent fellow you are,
and you can continue your deep thoughts.'

He could not take his eyes from her. Creamy skin, black
hair in a shining coil on the crown of her head, ears studded
with tiny jade pagodas, a willowy body in a clinging dress
of ivory silk, and graceful hands holding a cut-crystal glass.
More than enough to set his pulse racing. But it was her
submissive allure seldom found in Western women that unexpectedly excited him.

She seemed unperturbed by his scrutiny. 'Are you a friend
of Ferdy or Kim?'

'Neither. The Wellnuts brought me along. I'm staying with them. Do you know James and Joyce?'

'Very slightly. So you are a diplomat?'

'I'd make a poor one, skulking in a corner at a social gathering.'

'Then what is it you do, Mr . . .?'

'Hawkwood. Nick. I'm an Army pilot. On leave.'

Her almond eyes glowed with amusement. 'So now I understand why you are unwilling to circulate with these people who talk business, business, business. Have you come from Australia?'

He shook his head. 'I flew in from England yesterday.'

'Your first visit to Singapore?'

'Yes.'

'There is much for you to see, in that case. What interests you?'

'Sunshine. Open spaces. The breeze on my face. Calm people like you,' he said without thinking.

'You do not have to leave England for that,' she said, studying him with evident curiosity.

'I did.'

A Chinese in a dark-red dinner jacket approached her. 'John Vydecker has to leave in ten minutes and needs to speak to you about his daughter's birthday.' He flashed a smile at Nick. 'Excuse the interruption. Business sometimes has to be conducted over cocktails.'

The girl waved a slim hand in the air in a dismissive gesture. 'Tell him I shall come in a moment. It is not so urgent, and I am busy.'

The expression on the man's face changed as dramatically as sudden clouds over the sun. He was *not* happy. Nick was. The girl did not want to end this stimulating encounter, and neither did he.

'That didn't go down well,' he murmured, as the man moved away.

'Ah, it is not possible always to do what others wish. Especially when one strongly wishes to do the opposite.'

45

He wondered if that was a Chinese come-on, but she soon hit the notion on the head. 'So you do not plan to study our customs and ancient cultures? You have no interest in our trees and flowers? We have a multiracial society in Singapore. Does it not inspire you to discover the secret of its success when other nations have failed?'

'Right at this moment I want only to get to know you,' Nick told her. 'The rest can wait.'

She gave a faint frown. 'You are a most unusual person.'

'No. I can't believe every man you accost in a corner doesn't react the same way.'

'I do not make a habit of accosting men in corners. It was simply because you looked bewildered and rather unhappy that I spoke to you.'

'Whatever the reason, I'm glad you did,' he said, still optically savouring her petite perfection.

The pleasure was broken by a strident American voice, as a thickset man with silvering hair and a pseudo tan closed in on them.

'See here, Fleur, this is important to me. *Damned* important. We have to settle the details before Sunday.'

The girl half turned, saying soothingly, 'I said I would be just a moment, John.'

'My moments are precious. I have to leave in five minutes.'

'There is time,' she insisted coolly. 'Have you met Mr Hawkwood? He is a guest of the Wellnuts.'

Nick was given a brief nod, no more, before a hand was put beneath the girl's elbow and she was led firmly away. He watched with deep resentment as she was treated to a monologue in a booming accent audible above the general conversation. He was so intent on trying to catch what was being said it was a while before he grew aware of someone beside him.

'Exquisite, isn't she,' said Ferdy. 'You should see her designs. Hellish expensive, but each piece is a one-off.'

Nick frowned. 'Who is she?'

'Fleur Yang. I suspect Vydecker is commissioning

46

something for his wife or daughter. Most unlikable women. Well, *she* is. The daughter is catching up fast. You can afford to ignore him, but anyone in business here can't. He's the leading merchant banker; his wife is a member of one of America's most influential families . . . as she frequently reminds us.'

Realizing he had just encountered the sister of Philip Dunne's unfortunate crewman, Nick murmured, 'Miss Yang looks to be flavour of the month with him.'

'Mmm. Rumour has it Vydecker set her up in business and also subsidized her brother's legal studies.'

Nick glanced round swiftly. 'You mean she and Vydecker . . .?'

'If they are it's very discreet. I personally believe it's a purely financial tie-in. She's so talented she wouldn't need to spread her legs to win anyone's backing.'

'How about the brother?'

'Was he a bum boy? Nah. He was a crazy, that's all. A lawyer who should instead have been a wing walker, a skydiver or a film stunt man. Thrived on thrills. He teamed up with James Wellnut's predecessor, who was pretty much as crazy as Jimmy. He crewed for Phil in nautical escapades and went with him up country on jungle survival treks. Mad, the pair of them!' He pulled a face. 'They took up one of my aircraft whenever they could, and Phil pulled off some wild aerobatics. Stunts I'm too bloody long in the tooth to tackle now. When they landed they'd be as high as if they'd had a shot. I was considering doubling the insurance on that plane when the partnership came to an end. They went off in Phil's boat one day and never came back.' He signalled a steward. 'You've an empty glass. What's your poison?'

'Scotch and water,' Nick told the Malay, then pursued the conversation further. 'What happened?'

'Eh? Oh, it's anyone's guess. A one-way trip into the sunset. The two bodies will go the way of all flesh in the ocean depths. They took one risk too many, I guess.'

'How did Miss Yang react?'

'Philosophically. There's a streak of fatalism in many Chinese. It's all written. There's nothing you can do about it.'

'That's not exclusive to Chinese. A lot of us feel that way.'

'The bullet with your name on it? Been in any tight spots, Nick?'

'Not really.'

'So how about the Apache attack helo you Brits are buying? I read it's so hi-tech only computer maestros can fly them. James was just saying you're a very bright guy, so I guess you've done the conversion course already. Does it live up to its reputation?'

Physically tensing, cursing the man for raising the subject, Nick nodded. 'It's rated top security. Not allowed to talk about it.'

The arrival of their drinks caused a natural pause, and Nick deliberately turned the spotlight on his host by asking about Collins Air Charters. It was a fascinating success story and they talked professionally for some while until Kim Collins approached with someone in tow.

'Ferdy, look who's here.'

Collins's face lit up with pleasure as he seized the man's hand. 'You old bastard! Where the hell did you surface from? Typical! Turn up without letting a bloke know.'

The newcomer was around fifty but as trim and fit as a younger man. His deep tan was natural. 'You know how it is, Ferdy, never know where I'll be till I get there. This time I've brought someone with me.' He drew forward a woman talking to Kim. 'On the flight over I asked her to make an honest man of me and she agreed. Lara, this bloke knows more about me than he bloody ought. If he tries to tell you any of it, just walk away.'

With typical Australian frankness Collins said, 'It's a brave woman who'd agree to become wife number three to this reprobate. Happy to meet you, Lara. He's a lucky bastard. Always was.'

He turned to complete the introductions, but shock waves

were already racing through Nick. Two and a half years had gone by and she looked just the same . . . until she grew aware of him. Her eyes darkened with apprehension and the vivacity drained from her face. She held out her hand to greet Nick as a total stranger.

He responded the same way, hardly aware of what he was doing, and she turned swiftly back to Kim. The conversation, the laughter and rough leg-pulling rose around Nick and became a cacophony of personal ridicule that beat against his ears unmercifully. Nausea rose in his throat; the room began to spin as heat overwhelmed his body. Panic ruled. He had to fight free; had to breathe before he suffocated.

It was bad. Impossible to deal with sober. He stood by the unshuttered windows of his unlit bedroom with a couple of bottles on the sill. The first had held only two measures, so he had opened a second. His hand shook as he put the neck of it to his mouth and drank deeply. Taking the road to oblivion once more. Trying to drive away the sound of her voice (How do you do, Captain Hawkwood) and the memories of all she had been to him.

Four of them had driven to London for an engagement party, after which they had planned to go to a strip show and end in a night club. Only three saw the strippers because Nick saw Lara first. (My mother was reading *Dr Zhivago* during her pregnancy.) She was an Australian in England to extend her studies in marine biology. Nick swiftly decided to extend his studies in female anatomy. Lara had her own ideas on that, so he tried again the following weekend. And the next. And the one after that. By the time he had persuaded her to share a bed he was seriously in love.

They were engaged two months later and planned to marry when Lara finished her degree course that summer. After the acrimony of his parents' divorce, and the stress of Jon's injuries, Nick felt life was promising to be good again. His wild oats had been sown, his career was flourishing. He was ready for marriage.

There were the usual hang-ups over the wedding plans. Nick's mother was abroad with her new lover, his father was back on the booze and on course for destruction, so he was all for a swift civil ceremony and a honeymoon in an exotic resort offering hot sun and water sports. Lara's people wanted a slap-up affair in church with a team of bridesmaids and men in heroic uniforms providing an archway of swords. She was their only daughter and they could afford to fly over assorted relatives for the event of their lifetime. Nick had surrendered with mildly bad grace.

The church in the Cornish village where Jon and Lucy lived was old, beautiful and exactly what Lara's parents had dreamed of for a wedding in 'the old country'. Nick's stag night followed the usual pattern so he and his friends, with dress uniforms and swords carefully packed, travelled to Cornwall by train and slept most of the way.

Next morning, when Nick saw the church full of flowers, his brother officers resplendent in blue with swords at their hips, women in glamorous hats and dresses, and crinolined bridesmaids waiting at the door, he admitted this was the only way to celebrate his legal union with a girl he adored. Maybe they should also have had a fanfare of trumpets!

Brides are allowed to be late. After half an hour Jon, as best man, telephoned the hotel to check on the cause for the delay. Lara's father broke down. While he had been seeing the bridesmaids settled in their limo, Lara had taken off the dress she had just been photographed in and left by a rear entrance. A waitress who saw her go said she was crying.

After several poor performances in the air, heavy nightly drinking and verbal aggression towards everyone around him, Nick had been grounded by James, who suggested he should apply for a transfer. It had been good advice. His SAS colleagues neither knew nor cared what lay in his past, and Nick buried his need to hit out deep in the physical and mental demands of his specialized work.

Until five days before Christmas!

He tipped the bottle again. The anaesthetizing spirit

dribbled down his chin to soak into his shirt. Tonight, Lara had turned to face him and revived the pain and humiliation; stripped him naked before that party crowd, degraded him, rendered him helpless. As *they* had.

James found him on the floor out cold, and thanked God he was not faced with searching the bars of Singapore for most of the night. He put Nick to bed and closed the shutters before joining Joyce in their room. He held up the half-empty bottle.

'Precaution in case he revives and attacks it again.'

'That bitch! Standing there as cool as you like and acting as if we had never met. She has ice where her heart should be!'

'Give it a rest,' he said heavily, pulling off his shoes. 'You've been at it all the way home. And if you say just once more I shouldn't have taken him with us tonight I'll not be responsible for my actions. Nick's tough enough to work his way through this.'

'Go on. Add that he's been trained to put his life on the line without hesitation. Remind me that he's been working with the SAS who have bodies like Hercules and nerves of steel,' Joyce countered with continuing heat. 'Nick's still a person, James. A human being with needs and feelings. This isn't some *scare* he's had; something he can banish over a few drinks with the lads.'

'I didn't suggest that. I know him better than you on a professional level. He has a steel will; immense strength of purpose. He'll fight this all the way – has done right from the outset, according to Chris Franklin. We have to support him in that by behaving normally, treating him as the chap we knew when he was with the squadron.'

'But he isn't! That's the point I'm trying to make. He used to be great fun. Wicked sense of humour; up to mischief whenever there was the opportunity. Some of the most audacious squadron pranks were instigated by Nick. And he could charm girls from the age of four to ninety-four. *I* know him better than you on the sexual chemistry level,' she pointed out. 'But *now*. He's wound up so tight it's impossible to reach the Nick who used to be so entertaining. He hasn't smiled once since he arrived, and he sometimes seems to be looking right through me while I'm talking, as if he can see something beyond my face.'

'He probably can. By ignoring it, carrying on as we would with any guest, he'll gradually relax. He needs to be kept occupied; kept from brooding. He's getting psychiatric help to rehabilitate. What he needs from us is a reminder that normal life is there for him when he's ready to rejoin it.' He regarded her with concern. 'You don't regret having him here?'

'Of course not! I just wish I knew how best to get through to him.'

'You're doing wonderfully well simply by being yourself. Don't attempt anything else. Leave that to the psycho boys. I've got him interested in Philip Dunne's file. You can take him to the normal tourist places; chat away as you usually do. Ignore his lack of response. He needs us right now.'

'Mmm, what he certainly *doesn't* need is Lara Scott turning up here. It's a hellish twist of fate.'

'Agreed.'

'I won't ever forget the way he looked in that flower-decked church when Jon announced that the ceremony would not be taking place. I could have wrung Lara's neck *then*. I could have done even more to her tonight when she pretended we'd never met. Dammit, she'd eaten dinner in our house several times when she was engaged to Nick.'

James folded his trousers and began unbuttoning his shirt. 'That was several years ago. Nick's certain to have had a procession of other girls since then.'

'No doubt, but he still came back here and drank a lethal cocktail tonight. We didn't witness their meeting, but Kim said he looked to be in deep shock when he suddenly walked away. In another world, she said, and she's an expert on the subject.'

'If he's still hung up over the girl there's nothing we can do about *that*. Nick's dealing with it in time-honoured fashion.'

As he headed for the shower Joyce said tartly, 'Getting pissed never made any problem go away, as you've discovered often enough.'

He glanced back at her, grinning. 'But it doesn't seem nearly as bad when viewed through an alcoholic blur, sweetheart.'

When Nick left his room, the morning was well advanced and he felt distinctly fragile. Even the liquid notes of a golden oriole outside increased the pounding of a myriad tiny hammers in his head.

Joyce was writing at a small desk and glanced up at his entry. 'You look terrible!'

'That's how I feel. If you're compiling a shopping list add replacements for the bottles I apprehended last night, and give me the bill.'

'Fair enough.' She wrote briefly, then swung round to study him. 'I guess you couldn't face breakfast, but dry toast and a river of black coffee should do the trick. It's what I give James when he's been on a bender.' She crossed the room to ring for the maid. 'I'll join you for some coffee. Time for my elevenses.'

'You're a thoroughly nice woman, Joyce. I should have married someone like you years ago.'

'Someone like me wouldn't have you,' she countered lightly. 'You're too harum-scarum.'

He sank slowly on to a chair, wincing at the pain movement brought. 'Sorry about last night.'

'Don't be. Came as something of a shock to us, too, which is why we let her get away with treating us like strangers. If my wits had been functioning normally I'd have made everyone aware that she'd been our dinner guest several times, and was a regular at squadron events. I imagine her act was for the benefit of Gray Attard, the fiancé twice her age and twice divorced. Some catch!

'According to Kim Collins he's a top man in the marine science field. Lara's in his team. They've flown in to check on marine life around Pulau Pelingi; the effect being made by a particularly virulent type of weed that's threatening to grow out of control and change the normal balance of life in the waters around this part of the world. Sounds like *The Day of the Triffids*, doesn't it? Ah, here's the coffee.'

Although it scalded his tongue, Nick drank it quickly and nibbled a slice of toast while he absorbed what Joyce had said. Lara's right to a career of her own in her chosen field had never been a real issue between them; had never quantified their passion. But an army captain was not the top marine scientist. Attard's age and the number of wives he had gone through was apparently immaterial. She was in his team . . . and in his bed. Lara had all she could desire.

Pushing that thought aside, he concentrated on what else he remembered of last night. The priggish Cranford Fielding, John Vydecker, the kingpin banker who held something of a grip on the business community, and a stunning Chinese jeweller, who might be his mistress.

'Did you know most of the people who were at the party, Joyce?'

'No, we've been here too short a time.' She gave a wry smile. 'We'll soon catch up. James has three invitations for tomorrow evening. Not unusual, I gather. Goes with the job. We'll spend half an hour at the first, then move on to the next. Then the next. I'm learning to make a drink last a long time.' She broke off to answer the telephone beside her chair, and her voice turned suddenly glacial. 'Sorry, *who* did you say you are? Do I know you?'

She turned to hold the receiver towards Nick. 'It's for you. A woman calling herself Lara Scott.'

They exchanged a long meaningful look before Nick crossed to take the call. 'Nick Hawkwood with latest sitrep. Position untenable. All contact severed. Over and out!'

He replaced the receiver and returned to drinking his

coffee. Joyce made no comment and he asked, as if there had been no interruption, 'What do you know about John Vydecker?'

'Only what Ferdy Collins told us. The American bank has financed a number of projects, some of them rumoured to be a trifle dodgy. James has been approached by a local company that obtained a hefty loan from Vydecker. They're offering to undercut the firm presently providing small components for a UK manufacturer selling to the MoD. James thinks Vydecker has a personal interest in the deal because one of the invitations for tomorrow came from his wife.'

Nick nibbled toast while his dulled brain assimilated the information. 'He could have talked to James last night, if that's the case.'

'He had bigger fish to fry, I suppose.' She poured more coffee, then said casually, 'I'm aware that James has passed on his suspicions concerning Philip Dunne and asked you to get to the bottom of what he sees as a mystery. Wicked of him.'

Nick was instantly defensive. 'Why? I think he might be on to something. I'm the obvious guy to follow up on it. He's tied up with the job and I've nothing else to do while I'm here.'

'You should relax and have some fun. Fly up to Penang; swim, sunbathe and chat up the sexy Australian tourists.'

'I'm off Australians right now,' he said carefully, knowing she had spoken without thinking. 'Do you know where I can find Fleur Yang's shop?'

'Her showroom, you mean. Women like Fleur Yang don't have *shops*, Nick. You can buy her jewellery in Raffles Mall, but I imagine the actual workshop is elsewhere.' She studied him shrewdly. 'The girl's truly lovely, but I wouldn't have thought she's your type.'

Remembering that air of submission in her manner, he said, 'She is now.'

By 3 p.m. Nick reckoned he looked and felt respectable enough to seek out Fleur Yang. As he strolled through Raffles

Mall he appreciated Joyce's admonition regarding a shop. Designer names abounded on the elegant carriers toted by shoppers.

The showroom was situated on a corner. The black façade bore the word 'Yang' written in flourishing white script. The windows contained a few items discreetly highlighted against an ultra-modern abstract display design. The message was clear. These premises should only be entered by those who have no need to ask the price before buying. An army pilot who did not fit that category went in and began to study the unusual jewellery in the narrow showcases set in the walls.

A smart young Chinese woman left him to browse for a while before approaching. 'We have a number of other pieces which are not on display, sir. If you have a particular stone in mind I can show you a selection of items, or suggest something suitable for your requirements.'

He turned. 'I'd like a word with Miss Yang.'

'Of course, sir.' She crossed to open a door to a small room containing three black leather armchairs grouped around a low table. 'Miss Yang will join you in a few moments.'

Nick was impressed. This must be where special commissions were discussed and assessed. He wondered how much American backing had been needed to finance this set-up. Had the deal given Vydecker shares in the business? Did he also own shares in the talented designer? Jimmy Yang died only three years after qualifying as a lawyer, so the American would have had little return on that investment. Did he seek regular compensation from Fleur?

'Do you like it, Captain Hawkwood?'

He turned from studying a startling photograph depicting a diamond of such fire light appeared to spill from it like lava from an erupting volcano. Deep in the source of this fire was a face that amazingly incorporated the features of Eastern, Western, African and Native American women so that she became 'everywoman'.

Fleur Yang stood just inside the door, dressed in a fitted black gown with one wide pale satin lapel. Nick thought her a greater work of art than the picture on the wall. She smiled and advanced, closing the door gently. 'People either love it or hate it.'

'How about you?' he asked.

'I'm never sure, and therein lies its brilliance, because it compels me to assess it each time I enter this room. If I loved it I would simply accept that it will always be there and forget to look at it. If I hated it I should not have it on the wall.'

Charmed anew he said, 'That sounds remarkably Confucian.'

She gave a soft laugh as she gestured an invitation to sit, then settled on another chair with the third between them.

'I followed your advice last night, mingling with the guests, nodding every so often and saying nothing. Between the nods I learned that I'd been befriended by the renowned Fleur Yang.'

She accepted the compliment with composure, sitting quietly as she waited for him to continue.

'I also learned that much of your work is commissioned; that you've several times made items for the merchant banker John Vydecker.'

'You wish me to make something for you? A gift for your wife?'

She had neatly sidestepped the subject of the American and put him on the spot. 'I'm not married, Miss Yang.'

'For your fiancée, perhaps?'

He decided to go along with her and pursue a different line. 'My sister.'

'I see. It will be helpful if you describe her to me; tell me the style of clothes she wears.'

He enjoyed her close proximity while he gave answers to questions on the non-existent Virginia Hawkwood, who, she eventually decided, would most appreciate a pair of earrings.'

'Would Miss Hawkwood prefer any particular stone?'

Bingo, the perfect cue! 'She's very fond of lapis lazuli.'

Nick was trained to read and interpret people's reactions, but

57

he saw nothing in her dark eyes or in her manner that told him the words held any special significance for her. So James was mistaken in his surmise that Philip Dunne's mention of the blue stone could be connected to this cultured woman.

He set about getting himself out of a commitment to spend a year's salary on a pair of designer earrings. 'I must point out that I have to return to the UK very shortly, so I'll understand if you're unable to take on a rush job. You must have a backlog of commissions to meet.'

She got to her feet in a fluidly elegant movement, leaving him to struggle up from a soft chair in which his weight had settled too deeply.

'There will be time. I merely create the pieces. My craftsmen make them up. It will be an enjoyable challenge to find an image that will compliment the colour and texture of lapis lazuli. I will show you the design on paper, then you must decide on silver, white gold or platinum for the setting. It will affect the price.'

'How about discussing that over dinner? Your business demands interrupted our conversation yesterday. Couldn't we continue it by combining business with pleasure tonight?'

She studied him gravely. 'The British have a saying about not letting grass grow under the feet. I think you are following that advice, Captain.'

He gave a faint nod. 'I did tell you I'll be in Singapore for only a short time. And is that a yes or a no, Miss Yang?'

James was already at home when he got back, so Nick lost no time in tackling him over a sundowner on the verandah. 'If you want me to be your leg man I'll need to read that stuff in Dunne's file. I'm working in the dark.'

James raised his eyebrows. 'Thought you'd turned the job down.'

'I chased a wild goose on the lapis lazuli. Fleur Yang knows nothing on that score, but she was reluctant to talk about Vydecker. Could be there *is* something going on between the sheets. If so, she's certain to know a hell of a lot more about him than the size of his balls. Joyce said he's backing a company that's after you to support their bid on a defence deal with the UK.'

'That's right.'

'I thought you were here to assist British sales to Singapore.'

'So I am, but this is slightly complex. Senoko Components are keen to sell switches to Rees and Hardy at a price well below what the UK company is presently paying the Japs for them. As you know, Rees and Hardy supply the MoD with inertial navigation systems, some of which are then sold on to the Singapore Air Force. You'll appreciate that the defence roundabout often results in the enemy being killed by weapons the poor buggers' countrymen helped to manufacture. The arms market is highly lucrative and therefore just as highly competitive. Hence why there's so much dirty dealing in that line.'

'Will you give Senoko your support?'

'It's not really necessary. They could deal direct with Rees and Hardy, but I could smooth the way for them. It's a small company wanting to break into the world market, so they'd be grateful for official backing of any kind. I was taken over their workshop last week and met the two directors.'

'And?'

'I discovered they already supply switches to AXK Systems in Jakarta; a company on our black list which is mentioned in Dunne's file. It doesn't necessarily mean Senoko are also dodgy. Rees and Hardy are free to decide who they deal with, but I've a feeling Vydecker is set to have a persuasive word in my ear at his place tomorrow. Fielding has been invited on the odd occasion, but the American normally consorts with the mercantile rather than the diplomatic brotherhood of the East. There must be an ulterior motive behind this invitation. I'm very small fry on the Singapore scene.'

Nick drank his whisky thoughtfully. 'Umm, regardless of anything else, John Vydecker appears worth investigating. I'll see what I can find out from his protégée tonight.'

'Oh?'

'I'm taking her to dinner.'

James's smile widened. 'A leg *and* tit man. Go to it, Hawk!'

'If I'd known you were having a *man's* conversation I'd have stayed in my room,' said Emma, arriving silently from the corridor and sinking dramatically on the settee facing Nick.

James said equably, 'If you will creep about the place you're sure to hear all manner of conversations not suitable for your ears. Much better to have stayed in your room where you could talk quite acceptably to yourself.'

She made a great show of ignoring him and, with colour high, asked, 'Who are you taking to dinner, Hawk?'

'It's *Nick* to you, Emma. I have a date with someone I met at last night's party.'

Her flush deepened. 'Surely not with *her*. Not after what she did.'

'Who d'you mean?'

Confused, she shook her head. 'I don't know. Tell me.'

'A Chinese woman who designs expensive jewellery. I hear she's quite renowned.'

'You don't mean Fleur Yang!' She breathed the name with adolescent awe. 'Her stuff is *fabulous*. It's absolutely tops! She designs for Schiffer, Martinez, Fergie . . . oh, *crowds* of famous women. Why are you taking her to dinner, and what information can she give you?'

Nick found her intensity irritating and tried to counter it. 'She's going to tell me the estimated price of a pair of earrings I commissioned for an imaginary sister. I'm aiming to slide out of the deal, otherwise James will have to buy them for your mother.'

He did not meet Fleur Yang that evening. The young woman assistant rang an hour later to give Miss Yang's apologies. An emergency had arisen. Nick was disappointed. Apart from being frustrated in his investigation of Vydecker, he wanted to see her again. He found her fragile beauty and gentle manner very appealing.

The Wellnuts had no official engagements so they spent the early evening playing board games with their children. James was accused of cheating, as usual, and chaos reigned until Emma said the children should go to bed.

Gina rounded on her. 'You're children. *You* should go to bed.'

'Don't be impertinent,' Emma snapped. 'I'm twice your age . . . and I know things *you* are far too babyish to understand.' With a significant glance at Nick, she added, 'Don't I?'

Joyce tactfully took them all off, the younger pair to bed and Emma to give her opinion on the dress her mother should wear to the parents' tea at her school tomorrow.

'They're great to have around, but only for short periods,' James observed wryly as he got to his feet. 'Drink?'

'Thanks.' The best part of the whole evening.

At the sideboard James said, 'I fear Emma has the adolescent hots for you.'

'They start young these days.'

'So what was behind that knowing look she gave you?'

It was said casually enough but Nick reacted with flash aggression. 'What the hell kind of bloody insulting question is that?'

'You're not obliged to answer. This isn't an interrogation,' James countered calmly as he crossed with the drinks.

Anger slowly died while Nick swallowed a good half of the whisky and water. 'Sorry. Still jet-lagged.' But he knew it was more than that and it worried him. He drank the rest in one gulp, then glanced across at James. 'Walls apparently have ears in a house with no glass in the windows.'

James worked on that for a few moments then swore. 'Didn't occur to either of us our bedroom was being bugged by that little madam when she should be asleep. Christ knows what she's overheard! How come you found out?'

'She offered to stand by me in my hour of need.'

'Oh God! Now it's my turn to apologize.'

Nick angled the conversation. 'Is that cryptic file of Dunne's here or in your office?'

'Here. Why?'

'I'd like to go through it tonight. It'd be helpful to have a nautical chart to refer to.'

'Can do. The chart's not bang up to date but it'll serve the purpose. So you think I'm on to something?'

'Not in connection with Dunne's death. Collins told me he and Jimmy Yang were a pair of madmen who thrived on taking risks. It's probable they took one too many that day. What interests me is why. I accept the macho element in Dunne's personality. To fly fast jets a guy has to acknowledge the danger involved, but gung-ho antics would have had him grounded fast. A strong sense of responsibility is as important as any other quality in a good combat pilot. Men come cheap. Harriers don't. You claim Dunne wouldn't have been selected for your job if he'd blotted his service copybook, and I'll go along with that, so his search for thrills must have started after he got here. I find that intriguing.'

'But you've already decided that he resented younger guys doing what he longed to do, and broke out as soon as he was no longer restricted by squadron limitations.'

'I was merely theorizing, although it makes sense. Your idea that he was being manipulated by local villains doesn't, because he'd surely have been over-protective of his wife not hellbent on making her a widow.'

'*I* was merely theorizing,' James retaliated. 'Until you do your leg man stuff that's all either of us can do.'

'Something else that's interesting is this Senoko deal you suspect Vydecker of backing. He seems to have too many irons in the fire. Men like him get my back up. I need to meet him.'

'Come along tomorrow evening. I'll introduce you as a colleague. These affairs are so transitory anyone can gate-crash.'

The telephone rang. Joyce sang out from the hall that she

would take the call. 'It'll be Cynthia Boswell about the charity concert on Saturday.'

It wasn't. She came in the room and caught Nick's eye. 'For you.' His surging anger died when she added, 'It's Ferdy Collins.'

'You sure it's me he wants?' he asked without moving.

'He mentioned a guy named Nick. That's you, isn't it?' She smiled teasingly. 'If I'd said Fleur Yang was on the line you'd have been on your feet like a shot.'

'She'd only be after my money,' he said, going through to take the call and wondering how to explain his abrupt departure from the Collins's party.

'Evening, Ferdy.'

'Hi there, Nick. If you've nothing on tomorrow would you like a helo trip? I'm going over to one of the outer islands. Thought you might like to come along. Do some sightseeing. Take off o-nine thirty. Are you on?'

Totally unexpected. His heart began to race. 'Yes. Thanks.'

'No worries. Catch you then.'

With the prospect of getting back in the air again, and in a helicopter, Nick soon headed for his room, leaving the Wellnuts to relax on their own. He was armed tonight with Philip Dunne's file instead of a bottle, and if the shadow of Lara Scott hovered it was not allowed to materialize.

With the aid of the chart Nick found no more significance in Dunne's grid references than James had, yet it had to be there somewhere. He noted a restricted live firing area on and extensively around Pulau Sudong, and mentally added a military cock-up to the list of possible fatal hazards encountered by Dunne and Jimmy Yang. Nick knew air-to-ground combat could occasionally be disastrously inaccurate.

He next studied the sets of initials. James had managed to link some to those of companies manufacturing defence equipment, but in today's world of initials each set could be alternatively interpreted. He scanned the list of dates James said matched shipping movements. Some were highlighted in blue, some in red. Inward and outward passages?

The comment 'check on lapis lazuli' appeared three times against these dates. Nick brooded on it for some minutes. There was an obvious link here. Jimmy Yang was in cahoots with Dunne on risky escapades: he was Fleur's brother. She worked with semi-precious stones. Yet she had not shown an unusual reaction at Nick's mention of the blue stone. Her relationship with Vydecker was uncertain, but the American had also invested in Jimmy Yang's career. More must be learned about the dead Chinese lawyer.

Nick turned his attention back to Dunne, who came over as something of an enigma. What had prompted his sudden craze for kicks? Had his wife's return to England been stage-managed? Could James be right about Dunne becoming forcibly enmeshed in illegal arms dealing? It might explain the move to get Alison safely home, and Dunne's reckless-ness with his own life. *Death before dishonour?* Come to that, had Yang also been coerced? A legal man who could bend the rules?

Nick sat for some time at the open window while ques-tions and part-answers ran through his mind. Then he real-ized he had forgotten one pawn in the game whom he had considered important when James first presented his suspi-cions. Sir Charles Fanshawe, one-time governor of Hong Kong and still influential in the Foreign Office! Dunne had been highly recommended for the post of Defence Adviser by his wife's grandfather. There had to be a significant reason for the old boy's intervention.

He reviewed the facts once more, but no sudden dawning of light in the darkness occurred. He needed more informa-tion. Glancing at the bedside clock he discovered it would be 4 p.m. in Cornwall. He crossed to the telephone and dialled.

'Hawkwood Books. Good afternoon.'

Nick took a breath. 'Hi, Jon.'

A short silence. 'Hi, yourself.'

A longer silence. 'How's Lucy?'

'Better now you've hoofed it.'

'The kids?'

'Also.'

Nick waited a moment. 'And how about you?'

They had always been too close for long-term bitterness. 'I chased Chris Franklin down. He told me where you are. Didn't it occur to you I'd want to know?'

'I've been in lots of places you didn't know about, kid brother,' he said.

'Hell, Nick! Well, have you found what you wanted; sun, girls, bars? Paradise?'

The ice was broken. 'I guess they're all here but my host has set me to work.' He gave Jon a run-down of James's suspicions. 'It all sounds cockeyed enough to contain an element of truth and I'd like to get to the bottom of it.'

'I'd be happier if you stuck to your original plan instead of playing Action Man again.'

'I'm hoping to combine the two. There's a stunning Chinese girl featuring strongly; the sister of the guy who died with Dunne. There's also an off-stage player I'd like some info on. Sir Charles Fanshawe, one-time governor of Hong Kong and presently a big shot in the FCO. Get in touch with Chris Franklin again; ask if he knows anything about Fanshawe that isn't in *Who's Who*. And find out all you can about Philip Dunne. There'll be press reports of his heroism in the Falklands, if nothing else. Oh, and Alison Dunne's mother lives not far from you in Mousehole. Take the family for a day out and ask around. Shopkeepers like to gossip; one's sure to tell you how awful it was that the old girl was told she was dying when she wasn't. If Alison is actually staying with her mother get what dirt you can on her, too.'

'Anything else?' asked Jon with heavy sarcasm.

'Not until I've delved further.' He was unsure what else to say. 'Good to talk to you again, Jon.'

'And to you. Keep at it, Hawk.'

Nick slept peacefully until the maid brought a cup of tea at seven next morning.

Four

The former RAF airfield and seaplane base at Seletar was home to the island's Flying College, Flying Club and charter companies. Nick resolutely pushed back images of a burning Lynx lighting the night sky as he walked past parked aircraft on a clear morning when a light breeze eased the humidity. It was a familiar environment; the smell of aviation fuel, the swarm of overalled mechanics, the roar of engines overhead. Men going places. Entering the office of Collins Air Charters, his heart sank. Ferdy was in conversation with Lara's future husband, Professor Gray Attard.

'G'day, Nick, how goes it?' he asked cheerily. 'Gray wants a look-see at Pelingi. He and his team plan to set their base on the island for a three-month project.'

Attard smiled a greeting. Nick nodded, straightfaced.

'Until I've spied out the land I won't know how far from the landing zone our gear will have to be transported. Ferdy says the island is largely undeveloped with just a small fishing village to the south. We'll be working from the northern shore.'

While Ferdy finalized his flight plan, Attard rambled on about the threat to marine life of a plant with a Latin name that rolled off his tongue as smoothly as everything else he said. Nick studied a girlie calendar showing a sloe-eyed nude beckoning coyly from behind a painted fan. He preferred Fleur Yang. Had she posed erotically for Vydecker in return for financial backing?

Ferdy issued helmets and they walked out to the helicopter. The friends sat together up front, and Nick was glad they could not see how his hands shook while fastening his harness. He spent the first five minutes of the flight battling against the impulse to free himself. Dear God, how could he hope to resume his career if restraint continued to induce panic?

His passion for this brand of flying soon dominated and he then contributed to the three-way conversation while studying the ground. Ferdy pointed out landmarks, reciting the history of areas surviving from the time Singapore had been part of Malaya and governed by the British. He was well informed on the tragic fall of the country when Japanese invaded overland instead of by sea, as expected. A number of Australians were slaughtered, or imprisoned in the infamous Changi jail where many subsequently died. Attard introduced a sour note by resurrecting the popular Australian belief that they were sacrificed by the British, who made every tactical error in the book. As the sole Briton in the aircraft, Nick decided to let the comment ride.

'Coming up ahead is Sentosa, an Asian Disney-style theme island that hasn't quite lived up to expectations,' Ferdy said. 'There are the usual formulaic attractions for kids, and a five-star hotel with its own artificial beach. You can cross to it by ferry, over a road bridge or by cable car. It's all there, but I guess the Disney magic and organization are lacking.'

'What's that coming up below?' asked Nick.

'A twenty-foot-high merlion said to be standing guard over the mouth of the Singapore river. It's floodlit at night and illuminated from within. The eyes glow with menacing colours as it spews water.' He chuckled. 'It makes a handy landmark coming in after dark with instruments on the blink.'

'What does it represent?' asked Attard.

'It's a creature from ancient Chinese mythology, not to be confused with what we know as a sealion. This is half lion, half fish. Same way a mermaid is a girl with a tail. Locals see it as a potent national symbol. If you want the full story talk to Kim. I'm not into that kind of stuff. Had enough of it back home with the Abos and their Dreamtime. Strictly down to earth, me.'

'Even when you're six thou above it?' joked Attard.

'Too right. Never had time for anything fanciful. Ghosts, poltergeists, witchcraft; a sackful of moonshine! Food for bloody loons! Yet take my Kim. Highly intelligent, crammed full of more brains than I've ever had, but she believes in *feng shui*. In my opinion it's no more than Chinese mumbo-jumbo, yet she consulted a so-called expert before placing a single piece of furniture in our house. I thought she was kidding me on. No sir, she was deadly serious. If the old guy had put the spooks on the house itself there's no way she would have lived there.'

'How many times have you avoided walking under a ladder, mate?' asked Attard.

'That's to ensure I'm not splashed with paint, not because I think bad luck will dog me if I don't.'

'And you're happy to fly on a Friday the thirteenth?'

'Sure I am. They're *lucky* days for me because it means I get paid a fat fee. Like you'll be paying me for shifting your gear,' he added with a chuckle.

Attard said, 'How about you, Nick. Any hang-ups?'

Yeah, being . . . He turned his mind from that. 'I fly with a model hawk in the cockpit. My squadron name. Wouldn't have felt happy without it there. Pilots are a superstitious breed. I'm surprised you really haven't a talisman of some kind, Ferdy.'

Collins reached into his breast pocket and held up a small medallion. 'This was given to Grandad by an early barn-stormer who made an emergency landing on our sheep station. The old folks took him in, treated his injuries and gave him a bed and food until he was able to leave. They wouldn't accept payment, so he gave them something he'd won as an RFC ace in 1917. It's a squadron medal celebrating his twentieth kill. He said it might be worth something when he and his pals are history.' He replaced it in his pocket. 'It prompted my urge to fly. I never take off without it.'

'You old fraud,' Attard accused with a laugh. 'No time

for anything fanciful? Food for bloody loons? You're right in there with them.'

'Does that mean you've no truck with anything in that line? You face more risks deep beneath the ocean than up here.'

'Not if you rigorously check your equipment and use a top back-up team. I don't need toys or medallions. I simply get on with the job.'

'You might wish you had some kind of lucky charm if you come across a merlion cruising the sea around Pelingi,' said Ferdy.

'Now that would be something! I've made some shattering discoveries before now. Found previously unknown species, proved others are not extinct, as believed. Come across corpses on a coupla occasions. Not pretty when they've been in the drink a while. Lara came face to face with one last year. Shook her up, but she's a game girl. Never backs away from anything.'

Except marriage to me, Nick thought. Then he was asked if he had ever done any diving by the man who was so self-confident he had no need of luck.

'I took an Army course several years ago.' He didn't add that he had perfected his expertise in Oman, nor that he had seen more bodies in war-torn Bosnia than Attard was likely to come across in his work. Those experiences had not made Nick top man in any field but they had taught him much about human nature.

'An Army survival course bears no comparison with marine exploration, Nick,' Attard said dismissively. 'I've dived all over the world in some pretty tricky conditions, and in areas known to be highly treacherous. I'm now the recognized authority on . . .'

Nick stopped listening and studied the scattered islands they were heading for. Although they were well past the huge mercantile heart of the famous harbour there was still a mass of shipping. Somewhere among it was the corpse of Philip Dunne – or what remained of it. Maybe Lara would come face to face with it and not back off, game girl that she was!

A few minutes later, Ferdy interrupted Attard's monologue to draw their attention to an island lying nine or ten miles from their destination. 'Harking back to our conversation on good luck, that's Pulau Gombak. The *feng shui* there is so bad no one will set foot on it and ships keep well clear.'

'Here be dragons,' quoted Attard.

'Or merlions,' Nick suggested. 'What's the story, Ferdy?'

'Kim can dot the i's and cross the t's, but it seems that centuries ago a Chinese deckhand called Wu was dumped on Gombak to die because he'd murdered another hand during a fight on board. He threw in his lot with the malevolent spirits on the island and was given their evil powers. He would conjure up storms when ships passed, and the spirits lured them on to the beach. Neither the vessels nor the crews were seen again. The legend claims Wu ate the men and used their ships and cargoes to build himself a luxury pagoda filled with riches from all over the world.

'The advent of steam and oceanographers changed things. A dangerous shoal was charted alongside the island, and evidence of wrecks containing human bones put paid to the myth. Almost.'

'Why'd you say that?' asked Attard.

'*Feng shui* is a potent force. Today's Singaporean is modern and greatly westernized, yet Gombak is still regarded as an evil place. To feed that is the rumour that during the Japanese occupation the island was used for obscene purposes. Screams and moans were heard; fast boats arrived there and departed in the dead of night. The British investigated when they took Singapore back but found no real evidence to support the story. But it persists. A number of people were apprehended by the Japs and simply vanished during those terrible years.'

They were over the island now, and Ferdy said, 'Look at it. Wall to wall vegetation! Not somewhere you'd want to visit, bad *feng shui* or not. Pelingi coming up at ten o'clock. A better prospect altogether.'

Nick was mentally in another place where obscene purposes had been perpetrated; where the screams and moans were his own. In consequence, he released himself from the harness long before Ferdy set the helicopter down in a small clearing from which the sea could be glimpsed.

He walked behind the other two as they assessed how much of the wild growth would have to be hacked back to allow the equipment to be carried through to the shore. Attard had gained permission to do this, and it was easy to see why. The people of the fishing village to the south hugged their side of Pelingi, receiving supplies and transporting the fish they caught by a twice-weekly boat. The rest of the island was deserted save for wildlife.

The beach was little more than a narrow strip of sand and shingle littered with stinking seaweed and jetsam from the heavy ocean traffic. The water lapping it was dark and deep. Attard was excited.

'Perfect! The land falls away sharply, giving us deep water close in. Saves wasting time getting out to where we can work.' He indicated the murky water with a sweep of his arm. 'You can see the damage already being done by that bloody growth.'

Nick saw nothing, but he was not in Attard's game. He could not get het up over a voracious weed beneath the sea, although he was prepared to accept that it might ultimately affect mankind. He wandered along the ugly shore, leaving the two men to discuss the transportation of a vast amount of equipment in the shortest possible time. To keep himself from looking out to where Gombak was a dark blob on the horizon Nick thought about the upcoming Vydecker party. Tonight should give him the opportunity to confirm whether or not the banker was linked with whatever Dunne had vaguely documented in his file. Loath as he had been to take James seriously, he now saw that sleuthing was just what he needed to fill his days here. Jon had been right. Getting pissed and shagging was not the way back. He had had a good go at the first, which had simply deadened feeling and been unfair on his hosts. As for the second . . . which led his thoughts to Fleur Yang. She would have to make contact to show him her design for those damned earrings . . . which led his thoughts to lapis lazuli. There *had* to be a connection!

'Nick, come back. All is forgiven.'

He turned at Ferdy's shout and retraced his steps. They had sorted out the logistical problem and were ready to leave.

'Can't say I envy you a spell in this place,' Nick said, 'Bad *feng shui* here would get my vote.'

Attard cast him a superior look. 'The Army of today is mollycoddled. Every comfort wherever you go. You should try living in some of the conditions I've endured.'

Nick's flash of anger was swiftly doused by Ferdy's invitation to take on the return flight. 'Indulge yourself, Nick.'

Attard spoke up swiftly. 'I'm paying for this, Ferdy. Don't care to be flown by holiday amateurs.'

'Nick's far more qualified than me. He's been trained to fly even under battle conditions. That's no holiday amateur, mate.'

'I want a safe flight, not military histrionics.'

Nick's anger returned in a rush. 'You might be king of the depths, Attard, but you're presently in the hands of princes of the air. Upset us, and the only way you'll leave here is on one of the twice-weekly fish boats.'

Ferdy grinned. 'So let's roll, Nick.'

Seated at the controls, Nick secured his harness with no thoughts other than those needed to run through pre-flight checks. Before long the engine roar, the whirr of rotor blades, the shaking as the aircraft battled to rise while held on the ground all brought an intense rush of adrenalin that set his heart thumping against his ribs. He was really living again.

Taking the helicopter gently and smoothly to treetop level, Nick hovered to get his bearings before swinging round to head fast and low over the sea. He was on the road to re-discovering Nick Hawkwood. He had lost none of his skill.

They would *have* to reinstate him as a squadron pilot. He was good. No, more than good.

They were halfway back when Nick's super-elation created an urge to take Attard down a peg or two. He spoke to the man beside him. 'OK if we dance around a bit?'

Ferdy waved a hand. 'You have control.'

The potent words! Nick began modestly, but mounting stimulation soon encouraged him to indulge in aerobatics that completed his sense of freedom up where he knew he belonged. This *was* living!

Attard complained forcibly. 'Stop this kids' stuff! If this is how you treat your clients I'll deal with another charter company.'

'Aw, keep your cool, mate, we're just having a little fun.'

'Fun be buggered! My guts have twice travelled to my mouth. Once more and your back'll be covered in vomit.'

Ferdy made signs with his hands. 'Head for home, Cap'n.'

Nick flattened out, smiling maliciously as he said over the intercom, 'Today's flight passengers are mollycoddled. Every comfort wherever they go. You should try flying in some of the conditions I've known. Airsickness would be the least of your worries.'

The resulting silence completed Nick's sense of well-being and he made a copybook landing. Looking pale beneath his tan Attard headed for the office, ignoring the two pilots.

'Hope I haven't ruined a beautiful friendship,' said Nick.

'Nah. We used to be mates way back, but he's become an opinionated old fart. Success has gone to his head. I'm the first guy to appreciate expertise in any field, and he's a bloody master in his, but we're all just flesh and blood when it comes down to basics.' They had almost reached the office when he added, 'Sorry you had to leave us early the other night. Kim said you didn't feel too good.'

'That's right,' he murmured, coming down to earth abruptly.

'She wants you to have dinner with us; said she had no

chance to talk to you. She'll ring Joyce to fix it.' He pushed open the door. 'How's about a cold beer?'

'Great!' The word froze on his lips as he saw Lara having her ear bent by her irate fiancé.

She turned calmly from his tirade, having had a few moments' warning of the situation. 'Hallo again, Captain Hawkwood.'

Nick nodded woodenly.

'Who's for a beer?' asked Ferdy, walking to a large refrigerator. 'I can get your team a discount from my supplier, Gray. Him and me have an understanding. Any pals I introduce get a special rate.'

'How much of backhander do you take?' asked Lara. It was a jokey comeback, but there was no humour in her voice. She was just covering an awkward moment.

Ferdy handed ice-cold cans to them all. 'I have a permanent discount. And I get a gift each Christmas. We have more teasets in our house than we have chairs for guests, Lara.' Nobody laughed, so he said, 'When d'you want to start the move to Pelingi, Gray?'

'Around midweek. Rest of my team arrive then.'

'Good. Ronnie Chan gets back from Bangkok with a Sikorsky tomorrow. I'll book him to start Wednesday. Should be able to get it all in place end of the week. That suit you?'

Attard nodded coolly, so Ferdy continued to mend fences by questioning Lara on what she would be doing on Pelingi. Nick studied her as he drank his beer. She was worth looking at. A yellow shirt that moulded her breasts was tucked into close-fitting shorts. She had always liked displaying her body. 36–22–34. He remembered her vital statistics. His gaze moved to the long brown legs that made her only two inches shorter than his own seventy-three. He recalled the smoothness of them when they had entwined with his, and the wicked things she could do with them in a shared bath.

He had dubbed her accent 'educated Strine'. She had retaliated by calling his 'Sandhurst Arabic'. Watching as she spoke to Ferdy, he remembered a lot more about the times they had spent together. Heated intellectual discussions, wild water-skiing races, hotly competitive swimming sessions: shared passions for jazz, lobster and *Dad's Army*. Her favourite position for lovemaking, the glory of her nakedness, the softness of auburn hair lying across his chest after sex. *The non-wedding!*

He turned for the door as visions of stained-glass windows, bridesmaids and guests' pitying glances superimposed themselves on office furniture. He had come on the MRT and faced a longish walk back to the station in afternoon heat. He could have rung for a taxi in the office if he had not had to distance himself from Dr Scott-soon-to-be-Attard. The move had failed. She came up beside him, slightly breathless.

'Nick, we have to talk.'

He kept walking; refused to look at her.

'There are things to be straightened out between us.'

'It's two years too late.'

'We have to clear the air.'

'Comment as before.'

She grabbed his arm; forced him to stop. 'This is as difficult for me as it is for you.'

'Is it really?' he flared. 'That's why you're flaunting all you've got and dogging him like a smitten teenager, is it?'

She ignored the outburst. 'Why are you in Singapore?'

'You've no interest in my life. All you want to know is will I put it around that you chicken out at the eleventh hour. No, actually it's the eleventh hour and fifty-nine minutes. Don't worry, I'll let him find that out for himself. It's a once-in-a-lifetime's experience, believe me.'

'Nick—'

'Maybe what you really wanted all along was a sugar-daddy with matrimonial know-how and an ego big enough to compensate for the size of his ageing dick.'

She held his arm as he made to move off, and there was real distress in her voice. 'I explained why I did it in my letter.'

He shook off her hand. 'You mean the one you wrote three months too late? I binned it unopened. I had a successful career to get on with. No time for immature confessions. Go back to your arrogant deep-sea lover, Lara. You're two of a kind.'

He walked on alone.

Nick arranged to meet the Wellnuts outside the Vydecker home. He had not wanted to attend a bash given by a French captain of industry. Cocktail parties were not his favourite scene. He mused that James must have sobered considerably to apply for this post that was awash with them.

During his brief wait in an air-conditioned taxi, Nick told himself the flight that morning had proved he had a future with the AAC if they would reinstate him as a pilot. He saw no reason why not. Encountering Lara again had initially been a serious setback, but anger had now replaced the humiliation. And she would be out on Pelingi by the end of this week.

His thoughts turned to that other island: wall to wall vegetation and malevolent spirits. His service with the Army had shown that evil was a powerful force in today's world. History proved it always had been. No reason to doubt that places could emanate evil the way humans did. His father had experienced and reported it; school holidays in the Middle East had persuaded himself and Jon there were forces beyond human understanding. It had sometimes scared them to think they might not be always in control of their destiny. They both now knew that to be true.

Instantly, images of Jon, white-faced and bitter, effing at the Army, his nurses, his own stupidity, his brother and even Lucy, rose up once more. Close on them came vivid recollections of their father, dishevelled, unshaven, loudly and drunkenly calling down curses on the fates that had ended his career. Then the church, and the expressions of his brother officers in full dress uniforms, girded with swords that would not form a triumphal arch.

A sharp rapping sound brought him from the past to see Joyce's face outside the taxi window. Nick paid the driver with sweaty palms, then climbed from the car with his pulse pounding in his temples.

'A few more months of this and it won't surprise me if James starts going off the rails like Philip Dunne,' she said jokingly. 'It was a real stinker, Nick. Let's hope this will prove jollier.'

Nick silently followed his friends into the house, fighting off the threatening images.

Binnie Vydecker was large and opulent in a dress smothered with diamanté, and with jewels flashing at every point where women traditionally wore them. Her personality seemed dull, in comparison. She greeted the Wellnuts with little interest, but when James introduced Nick, he sensed he was being closely assessed. As the Wellnuts headed for someone they knew, Binnie held Nick back.

'My daughter will take care of you, introduce you to other younger guests who are here merely to enjoy themselves.'

Next minute he was confronted by a young woman in her early twenties with a voluptuous figure on the brink of bursting from a dark-red, close-fitting dress slit from hem to thigh, cheongsam style. There was nothing Chinese about her all-American gloss, however. Shoulder-length bouncy brown hair, artificial heavily mascaraed eyelashes, lipstick so shiny he'd hesitate to kiss her for fear of it being transferred to his own mouth, and very long, polished fingernails. When she smiled it was impossible not to admire the orthodontist's workmanship.

Three of Nick's less than perfect teeth had been smashed during his interrogation. A military dentist had repaired the damage reasonably well.

'Let's go get a drink,' she said, linking her arm through his and leading him to a Malay steward filling glasses. 'I'm Zona. That's the shortened version. I was born in Arizona, so Daddy named me after the state.'

'I was born in Damascus, but I'm called Nick.'

She seemed to find that hugely funny and aired her perfect teeth for him to admire again. 'You British are so quaint!'

Nick accepted a glass from the steward and sipped experimentally. It was a pretty potent cocktail with a whisky base. Vydecker clearly liked to relax his guests before talking business. 'How long have you lived in Singapore, Zona?'

She waved her hands expansively. 'We spend time all over. The bank has branches in Hong Kong, Bangkok, Shanghai, Jakarta. We have apartments in each city.'

So Daddy had fingers in many Oriental pies, including volatile Indonesia! Nick decided he could probably find out more about Vydecker from this girl who was coming on like mad to him than from the banker himself.

'We always go home for Thanksgiving, of course.'

'To Arizona?'

'*Boston.* Mommy's a De Witt.'

Nick nodded understandingly, only because Ferdy had told him Binnie was a member of one of America's foremost families. 'You're a much travelled lady, then.'

'I guess. Europe, too. But we've always avoided the Middle East. Daddy says it's too unpredictable. They're not easy people to understand and hostilities can flare at any time. Don't you agree?'

'Yes.' This was not the way he wanted to go. 'Your father must have greater empathy with Orientals as he spends so much time among them.'

Zona smilingly exchanged his empty glass for a full one as she gratifyingly embarked on her family history. 'Grandaddy Vydecker was a naval commander with the Pacific fleet. He made some shrewd contacts during that time, so when the war ended he got into the market early. People who'd suffered under the Japanese were just so grateful to the Americans who liberated them, they were happy to have them run things while they got back on their feet. When Daddy became president of the bank, business was booming, so none of the shareholders voted for change. That's the way it's been ever since.'

With most of the second cocktail inside him, Nick asked, 'And Arizona Vydecker is all set to take over as the bank's first woman president when her father retires?'

She touched his arm, glowed up at him. 'I am to be the feminine power *behind* the next president. When I find the right man.'

You haven't found him yet, Nick thought, easing away from her close proximity. He glanced across at Vydecker. 'There's no rush. Your father appears to be in the peak of condition. I'd like to meet him.'

Zona glowed further. 'Sure thing, but as you said, there's no rush. Tell me more about yourself, Nick.'

'I fly military helicopters. Big business, boardroom battles, cementing big international deals are beyond me. All I know about banking is they keep telling me I'm overdrawn.'

'Take out a loan, big spender.' Her shiny lipstick came perilously near his shirtfront. 'Are you married, Nick?'

'Too busy. And Army life doesn't appeal to many women.'

'But I guess Army *fliers* do. How long is your R and R? We could have a little fun while you're here.'

When Vydecker approached at that moment Nick had the wild idea he was coming to save his daughter from the lure of Army fliers. But he was wrong.

'Honey, Mr Shen has to leave shortly and wishes to speak to you very particularly. I believe he has a birthday gift for you.'

This caused no excitement in a girl to whom gifts were possibly an everyday event. Army fliers clearly were not. She was reluctant to leave.

'Daddy, this is Nick Hawkwood. He's a pilot with the British.' She giggled. 'I think he needs advice on his finances.'

Cool eyes flicked over Nick without interest. Finances nowhere impressive enough to warrant this man's attention. Nick offered his hand deliberately.

'You hadn't time for a proper introduction at the Collinses' party, although Fleur attempted one. Your moments were precious, you said.'

Vydecker hesitated, then gave a brief handshake. 'I'm a very busy man, Mr Hawkwood.'

'*Captain* Hawkwood. So am I when I'm not on leave. No expense-account lunches in my job, of course, but I could be useful to you in a small way. I'm staying with my close friends, the Wellnuts. Could have a word with James about this Senoko deal you're backing. Rees and Hardy supply a lot of our equipment. It's good stuff. I recommend it.'

The American gave a sour smile. 'Glad to hear that. Have yourself another drink, Captain, then go get a bite to eat from the buffet. Binnie caters for the five thousand.' He turned to his daughter. 'Zona, Mr Shen is waiting.'

And that's as far as I'll get with Daddy, thought Nick as the pair walked away. Yet he had gleaned much from Zona. Any man whose father had made 'shrewd contacts and got into the market early' with oppressed people eager to show their gratitude to their liberators had to be suspect. Exploitation had surely been the basis of Grandaddy's success. Was Vydecker continuing the trend?

For fifteen minutes Nick silently hovered on the fringes of groups discussing markets, economies and exchange rates. Vydecker's name was frequently mentioned, and Nick understood Ferdy's comment about needing to keep in with the merchant banker in order to prosper. It was something of a relief when James approached to draw him aside.

'Joyce and I are moving on. The next one should be more fun. I saw you chatting to Vydecker.'

'For about ten of his precious moments. I introduced the subject of Rees and Hardy, but all I got was advice to have another drink and something to eat. I think he rated me at slightly less than two against his five-star guests.'

James grinned. 'I did rather better. He twisted my arm ever so slightly over the Senoko deal.'

'So did you make his day?'

'No, lad, I'm no pushover. I said I'd go into the details more thoroughly when I had time. Rather surprisingly,

Fielding seems keen to put our official seal of approval on it.'

'I'll go into them with you, because I discovered some interesting facts from the daughter.'

'Watch your step there. She's been known to eat men for breakfast. After snacking on them all night.'

'Vydecker's bank has a branch in Jakarta. Now, didn't you say Senoko already sells switches to a company there that's on your black list? So what other links are there between his bank and dodgy companies? More importantly, is Vydecker involved in the sale of complete weapons as well as small components? He travels regularly between Bangkok, Shanghai, Hong Kong and Jakarta, and returns to the US for Thanksgiving. Sounds like a very convenient working routine to me. No wonder Dunne was investigating him.'

'He wasn't. There's no mention of Vydecker in that file,' James reminded him. 'You're the person who's fastened on him.'

Nick regarded his friend shrewdly. 'You know that rodent you claimed to smell. I'd lay even money he's it. I learned a lot about him tonight.'

'Tell me tomorrow.'

'No. Zona's planning on me for tomorrow's breakfast. I'll leave with you. No, I won't,' he immediately contradicted, seeing a slender woman enter the room. 'I'll stay for a while.'

James followed his glance. 'You said you chased a wild goose.'

'Now I'm chasing an elusive swan. Cheerio, Cracker.'

There could be no greater contrast with the Vydecker girl than Fleur Yang in a pale gold sheath, hair in a simple chignon and her mouth touched with apricot. Eminently kissable!

Nick crossed to where she stood with a small group. 'Miss Yang, I need to speak with you urgently.' He nodded at her companions. 'My apologies, but business has sometimes to be conducted over cocktails.' He took her elbow and led her firmly to a space beside a window.

She turned to face him, unsmiling. 'That was rather rude, Captain Hawkwood.'

'Not at all,' he replied calmly. 'Your friend in the red DJ did it two nights ago, and so did John Vydecker. It's perfectly acceptable. We were to have had a business discussion over dinner last night. As your emergency appears to be over, let's switch the plan to tonight and go somewhere for a meal.'

'I have only just now arrived.'

'I haven't. I've spent an hour silently nodding on the periphery of groups talking high finance. Now I want to go somewhere quiet and talk to you.'

After studying him for a few moments she gave a small nod. 'I will explain to John.'

Feeling he owed his host no official thanks, Nick waited while she held a short conversation with Vydecker, who glanced across with narrowed eyes, then he escorted her from the house and hailed a cruising taxi. Once they were seated, he turned to her.

'As I'm a stranger here you'll have to choose where we go, bearing in mind I'm no great shakes with chopsticks.'

She told the driver to take them to the Silver Troika, then asked, 'What is "great shakes"?'

'In that particular context it means I either ask for a fork or spend the entire evening getting to grips with the first course. I'm fine with borscht and blinis.'

It was difficult to judge her mood. Although she had surrendered to persuasion easily, she sat as far as possible from him and wore a straight face.

'Did you go alone to the party?' Polite small talk!

'With the Wellnuts. They've moved on to this evening's third venue. Diplomacy appears to be a hectic profession. It wouldn't suit me.'

'I think your profession must be hectic. I also think you are used to telling people what they must do.'

'In the Army they're obliged to obey. I have a feeling you rarely do anything against your wishes.'

'You are persuading yourself you did not bully me just now?'

'I'm suggesting bullying was unnecessary.'

After a few moments of silence during which their driver turned from the mass of humanity and blaze of lights in Orchard Road and headed along a tree-lined avenue, she said, 'I do not have the drawings with me.'

Coming from erotic thoughts of the kind of bullying he would like to try with her, he frowned. 'Drawings?'

'The designs for your sister's earrings.'

God, was she really expecting a business meeting? 'Well, you weren't to know this would happen when you came to the party. I heard you're also designing a birthday gift for Zona.'

Her dark eyes challenged. 'You're very well informed, Captain.'

'Because of all that silent nodding I do. You'd be surprised what I overhear. Do you think you could call me Nick?'

The taxi slowed and turned on to a half-moon driveway fronting a discreetly lit restaurant accessible from a zig-zag flight of steps. Fleur was greeted with evident pleasure by a Russian Nick guessed had never set foot anywhere north of Kuala Lumpur. Heads turned as Mikhail led the way to a window table, and Nick enjoyed the envy he was arousing in male breasts. The menu was international with a few token Russian dishes. The wine came from Australia, the USA and Europe. It was all expensive.

When Mikhail went off with their order Nick looked across the table at his stunning companion. 'Is Fleur a professional name?'

'It's French.'

'I know.'

'My grandmother married a silk importer from Paris.'

'He chose that name for you?'

'No. He disappeared during the Occupation. We do not know what became of him.'

'Haven't you been able to trace him through the official sources?'

She shook her head.

'When the Japs surrendered they must have handed over a list of casualties and prisoners.'

'He *disappeared*,' she insisted. 'My mother and grand-mother believe he was taken to Pulau Gombak.'

Nick clearly visualized that dark blob ten miles from the beach he had walked along this morning. Wall to wall vegetation! 'I flew over it today. It looked pretty grim. Fleur, do you believe in *feng shui*?'

'It is not something to be believed or not. It *is*.'

His fascination with her grew. Western glamour, Eastern mystique. 'Was it another undeniable Eastern influence that led you into jewellery design?'

Her dark eyes narrowed. 'Please don't mock our culture.'

'I wasn't. I'm trying to learn more about it; trying to absorb in three weeks as much as I can of centuries of Chinese wisdom.'

'I have only learned a fraction of it in twenty-five years. You have set yourself an impossible task.'

Mikhail opportunely arrived with the wine. Nick nodded his approval and some was poured in Fleur's glass. She immediately drank, preventing Nick from making any kind of toast or statement. Then, when he began on his, Fleur embarked on a lengthy description of myths and festivals that was worthy of a tourist guide. He sat quietly, enjoying the lilt of her voice and the self-effacing quality that attracted him so strongly. When a waiter came with their meals, she brought the commentary to an end and suddenly smiled.

'I have bombarded you with so many details. How much will you remember?'

'Oh, you'll have to go over it all again over dinner tomorrow, just to be certain it sinks in,' he said.

She began to eat, treating the comment with a lightness

that dismissed it, so then Nick once more raised the subject of her jewellery. He learned that as she had a showroom, not a shop, so she had clients rather than customers. He made a note to tell Joyce.

'Even as a layman I noticed that you use mythology in some of your designs. Are you asked specifically for those?'

'No, my clients leave the artistic details to me, although they sometimes indicate that they would prefer an Oriental or Western theme. They see my design on paper before the work begins, of course.'

'Do they ever want it changed?'

'Rarely. You know that I ask many questions about who is to receive the gift so that I shall know what will be right for that person.'

'I find that intriguing. Did you inherit your talent from someone in your family?'

'Perhaps. My parents still have the import business my grandfather owned. As a child I would be given small corners of silks to play with. I loved the colours and patterns. I began to draw my own and my father gave one to the manufacturers, just to please me. It was exciting to see my design on the silk, but I wanted to produce something more dramatic. When I went to university to study art and design I realized the medium I should work with was precious stones.'

'You must have accepted that you'd need hefty backing for a project like that,' Nick said, leading her in the direction he wanted to follow.

She ate silently for a moment or two, then looked up at him again. 'You must understand that I am serious when I say it was written that I should be invited to the birthday party of a friend who also knew Zona Vydecker. I bought a small topaz and took my design to an uncle who is a goldsmith. He set the stone for me to take as a gift for my friend. Zona saw it and told her father she wanted a bracelet of my design. I was invited to show him my work.'

Feigning innocence, Nick said, 'Don't tell me he

immediately offered you a loan to launch your own business! It certainly *was* written.'

She smiled. 'You see? John decided that we must start out big. A showroom in Raffles Mall, the top shopfitter to design it, a private room for discussing special commissions. I was very afraid at the start. What if it failed? My father advised against trying to start a business at the top. He said I could only come down.' She sipped her wine, eyes shining. 'But John was right. It has worked well.'

'And he sent clients to you?'

'He knows many people.'

'And his bank had a great deal of money invested in you.'

'He took a big risk,' she said defensively.

'Oh no, Fleur, I don't think so. You're so highly talented you had to succeed. The Wellnuts' elder daughter practically swoons over your stuff. She gave me a rundown of your famous clients. The list is impressive. You must have significantly reduced Vydecker's loan over the five years you've been up and running.'

She took refuge in the sudden inscrutability she used to good effect, so Nick allowed a small silence before leading her in another direction.

'Your brother's tragic death must have affected your creative drive for a while. I heard the details of the accident when James told me why he was rushed out here to replace his predecessor. A sailing disaster, he said.'

She reflectively studied the glass Mikhail had just topped up with wine. 'Those two were crazy. Something was bound to happen one day.'

'It was written?' he suggested quietly.

Her head jerked up. 'Yes, but Jimmy would not see the writing.'

The suggestion of contempt in her tone surprised Nick. No doting sister, this. 'How about Philip Dunne?'

She shrugged. 'I hardly knew him. He was a man like you, used to telling others what to do. My brother was easily persuaded.'

'By Dunne?'

'By anyone.'

Now he was getting somewhere interesting. 'Didn't your father counsel him? It's usually the case when sons run wild.'

She shrugged again. 'Jimmy said I had ignored our father and so would he.'

'But he did well and qualified as a solicitor.'

'Only because . . .' She broke off, but Nick took her up before the sentence could lapse.

'Vydecker backed him, too?'

Avoiding a direct reply, she said, 'Jimmy liked the high life: designer clothes, sports cars, parties.'

'Along with the majority of young men, including me not so many years ago,' Nick told her ruefully. 'I daresay Jimmy's expensive tastes played havoc with his bank balance. I remember twice trying to squeeze a loan from my father. Unfortunately, my brother was playing the same game, so we both went empty-handed and had to pull in our horns.'

'What is that? "Pull in horns."'

'Another of our curious expressions. It means to practise economy; match expenditure with income. Difficult for rather wild youngsters like my brother and me. And Jimmy.' He took the bottle from the ice-bucket and topped up their glasses, asking deliberately casually, 'So, how long had Jimmy been acting as John Vydecker's personal legal adviser?'

'Three years.' Her eyes suddenly narrowed. 'I did not tell you that. I said nothing of that.'

'You didn't have to. It was clearly the most convenient way for your brother to repay his substantial loan. Deductions from his salary, unpaid overtime when something special came up. It's not uncommon, you know. Of course, Jimmy's death would have put an end to that, but Vydecker is solid enough to bear a few losses.'

'John is a very generous man.' The mask of inscrutability again descended, and she fell silent.

Nick was once more wondering just how generous the banker was to his gorgeous protégée when there was an

earsplitting explosion. Jumping nervously, he gave an invol-
untary cry. His heart raced; his hand continued to shake even
when a blinding flash told him a storm had arrived overhead
without warning. Joyce had said they were awesome in this
part of the world. She was right. Rain began to fall like the
chattering of a machine gun. Then it became a thundering
torrent that drowned other sounds.

Dazzled by the continuous lightning, Nick jumped again
when something touched his hand. He looked down swiftly
and saw slender fingers bearing an ornate opal ring.

'Are you all right, Nick?'

Her serene face and dark, concerned eyes again repre-
sented peace, tranquillity. Contempt for her brother, her aloof-
ness, had vanished. Nick swallowed the unexpected fear.

'You like your storms big and noisy, don't you?'

'It is simply the clouds bumping together.' She smiled.
'Isn't that what English children are told?'

This gentle teasing restored his equilibrium. 'And what
were you told, Fleur?'

'We have complicated stories to explain everything. You
will never learn them in three weeks.'

'I might manage an extra one.'

'Of course that would make all the difference.'

She was still teasing and, although his pulse had slowed
its mad racing, it remained faster than normal because this
woman was really getting a hold on him. So much so, he
was swamped with dismay because there was no need for
strategic placing of his table napkin. How the hell could
he feel so aroused yet have no physical response? He
forgot the raging elements outside. The rage was within
him.

'The British have no gods and demons,' she said, breaking
his train of thought. 'Everything there is very straight and
proper, isn't that so?'

'It's what other nations like to believe of us, but it's not
strictly true.'

'Then what is? Tell me now! You were a wild boy a few

years ago. You and your brother. Are you not so wild any more?'

The storm rolled slowly away to hit the outer islands while Nick gave an account of his childhood and his determination to be an Army pilot. He mentioned the way Jon had been disabled, and claimed his wildness had ended then. He made no reference to his parents' broken marriage, to Lara Scott or his own service with the SAS.

Lights were being dimmed before Nick grew aware that they were the only diners left in the Silver Troika. He settled the bill, and they walked out to the verandah at the head of the steps. The humidity in the wake of the storm was oppressive: way out over the sea the sky was being almost continuously slashed with lightning. It would be treacherous for ships navigating around the outer islands tonight. Nick's dark vision of Pulau Gombak went as swiftly as it came, as the taxi Mikhail had called for them swung into the driveway.

Fleur lived in a block of luxury apartments not far from the restaurant. The journey ended too soon for Nick, but Fleur surprised and delighted him by inviting him to go in with her.

'I have to show you the design for the earrings,' she explained.

It brought him down to earth. A business meeting! As he stood with her in the lift, then followed her along an empty corridor, he tried to think of how to wriggle out of spending a small fortune, but his thoughts were more occupied by the wriggle of her hips. He had not resolved the problem when they entered a large room furnished in ultra-modern style. He was impressed, his thoughts rapidly returning to John Vydecker. However successful Fleur Yang had become, a hell of a lot of backing would have been needed to set her up in style when she was virtually unknown. She would have had to sell an impossible number of her top-of-the-range pieces to get anywhere near to repaying the loan within five years. No way would there be enough cash for a place like this.

While Nick took in the stark lines of the black and white decor, it occurred to him that as special commissions were discussed in a private room, so this might be where the designs – and a whole lot more – were shown to the clients.

'A nightcap, Nick.' Fleur was beside him, holding a chunky tumbler. 'You were drinking whisky in your corner at the Collinses' party, I think.'

He took the glass, seeing her in a new light. Ferdy claimed she was too talented to need to spread her legs to win anyone's backing, but it was stretching belief that she would get this amount of it with no more than a winning smile. She either sold herself along with her jewellery, or she was being financed through some additional source.

'You're very observant,' he murmured, appreciating the top-grade whisky. 'We were in that corner together for no more than five minutes.'

She smiled. 'It's plain you are used only to telling people what they must do, knowing they will do it. In business it is necessary to *persuade*. So I observe those things that will make my clients relax and feel they are important. It becomes automatic.'

'I'm already relaxed, so the whisky is to make me feel important, is it?' he said. 'At what point do you show me the drawings?'

'There are no drawings, Nick. You do not have a sister. I knew it from the start. Tonight you confirmed it. You told me of your parents and your brother, but there was no mention of Virginia.'

He had been careless. But this was no covert mission. It was not important that he had blown his cover, and here was his reprieve from heavy expenditure. 'You knew from the start?' he asked curiously.

'Oh, yes. No blonde woman would wear the colours you mentioned as Virginia's favourites. And you described the clothes of a sportswoman, not those a chic young woman would have in her fashion collection. It was all lies.' She came a little closer. 'You did not want to buy jewellery, so why did you come to my showroom?'

He was no longer relaxed. Despite her demure manner this girl was a smart cookie. Eastern promise had turned to Western feminism, but he could handle that easier than the other.

'You're very beautiful; you accosted me in my corner. I wanted to follow up on a promising encounter. My turn to ask a question. Was there a family emergency last night?'

'Who are you, Nick Hawkwood? A pilot on holiday, you said. A soldier. I think that is another lie. A soldier would not be afraid of thunder and lightning. You were tonight.'

'It took me unawares. I told you that,' he said.

'You do not stay in a hotel for your holiday, but part of the British High Commission. You deny that you are a diplomat.'

'James Wellnut is a military man *attached* to the High Commission. He and I are friends and former colleagues. He flew helicopters before taking up this post.' He frowned. 'Who do you imagine I might be?'

She gave the familiar little shrug and spread her hands. 'Singapore is not just a place of ancient Chinese wisdom and dragon dances and exciting things to buy. That is only what the tourists see. There are laws, restrictions. You do not know. It is necessary to be careful. You came to me and told me lies.'

'Only white ones.'

'You said you followed my advice at the Collinses' party to mingle with the guests, and they told you who I was.'

'And?'

'I saw you leave very abruptly after speaking to a late arrival who came with a red-haired girl. You did not stay and mingle with anyone.'

So she had been interested enough to keep her eye on him! 'I left because I was feeling unwell. Jet lag combined with the change in climate to prove more than I could take after a few drinks. If I'd told you that it wouldn't have impressed you as much as the white lie.'

'You wanted to impress me?'

'I wanted to get to know you; spend some time with you. I still do.' He put down the empty glass. 'If you didn't entirely trust me why leave the party tonight with me?'

'You bullied me. I had no choice but to obey,' she murmured.

Eastern promise was suddenly back with a vengeance. She closed on him, pulled his head down and began exploring his mouth with her tongue to indicate the promise was about to be realized.

With all his senses throbbing crazily Nick went with her to a bedroom of stark blue and acid yellow, where she unzipped her dress and stepped from it. Beneath, she wore only a satin thong. Her breasts were tiny mounds he could cover completely with his palms. Occupied with these while she unbuttoned his shirt, he grew aware of faint stirrings. Glory be, he was getting an erection!

Pulling his shirt free of his trousers, Fleur raised the temperature further by sucking his nipples while running her fingernails gently up and down his spine. Breathing hard, he lowered her to the bed and slipped the thong down over her feet. She parted her legs invitingly, but he was appalled to find he was losing it; couldn't sustain the erection. Sod it! *Sod it!* Struggling to unzip his fly, he lost control of his fingers. Lost co-ordination of mind and limbs. Couldn't think straight.

Through dawning awareness of what she had done, her lilting voice reached him as if through cotton wool before he pitched forward into oblivion.

Five

Knives were slicing through his head, cutting ever deeper when he moved it. He groaned as much in despair as in pain. How much more could he endure? When would they put a merciful end to him?

Something damp and ice-cold settled on his forehead; a gentle voice whispered consolation. Struggling from the depths of past anguish, his mind told him this was different. Brightness beat against his closed lids: *they* had kept him in darkness. He opened his eyes to slits. A girl's face swam mistily above him. Why was he surprised that it was not Oriental?

'Dear Nick, lie still and it won't hurt so much. I'll bathe your head until the pain goes away,' said the girl.

She *was* only a girl. He was in bed at the Wellnuts' and young Emma was sitting beside him, holding a hand towel across his brow.

'What are you doing here?' he demanded thickly, then groaned and closed his eyes as the knives again attacked his skull.

'Shh! You have a gargantuan hangover. Just lie quietly while I do this.'

His brain had so much to cope with he actually did as she said while it sorted through the jumble of impressions now slowly becoming facts. The icy bands were bringing some relief, but the emerging recollections soon slotted into unwelcome chronological order.

Pushing away the girl's hands, he squinted sideways. 'Where's James?'

'Still in bed. It's only five o'clock. He's not very pleased with you, I'm afraid.'

'He'll be even less pleased if he finds you in here dressed only in skimpy pyjamas.'

She flushed with adolescent pleasure. 'I thought you were too hungover to notice.'

He sat up, wincing with pain. 'I appreciate your wish to help, but what I need is a long cold shower and gallons of black coffee.'

'I'll fetch you some.'

'*No!* Cora can bring it. Go back to bed, Emma.' He badly needed a pee, but he was wearing no more than underpants beneath the sheet. He had no intention of getting out of bed while this infatuated girl was there. James was already keeping tabs on the situation. It could get ridiculously out of hand unless this child-woman was firmly discouraged. Or disillusioned. Unfortunately, she was at the age when idols were not easily toppled.

When the girl left, Nick staggered to the bathroom, where he emptied his bursting bladder, then vomited copiously in the lavatory pan. He sat for a while against the bath until the giddiness that had induced nausea gradually subsided. Whatever Fleur Yang had put in his whisky was potent stuff. Fast acting and surprisingly long lasting. A burning pain began in his breast; a pain caused by anger and remembered humiliations. That bitch had taken him for a ride. She had been in control, and he had been rendered helpless once more. Terror hovered.

He thrust it away determinedly; denied it. The shower cubicle was in front of him and he was soon under a deluge of lukewarm water. It was impossible to have a really cold shower in this country, but he felt refreshed and calmer when he finally emerged and towelled down. Dressing in a loose shirt and shorts, Nick downed several cups of the coffee left by the maid while he was in the bathroom. The caffeine went some way to clearing his head, but it was no aid to solving the mysteries of last night. Dragging a lounger from the verandah, he positioned it beneath the circling fan and sat, resting his aching head against the bright cushion as he tried to recall everything in sequence from the moment they had left the Vydecker party.

He must have slept because James was standing beside him when he opened his eyes.

'Cora said she brought you coffee two hours ago. I've asked her to bring some more. Presumably you're too hungover to face breakfast. *Again.*'

Nick sat forward, frowning. 'How did I get back here last night?'

'The manager sent you in a taxi.'

'The manager of the apartment block?'

'What apartment block? You were making a nuisance of yourself at the Silver Troika. Diners were complaining. The manager had no alternative but to get shot of you.'

'That's a load of bloody bullshit,' said Nick vehemently.

The maid entered with a tray of coffee. James immediately filled a cup to hand to Nick and, as soon as the girl left, challenged him. 'I had to ask the taxi driver to help me bring you indoors, where you threw up over the hall carpet. You'd already spewed half your meal over his rear seat. I gave him enough to cover the clean-up in addition to his fare. You couldn't stand even with our support. We had literally to carry you up here. Joyce cleared the mess from the hall. She didn't feel it was fair to rouse the servants. *I* don't feel it's fair when my wife has to mop up a load of vomit at two a.m. because a guest treats her house like a barrack room.'

Nick put down the cup and saucer. 'You're right. I'll move to a hotel.' The second time in a week he had become an unwelcome guest!

After a short silence James said, 'Getting wholly pissed night after night isn't the answer, Hawk. They must have given you some kind of counselling at the hospital – it's usual after incarceration and brutality – and I'm certain—'

'I wasn't drunk, James.'

'You were paralytic! I can tell when a man's been on a bender, and you've been on one three nights out of four. I invited you here because I thought it a good place to sort yourself out. It's an exotic environment, and no one but Joyce and me knows your history. I'd reckoned without Lara Scott, of course. It's God-awful luck that she should—'

'She has nothing to do with what happened last night,' Nick interrupted brusquely. 'I had a meal with Fleur Yang at the Silver Troika. We left together at around one a.m. – the last diners to go – and she invited me up to her apartment. To see her design for the earrings, she said. She gave me a nightcap, then told me she knew I had no sister. I'd slipped up badly over that. There was a short cross-examination about my true identity and motive for seeking her out. I believed I'd sorted it when she began coming on to me in a big way. I had her naked on the bed by the time my co-ordination began to foul up and I realized she'd doctored the whisky. I don't remember anything more until I woke in bed here a couple of hours ago.'

James frowned. 'You're claiming that woman *drugged* you?'

'Yes.'

'You reeked of whisky, man.'

'Someone must have poured it into me once I was out cold.'

'Oh, come on!'

He leaned forward intently. 'Cracker, you've seen me pissed often enough to know I don't get noisy and aggressive under the influence, especially in public places. In fact, I never drink to excess in public. I leave and finish the job in the Mess or my quarters, if the occasion demands. Didn't it strike you that I was acting out of character last night if what was inferred was true?'

There was a significant pause. 'You're not the man I used to know on the squadron. Too many things have happened to you since those days.'

Anger raced through Nick, sending him to his feet. 'So

I'm now a sot like my father, and a liar to boot? Two days ago you even suspected me of playing around with your underage stepdaughter. Thanks for the sodding vote of confidence, pal! It's definitely time I cleared out of here. And before you get to hear of it, I'll tell you Emma was with me earlier while you were all asleep. She came to perform a Florence Nightingale act, but if she claims she was violated, you'll know who's guilty. That guy Hawkwood whose mind's been bent by ragheads.'

'Has it?' asked James calmly. 'Chris Franklin and Pete Higham think otherwise. I checked before I called to invite you here.' He poured more coffee in both cups and held one out to Nick. 'Let's get to the bottom of this Silver Troika business.'

Nick's pulse still raced as he took the cup and saucer, but the red cloud of rage had passed. He drank the black liquid in one draught, then sat back in the lounger.

'OK, I agree I'm not the same balanced guy I was when we flew together. I'll be a different person from now on. Pete warned me of that, but I'd already seen it happen to Jon and guessed I'd be permanently scarred by what happened. It's not easy to accept. It'll take time to adjust.' He tipped the coffee pot again. 'Look, about Emma . . .'

'You sent Florence Nightingale packing?'

'She's another reason for me to move out.'

'About the Silver Troika; we could call the manager. Get the truth.'

Nick shook his head. 'He'll corroborate the taxi driver's story. Fleur Yang's intimate with Mikhail. That little bitch put one over on me too easily. Her gorgeous exterior hides steely self-interest. Now she's shown her hand she'll discover I have some hidden aces. I learned a great deal during our meal. She's in this business right up to her diminutive tits.'

'What business is that?'

'The one you wanted a leg man for.'

'To ask a few casual questions about Philip Dunne, that's all.'

97

'Oh yeah? "Latch on to Jimmy Yang's sister. She's just your type and she handles semi-precious stones," you said. Remember?'

'Mmm,' James agreed resignedly. 'What was all that about a cross-examination on your true identity?'

Nick told him of Fleur's suspicions, then related what he had gleaned regarding her brother and John Vydecker. 'She had little sibling fondness for Jimmy; claimed *it was written* that he'd come to a sticky end. He and Dunne were pushing their luck. Funny how we keep hearing that. I've no doubt Vydecker's tied in with some dodgy dealings. It doesn't take a great brain to figure that Yang was in debt to him for a personal loan apart from the financing of his studies.'

'That's pure speculation.'

'Maybe, but how useful to have a legal man in the palm of your hand to deal with the illegal sidelines you're running. Fleur confirmed that her brother worked for Vydecker when he qualified. It's my guess the poor bastard was so deep in hock to the man he'd have been under pressure to do anything. It's also my guess the girl is in the same predicament. Vydecker must have put millions into that jewellery outlet – have you seen the showroom? – and she admitted he often sends clients there. You've certainly seen *her*. Designer clothes; professionally coiffed and manicured. Eats in the best restaurants; seen at the up-market parties. And her apartment is top-of-the-range. Who pays for it all?'

'An inheritance from a rich uncle in Australia?'

Nick was too intent to grin at the hoary adage. 'If it's all above board why should she be wary of my true identity? Who did she fear I might be?'

'A leg man asking too many questions? The Chinese are private people averse to anyone prying into their personal lives.'

Nick dismissed that. 'We're talking about a westernized woman who deals with the rich and famous. What she'd be averse to is someone discovering what's going on behind the genuine jewellery business. And, take my word, she's no inscrutable shrinking violet in the bedroom. Her clients are surely buying more than earrings and pendants from Fleur Yang.'

'She provides high-class nookie in her spare time? Maybe it's kinky and she merely overdid the rhino horn in your drink.'

'So you now accept that I wasn't kicked out of the Silver Troika?'

James looked uncomfortable. 'You have to admit your story's somewhat bizarre.'

'No more so than your theory about the Dunnes.'

'Yeah, well it was a while before *you* took that seriously.' He pursed his lips thoughtfully. 'I co-opted you on the mystery of Dunne's file, but you've started following a different trail with Vydecker as the leading villain. Back off, Nick, you're heading into deep, dangerous water.'

'Isn't that where you suspect Philip Dunne went? It's not a different trail, I'm simply approaching it along another direction.'

'Then stop now. If you're right about Vydecker et al., it's a police concern. Probably Interpol. Diplomatic personnel can't get involved in anything like that.'

Nick gave him a straight look. 'A couple of days ago you were convinced Dunne had been controlled by some gang which would see you as his natural successor.'

The other man looked even more uncomfortable. 'I may have gone a bit OTT on that. Look, when I arrived here at short notice I detected a curiously blasé attitude towards Dunne's presumed loss at sea. I told myself that twenty-four years of service life, many with Special Forces flights and in combat situations, had made me sensitive about the way men died and how their bodies were treated: that I was in a different milieu and should accept what everyone here found expedient. Then I found that file. It revived my suspicions about the nautical disaster.'

'You believe it was murder?'

He sighed. 'No, but the poor devil's death seems to have

been treated rather cavalierly. I suspect there'd be a greater stink kicked up over a lost document.'

'Referring to Cranford Fielding?'

He nodded. 'You've met the cold fish.'

'He was another who claimed Dunne was on a self-propelled collision course with disaster. You say no one seems unduly upset over his fate. Fleur Yang shrugs off the death of her brother; only got what he'd been asking for! Is there a case here of "he protesteth too much"? I'm getting a strong whiff of the rodent you mentioned.'

'But you named it John Vydecker, who doesn't feature in my scenario,' said James.

'He's not only in it, he's the main player.'

'I repeat: drop it!'

'I'm not diplomatic personnel, and I'm too involved after last night. At some point I must have set alarm bells ringing. Fleur could have conspired with Mikhail, she could have poured whisky over me, but there's no way she could have dragged me from the fifth floor and into a taxi single-handed. There were others involved, and not for the first time. That baby knows how to administer knock-out drops and how to accelerate the reaction with sexual excitement. What I don't know is why I was given the treatment. They either intended to finish me off in a dark alley, then discovered from her my slight link with the High Commission and ran scared. Or it was a warning to back off.'

'What I'm telling you to do.'

Nick rose as the burning sensation in his breast returned. He walked to the open window, breathing deeply to combat it as he tried to concoct an explanation.

'I have this aversion to being . . . *controlled*. Fleur Yang's apparent fragility got to me so strongly I played into her hands. I can't walk away. I have to retaliate.'

The two men decided to keep the truth about the previous night to themselves when Joyce immediately scoffed at Nick's intention of moving to a hotel.

100

'James has never seen fit to move out and I've lost count of the number of times I've dealt with the consequences of *his* nights of folly. Besides, what inference would the social gossipers put on it? They'd have a field day.' She adopted a schoolmarmish glare. 'Just see that you reach the bathroom before your innards reject everything.'

'I'm on the wagon from now on,' he promised with sincerity. 'You're a woman in a million. If you had a sister I'd marry her tomorrow.'

'If she was my sister she'd have more sense.'

When James had a free weekend he went with his family to their club. Nick welcomed this and felt sufficiently recovered to enjoy an invigorating swim in the huge pool. An uncle figure who could perform amazing aquabatics was a magnet to Gina and Robin, who laughed and frolicked around him in delight. But the morning caused havoc in Emma's breast. Throughout a casual lunch eaten on the terrace her gaze was glued to the scars on Nick's legs.

Like all sensible mothers Joyce insisted that her children should sit with books for forty-five minutes after eating. She had a novel and James settled with newspapers, but Nick opted for a period of deep thought with closed eyes. He must have slept because when he opened them the youngsters were back in the pool, Emma was sitting moodily on the side of it, and his hosts were chatting to a British couple.

James made introductions. 'Euan and Vicky Goss. Euan's my assistant, Nick. He's a Naval weapons expert.'

'And I'm a masseuse,' supplied the man's wife with a pert smile at Nick. 'If you want any work done on your pecs while you're here, I'm your girl.'

The dark-haired Naval commander flicked her with his towel. 'She does this with every ex-pat we meet to see how embarrassed they get. I'm trying to break her of the habit.'

'And failing dismally,' said Vicky, pulling a face.

They all laughed and, after a few minutes of general social chat, the pair rejoined their friends. Nick glanced at James.

'Weapons expert, eh? How often has he been invited to Vydecker parties?'

James frowned a warning not to discuss it in Joyce's presence. 'Vicky's irrepressible vitality almost cost him the job. Fielding took a dim view of her sense of fun and sent in an adverse report after three months. Euan's qualifications are impeccable, so he was simply cautioned to remedy the problem. Vicky was furious but toed the line for his sake. She breaks out now and again, when protocol hasn't to be observed.'

'He's nutty about her,' Joyce said. 'She told me Euan was prepared to throw in his hand and go home, but she knew it wouldn't help his career if he did. Anyway, they love it out here. Party animals, no kids. The ideal life for them. And, like me, she knows her husband won't be whisked off to a war zone without warning. That's worth behaving herself for.'

'Presumably, restrictions only apply to the wives, or Philip Dunne wouldn't have done all the crazy things everyone talks of.'

Joyce studied both Nick and James shrewdly. 'You're not still dabbling in that water, are you?'

'No,' they said unanimously.

'Good!' Then she took Nick unawares. 'Emma's discovered that she'll be in love with you until she dies, but I can fix you up with a partner more your age to provide light relief for a week or two, no strings attached. While you were sleeping, Jani Spencer stopped for a chat and the hope of an introduction to our friend. Your resounding snores didn't appear to detract from your general appeal,' she added poker-faced. 'Jani's Eurasian; a doctor of sociology and a hard-working member of the committee governing a charity providing help for deaf children. She's very attractive and amusing.'

'I'm sure she's delightful, if you say so, but no thanks.'

'So what are you going to do with yourself while you're here?'

He knew she was hinting that he couldn't stay under her feet the whole time, but he dared not reveal that he was going to continue probing the mystery of Dunne's death.

'I'll do the tourist round: Botanical Gardens, Chinatown, museums and art galleries.'

'I'll believe that when I see it! But it's really not a bad idea, Nick. Give it a go. Singapore's very culturally interesting.'

They swam again. Nick then left the Wellnuts larking with their children and headed for the Gents', where he encountered Euan Goss similiarly engaged. As they chatted side by side, Nick suddenly recalled Lara finding the prospect hilarious. *We girls don't make a social occasion of having a pee. We concentrate on the business in hand.* And his reply: *So do we – literally.* He pushed the memory aside and heard Euan praising his expertise in the pool.

'Vicky's run out of superlatives just watching you,' he added with a hint of pique.

Nick played it down. 'Did an advanced survival course. We're more often in water than on it. I've done some rowing during manoeuvres – crossing rivers and so on – but that's about my limit in boats. You guys are the experts in that area. It takes skill and bloody fine judgement to handle a warship. As for aircraft carriers!' They crossed to wash their hands and he said with some awe, 'I was told the Yanks have to start slowing down around six hours before reaching port in those floating colossi they man.'

They emerged and stood in the shade of trees. 'They can get too damn big,' said Euan. 'We don't go in for that. It's bad enough on ours. A chap can get lost and wander for a week searching for his cabin. In those mammoth US jobs they never meet the other three quarters of the crew, and they stay below decks the entire voyage. Never see daylight.'

A frisson of horror touched Nick's skin. 'I couldn't do that.'

Euan smiled. 'The pampered fly boys don't have to. Ever landed on a carrier?'

They exchanged professional experiences for a while until Nick broached the vital question. 'You've been out here almost two years and worked with Philip Dunne, so how does James compare? He's sobered somewhat since we served in the same squadron and I heard Dunne was a real live wire.'

'Phil was OK,' Euan replied non-committally, brushing a fly from his face. 'Knew how to handle people. Men. Not so hot with the ladies, but Alison took that on. They were popular with the locals, which was important. I'm afraid Fielding looked down his nose at Phil. Our Head of Mission's a bit of an old woman,' he added.

'So it wasn't a body blow to him when Dunne vanished?'

The other man frowned. 'He didn't vanish, he drowned.'

'But the body's never been recovered.'

'It wouldn't be, under those circumstances.'

'What circumstances?' Nick asked casually.

A bout of excited shrieking from passing children created a pause, then Euan continued somewhat obliquely. 'Pilots should stay in their own element. Phil was a typical macho type; had to be forever testing himself to the limit. He was handy in a small boat, but not experienced enough to make solo runs around these waters. The currents are treacherous and there are submerged hazards.'

'Surely he'd have studied the charts.'

'Huh! With his eyes closed! One time he showed up in the live firing area off Sudong; strictly prohibited to all shipping. The Singapore Army had to halt a gunnery practice.'

Interesting! 'What excuse did he give for being there?'

'Monsoon blew him off course. It happens: get caught in a sudden squall and the best of us are in trouble. He was bloody lucky the khaki gunners didn't sink him.' Euan's eyes narrowed speculatively. 'Didn't deter Phil as it should have done. Had to prove he could handle anything.'

Nick nodded. 'I've met the type. But Dunne was a Falklands hero, wasn't he?'

'Yes. There's no doubting his courage. No war to fight out here, that was the problem.'

'So what made him apply for the posting?'

'Alison wanted some peace of mind for once, I guess. Phil enjoyed the job, and he was an easy chap to work with. Not like some.'

'Is that aimed at James?'

'God, no! Instant rapport.' He grinned. 'His vices are simply the average amateur watercolourist's raving over a clump of flowers and a tendency to sing in the office. Drives his PA into raptures. She says he sounds like Bryn Terfel, whoever he might be.'

'No idea. I'm a jazz man.' They were straying from the subject. 'D'you reckon Philip Dunne was accidentally killed by the military, then?'

Euan looked startled. 'I didn't suggest that.'

'But it's a possibility?'

He studied Nick curiously. 'What's your interest in his death?'

'I was thinking of hiring a boat – and a skipper – for a trip while I'm here, but it sounds a bit too risky.'

'Not if the skipper knows what he's doing,' he replied, apparently accepting the lie. 'If you really want a look around I'll give you a buzz the next time I go out. One of the perks of the job, I'm glad to say.'

'Great! Thanks, I'll look forward to it.'

Hands suddenly seized him from the rear as a scream rang out. Nick instinctively swung round and lashed out with both hands ready to chop at throats. The attackers reached only to his hip level. The rampant mischief on their faces swiftly drained to leave wide-eyed awe as Robin, Gina and three of their friends sensed that their attempt to grab Nick and drag him back to the pool had somehow gone wrong. The man who had performed tricks in the water was glaring at them in frightening fashion. They backed away, then ran to the familiarity of the water slide, where they closed ranks and stared at him in silent bewilderment.

Nick's racing heartbeat gradually slowed as he came from the dark place that was never far away. With no experience as a father he could not bridge that moment of mutual fear and simply stared back at them. The children moved back to their parents' sides in watchful nonchalance.

'That survival course you took must have been more advanced than you let on.' He swung round to find Euan Goss regarding him with professional interest. 'Thought pilots were trained for combat in the *air*.'

'They can be shot down over enemy territory,' he said briefly. 'See you around.'

Walking down to the pool, he made a shallow dive and swam the length several times until the lingering shadows evaporated.

That evening James called Nick to his study while Joyce was getting the children to bed. 'Ploughing through my e-mails I found one for you.'

Nick sat to read the message from his brother.

Franklin cagey on subject of Fanshawe. Is there something on a strictly need-to-know basis? Recent move not in current Who's Who – has retired from the FCO to become a director of Rees and Hardy, who make inertial navigation systems for MoD. Driving to Mousehole tomorrow. If not arrested as suspicious snooper will send results or lack of them.

These cuttings are all I could find on Dunne's heroism in the Falklands. Why do all the good guys get the shitty end of the stick?

Regards to J and J

Nick glanced up at James. 'A link we didn't suspect. Alison's grandad is now on the governing board of the company Senoko wants to supply with switches: Senoko has dealings with a black-listed Indonesian outfit in Dunne's file. Was Dunne another of Vydecker's puppets?'

'No, *No!*'

'Why not? You suspect he could have been involved in dodgy dealings under duress.'

James rubbed his chin thoughtfully during a short silence, then sighed. 'I'm sorry, but this has to be said. I took a few interesting facts and bumped them up to give you something to work on while you're here.'

Struggling to hold down his anger, Nick could almost hear Chris Franklin saying: *Keep Hawkwood occupied. Don't let him brood.* He had been trying to make sense of a concocted placebo!

'You bastard!' he said with quiet venom. 'There *is* a consensus of opinion that those devils warped my mind.'

'I say again, no!' James sat in the swivel chair by his desk and attempted to explain. 'You're well aware I've had two tours with Special Forces flights, one during the Gulf War. I've picked up guys who'd been worked over like you. I've taken them out again six months later. They'd changed – less banter, even more coldly determined – but they still operated at top level. Top SAS level, at that. Chris Franklin knows what it takes to get a man past the barbarity barrier and back on track, Hawk. A slightly different track, maybe, but one running straight and true.'

Nick gave him a withering look and repeated, 'You bastard! Jon's going to Mousehole to ask questions about the Dunnes. He's been through his own ration of brutality and conquered it. Why involve him?'

'I didn't. You did.'

They confronted each other in silence for a moment or two, then Nick said, 'Tell me how much of that file is genuine and how much is convalescent's embroidery.'

'What you saw was exactly how I found it.'

'And the Senoko business?'

'As I related. They want to supply Rees and Hardy. Vydecker has invested in them and is courting my co-operation.'

'Fleur Yang?'

'Knowing your libido I thought she'd add sugar to the spice, and the lapis lazuli references proved a convenient link.'

'They weren't . . . although that beautiful bitch is such a consummate actress she probably fooled me on that, too.'

Spreading his hands apologetically, James said, 'I came here to replace Dunne and found surprising nonchalance over his death. I discovered a file that means nothing to his PA but suggests he was keeping tabs on what I take to be companies on our black list. I was mildly intrigued – still am – by circumstances that can be interpreted two ways, and it seemed the ideal puzzle to offer you. A *mental* puzzle. But the eternal action man had to get physical over it. You've gone heavy-booted into something far bigger than my exaggerated scenario suggested. That bloody woman gave you knock-out drops, for God's sake! You could have wound up in a monsoon drain with your throat cut last night. It's my belief that you didn't because of your connection with me. A brand of diplomatic immunity.'

'It didn't protect Dunne.'

James wagged his head. 'I think we must accept the coroner's verdict of death by drowning. As for that damn file, I'll take your initial advice to shove it through the shredder.'

Still very angry, Nick said, 'What a bloody U-turn!'

'Possibly, but I can't have my family put at risk through your interference with whoever the Yang girl works for. And it's more than my career's worth to tangle even indirectly with internal affairs. We have to be extremely careful not to act as if we're still colonial overlords. It's a sensitive issue.'

'You should have remembered that before you started the ball rolling.'

'What I should have remembered is that you're a hawk by nature – a hunter – who wouldn't just pussyfoot around with this. I suggested this morning that you back off. I'm now telling you to.' He frowned sympathetically. 'Go out and see the sights; enjoy the flip side of Singapore. There's a great deal to interest you if you look for it. Take up Euan's offer to go sailing, have a look around Sentosa, use your temporary membership of our club and swimming pool. Let

Joyce introduce you to Jani Spencer. She's a very cultured woman who'll be an undemanding companion.'

On the verge of a bitter riposte, Nick held his tongue. He had been in this house for four nights. On the first two he had raided the drinks cabinet and emerged hungover in the middle of the following morning. Last night he had been brought back in a drugged state and vomited over a valuable Chinese carpet. The Wellnuts had taken it all very well, and he owed them some return for their loyal friendship.

'OK, relax. My career as a gumshoe is over as from now.'

'No hard feelings?'

'Just a request. No introductions to available women. I'll find my own crumpet, if I feel the need.'

'Jani Spencer isn't crumpet.'

'That's what I feared.'

James summoned a smile. 'Fancy a nightcap?'

'Bloody good idea.'

Nick breakfasted with the whole family, then embarked on the tourist round after James had left for the office. Joyce regarded her guest with suspicion.

'The Botanical Gardens – *you*?'

'It was your suggestion.'

'You're up to something, I know it.'

'Don't worry, I'll stay on the wagon.'

'I doubt they'll serve alcohol in the Gardens. It's where you plan to go afterwards that worries me. Take care, Nick.'

He walked through the garden for forty-five minutes deep in thought, then sought the air-conditioned restaurant and sat with coffee, still wrestling with the puzzle. If Vydecker was gun-running where did Fleur Yang fit in? He could see no possible link between weapons and jewellery, and the Yang showroom was an unlikely front for arms dealing. The actual workshop might well be. He would check it out.

He switched to the other possibility: the other big earner. Drugs. A swanky place in Raffles Mall could provide the perfect façade. Heroin, cocaine. Easily transported. There was that room for discussing special commissions. Who would be curious of expensively dressed men with briefcases demanding private meetings with Miss Yang? Nick had been ushered into the room without preamble. And the East had long been a rich source of opiates.

Formerly convinced that Dunne's comments *check on lapis lazuli* must be linked to a woman working with semi-precious stones, Nick now wondered if it was simply a password. Fleur had shown no reaction when he mentioned it, but she had proved to be the ultimate inscrutable Chinese. He determined to settle the score with her before he flew home. And that formed the core of the puzzle.

He had gone over and over their conversation at the Silver Troika. Apart from confirming that Virginia Hawkwood did not exist, nothing he had said would arouse suspicion of his motives. Attractive women invariably accepted that men often lie to further their chances. Fleur must be used to sexual pursuit. Had *she* let slip information that drove her to make it appear Nick had been too drunk to remember the evening clearly? He thought that a more likely explanation than James's claim of diplomatic immunity saving his throat from being slashed. His friend read too many thrillers! Yet *something* had scared Fleur into luring him to her apartment and setting him up. He had once been sharp enough to get the answer to any puzzle. Not now.

Moodily drinking a second coffee, Nick reviewed the press reports of Dunne's exploits in the Falklands that Jon had e-mailed. The Harrier pilot and his wingman had repeatedly repulsed Argentine aircraft before they could reach the islands, twice shooting down the leaders. Dunne earned his decoration for a solo action. Returning to base because of a defect in his weapons system, he came upon a lone enemy who had slipped through the defence. Instead of hightailing it, Dunne entered the lists, harrying the intruder with dazzling manoeuvres that prevented him from locking on to Dunne or to the ships in Stanley Harbour. Unnerved and certainly dangerously low on fuel, the enemy had finally run for home.

Dilute the media dramatics and it still described a man unlikely to let himself be threatened, much less intimidated into some kind of skulduggery. Nor did he seem the type to go for a diplomatic attachment. Unlike James, who wanted to spend time with his growing children. The Dunnes' daughter had left home. So, *had* Lord Fanshawe twisted the man's arm for some reason? It was a possible explanation and also made sense of the macho craziness everyone referred to. Men of Dunne's calibre frequently found it difficult to slow down after living in the fast lane for any length of time.

Thrusting away the dread that he, himself, might be driven to that unless he fully mastered the aftermath of Iraq, Nick left the gardens and took a taxi to Orchard Road with the intention of buying Joyce an apology present. She well deserved one from him.

Circling the beauty department of a large store, he was undecided. He had bought perfume for a number of women but he had always known what they liked. Joyce was an unknown. Maybe flowers would be safer.

'You look as bewildered as most men in these places.'

Vicky Goss stood beside him, smiling. 'I recognized you although you have clothes on today.' When he failed to rise to her flirtatious banter, she asked, 'What is it you're looking for? Maybe I can help.'

'A thank-you present for Joyce. Any idea of her favourite perfume?'

''Fraid not, but you can't go wrong with Chanel Five. Some of the sexier fragrances don't do well in this climate, and Joyce is hardly the hot, passionate type, is she?'

She went with him to the counter, where he arranged for an extravagant boxed set of Chanel products to be delivered to the Wellnut home. Then she linked her arm through his.

'Euan has a heavy day with the Singapore Navy, so how about buying me lunch in return for helping you out?'

Seeing another way in which she could help, Nick said, 'Yes, but you'll have to choose the venue. I'm a stranger in town.'

Vicky chose the nearby Marriott and they were soon seated at a table in the grillroom. Nick fully understood why Euan was defensively in love with his wife. Blonde, tanned and irrepressibly flirtatious, she was the kind of girl Nick had dated over the past two years. He presently appreciated the curve of her thigh beneath the linen skirt, and the generous glimpse of cleavage revealed by her low-buttoned shirt. But sex was a secondary consideration as they waited for their food. Vicky Goss had known the Dunnes and she was chatterbox enough to reveal more about them than had her husband or Cranford Fielding.

Nick broached the subject casually. 'You said Joyce isn't the hot, passionate type. That's surely important for her role as James's wife. I guess in the old colonial days there would have been a few ripe scandals before air-conditioning cooled fevered emotions.' He paused, 'Although I can't imagine Fielding's wife breaking out, no matter how hot it was. Typical memsahib type from the no-nonsense school.'

'Barbara's OK, it's *him*.' She pulled a face. 'If he'd drowned instead of Phil, Euan would have found a secret hoard of porno stuff when he packed his things. I swear he slips out in disguise to kinky clubs and does disgusting things to other creeps like himself. Euan says I'm fantasizing, but I've met men like that before and they emanate perversion. I'm psychic, you know.'

He tried to sound impressed. 'Then you're probably right. What did the Dunnes make of him?'

'Phil found him heavy going, which wasn't surprising. Phil was great fun, especially when he'd had a few. HOM looked down his nose, of course.'

'Hom?'

'Head of Mission. It's less of a mouthful than his name. Euan had a set-to with him soon after we arrived.'

She told of the adverse report Joyce had mentioned, and Nick let her chatter on until their meals were brought.

'He sounds like a commanding officer I had the misfortune to serve under in Northern Ireland. Great soldier,

112

terrible man. How did Alison Dunne rate in Fielding's joyless estimation?'

'Oh, she was a chameleon; changed her approach to suit the occasion.'

This was a new angle on the woman. 'So Fielding found no fault with her?'

'No one found fault with her. She made certain of that.'

'And you didn't like her?'

'It was impossible to get to know her. At official dos she was all smarmpots and *terribly, terribly* in agreement with what was said. At more intimate parties she acted the perfect understanding wife. But she played havoc with her Chinese dressmaker. Nothing was ever right. Same with hairdresser and manicurist. Had the role of an English lord's grand-daughter off pat. And the way she spoke to her domestics!'

All this was rattled off between mouthfuls of prawns. Nick found it illuminating. 'Yet she was the perfect understanding wife?'

'On the surface, yes. Euan was taken in – you know what men are – but I could see behind the public performance.'

'Your psychic powers?'

Her eyes sparkled. 'I suspect you can be very naughty when you let yourself go. I hope I'm around when you do.'

'What did you see behind the public performance, Vicky?'

'A woman who had her life well sorted. She had money – lots, I believe – and an influential grandfather. I'm not saying Fanshawe pushed Phil's career along, but he certainly shoved a little when Alison chose to come out here.'

'*She* chose to?' he asked with swift interest.

'Stands to reason. Phil was a squadron guy. Falklands hero and the rest,' she said breezily. 'Wouldn't want to give all that up, would he? No, she was the one who set her heart on this posting. And Grandpa got it for her.'

'But surely Dunne had to meet the requirements.'

'He did. I guess Phil could've got any job he applied for. Impressive service record, good mixer, looked great in uniform, faithful husband . . .'

'But pretty crazy, I heard.'

'No more than the average serviceman. A bit of a lad, that's all; took a risk or two. But so does Euan when he climbs aboard his beloved *Felice*. Phil wasn't as experienced in small boats as Euan, but I still find it odd that he died out there. He had a ship-to-shore and emergency flares. His death upset me a lot. Phil was bursting with vitality. It seemed such a sad end to a man like him. Eaten by the fishes!'

At last here was someone who cared about the loss of Dunne! Vicky might have been infatuated with the heroic fighter pilot, but she was the first person to agree with James that there was an element of mystery over the tragedy. Beneath her perky manner this young woman was shrewd.

The waiter brought a dessert menu. Bad timing from Nick's point of view. If Vicky had been fond of Dunne, talking about his death did not stop her from ordering an apricot sundae smothered in cream. Nick opted for cheese and swiftly returned to his questioning.

'Awful shock for Dunne's wife on top of the scare over her mother's condition.'

'Huh, another chameleon change there! Never mentioned her mother in my hearing, and I was necessarily in her company a lot. I had assumed both her parents were dead. Everyone was surprised when she jumped on the first flight home because the old girl was on her way out. Except that she wasn't. But Alison had had to demonstrate that she was the ever-loving daughter. Baloney!'

Another interruption with the arrival of dessert and coffee. Heaping sugar in his cup, Nick asked, 'How sincere was the widow's grief when she arrived back?'

'Hard to judge. Alison was never less than controlled. Euan arranged for her to cast a wreath on the water, but as no one knew where Phil drowned it was a hit and miss affair. She looked upset during the business, yet the memorial service at St Andrew's left her outwardly calm.' She forked ultra-sweetness into her mouth. 'Probably missed the flag-draped coffin and volley of shots over the grave. Much more impressive!'

Nick's hand stilled as he made to drink. 'You *did* dislike her.'

'I couldn't figure out what made her tick. That always makes me suspicious. No one can be perfectly nice to *everyone.*'

'Not to her dressmaker and hairdresser.'

'Ah, they were paid for their services. She believed that entitled her to treat them however she chose. Same with her domestics.' Another forkful of death-by-calories went into her mouth. 'Forget her. Let's talk about you, Nick. Tell me what you've been doing in cold, grumbly but dear old England.'

'Flying helicopters.'

'And?'

'The usual things one does in cold, grumbly but dear old England.'

She put down the fork and grew quietly serious. 'Nick, your name and picture made the front page of every western newspaper. We're all aware of what happened to you.'

'And to my brother. *And* how our father threw away his marriage and career because he's a hopeless alcoholic,' he added bitterly.

'Bloody media! Euan said I mustn't bring up the subject; that you wouldn't want to talk about it.'

'I don't.'

'Fair enough ... but tell me why a gorgeous, sexy guy like you has flown halfway across the world at a time like this to join a heavily married couple with three children.'

'The Wellnuts and I go back a long way.'

She studied him searchingly during a short silence, then said softly, 'Whoever the girl is needs her brain sorted. Men like you don't grow on trees.'

'Joyce must be heartily thankful we don't. I haven't been the ideal guest so far. Hence the Chanel. Now, if you've finished that gooey concoction, I'll settle the bill and we'll face the heat and crowds in Orchard Road again.'

Vicky was quiet as they quit the hotel and walked towards the taxi rank. The humidity closed in on them as they fought their way between the tide of people flowing in the opposite direction.

'I guess Euan's day will have been cooler and quieter at sea,' Nick said, guiding her across a busy side street.

'Not at sea. He'd have been chirpier at breakfast if it was. He hates long meetings ashore. They never resolve the issue.'

'What issue is that?'

'Piracy on the high seas. The local Navy and Police know they'll never stamp it out. Euan says they chew all round the subject to arrive at no conclusion. He has to attend, although British Naval vessels are never targeted.' Nearing the site of the taxi stand, she glanced up at him. 'I'm going to the club to swim and laze the afternoon away. Why don't you come? Seems a pity to break this up when we're getting on so well.'

He shook his head. 'Sorry, Vicky. I'm not in the game of making husbands jealous, and Euan's crazy about you.'

'I know,' she agreed on a sigh, 'but there's something very daunting about being adored. It puts tremendous pressure on you to be worthy of it.' As her taxi drew up she kissed his cheek. 'Lunch was lovely. Don't be too much of a hero and end up like Phil. You're a great deal like him.'

He stared after the departing car, struck by her words. Had Lara felt so pressured by his love she had run from it? Four girls pushed past him to take the next taxi, bringing him from speculation. When the following car pulled up he occupied the rear seat hastily. The ageing Chinese was already weaving into the flow of traffic when Nick asked if he knew the Yang workshop. A curious nasal grunt by reply told Nick nothing, so he asked again in a louder voice.

The taxi screamed around a corner, throwing Nick against the side, then raced no more than a foot from the flank of another cab down a long palm-lined street and over a high-arched bridge to land with a thump on the far side. Nick would not care for this driver as a co-pilot, although he seemed sure of where he was going.

It came as little surprise when wide roads gave way to meaner thoroughfares. The back streets of Singapore; the reality behind the tourist glitz! Nick had seen enough of the world to know that workers who produced articles of beauty all too often did so in badly lit, airless, unhealthy premises for less than a basic wage. His contempt for Vydecker and his exquisite protégée increased. The Yang showroom, Fleur's showy apartment, the price of the jewellery were all obscene when compared with the standard of living of those who made it all possible.

The taxi turned continually through a maze of streets hung over by buildings that had stood for more than a century. The people who shuffled along the broken pavements were poorly dressed and listless. Modernization had not reached this far. Nick tried to imagine Fleur in these surroundings and decided she more likely summoned the foreman to the city for his instructions.

The taxi stopped with a jerk outside a narrow open-fronted shop hung around with dried plants, animal parts and posters advertising Tiger Balm Ointment. A Chinese apothecary!

'Why have you stopped?' Nick demanded.

The driver pointed. 'Yang.'

'No, I want the workshop for Yang jewellery.'

The man nodded. 'Yeh, Yang.'

Nick had seen enough of the world also to recognize the futility of further argument in situations like this. He leaned back in resignation. 'Just take me back to the city.'

Five minutes later, still crawling through the criss-cross of streets, Nick suddenly sat forward and snapped an instruction to stop. Settling the sum on the meter, he stepped out into stifling heat laced with the stench of incense, overripe mangoes, durians and bad drainage. He turned back to walk to the junction where he was certain he had seen Gray Attard paying off a taxi. What was a top marine biologist doing in the back streets when he should be organizing the transfer of his team and equipment to Pulau Pelingi?

The Australian had disappeared: his taxi was being occupied by two Indians who had emerged from a garishly pink building fifty yards along the street. Undoubtedly, a favourite venue for men of certain tastes. Nick felt vicious satisfaction. Did Lara know her arrogant, master-in-his-field lover frequented places like this?

The Golden Orchid Club proclaimed itself to be an open-all-day night club. Knowing he would have to pay over the odds for temporary membership that would allow him to follow Attard inside, Nick was stopped in his tracks by a large poster on the wall beside the entrance. It showed a striking girl of mixed Asian origin seductively draped and veiled with diaphanous blue scarves.

PERFORMING SIX TIMES DAILY
THE EXOTIC SLAVE DANCER
LAPIS LAZULI

Six

A coffee-skinned girl in a tight glittery sheath relieved Nick of a wad of dollars as she smiled a greeting with sticky scarlet lips. Her eyelashes were weighted with mascara; her ears with six-inch tasselled drops. Her breasts thrusting against the gaudy material were amazing. He smothered the urge to test if they were real.

The dim interior smelled of pungent tobacco, sour sweat and the cloying sweetness of incense. Chinese, Indians and white clients sat at small tables drinking, talking together, laughing while missing nothing that was happening on the small raised platform. Another amazingly endowed girl brought Nick his first 'free' drink; asked if he required anything else.

With his gaze on Attard at one of the front tables, he murmured, 'When is the next performance by Lapis Lazuli?'

'Soon,' she promised with the smile that never reached the eyes of these girls.

Performing at present were a Chinese pair who were identical twins. Dressed in skintight lurex their routine suggested a girl and her mirror image as they moved together so exactly it seemed they could be just that. Their acrobatic contortions had Nick wondering if they had rubber bones.

He began to sweat in the sultry atmosphere. The drink was the usual kind of cocktail of raw spirits designed to reduce a man's resistance to buying more of the same. It delivered a hefty kick. He kept his eye on Attard, who had accepted a second drink and was enjoying a worm's eye view of the pliable young Chinese. Nick's mouth twisted. If Lara could see him now her admiration might take a nosedive.

The act ended with the girls so intertwined it seemed they would never manage to disconnect their limbs. When they did, they walked from the platform as unconcerned as if they had been demonstrating a household cleaner.

Lost in contemplation, Nick jumped nervously at a sudden deafening cymbal crash. The girl who then sidled on to the platform was dressed in blue silky harem trousers and a bra trimmed with gold beads. Lapis Lazuli was draped with trailing blue scarves and sexily veiled.

She began with the standard voluptuous gyrations to bazaar-style music. Nick studied the audience more closely. *Check on lapis lazuli.* If this dancing girl was involved in whatever Philip Dunne had been investigating she was surely no more than a link in a chain. A chain leading to John Vydecker? The American dealt mostly with Orientals, so he could easily be backing a set-up connected with someone in this club.

More cymbal crashes, faster music as she began to shed scarves more sexily than Nick had seen in distant Arab dives of his youth. Or perhaps he was more maturely appreciative now. A swift glance away from the performer showed Attard on his feet and pushing through red velvet curtains along-side the bar. Was he after more active enjoyment in the rear rooms?

Not so Nick. The girl on stage had a superb body, fully rounded and so firmly sculpted there was barely a fold in her brown flesh as she bent and swayed. He watched with pleasure as the scarves were discarded, the bra removed to leave gold discs that shimmered as she wriggled. With sinuous grace, the girl sank to the floor in a split position, arching back with her arms raised in a gesture of supplication to the heavens.

Nick's nerves reacted wildly again when the thunderous crack of a bass drum heralded two dusky men with ropes and a whip.

The mood changed drastically. The girl was dragged to

her feet, bent forward and back, lifted high and tossed from one half-naked man to the other. She was caught and held by one, feet and hands tied together by the other, before being flung down flat. The whip lashed down on each side of her beautiful body as she writhed around in simulated pain.

As the drumbeat thudded louder and louder agony began rioting through Nick's body. He could see nothing, yet he could smell them near. He did not know who they were, did not understand why this was being done to him, had no indication when it would stop. His balance had gone adrift; he was toppling into a black abyss. The world was closing in on him, crushing the breath from his body.

'Please, sir, allow me to help you.' The voice spoke to him in English. It was a gentle voice. 'Come, it is just a short distance.'

The man's eyes were dark, but they held only concern. His features were Malay, not Arab, and Nick could *see* him. They were in a narrow street where drab awnings hung over uneven pavements.

'I am Dr Rahman. My clinic is nearby. Please come and rest for a while away from the heat.'

Nick's arm was taken in a gentle grip and he was led beneath the striped awning. He felt drained of energy, unable fully to understand what was happening. Women and children were occupying several chairs in a small room; a few elderly men sat apart from them. Whirring wall-fans cooled the air. The doctor took Nick across the mosaic floor to an inner door. The small consulting room was air-conditioned. A young Indian nurse turned from a cabinet with a greeting.

Their short exchange was mere background sound as Nick slowly sorted his thoughts out. He had entered a seedy club because of a poster bearing the name Lapis Lazuli. The girl's dancing had started to arouse him until the slave element had turned seduction into brutal domination.

Nick was persuaded to sit on a hard polished chair. 'This

is merely a reviving mixture of glucose and water,' he was told. 'I suspect from your pale skin that you arrived here just a few days ago and forgot the power of our tropical sun, sir.'

Nick frowned up at him. 'Where is this place? What happened?'

'You stepped in front of my taxi without seeing it. The driver fortunately had good brakes.' He studied Nick closely. 'Are you an epileptic?'

Nick shook his head.

'Then may I ask, without causing offence, if you have been visiting a Chinese healer? Some are excellent practitioners; others are charletans who put their patients in a trance without their consent. You were totally unaware of your surroundings when I came upon you. I could tell you were neither inebriated nor drugged, so I thought it best to bring you here.'

'It's very good of you.'

If Rahman expected an explanation he did not show it, merely asked where Nick was staying. 'You should take a taxi there and rest, then you should make an appointment with the doctor who attends the High Commission staff. Whatever problem you have it will be better to consult him. I warn you this hypnotic state might return. Several times, in fact. Tampering with the mind can be dangerous.'

James had a rare free evening so the Wellnut family went to the cinema. Nick opted out, saying he would catch up on some reading. In truth, he was deeply shaken. He had no recollection of leaving the Golden Orchid club or of walking the considerable distance to Rahman's surgery. The doctor's parting words haunted him. If the mere witnessing of simulated aggression could have so drastic an effect, *they* still controlled him. What, in God's name, would it take to find Nick 'the Hawk' Hawkwood again?

Sliding off the wagon, he downed a couple of whiskies, then forced himself to concentrate on the girl, not her bondage act. He did not believe it just a coincidence that her exotic stage name linked with Dunne's comments. A porn club was an excellent front for shady business – more so than the Yang showroom – and the girls in such places more often than not were prepared to do anything for money. Which meant they would also blab for payment. A session with that girl was the next step.

Remembering James's intention to shred Dunne's notes, Nick went to the office and the drawer where his friend kept the file. It was still there, but he was taking no chances and swiftly photocopied the pages. Then he checked the computer for e-mails. There was one from Jon which banished introspection.

> Nick,
>
> You were right. Gossips in Mousehole related scandal to Lucy.
> 1. Jacqueline Farley is local celebrity. Writes poetry no one understands but wins prizes. Was ill with viral pneumonia, not cancer. Not life-threatening.
> 2. Daughter Alison arrived from Singapore at time you gave. Made daily visits to Penzance hospital to see cousin hurt in road accident. Convalesced at Farley's cottage. Mousehole unconvinced about cousin. He and Alison more like lovers.
> 3. Name: Squadron Leader Tim Rourke. Married. Former colleague of Philip Dunne.
> 4. Alison and Rourke now frequent occupants of isolated annexe to Farley cottage.
> 5. Main problem: both lovers in Cornwall, so couldn't have bumped off Dunne.
>
> Does this help or hinder? Keep out of trouble. (What a hope!)
> Ciao,
> Jon

Loose ends suddenly tied up in startling manner. Fanshawe had sent granddaughter not Dunne away from looming scandal! It explained why Dunne would have gone along with it. His wife and a married brother officer were having a hot affair. The Falklands hero was being cuckolded and, unless they had been amazingly discreet, it would have been discussed throughout the squadron. How would the macho Dunne then appear?

If the press had got on to it there would be headlines. Fanshawe would deplore the publicity. So would the RAF. Two men's careers would suffer. Far better to put half the world between the lovers.

The only person failing to condemn the situation had been Alison's mother, who presumably viewed passion through a poet's romantic eye. Had she stage-managed the emergency flight home when Tim Rourke had been injured in a car smash? Had Dunne known Alison was rushing to the bedside of her lover, not her mother?

The affair between Rourke and Alison possibly explained Dunne's craziness in Singapore. If he had loved her, risky exploits would provide an outlet for his anger. If he by then despised her they would have eased his bruised masculine ego.

Nick had a sudden thought. If Dunne, believing his mother-in-law to be dying, had somehow discovered the true reason for his wife's return to England, was it possible that he had committed nautical suicide that day? Would he have willingly sacrificed Jimmy Yang's life? Unlikely. Yet it made neat sense of rough supposition regarding that sailing disaster.

Vicky Goss this morning said Alison had appeared upset when casting a wreath on the water. Remorse? At the memorial service her calmness could have cloaked her sense of freedom to indulge her passion for Rourke. A chameleon, indeed!

A feeling of fellowship with Dunne invaded Nick. Another man who had been heartlessly dumped by a woman he loved. His mouth twisted cynically. Between sessions in the Mousehole cottage with Alison Dunne was Rourke visiting brothels, like Attard? Having their cake and eating it!

*　　*　　*

At breakfast no mention was made of the printout of Jon's e-mail that had been pushed beneath Nick's door overnight. At the bottom James had written: *Let sleeping dogs lie.* Nick agreed, yet there was an element of satisfaction over the explanation for Dunne surrendering his fulfilling squadron life for a diplomatic attachment. But Nick was still determined to get to the bottom of the man's cryptic file, which would surely lead to whatever Fleur Yang and Vydecker were involved in.

He had fifteen days in which to tackle it, but this one promised little chance for sleuthing. Euan Goss had phoned early inviting Nick to go sailing at 13.30, and Joyce was so pleased with the gift of Chanel she declared that she would devote the morning to her guest before driving him to the sailing club. They were then engaged to dine with Ferdy and Kim Collins.

'I hope you haven't plans of your own for tonight, Nick,' said Joyce.

'No, look forward to it. I'll get Kim going on merlions and *feng shui.*'

Joyce took him to Ming Village, where visitors can see Ming designs being reproduced on porcelain by highly skilled painters – mostly women – whose steadiness of hand and sharpness of eye create works of art. Knowing Lucy would love it, Nick bought a small bowl to take home for her. The second apology gift he was obliged to give! He left it with Joyce when she dropped him off after a light lunch.

'Remind Euan you have a dinner date,' she advised. 'He's inclined to sail into the sunset forgetting how long it will take to get back.'

It was an ideal day. Nick enjoyed the chance to crew for a man who knew well his vessel and the waters they were in. The breeze over the sea eased the energy-sapping heat and it was good to engage in activity that tested muscles and coordination. *Felice* was a graceful craft, clearly the second greatest love in Euan's life. Nick had been surprisingly relieved that Vicky was not joining them. His concentration would have wandered if she was aboard in brief shorts and bikini top.

Euan explained that his wife suffered from motion sickness. 'First time I took her out we were still in sight of Plymouth Sound when she threw up over my feet. Should have ended the affair, but it turned me on in a weird kind of way. Wanted to look after her, make sure she was OK. When I asked her to marry me she agreed, providing I added to my vows, *in sickness and in health permanently on dry land.* Euan laughed, but Nick's stomach muscles tightened as he stared out to sea. He and Lara had once spent an intoxicated evening dreaming up additions to the marriage vows each would demand from the other. He recovered quickly, but thoughts of Lara hovered as they got underway.

For a while they talked of service matters. Nick questioned the Navy man on ships' weapons and their effectiveness. They both let forth on the need for updating equipment in all branches of British services – a constant demand of the men who had to use them – then Euan touched on the subject of his liaison with the Singapore Navy.

'The most up-to-date, maximum effect stuff is American, of course, but it costs, and how! This small nation doesn't envisage waging a major war, so I mostly advise on sales of British components. Maintenance stuff from firms like Rees and Hardy. Crazy, really. In many instances *they* buy even smaller components from the Japs or Taiwanese to make their systems, then export eastwards again. Dealing in arms is one of the most lucrative and convoluted trades. We all know that in a combat situation the weapon that knocks us out is liable to have parts that were made by our own countrymen.'

'Is Rees and Hardy fully on the up and up regarding customers?' asked Nick, hanging out over the green flecked water as *Felice* raced before the wind.

'God, yes! Been established a hundred and fifty years. Mind you, it's not unknown for reputable firms to sell to customers who simply ship the stuff on to renegade nations at a stiff profit. It's then used for a purpose the manufacturers didn't suspect. Mad tyrants making superguns or nukes. I guess R and H could have been used that way.'

'What do you know about Senoko's bid to deal with them?'

Busy negotiating between several eyots, Euan answered abstractedly, 'James is handling that. I concentrate on seafaring stuff.'

The rest of the afternoon passed very pleasantly out on the water. Nick relished the sensations of sun on his bare skin and the wind ruffling his hair; enjoyed agreeable male company and the wonderful sense of freedom when nothing blocked his view in any direction.

After an hour or so Nick noted dark blobs over to the west and, his thoughts heading elsewhere, asked if one of the islands was Pelingi.

'No, it's some distance beyond that group. What's your interest?'

'I flew out there with Ferdy Collins. Landed to suss out a camp site for a team of scientists.'

'Gray Attard and his men? My Aussie counterpart mentioned it to me. We keep each other informed about anything like that. They're very welcome if they manage to halt the advance of that bloody growth.'

'I'm afraid I know nothing about it,' Nick confessed.

'You wouldn't. You spend your time up there.' Euan pointed skyward, grinning. 'Nothing to clog up all that lovely open space you lucky guys enjoy.'

'Is this rogue weed a really serious problem?'

'Serious enough to employ the top man on a three-month survey. Left alone, this harbour could be choked up within ten years.'

'So Attard's commission is to get rid of the stuff?'

'He's here to find out how. So far, no one has any idea how to kill it off. His team are scientists. They'll cut samples and bombard them with chemicals in the hope of a breakthrough. Trick is not to kill off everything else with it. The people who live on Pelingi catch and sell fish for their

127

livelihood. They're not altogether happy about scientists messing in their fishing ground. Understandable. Alex Foyle, my Oz colleague, went out there to explain.' He gave a slightly malicious smile. 'He thought it would help his case if he made the trip in one of their twice-weekly boats – getting down to their level, was how he put it to me. They sussed him. Sat him in the stern beside baskets of durians on the way out, and surrounded him with fish on the way back. Alex brought up his guts over the side both times, and him a sailor! He'll never live it down.'

Nick reflected that a similar experience would do Attard a lot of good. But that man would never try to get down to anyone's level from the heights he believed were his alone.

'Did Foyle get his point across?' he asked.

Euan shrugged. 'Who knows? The Chinese living on the islands aren't like the city dwellers. Very clannish, steeped in folklore and superstition, it's impossible to judge what lies behind their bland expressions.'

'They wouldn't sabotage the project, attack the camp?'

'Highly unlikely, but they're certain to be unhelpful and conveniently dense if approached by the members of the team. I don't envy Attard and his men.'

'One's a woman,' said Nick before he could stop himself.

'So I heard. A real stunner, according to Alex. Far too lusciously sexy to spend her time in the depths with voracious plantlife. Should stay on land with voracious manhood!'

'What d'you know about Pulau Gombak?' Nick asked to end that topic. 'Ferdy said no one'll go near it.'

'Mmm, bad *feng shui*. A strong deterrent. It's an unattractive chunk of land, anyway. Smothered with vegetation, seven eighths surrounded by rock, dead in the path of incoming monsoon storms. Who'd want to go there?'

'According to local hearsay the Japs practised brutality on the island during the war.'

'People vanished. Large numbers of them. They've never been traced and locals believe they were taken to Gombak for some terrible purpose.'

They were running for home now, letting the wind take *Felice* more gently over water turned pale gold, as Nick recalled his conversation with Fleur. She had surely not been acting a part when she asserted that her grandfather had been taken and put to death on that island.

'Didn't anyone investigate at the end of hostilities?'

'Sure, but they found nothing conclusive. There was a cluster of huts where a clearing had been hacked out, but the presence of a tower suggested the Japs had used it merely for advance sighting of approaching shipping. Two Dutch vessels bound for Indonesia foundered on the rocks soon after Singapore fell, and there were others. Older Singaporeans claim the Japs lured them there like the chap in the ancient legend. Have you heard about Wu and his evil powers?'

'Yes, Ferdy filled me in.'

'I suppose it's possible. Jam the air waves, realign buoys to decoy enemy ships on to the reef at night. Cheaper than depth charges.'

'Bloody archaic, though.'

'They were. Rode on bicycles through jungle right down the length of the Malay Peninsula to take Singapore. Impossible, but they did it. One has to hand it to them, the poor bastards were given pedal power only and had to scavenge for food as they advanced. No tents and hard rations. Allied commanders had road blocks, guns and troops in place to counter a conventional invasion. Must have been a bitter pill to swallow, losing a strategic colony to blokes on bikes!'

'Don't get too carried away with admiration for their ingenuity. Their treatment of prisoners was archaicly imaginative, too,' Nick reminded him curtly. 'To get back to Gombak, presumably it was deserted when the search got underway.'

'Clean as a whistle. No sign it had been used as an outpost, or whatever.'

Nick frowned. 'You mean they'd buried cans, cartons, all the wastage of day-to-day living before they left?'

'No, seems they must have deposited everything in the

tangle of vegetation surrounding the clearing. I've read the report by the investigators, out of interest. The earth around the huts hadn't been disturbed – no sign of digging. It states that they started to penetrate the solid growth but had to abandon the attempt. The Allies had just recaptured the entire Malay Peninsula. Had their hands full liberating the poor devils in Changi, giving succour to the locals and investigating those war crimes of which there was abundant evidence. Far as I'm aware, Gombak was shelved.'

'And the missing people?'

Euan shrugged. 'Happens in every war. Some eventually turn up telling amazing yarns. Ever hear about the Nip soldier discovered on a Pacific island forty years after the war ended? He'd been hiding in the jungle; didn't know Japan had surrendered. Sounds crazy, but I guess if you're completely cut off from the world there's no way of knowing what's going on. Weirdos deliberately turn their backs on civilization.' He gave a short laugh. 'Maybe they have the right idea. Could be very peaceful.'

No, it's anything but peaceful; it's total and frightening isolation, his senses screamed. He would never forget it. Deprived of light it had been impossible to count time passing. At first, he had calculated each day by the delivery of meagre food and water. Then he had grown progressively confused. Hearing the key in the lock, the clink of the bowl on the stone floor: *smelling* their presence. Yet there had been no bowl when he explored as much of the floor that his chains permitted. He would hear them come again. Explore again. No bowl! Then it would suddenly be there beside him when he turned to ease his agony. How had it got there? He had believed he was hallucinating, but it had been just one of their subtle torments designed to induce mental deterioration. If he had remained there much longer . . .

'. . . made an exploratory pass, but the place looked pretty well impenetrable.'

Nick grew aware of Euan as he came from the ever-hovering darkness. 'Sorry?'

130

'Gombak. Alex Folyle and I were prepared to challenge the *feng shui* and land there, but the shoreline opposite the narrow channel between the rocks consisted of no more than a thin strip of greyish sand fronting thick growth. That wartime tower is now probably little more than a ruin.' He gave a rueful grin. 'Our plucky "boys' adventure" was abandoned by mutual cowardly agreement. As I said earlier, who'd want to go there, anyway?'

They returned to the marina in time for a sundowner. Nick had mentioned his dinner engagement at the outset, and Euan said he had to attend a drinks party followed by a meal with some Indian friends. Drinking his gin and tonic in the clubhouse, he told Nick these friends always produced wonderful food, but the meal ran on well past midnight.

'OK if you can put in a late start next morning. Unfortunately, a couple of our destroyers are due to dock at the crack of dawn and I have to be there. They'll probably head a convoy of merchantmen of all nationalities. Always happens when warships come in. They offer protection from marauders.'

'Piracy's that prevalent?' asked Nick from his chair beside the long window.

'God, yes. You name it, there's a market for it in the East. Weapons, drugs, silk, currency – even kids. They're sold to brothels as young as four or five. It's obscene!'

'Vicky mentioned you'd been roped in for another meeting on the subject yesterday. I guess—'

'You spoke to Vicky yesterday?' It came out sharply suspicious.

'Met by chance in Tangs.'

'She told me she'd swum and lazed all day. No mention of meeting you in Orchard Road. It's a long way off the direct route from our place to the club to encounter someone by chance.'

Nick set his glass down so hard the spirit slopped over the side. 'Are you suggesting the meeting was by arrangement?'

The other man looked uncomfortable. 'Of course not.'

'Then what are you suggesting?' he demanded.

'I simply said Vicky didn't mention it. It just seems curious that she should keep quiet about it.'

'Perhaps it was because she knew you'd react like a bloody adolescent prat,' Nick flung at him, his voice rising. 'You had better know I took her to lunch as a thank you for helping me choose a present for Joyce. We shared a table at the Marriott, not a bed. *OK?* I'm getting sick of these insinuations on my motives.'

'For Christ's sake calm down,' Euan hissed, glancing round at members who were staring in their direction. 'No need to behave like a flaming lunatic.'

It was the worst thing he could say to someone who had that afternoon briefly travelled back into a nightmare. Nick got to his feet, fists bunched. 'I'm a bloody sight saner than a jealous bastard who sees a violater in any man who speaks to his wife.'

He pushed his way through blazered yachtsmen and women to reach the stifling late afternoon freedom outside. He was still breathing hard when his taxi came to a standstill in the rush-hour gridlock ten minutes later. Slowly, he faced the daunting fact that there would be no hope of reinstatement as an operational pilot until he could maintain complete control of his reactions in any situation.

This was put to the test a few hours later when Nick arrived with the Wellnuts to find Lara on the Collinses' verandah, chatting with Kim. Attard was standing with Ferdy at the far end, engrossed in a sheaf of papers. Ferdy glanced across and waved.

'Be with you folks shortly. Grab yourselves a drink.'

Kim smiled. 'Welcome. Please come and join us.'

Nick hardly noticed Joyce's swift scrutiny of his face as Lara gazed directly at him. 'Hallo again, Nick. I've just been telling Kim how I'd suddenly remembered we'd met before, at an engagement party when I was in London at uni.' She turned her lying eyes on the Wellnuts. 'I should also have recognized you both when we were introduced. A group of us came to several of your squadron parties. Pretty hectic affairs, but great fun.' Her smile gave her away; it was clearly an effort. 'Please forgive my lapse of memory. I'd been working like crazy to get everything ready for the trip – so much to check out – and we came to the party straight from a long flight. I guess I was too tired and jet-lagged to think straight.'

'And you'd just agreed to marry your boss. Enough to make a girl forget anyone else but him,' Nick said deliberately.

Joyce was true to form. 'As you said, those squadron dos were somewhat riotous. I really don't remember half the people who came to them. What did you say your name was?'

She accepted the challenge. 'Lara.'

'How pretty! Are you Russian?'

James moved to end the female skirmish. Taking Joyce's arm, he turned her towards him. 'Here's George waiting to hear what you'd like to drink. The usual G and T?'

The Chinese steward greeted Joyce warmly as a frequent guest. During her brief enquiry about his parents' health and the progress at school of his sister Betty, Nick said all the right things to his hostess and sat in the chair she indicated. He was acutely aware of Lara on the red-cushioned carved settee facing him. She wore a cream trouser suit enhanced by a necklace of flat turquoise stones forming an arresting ethnic design. A Fleur Yang piece given as an engagement present? No, Attard was more likely to consider as a suitable gift a framed photograph of himself holding up a previously unknown fish he had discovered for mankind. And was Lara's sudden feigned recollection of three people she had initially treated as strangers mounted for that opinionated sod's benefit, or because she knew she could not brazen out an entire evening in their company? Whichever, it was going to be a long, difficult one. The Collinses had no idea what they had done when planning this dinner party.

133

It was a huge relief to Nick when, fifteen minutes later, three more guests arrived. The tall, bearded Professor Hendriks was a psychiatrist; his dumpy Australian wife taught deaf children and used her hands a lot when talking. Their daughter was a concert pianist who had just completed her first tour of Europe.

She was a total contrast to the other young woman present. Briony Hendriks was blonde, pale-skinned and petite, with a soft high voice. Lara resembled burnished gold with her deep tan and Titian hair. The moon and the sun. Nick found the former more restful. As he was plainly meant to partner Briony he was able to hold his attention away from Lara.

Once they sat at the table Nick began to relax. Ferdy had known Beattie Hendriks from way back. They told amusing reminiscences of life in the backblocks of Australia. Nick then asked the gentle girl beside him about her tour, which easily led on to a general discussion of the merits of European cities. All this prevented Attard from giving an ego-monologue on marine science. Lara, sitting across the table from Nick, said very little. Aware that she was watching him, he avoided meeting her eyes. And Joyce's. The light of battle was still in hers. He dared not guess what showed in his.

When they moved back to the verandah for coffee, James centred his attention on Briony and Joyce was in mid-conversation with the girl's father. The four Australians clustered together, standing as they talked. Kim beckoned Nick to join her on a corner seat for two.

'Ferdy said you expressed an interest in *feng shui*,' she said. 'Were you merely being polite?'

'Not at all,' he replied, liking this calm, cultured woman. 'My brother and I spent our school holidays in the Middle East, so we learned quite a lot about Arab and Muslim cultures which are fascinating. I'd like to know more about *feng shui*. Would you really not live in a house, however much it appealed to you, if the *feng shui* was adverse?'

'Of course. It would take you many months, even years, fully to understand the influences. I can recommend some good literature on the subject if you wish to delve deeply, Nick. But I will give you a brief outline of how it is possible to create harmony and wellbeing in your lifestyle through the ancient art, if you are truly interested.'

Nick became lost in all she said; she was a magnetic speaker and he found it easy to accept what she said. In his youth he had witnessed strange, inexplicable happenings in the Middle East, and there had been experiences in his military career that inspired a strong belief in fate; a Divine plan.

'Ferdy said you would also tell me about the merlion,' he then prompted.

Kim shook her head. 'That is a different matter altogether. You know that Singapore is called the lion city? The first explorer to land here saw a wonderful beast and, in his ignorance, claimed it was a lion. The beast was a tiger. There were many here until hunters killed them off. The lion has become our national emblem. It symbolizes strength and nobility. When Singapore became an independent nation, the old myth surrounding a creature that was half lion, half fish manifested into the merlion that can defend our country on land and at sea.' She smiled at him. 'You have your St George and the dragon. We have our merlion.'

'Maybe these marine explorers will find proof that merlions really exist,' he said, nodding towards Attard.

She regarded him silently for a moment or two; a small, striking woman in a green silk skirt and loose jacket, with pearls at her throat. 'You told me that men who cavort around the sky will talk about it at every opportunity, yet you have said nothing this evening about this unique passion. I would like to hear more.'

'You have a pilot husband. You must be sick of the subject,' he said.

'I would not invite you to speak of it if I did not wish to learn of your individual fulfilment in your career.'

It came over almost as a reprimand, and Nick realized that for all her westernization, this woman retained her inbred Chinese qualities. So he gave her a brief rundown of the

135

pleasure and sense of achievement his professional life offered him, travelling back in time to the golden days.

She nodded understanding when he finished. 'Your enthusiasm is almost infectious. I think I can appreciate that. You spoke of a sense of freedom. From life on the ground?'

'Lord, no.'

'From what, then?'

He frowned. 'Not *from* anything.'

'Perhaps freedom to express yourself in ways not possible under the influence of the element earth?'

Nick realized she was thinking as a Chinese. 'I'm afraid I've never considered it that deeply.'

'Everything should provoke deep thought, Nick. Freedom means so many different things to people. Maybe to do as one pleases without regard to legal or moral considerations. To speak out against what one sees as injustice, without fear of retribution. To be able to end a destructive marriage or a bad business partnership. To rise from a wheelchair and walk again. To escape from captivity.'

Nick had tensed. Her deep thoughts were getting too close to home. They had changed from those of an ethnic Chinese to those of a qualified psychologist.

'Captivity is the most obvious example, of course, yet there is the reverse. A long-term prisoner can see the outside world as too great a threat. He regards his ordered life behind bars as freedom from the burden of surviving out there in the human rat race. A person can also see even an unhappy marriage as freedom from loneliness. An invalid can welcome his bed or his wheelchair as freedom from the obligation to submit to painful physiotherapy, or from the indignity of appearing helpless in front of others. The hermit finds freedom in the solitary confines of his cave. Amnesia is also a form of it; the mind escapes from the unacceptable.' She looked searchingly into his face. 'And Nick Hawkwood seeks freedom in the element metal, which is the great dome of sky over the earth. I find that very interesting.'

He said through a jaw grown stiff, 'I can't think why. Ferdy also chooses to chase the clouds.'

'Ah, he takes to the air because of an early wartime ace who became his boyhood idol. When Ferdy leaves the ground he becomes Captain Felix Knowles, Royal Flying Corps.' She gave a fond smile. 'Freedom from being a non-hero himself, perhaps.'

A burst of laughter drew their attention to the four Australians who were enjoying an anecdote of Ferdy's. 'One looks at Dr Scott and sees a lovely, vital young woman. The mind subconsciously adds a background of wealth, glamour and self-indulgence. But the mind is stereotyping. It cannot equate that vision with endeavour, rough living and courage enough to probe the ocean depths. She clearly has an affinity with the element water.'

Nick had no difficulty visualizing her in a workmanlike swimsuit, as confident far beneath the waves as above them. He had been there with her. And in a bedroom afterwards.

'She is not a person one would forget having met before, I think.'

'No,' he murmured, lost in recollection.

'Neither are you, Nick. Perhaps Lara was seeking freedom by forgetting that meeting.'

Nick turned to face her again. This woman was a damn sight too perceptive. Time he broke up this one-to-one. 'Let's hope she discovers the means of freedom from the weed that's threatening the seas around here. Short of blowing it up, I understand only science can come up with a solution.'

Brilliant light momentarily flashed over the verandah, followed by the growl of thunder. Kim stood. 'A storm is coming. The elements fire and water will soon overtake us. We should go in.'

There was a general move into the house, but Nick hung back and walked to the far corner from where the lights of the city could be seen as a yellow glow above the surrounding trees. He was not ready for social chit-chat. Kim Collins had unsettled him, brought too near to the surface all he was fighting to keep buried. The spectacular on-off effect of the lightning and the increasing volume of the thunder echoed his inner unease. Only the waft of her perfume told him when Lara approached.

Without turning he asked, 'How much have you told him?'

'I merely had to explain why I had run after you at the airfield.'

'That was the moment when you suddenly remembered we'd met before, was it?'

Her arm brushed his as she moved up beside him. 'We're moving out to Pelingi tomorrow. There won't be another chance to talk.'

'Good.'

After a moment she said, 'Did you really not read my letter explaining everything?'

He faced her. 'You let *three months* pass without a word. Your father managed a short note of apology four days later, but even he was in the dark about where you'd gone and why. I was posted, and by the time your letter caught up with me I had no interest in it, or you. And if you think I want an explanation now, save your breath.'

'Don't worry. You've got the message over loud and clear.'

Lightning flashed across her face like an alternating neon sign as he accepted that he was not completely over what she had once meant to him. 'Lara, what are you out here for?'

'I'm not sure,' she said on a sigh. 'To make peace?'

'We were never at war. For that, belligerents slog it out face to face. It's very different when one delivers a coup de grâce then puts oneself out of reach. At Sandhurst they'd call it terrorism. What do marine scientists call it?'

Rain began to fall in heavy drops that became a deluge in seconds. It pounded on the verandah roof to spout off it like a mini Niagara. The breeze carried spray from it to dampen Nick's shirt against his body.

'Are you in love with him or just making a good career move?' he asked between thunder rolls.

'You have no interest in me, remember?' She had always been sharp at verbal sword-crossing.

'It's your fiancé I'm concerned about. At his age a sudden shock could kill him.'

The storm arrived overhead and they instinctively drew back against the wall of the house. She looked wonderful with fine spray sheening her face and bright hair, eyes dark with emotion. This was the girl he had planned to spend the rest of his life with. Would it be different now if she was his wife? Would her nearness banish the darkness that haunted him? Would he tell *her* what he could not admit to anyone, even himself?

'I'm not proud of what happened that day,' she said suddenly. 'I hurt so many people, caused so much distress. It's overshadowed my life; changed the person I used to be. I believed I was *so* in control, yet I fell at the first hurdle. I was so ashamed of my weakness I tried to purge it by staying clear of anyone who knew me. After three months of misery I could stand no more and faced up to what I had done.'

Another ear-splitting medley of thunder claps left them gazing silently at each other. When there was merely the thunder of rain and spasmodic lightning around them she reached up to kiss him softly on the mouth, her breasts warm through his damp shirt.

'Try to forgive me, darling.' She turned and went in to the house.

Nick remained on the verandah until the storm subsided.

Seven

The following afternoon the coffee-skinned girl at the door of the Golden Orchid again relieved Nick of a wad of dollars. The same hostess with pneumatic breasts served him with his 'free' drink. She was surprisingly straight-faced, and slipped through a mirror-fronted door as Nick took the cocktail across to a viewpoint beside a pillar. On the platform a dusky Amazon dressed in bra and loincloth was performing a sinuous dance with a trio of snakes coiled around her body.

Nick scanned the tables. Gray Attard was not present. Ah, of course, the god Neptune was moving his team out to Pelingi today. Lara would have to keep him satisfied for the next three months. He did not deserve her. Maybe she deserved him!

Someone tapped Nick's arm. He turned to see a small man in a white linen suit. Thinking he wanted a clearer view around the pillar, Nick moved aside to accommodate him. The man gave an uneasy smile and asked if he could have a word in private.

Nick shook off the hand on his sleeve. 'I'm here to watch the performance. Find someone else to talk to.'

'I'm the manager, sir. If you would come to my office . . .'

'I said no thanks.'

'It's a delicate matter.'

'There's nothing delicate about what goes on here.'

'That is what I wish to talk to you about. I will be much obliged, sir, if we could discuss it in private.'

Although mystified, Nick saw an opportunity to find out

140

more about what went on behind the scenes here. 'Right, lead the way.'

They went through the mirror-fronted door and along a short corridor. The manager was neither Asian nor Oriental. His features and accent suggested eastern Europe. The office was air-conditioned. Nick was invited to sit on a black leather sofa. He declined. The brawny bouncers he had half expected were not apparent.

'What's this delicate matter, Mr . . .?'

'Stanislav Ivanovich Vinnikov, which I'm sure you already knew. And you are?'

Not a bad guess. Russian. Mafia? 'I'm John Smith. What's this all about?'

'Do you live in Singapore, Mr Smith?'

'I'm here for a short holiday.'

The Russian's eyes narrowed. 'Shall we leave out the jokes and get down to business?'

Nick was even more mystified. This was clearly a case of mistaken identity. Was he about to learn what lay behind Dunne's *check on lapis lazuli*? Could he be that lucky?

'We have many regular members at the Golden Orchid. Very many. When a stranger enters, the girls naturally take notice of him. When he is young, virile and European he is *most* noticeable. When he has only one drink then leaves, the girls feel they have somehow failed.'

Did they check on how long everyone stayed? Nick wondered.

Vinnikov continued smoothly. 'It is even worse when the man leaves very suddenly, pushing the girls roughly aside and looking most . . . intense. They grow afraid. They ask themselves why a handsome young man should come to the club and not remain to enjoy their dancing.'

'And what answer do they come up with?' asked Nick.

The small man grew fidgety. 'My girls provide a cabaret for club members. No performance involves nudity. It is all highly artistic.'

'And highly erotic.'

141

'I can't be responsible if—'

'Members have lewd imaginations,' Nick finished for him, sure of the mistaken identity theory. He cashed in on it. 'You're treading a very fine line out front, but what goes on behind the red velvet curtain?'

Vinnikov's pale eyes flickered uneasily. 'The artistes' dressing rooms are at the rear of the club. If you saw members go through the curtain it was to personally express their enjoyment of a particular performance. The girls often receive presents from admirers. They are all very attractive, wouldn't you agree?'

Nick gave a crooked smile. 'You're putting a high-class gloss on a pretty earthy set-up. The "presents" from admirers are down payments for sex. Admit it.'

Vinnikov's forehead was beaded with perspiration, like his upper lip. He was scared, no hiding it. 'What the girls do in their free time away from the club is not my responsibility.'

'You're the manager. What *do* you accept responsibility for?' In the face of the other's silence, Nick said, 'You claim there's no facility for prostitution here?'

'None.'

'Nor for anything else?'

The Russian looked puzzled. 'What else is there?'

Certain he had been taken for some kind of inspector of moral issues, Nick recalled Fleur Yang's suspicions of him. *There are laws, restrictions. It is necessary to be careful.* What were these people afraid of unless they had cause to fear officialdom? Why be suspicious of an Englishman? Officials would be Singaporean. Surely they did not have him cast as a snooper from Interpol. They would have to be running something really big for that.

Nick revised his assessment of Vinnikov. He was too feeble to be connected to Mafia. There would be no discussion; no nervous explanation. The strong-arms would be present now. It would be a knife in the gut and a posthumous meeting with Philip Dunne. Strange that there should be another Russian on the scene: Mikhail at the Silver Troika. Two

Russians, Lapis Lazuli, Fleur Yang, Jimmy Yang, John Vydecker, all surely linked. Were some of the shipping schedules marked in Dunne's file details of Russian vessels? If so, the leg man had just taken another step forward. And further into confusion.

Vinnikov brought from a drawer a metal cashbox and set it on the desk, his smile betraying nervousness. Sensing that he was about to be offered a bribe, Nick felt a sadistic thrill run through him. He was in control here; Vinnikov the victim. This man could be forced to plead, to beg. A stimulating game could be played making the Russian jump through humiliating hoops.

The impulse was overwhelming, but for no longer than a few moments. Then it faded, leaving Nick deeply shaken. He had never found pleasure in another's misery. He had killed two men in a Northern Ireland booby-trap attack on troops he had flown in to pick up. He had finished off a Serb lying wounded, who suddenly produced a gun and attempted to shoot a UN medic as he walked across to the casevac helicopter Nick was piloting. The acts of a soldier operating within the rules of engagement. There had been no sense of enjoyment in ending those lives. He had done what his profession demanded of him. Like flying a covert mission into Iraq.

'Please do not imagine I would insult you by offering a . . . gift, Mr Smith.'

The ingratiating voice broke into Nick's racing thoughts, and he stared at the Slavic features as he slowly returned from elsewhere.

'I am merely happy to refund your fees for temporary membership, as I would for anyone who found the club did not please him.' Dipping into the cashbox, Vinnikov brought out a thick pile of banknotes held together by a rubber band. He pushed it across the desk with a nicotine-stained finger.

After a short hesitation Nick picked the money up. He would use it to persuade Lapis Lazuli to answer his questions. Ironic if Vinnikov had just funded his own downfall.

'Very generous of the Golden Orchid. I'd like to leave by the rear door through the red curtain. I'm sure I'll find things exactly as you say they are,' he added with heavy emphasis. The Russian's relief was plain. 'Yes. Indeed, yes.'

The Chinese twins were going through their mirror routine when Nick reached the bar again. He nodded reassuringly at the pneumatic hostess, then made for the curtain through which Gray Attard had slipped two days ago. Lapis Lazuli had to be there ready to follow the twins.

Behind the faded velvet was a corridor leading to a door with heavy bolts top and bottom. It was stuffy and smelly: incense, perfume, pungent food and open toilets. Nick pitied the girls whose circumstances led them here. What happened to them when they grew too old for this degrading work?

He passed two small cubicles containing beds; the curtains were pushed back because they were presently unoccupied. Dressing-room was too grand a word for the door-less area halfway down the passageway. Concrete floor, naked bulbs, fly-spotted mirrors, plastic-coated shelves with drawers beneath, rows of coathooks along distempered walls. It was tawdry in the extreme.

The snake girl, wrapped in a cheap cotton kimono, was slumped on a stool, eating rice from a blue bowl with her fingers. Others, similarly clad, gossiped noisily. Lapis Lazuli was draping her smooth curves with blue scarves ready for her performance. As Nick hovered, taking this all in, a woman of indeterminate mature age rose from a stool just inside the room and stood four-square before him. Malay? Indonesian? Possibly a result of several generations of cross-breeding. Dressed in full-length batik, her expression was tougher than her physique. She could hardly protect the girls from a determined punter, but a concerted effort by them all would surely floor a man who tried to overstep the mark.

Nick still had the bundle of dollars in his hand. He held it up.

'Vinnikov said it's possible to meet the girls when they leave the club. I'd like to arrange that.'

The ochre face remained semi-hostile while brown eyes raked him from head to toe assessingly. 'Koz chew,' she said harshly.

'Can I have that in English?'

'*Is* Inglis.'

The penny dropped. 'I know I have to pay. Vinnikov said—'

'Hoo yew wan?'

He translated that well enough. 'Lapis Lazuli.'

The girl herself glanced up from scarf-tying to give him an optical once-over. She nodded at the woman and resumed work on her slave costume.

'She koz eggstra. Pay now.'

'Oh no!'

'Pay harv, or deal off!'

Nick counted out the sum she named, pretty sure this ageing bodyguard would be lucky if Vinnikov gave her even one percent of it. The girls more probably paid the woman a small amount each time they had a 'date with an admirer', which would leave them poorly paid for submitting to men's lust. Vinnikov was undoubtedly a pimp and Nick was glad he had taken the bribe off him. Lapis Lazuli would get the bulk of it even if she had no answers to Dunne's notes.

The rendezvous was arranged for six that evening at an address crudely rubber-stamped on an oblong of blue card. As Nick took it from the woman the Chinese twins appeared, shouting coarsely and gesticulating that the slave girl should get her act underway. The perfect body adorned with blue scarves slid past Nick and ran down the corridor. The woman resumed her place on the stool. The cabaret prostitutes continued eating, gossiping – a routine day!

James and Joyce had to attend an embassy dinner, and Emma was staying over with a schoolfriend, so it was easy for Nick to say he would get a meal for himself in one of the restaurants

145

serving Malay specialties. No one had mentioned the meeting with Lara the previous evening, for which Nick was grateful. Thank God she would be out on Pelingi for the remainder of his visit. No need to face further disturbing conversations. She already had him wishing he had read her letter; puzzling over what had led her to run from him. After those initial humiliating few weeks he had closed his mind to the subject. It was now open again, damn her!

He took a taxi to what he assumed would be the girl's living quarters just before five forty-five. To his surprise the driver turned away from the gridlock in the city centre and on to a highway that was busy but mostly free flowing.

'Is this a diversion to beat the rush hour?' Nick asked.

The young Chinese looked at him in the rearview mirror. 'This way to Sembawang. Good road. Not many red lights we get there in three quarter hour.'

'That long? I've an appointment at six!'

The driver smiled cheerfully. 'You be late.'

He should have checked the location on the large-scale map in James's office, but he had assumed the girl lived near the club. If she had clients on an hourly basis Nick would have only a short time to question her. Not long enough. The subject would have to be approached slowly. Warm her up first, flash dollars in sufficient quantity, then start the grilling. If he was offered a drink he knew how to deal with that!

The sun had dropped below the horizon, leaving a rose-tinted dusk by the time the taxi approached a veritable forest of high-rise blocks in rainbow colours. Close together, and spangled with lights from most windows, they stretched as far as the eye could see in every direction. Housing for the multitude. The driver snaked his way to the heart of this complex, then drew up for a swift exchange with a woman pushing a pramload of black-haired, black-eyed children.

'Are you lost?' Nick demanded.

'Jus checking,' came the cheerful response. Chinese hated to admit to not knowing things, even when it was plain they didn't.

It was six fifty when they finally stopped outside a small shop in a block of four, with accommodation above. The address tallied with the one on the piece of blue card. Nick was puzzled. A flickering neon sign in the window was in Chinese. Beneath it a large card bore the probable English translation.

CHENG LI (CHARLES)
Bespoke Tayler

As Nick continued to puzzle over rendezvousing for sex in a tailor's shop, the driver said, 'If you come to collect suits I wait. If not, better you take MRT back. Taxi not pass here much.'

'Thanks, I will.' Nick paid him and left air-conditioned comfort for the smothering heat outside. The taxi shot off.

Cheng Li (Charles) was doing brisk business. Tall, thin, greying hair, he had unrolled lengths of cloth over the L-shaped counter for two men to study, and was busy measuring a third for trousers. He glanced up as Nick entered. Gold teeth flashed.

'Be with you soon. No one wait more than ten minute here.'

'I'm already late.' Nick waggled the card without much hope of a response.

The smile vanished; dark eyes hardened. 'Outside! Stairs at back.' He continued wielding the tape measure.

Nick had to walk along an alley beside the general store adjacent to the tailor to reach another that ran along the rear of the block. Lights were on in both floors of each premises. Windows were open. Cooking smells wafted on the still air. So did conversations of residents. It seemed to Nick that Chinese invariably spoke to each other at full volume.

He reached stone steps faintly illuminated by a naked bulb at the top. Looking up at peeling paint on a blue door, he thought it nothing like any tart's place he had ever known. But to some men surroundings were not important. Sex in

147

a cowshed, a railway wagon, the back of a lorry, against a wall in any dark corner. For them the instrument of their lust was not important, either. Nevertheless, this was not what Nick had expected tonight. In high curiosity he rapped the brassy knocker, noting that he was more or less an hour late.

She wore a loose cotton gown reaching to her knees. Her black hair hung past her waist; her feet were bare. Without the diaphanous yashmak she looked disturbingly younger than her voluptuous body had suggested. Sixteen? Seventeen at the most. Nick thought of the average age of the voyeurs at the Golden Orchid. Thought of Gray Attard.

'I decided you not coming. I start to eat,' she greeted through a mouthful of food, then turned back into the passage.

'I didn't expect you to live so far from the Golden Orchid.'

Nick shut the door and followed her, breathing a blend of cooked fish and joss-sticks. Hardly conducive to erotic arousal! She went into a room and beckoned him to follow. From the other side of the passageway came the sound of children playing and the voices of women conversing at full blast. Good God, were clients expected to perform with that going on a few feet away?

The room had a semblance of one in a brothel, but there was room only for a small double bed covered in cheap satin and a bedside table painted a garish blue. Several mirrors hung on the walls; there was a full-length one on the door that the girl closed behind him. A coathook in a corner held several plastic hangers for the fussy to hang their shirt and trousers neatly before getting underway.

Turning from surveying this, Nick found the girl had stripped off the gown. In spite of everything, it was impossible not to react to the perfect breasts crying out to be caressed and played with, to deny the urge to run his hands over curving hips leading to firm brown thighs and the ultimate pleasure ground between them. Asian girls matured early, he remembered, and this one was superb. What was she doing in this situation? She deserved better.

'You wan take off clos or wan me take them off?' she asked. 'What you see at club jus pretend. I not do whips. No ropes. Jus sex. How you like it?'

'How old are you?' he asked.

She began to unbutton his shirt. 'Nineteen.'

'Give or take a few years.' He gripped her busy fingers. 'I don't like to rush things. Prefer to talk for a while.'

'Can take clos off and talk,' she persisted.

'Too distracting.' He pulled her hands gently from his open shirt. 'Have you another client coming tonight?' She shook her head. 'Then we have time to get to know each other.'

She backed away looking nervous, unsure how to deal with him. The brutal, the contemptuous, the pathetic she must be used to. A man who wanted conversation before he violated her must be some kind of screwball.

'Koz chew,' she said eventually.

'I'm a very rich man.' He sat on the bed. 'Put your dress on and come over here.'

Covered, she sat, still looking wary.

'What's your name; your real name?'

'Muna.'

'Just Muna?' She buttoned her mouth. 'So what made you choose Lapis Lazuli for your stage name?'

'Is pretty.'

'Very. No other reason?' In the silence the voices of women and children bawling companionably to each other sounded even closer. Nick frowned. 'Whose are those children? Do they live here with you?'

Button mouth again. Nick took out his wallet and began putting dollar notes on the satin cover; enough to sparkle her dull eyes. 'Why do you entertain men way out here? You'd do better with a place nearer the Golden Orchid. Come on, Muna, it's a simple enough question. And I'm prepared to pay well for a simple reply.'

Watching him carefully, she reached out to gather up the money. 'My sisters live here. Five chillen. Cheng Li not like me here. Get very angry. My sisters say jus for while. Pay him good.'

'For a while?'

'Until Vinnikov find other place. We had room near club. Fire burn it up.'

It made sense. Some of the narrow streets around the club were closely packed with old buildings that would constitute a real fire hazard. 'How long ago was this?'

'Two week.'

'Anyone hurt?'

She shook her head, then suddenly laughed. 'Men run out in street with no pants. Was funny.'

Nick nodded, knowing she was starting to relax. 'I bet it was. Muna, you're very beautiful and your stage performance is too good for a place like the Golden Orchid. Why stay there?'

'Kos too much to leave.'

'It would cost too much to *leave*?' he queried. 'How's that?'

'Girl have to pay Vinnikov to dance at club. He give paper to sign say you pay him two thousand dollar.' She looked pointedly at Nick's wallet. 'Take long time earn that much.'

He spread another handful of notes on the bed. He was getting where he wanted with her. Vinnikov was clearly a very greedy pimp. Small wonder he had been prepared to silence a suspected snoop with a bribe.

'A very long time,' he agreed. 'So when the girls have sex with club members Vinnikov takes most of what they earn? That's not right.' He pushed the notes towards her. 'This is all yours. Vinnikov need know nothing about this money.' Watching her slender brown fingers scooping up the money, he said, 'There are surely other ways you could earn some extra money. Do something Vinnikov would never hear about.'

Counting the money, she answered almost automatically. 'Three times I dance at private party. That nice. Big house. All rich men. I sit on lap, they tuck dollar in knicker. Make plenty.'

'And Vinnikov didn't know? What about the two in the act with you at the Golden Orchid?'

'I not say to them. Men at party jus wan me.' She smiled proudly. 'I take off all clos dance for them.'

Nick followed up on the promising lead. 'How do these men make arrangements with you so that no one else gets to hear about it?'

'Come to club tell me,' she said in a tone that suggested he should see the obvious.

'The men giving the parties are club members?'

Muna shook her head. 'Same man come each time. Say he work for big boss.'

Nick scattered more of Vinnikov's money on the satin cover. 'So what's the name of the big boss?'

She gave him a pitying look. 'Men never give name. You no give name. Make no matter when clos are off.'

It brought a fresh frown from him. 'So you've no idea whose houses you went to to give these exciting performances?'

As she made to pick up the dollars he put his hand on hers, repeating the question. She shrugged. 'One American, two Chinese. Big house each time. Many men friend come see me dance.'

Nick told himself Vydecker was not the only American in town. In any case, he was unlikely to hold a stag party in his own home. No reason to rule him out as a guest at such affairs, although he was more likely to get his sexual kicks from Fleur Yang. A safer bet than this voluptuous child-woman.

'The man who claims to work for a big boss takes you to the houses and home again afterwards, does he?'

Her dark eyes shone. 'Come in big car take me both way. Same car he come in to collect letter.'

'Oh, what kind of letters?' asked Nick casually.

A shrug. 'Who care? He pay me, I give him letter.'

'Who writes the letters?'

'Son of my uncle.' She frowned. 'Why you wan know?'

151

Easing more money from his wallet Nick said, 'I might have some letters you could pass on for me. But I wouldn't want Vinnikov, or anyone else, to know about it.'

Her eagerness overrode any suspicions. 'I say nothing. Always I say nothing. When you wan give me letter?'

'Soon. Quite soon. So how often does the son of your uncle come to you with letters?' he probed, and received the sweetest of answers.

'Each time his ship come in. He sailor.'

It was well past eight when Nick left the room above Cheng Li's premises. Vinnikov's bribe had been fruitfully spent. He could not wait to get back to the Wellnut house to analyse all he had learned through Muna's greedy innocence.

In truth, he was glad to get away from that stifling room with its sordid overtones. Even if he had been able to hack it right now, the cooking smells, the strident chattering from the other side of the wall, and the images of her bondage act would have kept his fly firmly zipped. He gave an ironic grunt. After being handed a hell of a sight more money than she had ever received for an hour of soulless sex with a punter, Muna took as an insult Nick's disinclination to get his kit off.

Outside the tailor's shop Nick stopped a small family to ask the way to the MRT station. They gave complicated directions at top speed in heavily accented English, and Nick headed down the street with their words echoing in his head.

Turn right twice, then left. Go round the circle of trees, turn right, follow the raised path between two green buildings. Turn left at the small square, pass McDonald's, then turn right at the school. Straight past the medical centre, through the underpass, up steep steps, then along a path beside a high wire fence. More steps and there is the station.

Circle of trees? Yes. Raised path between green buildings? There they were. Small square. McDonald's. How did fast-food joints give off smells that pepped up the gastric juices to suggest the one thing you had to have right there and then was a triple burger with a fat bag of fries? Nick was tempted, but pushed on until he passed the school. That was distinctive enough, but he must somehow have missed the medical centre because he next came upon what looked like a perimeter road curving away into semi-darkness alongside a high grassy bank.

He turned and began to retrace his steps. Two thickset men in dark clothes some fifty yards behind him hesitated, then also reversed direction. Nick's heart jumped as he sensed danger. How long had they been following him? He mentally reviewed the directions he had been given. Past the medical centre, *through the underpass*. That was where they had intended to jump him. But he had somehow missed it, so they had stayed on his heels.

No way would he enter that subterranean tunnel. Spinning round, he set off at a fast pace along the perimeter road, heading for a path turning at right angles between two pentagonal housing blocks a short distance away. A swift glance over his shoulder confirmed his suspicions. The men were following. Why?

There surely had not been time for Muna to call up two heavies, so they must be local muggers who tailed lone walkers to the underpass. A blond head and a pale face in an estate of this kind would stand out. It would suggest credit cards, cheque book, traveller's cheques. If they had overheard him asking for directions they would know he was unfamiliar with the layout of this vast community. The perfect victim!

A shallow flight of steps led down to the path. As Nick reached them, a group of teenage girls began to mount them. Another backward glance showed the pair pressing on fast. Nick took a flying leap down the bank, astonishing the girls into silence, then he made a headlong dash between the looming buildings as he revised his ideas. Opportunistic muggers would have chosen to wait in the underpass for a stranger who must eventually go through to reach the MRT. He now felt these men were a more serious threat; sensed that they had instructions to deal with Nick Hawkwood, whatever!

If Cheng Li had conjured up two thugs at short notice the immediate future might be tricky. They would know every path and apartment block on the estate, but he would become swiftly disorientated with no time to pause and get his bearings. As his shoes pounded concrete slabs his brain also raced. He could, of course, have been followed right from the Wellnuts' house. This duo might have seen his taxi drive off and waited outside Cheng Li's, banking on their quarry using the MRT to return. In which case the three of them might be running for hours like mice on a treadwheel, getting nowhere.

Ahead, the path split three ways. Too canny to leave himself open to a pincer movement, Nick instinctively swerved left. It would more likely lead him back on course. Would it hell! Twenty yards on it bifurcated to run narrowly between tall towers. He turned left again. A quick glance behind. The pair split up at the junction. Bad tactics on their part, unless they knew for certain that the paths converged again. Better not risk it.

With military precision Nick 'about turned' at the run and charged straight at the single pursuer. They closed so rapidly the other was caught unawares. Nick's head went down ready to shoulder him in the solar plexus. Hard. He hadn't been a scrum forward for nothing. An express train hit a buffer. Totally winded, the man staggered backward three or four paces, doubled over in pain and temporarily out of action. Breathing heavily, Nick added a neck chop that felled him.

The way ahead showed no more than a dog-shaped shadow moving there, so Nick hared back the way he had come, heading for the perimeter road. Ten yards from where the way branched he was abruptly halted by a crowd of rowdy youths who spilled from the stairwell of an apartment block and filled the narrow way. Another express train had met a buffer!

The Chinese were all riotously merry, in no state for cold

reason. Any attempt to push between them could stir up aggression. Nick's only choice was to allow himself to be swept forward until they came upon the unconscious body. Then he would make a break for it while their attention was elsewhere.

It soon dawned on Nick that he had joined some kind of wedding party. Whatever language was spoken, the antics of inebriated pals towards a prospective bridegroom ran along much the same lines. The hapless victim, who could barely stay upright, had pink ribbons all over his head, a placard hanging round his neck, bare feet and a rope tail with clanking Coke tins attached. He was sure to be dumped in a fountain, tied to a very public lamppost, humiliated in some way in the name of friendship. They could actually provide the perfect cover. Nick now cursed the body that was certain to divert them shortly.

It did! It also semi-sobered them. Loosing their hold on the bridegroom, they clustered around the inert man in sudden silence. At that moment Nick grew aware of a dark, bulky figure running towards them from the opposite direction. No time to check on identity. He thrust his way between the erstwhile revellers and doubled back as before. *Lure enemy from position of advantage and reverse situation.* When the moment was right he would deal with this second man as he had with the first.

Sweating heavily in the sweltering heat, Nick raced on, aware of alarmed cries starting up behind him. He rounded a corner, searching visually for cover. Swerving across spiky grass, he dodged into a bay filled with bicycles propped in near-vertical racks. It was dimly illuminated overhead at the far end. The light above him was broken.

The man swung around the corner. His momentum took him several yards beyond the racks before he saw the empty path. He halted, turned his head back and forth, then walked stealthily towards the only hiding place. Nick crouched low. The advantage was his; he could see his opponent as a well-defined shadow. It was a brave man, or a fool, who offered himself as a clear target, Nick thought. But that was before he spotted the glint on a hand-held blade.

A renewed adrenalin rush highlighted this greater, more deadly danger. It was no longer unarmed combat. Breathing hard, nerves raw, Nick watched the man studying the recessed bay from a safe distance, knowing his quarry must be there. He looked set to wait until Nick broke cover. The Hawk had other ideas.

Lying flat, he elbowed his way along behind the metal racks, judging the distance carefully and collecting several small lumps of concrete from the crumbling wall. He selected one weighing roughly the same as a small grenade. Levering himself on to one knee with practised stealth, he lobbed the stone at the ceiling light. Crash! It went out.

As Nick anticipated, his pursuer instinctively moved towards the newly dimmed end, then swung round unsure what to do. He had to watch both exit points now. He hovered midway and copied the head movements of Wimbledon spectators. Nick knew he had a greater advantage. He could not be seen in the deep bay, but the man had light enough behind him to show up his every move.

Time for further action. Nick thrust the front wheels of two adjacent bicycles from the grooves that held them steady. They fell back with a clatter that caused the watcher to start forward. Nick began destabilizing bicycles willy-nilly, moving in a fast crouching run in each direction until he felt he had confused his opponent into wondering if there could be more than one person behind the heavy racks. At that point Nick stopped the activity and let total silence unnerve the man further.

It clearly did. Nick watched him twist and turn in the expectation of being rushed from either direction, shifting in agitation several paces back and forth yet unwilling to surrender that central viewing point.

Still crouching, Nick lobbed some of the smaller stones he had gathered. They rattled against metal to suggest progressive movement to the end where he had smashed the light.

Thoroughly unsettled, the man's attention was drawn that way for just long enough. Living up to his Sandhurst reputation, Nick emerged and swooped hawklike. A knee in the kidneys; an arm tight around the throat. One sharp . . . God, *no!*

Swift sanity halted military aggression. He was not tasked to kill, to commit murder! Nick straightened his knee, eased the lethal pressure on the man's windpipe and prepared to deliver a neck chop that would drop him like his partner. In that split second of mental hiatus the knife entered Nick's thigh as his struggling victim thrust wildly backwards.

Gasping in pain, Nick's combat skills led him to seize the man's arm as it swung forward to make a second stab. No restriction on breaking bones! A howl of agony rang out as Nick neatly dislocated his aggressor's right shoulder, crushing his wrist to force him to release the knife. It dropped to the grass, glinting wickedly in the pale light. Someone had given this bastard a licence to kill; the weapon was designed for the purpose. Nick's hard chop to the neck was only just on the prudent side of fatal. The man stopped feeling pain; stopped feeling anything.

Nick's thigh was throbbing. The warm stickiness of blood oozed down his leg as he bent to pick up the knife. No way would he leave it for the thug to use again. He would ditch it en route to the MRT. If the medical centre was still open he would get an emergency dressing slapped on the wound.

A shout reached him from the semi-darkness. He glanced up to see a knot of people on the path looking his way. He was standing over a huddled body with a knife in his hand. A blond Caucasian; an ethnic intruder in this Singaporean estate.

They burst forward in sudden united anger, shouting and gesticulating as they ran. Nick took flight. He was now outnumbered around twelve to one and he had little faith in James's famous diplomatic immunity being of any help to him in this situation. He grunted with pain as he ran. The ooze of blood became a gush.

The instinct to escape kept him going although he was bathed in sweat and each pounding stride stretched the wound in his leg. His mind told him this was a lost battle, but his martial spirit dominated. Four months ago he had been captured while unconscious, yet he somehow relived that disaster while running with a hostile crowd at his heels. Their yells revived dark demons; became echoes of his own screams. Terror spurred him on. It could be any country, any mob set on torturing and degrading. He had seen it happen all over the world. It would never again happen to him!

The estate was a poorly lit maze. He lost count of how many times he turned, branched left or right, leaped up or down short flights of steps. Amazingly, his pursuers followed like the long tail of a kite. No strategy: no military training, of course.

The propelling fear kept him going although there was no sure promise of safety ahead. His stride was growing uneven. His right leg was on fire. But this was pain he could withstand. He had known another kind of agony. Nightmare images forced a spurt of renewed speed. He could almost feel their hands grabbing at him. Dragging him back into a dark hell.

The path ended abruptly. Garish concrete towers no longer reared on all sides. Ahead was space and darkness. Two shades of darkness. The denseness of land, the rarity of sky. Beneath his feet was a shifting, crunchy surface. He identified the salty smell before his eyes picked out the third shade of darkness that glinted as it heaved. He was on a beach. His pursuers were fanning out, sensing that he was trapped. How wrong they were!

They so little expected it they were still standing in a noisy half-circle when Nick entered the sea, took a flying dive into the swell and began to swim out to deep water, confident no one would follow. He was right. Glancing back, he saw the shadowy huddle gesticulating on the beach. The ever-lurking terror, raw memories melted away. He was free!

Swimming was easier on his leg. He made his arms do

most of the work in a leisurely crawl. Then he floated for a while to rest and think. Singapore was an island. He could go ashore anywhere whenever he chose so long as he swam parallel with the twinkling lights of habitation. Ordinarily he could keep going for hours, if necessary, but he must have lost a deal of blood during the chase. He was also hampered by clothes. Making his way back to the Wellnut residence in underpants would arouse more than curiosity. Wet but fully clothed would be easier. Aware that his mind was drifting, he rolled over and resumed the easy crawl. Fatal to sleep and float out to sea.

Before long he found it heavier going and guessed the tidal flow was turning. Euan Ross said the currents were very strong in these waters. Time to go ashore. Raising his face, Nick was surprised to see arc lights, cranes, ships. Sembawang Terminal! It had been marked on James's map. Bingo! What could be simpler? 'I was walking along the jetty, slipped on a patch of oil and fell in, gashing my leg.'

The distance proved deceptive, yet Nick summoned enough staying power to reach the ladder fixed against the slime-covered wall of the nearest jetty. He had had to swim through garbage and patches of bilge effluent along the inner reaches, so it was with relief that he hauled himself up the slippery rungs to lie flat recovering his strength and wits.

The rusty hull of a cargo ship rose up alongside the jetty. The familiar mixture of dockside smells wafted over Nick as he gazed at a star-filled sky, savouring its wide infinity. Kim Collins had questioned him closely on what he found freedom from up there. Right now he yearned to be flying through the calm, quiet night with just one man he liked and trusted beside him in the airborne bubble of a cockpit. Andy Lisle. No, not poor Andy. He was dead. Had wings of his own now. Could fly anywhere.

He was mentally drifting again. Fatal. Time for action. Pain sliced through his leg as he stood. Blood further darkened the leg of his pale trousers. The MRT was out of the question. Taxis should be more available here. There would, in any case, be telephones he could use to summon one. First he must deal with the blood loss. Taking off his shirt he folded it thickly then tied it around his thigh. A tourniquet would be better. He would see what he could do about that while waiting for the taxi to arrive. First priority was to secure transport back to the city centre.

He limped past piled crates and boxes, past bollards, anchor chains, coiled, oiled ropes. At the end of the jetty he faced the main access road stretching into the distance. He wearily contemplated the distance to cover before any hope of a telephone, then set off through docks that appeared deserted. The matelots must all be on the town tonight, drinking, seeking out the tarts. Passing them letters! *Check on lapis lazuli.* How much had Philip Dunne discovered when he wrote that? Nick had no doubt his assailants tonight had intended to kill him. As they had Philip Dunne?

The offices on his left were all unlit. No hope yet of a telephone. Screwing up his tired eyes, he thought he saw a light on a third floor way ahead. Keep putting one foot in front of the other. Like that time on exercise in the frozen Brecon hills in December. Like that desert training march with full equipment in Oman. Like the escape and evasion hunt over fog-bound Dartmoor with sadistic Commandos and trained dogs on your heels. Like the punishment run he had undergone with three other cadets for failing to return to Sandhurst on time after a wild weekend in London. He remembered their faces clearly; the strain on them during the last deadly four miles. His must have looked the same. But it had been a riotous weekend. The girl had had fantastic breasts. The rest of her had been pretty hot, too. Lara Scott. No, she had come along several years later. And she had gone again. Gone in about the worst bloody—

'I tell you it *is* Nick Hawkwood, Euan. Yes, he looks like a dropout and no, I don't have any idea why he would be down here half naked, but it's him all right. He needs help.'

The woman's voice broke into Nick's wandering thoughts.

He glanced up uncertainly. A man in a starched white RN uniform and a blonde wearing a low-cut shimmery dress were walking across from a shiny black car. God, had he reached the hallucinatory stage already?

Eight

James gave Joyce one of those imperceptible messages exchanged between husbands and wives without uttering a word. She took Vicky's arm. 'Now Nick's cleaned himself up and smells fresher than when you found him, James and Euan are eager to hear the details of his latest escapade. I'm not. I had my fill of boys' jolly japes when we were with the squadron. Let's have some more coffee on the verandah while we gossip.' She propelled a reluctant Vicky from the room, leaving the men to thrash things out.

Nick knew he owed them an explanation and it would have to be the truth. Euan had taken him to the doctor who served High Commission staff. He appeared to accept Nick's story of slipping on oil and falling into the dock, but he had shown concern over the wound's proximity to the puckered scar already on Nick's right thigh. The cuts he had sustained in the Lynx crash had become badly infected during his incarceration, and had only recently healed. He was lucky not to have suffered serious muscle damage; his tormentors had not decided to inflict pain by opening his thighs to the bone.

Dr McIntosh had given a pain-killing injection and two strong sleeping-tablets in a packet. No alcohol! A slightly hostile Euan had driven Nick home, then got a message to James. The Wellnuts had excused themselves from the coffee stage of their embassy dinner. It was now time for the debrief. Sleeping tablets and bed would have to wait.

James poured whisky for himself and Euan. He was too angry to sit; stood gripping the glass and glaring at Nick. 'I

162

told you to leave bloody well alone! Euan and I can't afford to be involved in messy affairs like this. We have to tread carefully. No echoes of colonial rule; and definitely *no* interference in national or police business.'

Nick nodded. 'So you said. Your predecessor didn't observe the rules so scrupulously. Hence that file.'

'What file is that?' queried Euan, who had unfastened his high collar but still looked hot and uncomfortable.

'Will you tell him or shall I?' Nick asked James. 'I now have one of the keys to the mystery of those shipping movements. Euan ought to be brought in on it.'

'What file?' demanded Euan again. 'How does it affect me?'

'It doesn't. It shouldn't,' James told him fiercely. 'I wish to God I'd shredded the flaming thing straight off.'

'Instead of showing it to me to keep my mind occupied?' countered Nick with his own spurt of anger. 'You led me to open Pandora's box, then tried to slam the lid. Too late! Things had flown out. You explain the basics to Euan, then I'll give you both the latest sitrep.'

While James reluctantly regaled his colleague with details of Philip Dunne's file, Nick looked longingly at the whisky decanter. He could do with a stiff drink. The anaesthetic was wearing off. The nerves in his thigh were throbbing heartily once more. He was shaken by the fact that he had let this happen. Fleeting hesitation at the vital moment. An enemy could kill in that moment. Nick had had that drummed in over and over again, like every soldier during training.

'Why haven't I been filled in on this before?' Euan was protesting. 'Shipping data is my province.'

'I broached the subject with Fielding when the file first came to light and was sent off with a flea in my ear. Don't make waves, was the message. So I didn't.'

'Yet you showed the file to Nick.'

'Oh, didn't he explain why?' asked Nick, re-entering the lists. 'He asked me to make some sense of Dunne's cryptic notes, imagining it would occupy my time in Singapore. I thought he really wanted answers so I set about getting them. They began adding up to something so big I was drugged, drenched in booze and sent back here in a taxi as a warning to back off. That was when my good pal here confessed that he had set me up. A busybody colonel at home issued instructions that I should be given something to think about to stop me going off my rocker. The exercise went off half-cock. Hawkwood isn't barmy, just insubordinate. When a person puts one over on me I have this urge to retaliate. And when a woman manages to make an utter fool of me the urge is even stronger. So I ignored James's speech about diplomatic staff not getting involved in anything beyond their sphere of duties, and carried on looking for answers. Tonight, two men tried to wipe me out.'

Euan looked heavily confused. James looked resigned. He sat prepared to hear the rest. 'What happened?'

'Last I saw they were both out cold. I dislocated the shoulder of the one who stabbed me before I finished him off.' He added reflectively, 'Just stopped myself from snapping him in two.'

'Where was this?' Euan asked faintly.

'A large estate in Sembawang. A crowd of residents then turned up. Probably heard the bikes falling.'

'Bikes?' queried James.

'I pushed quite a lot from their racks. The noise must have alerted the owners. They found me standing over a body with his knife in my hand and gave chase. We ran around for what seemed an age until we reached a beach. They thought they had me then. Never guessed I'd swim for it. Left them howling with frustration.'

'Oh, my God,' groaned James, rolling his eyes heavenwards.

'You swam from the estate to the terminal!' exclaimed Euan incredulously. 'The currents are notoriously treacherous in that area. You must be a bloody fine swimmer.'

'Inter-services gold medallist,' put in James dryly. 'That

was without a stab wound in his leg, of course. This guy is the original Action Man.'

'Just as well, or we'd now be rescuing him from a lynch mob.'

'No, Euan, we'd be disclaiming all knowledge of him,' James corrected heavily. 'Nick, what were you *doing* in Sembawang?'

'Solving a riddle. Dunne's lapis lazuli doesn't refer to a precious stone but a girl. A sexy, voluptuous girl who dances with blue veils at the Golden Orchid Club. She also takes messages from sailors.'

'I bet she does,' commented the seafarer among them.

'And it won't surprise you to learn that in her free time she offers sex to club members. That's why I went to Sembawang. Correction. That was the cover story that allowed me to question her.'

'Prostitution in a Sembawang housing estate? It'd never be sanctioned,' declared Euan.

'It's a temporary arrangement. The usual place was destroyed by fire two weeks ago. Clients ran into the street starkers. Hilarious, she told me.'

James exploded with anger again. 'This is no sitrep, it's a load of bollocks. For God's sake give *facts*, and in some kind of order, man. What put you on to this dance of the seven veils? Why not question the girl at the club where she works? Who lured you to Sembawang? Why were two heavies tailing you? Did they know of your connection with the High Commission, and what's all this crap about taking messages from sailors?'

Nick spoke of his sighting of Gray Attard entering an erotic club, and his discovery that the star performer was named Lapis Lazuli. By the time he got around to that evening's events, James was sitting with his head in his hands.

'She didn't know the names of the men giving the stag parties but one, if not the rest, is linked with this guy who comes in a big car to convey her there and back. He's the one who picks up the letters from her cousin.'

'*Billets doux* from a married woman,' grunted James, still holding his head in despair.

'There's no name on the envelopes, just a rubber-stamped merlion, Muna said. But here's what puts an interesting perspective on the whole business. The cousin isn't one of a permanent crew. He prefers to sign up when captains are taking on new hands; likes to go to different places each voyage. She remembered the names of two ships he's worked on. They're both on Dunne's list. If Euan checks them out we may find out why Dunne starred them.'

'Phil never consulted me on any of this,' Euan said peevishly. 'If he was on to something dodgy he should have filled me in.'

Nick hazarded a guess. 'Vicky liked Dunne – told me he was great fun. She's the only person I've come across who was upset by his death. You probably made your jealousy too obvious. Dunne had his own problems. Couldn't be doing with your attitude.'

Nettled, Euan retaliated. 'He had to prove he was the ultimate macho man.'

'Maybe he had reason to,' said Nick, thinking of Tim Rourke in the Mousehole love-nest with Dunne's wife.

'You mean heroics in the Falklands weren't enough to satisfy his giant ego?'

'No, I didn't mean that,' he replied quietly.

James intervened. 'None of this comes under our aegis. Neither Euan nor I can take this on and delve further.'

'Dunne wasn't so faint-hearted.'

'And he's now dead. If you had been eliminated tonight there'd have been hell to pay.'

'I've always hoped to go in an upward direction.'

'Don't be bloody flippant! You're dabbling in deep waters. If someone is prepared permanently to silence you it's an internal affair.'

'So let's inform the relevant authorities.'

'Of what? That you were drugged by a glamorous jewellery

designer who counts the rich and famous among her customers . . .'

'Clients,' Nick corrected.

James glared. 'It's only your word against hers on what really happened that night.'

'Such touching loyalty!'

'For Christ's sake!'

'OK, so perhaps I also invented Lapis Lazuli, the angry bike-owning residents and swimming through tidal currents that should have swept me out to Pulau Gombak to meet up with the ghost of Wu, the deckhand. Maybe I really did slip on oil on the jetty and fell in the dock,' Nick countered with anger more bitter than his friend's. 'Maybe those weeks as a guest of ragheads *did* unbalance my mind. Who knows?'

There was an uncomfortable silence. Nick thought of those sleeping pills and bed. His thigh was on fire again. He got to his feet. 'Let's drop the whole thing. I'm bushed. Thanks for sorting out the doctor, Euan. Say goodnight to Vicky for me.' He glanced at James. 'Nothing of what happened tonight endangers you and your family. I gave my name as John Smith. No hint of any connection with you. And I doubt there was a direct link with the drugging by Fleur Yang, either. Once I came face to face with them I recognized my attackers as the two who play in Muna's bondage act – heavily-muscled, vicious-looking brutes. Vinnikov would know I was visiting Muna – he takes at least fifty percent of the girls' earnings. I guess he guessed he'd failed to buy me off and opted for safer measures. He had me down as some kind of morality snoop; better off dead! Sorry I spoiled your embassy dinner. I'll move to a hotel tomorrow.'

'Better still, fly home,' James said more sympathetically.

Nick shook his head. 'Can't pull out now. Someone owes Dunne an answer to why he died. It was surely no accident.'

The pills made him sleep, but nightmares came with it. He was being pursued through endless dark tunnels, naked and hung around with chains. They were slicing into his flesh with knives. He screamed; begged them to stop. They told him he was imagining it all and immobilized him in a straight jacket. Freedom had been an illusion.

Due to the unusually healthy state of his bank balance, he took a club room overlooking the harbour entrance in the elegant Oriental Hotel. The room was air-conditioned, quiet and beautifully appointed, but Nick missed the trees, the birdsong and shutters that could be thrown open to fresh air night or day. He missed his friends, the chatter of the children. Joyce had made no protest at his departure. James had worked on her, without doubt. Kissing Nick fondly, she had reiterated her husband's advice to fly home.

'You've had more than your share of danger, Nick. Find a good woman prepared to take you on, and settle down.'

The hotel had a huge open-air pool with a bar and restaurant alongside. Unable to swim because of his leg, Nick bought a paperback, ate lunch, then settled on a lounger to read and get a tan on his unusually pale body. He fought drowsiness throughout the opening chapter, finally losing the battle.

An insistent jingle woke him. Still sleepy, he plucked his mobile from beneath his towel. 'Hawkwood.'

'Euan Goss here.'

'Oh . . . hi,' he said, surprised and wary.

'Had cause to go through back shipping lists,' he said ultra-casually. 'Spotted those two vessels you mentioned, so I checked their movements over the past year. They make the same run each time. One does the round trip to Rangoon; the other is registered in Timor and chugs along from Dili, calling at all the main Indonesian ports, Singapore, and doing the turn around at KL. I have a note beside them saying that they have both been boarded and robbed on the high seas in the past twelve months.'

Nick sat up. 'Piracy?'

'It's not my direct responsibility, but I'm often invited to attend meetings on the subject. Our warships are notified and asked to keep a watch for these daring bastards, but they lie low then. It's been my practice to make a note of these light-ning raids and what's taken off the ships. They've been known to seize the ship itself and spirit it away. You'd think it impossible today, but once in international waters they change her name, fly a different flag and put into some port where they get busy with the paperwork to create a new vessel.

'Shipnapping?' asked Nick in amazement.

'In a nutshell. But it's more often cargo, and valuables from the captain's safe.'

'Big stuff?'

'Depends on the size of the pirate ship.'

'You mentioned children – slaves – that day we went sailing.'

'I think I said you name it there's a market for it in the East. Every so often something bizarre like that crops up, but it's usually merchandise they can move on easily. Electrical goods, mass-market clothing, handbags, shoes, household stuff, medicines. Not prescription drugs. They're invariably transported by air.'

Gazing at the relaxed bathers and baskers around the shim-mering pool, Nick thought how strange it was to be having this conversation. Then he remembered Fleur Yang's words. And he remembered last night. The two faces of the dazzling East!

'Are you still there?'

Nick hastily assured Euan he was. 'Does James know all this?'

'He's aware of piracy, not the details. That's my province.'

Here again was evidence of the Naval man's possessive tendency, whether it was wife or job. 'You claim both vessels Muna's cousin worked on have been attacked this way. Coincidence?'

'What do you think?'

'I think it would be valuable to learn the names of other ships he's crewed on. If I get that info would you check if they've also been boarded?'

'How can you find out?'

'Leave that to me. Would you check?'

'Well . . . OK.'

'You don't share James's reservations?'

'Certainly I do . . . but as you said, we owe Phil an attempt to interpret his damned file.'

So those words had touched a chord last night, had they? 'James showed you the file?'

'This morning. Felt he had to, I suppose. We can't get officially involved,' he added swiftly.

'I appreciate that.' Nick watched a shapely blonde in a gold lamé swimsuit dip her toe in the pool then return to her lounger. Shame to get that suit wet!

'You can call me at the office, or at home. Here's the number.' He gave it, adding with a touch of reluctance, 'Glad to help.'

'Thanks.'

'No probs.'

'Oh, Euan, one more thing,' he said hastily. 'Do you have notes on what was actually lifted from those vessels?'

'Hold a mo. If it was weaponry we'd certainly be interested.' Pages turned noisily. 'Here we are.'

The list he read out seemed mundane enough in both cases. No weaponry. Then Euan said thoughtfully, 'It appears the safe on each ship was robbed of currency and precious stones. Rubies, pearls, sapphires. Worth a bit, apparently.'

Nick forgot the blonde in the gold lamé. 'Isn't that unusual?'

'I scribbled something in the margin at the time. Hard to read now, but I think it refers to a courier travelling as a passenger. Fewer official checks than air travel. Sounds a bit dodgy, doesn't it?'

'Smuggling?'

'There's plenty of that out here. Small boats, dark nights. This seems too open for that.'

'But dodgy. How come it didn't strike you at the time that it was worth investigating?'

'Why should it?' Highly defensive again.

170

'Dunne certainly thought it was, hence his file.'

'That bloody file again! Why was he snooping in my office, searching through my records? There's no other way he could have latched on to all that gen.'

'Don't you pool it?'

'On a need to know basis.'

'So you thought Dunne had no need to know about the rampant piracy, which involved the theft of valuable gems?'

Euan hesitated. 'In general, yes . . . but *I* deal with shipping. In case you're unaware of the system, the Defence Adviser primarily liaises with the local and visiting Air Force and Army personnel. I'm more concerned with Naval affairs. Anything to do with shipping is my pigeon,' he repeated with emphasis.

'So why not the snatching of precious stones at sea?'

Euan fired up. 'Look here, this may be a diplomatic attachment but I'm still an RN Lieutenant Commander acting within the regulations of my service. They are very clear cut. The theft of jewels by foreign nationals from ships not registered as British does not come within my sphere of authority. Any more than it did Philip bloody Dunne's. That satisfy you?'

'Yes, sorry,' Nick returned grittily. 'I tend to think as a soldier. As well as fighting in wars and keeping the peace between non-British belligerents, we're called in during strikes to man fire-engines, ambulances, petrol-tankers or refuse lorries. We're roped in to kill livestock and burn their carcases during foot and mouth outbreaks, fill and pile sandbags to hold back flood water, deliver supplies to hamlets cut off by snow, defuse World War Two bombs found by small boys, and blow up suspicious items planted by today's terrorists. My own corps fights in the air; REs often operate under water. Our sphere of authority is elastic in the extreme.'

There was silence at the other end of the line. Nick knew he had gone too far with a man whose help he needed, but Euan's attitude riled him. He counted to five.

'So now we've cleared the air I admit I'm acting as a free agent in this. I do welcome your offer of help, and I do appreciate the limits of your status at the High Commission. I'll do what I can to discover which other ships were served on by our friend who sent letters through Muna. You shouldn't overstep any bounds if you simply check them against your records. I'll call you soonest.'

'You omitted something from your sphere of authority,' came the cold response. 'Flying secretly into Iraq to pick up non-existent passengers. You out-macho even Phil.' He disconnected.

Nick lay back beneath the shade of a huge parasol, chasing ideas around in his head. A deckhand who happened to serve on two ships boarded by pirates hands letters to an erotic dancer. She passes them to a man who arrives in an expensive car to collect the envelopes marked with a merlion symbol, to take them to the 'big boss'. The matelot has either to be notifying him of the ship he'll next sail on, or reporting on the cargo lifted from the one he's just left. Nick was sure Euan's records would show a similar pattern when given the names of those other ships.

Why the complicated system? Why not send messages direct? Could Vinnikov be taking his percentage on this, too? But he would then surely deal with the letters, not Muna. Nick was certain the Russian had sent those two to Sembawang after him: they worked in his club. Yet was Vinnikov the actual owner of the Golden Orchid? Probably not. He was too indecisive to be more than a puppet activated by . . . whom?' If only Muna had known the names of those men at whose parties she had provided a naked floor show. An American and two Chinese!

An American, stolen precious stones, Fleur Yang. Was there a link here with Vydecker and his talented mistress? That man had businesses all over the Far East. Burmese rubies, Sri Lankan sapphires, Japanese pearls, Fleur Yang jewellery! Surely the merchant banker was too big to risk dabbling in piracy, yet how many rich men forever wanted more?

What of the American's large investment in Senoko's bid

to make components for Rees and Hardy, of whom Alison Dunne's grandfather had just become a director? Did John Vydecker know Sir Charles Fanshawe? The peer had been a governer of Hong Kong. Vydecker's bank had a branch there. He also had a home. Had a business connection been formed some years ago between them?

'Your tea, sir.'

Nick's reflections were interrupted by a white-clad waiter who placed a tray on a small table beside the lounger, then held out a chit for signing.

Frowning, Nick took a moment or two to grasp the situation. 'I didn't order anything.'

'No, I did. My fault. I told them I was sitting right by the palm trees. I'm actually just across the way.' It was the gold lamé swimsuit. The blonde inside it was American. She smiled. Perfect teeth, glossy lips. 'Now I've disturbed your reverie can I compensate by sharing my tea with you?'

She signed the chit and asked the waiter to bring another cup and more tea. Then she sat beside Nick and gave him an optical once over, eyes gleaming appreciatively. 'Just arrived today?'

'That's right.' Nick knew he was being picked up, but she was exciting to look at and his libido needed perking up.

'Thought I hadn't seen you around,' she continued. 'What business are you in?'

'Aviation.'

'Aircrew?'

'You've got it.' He guessed she was thinking of 747s.

The waiter returned and arranged the extra china and teapot on the tray between them. Nick steered the conversation away from himself as she filled two cups and pushed one towards him.

'You here on business or pleasure?'

'Oh, *pure* pleasure,' she drawled sexily. 'Just been through an acrimonious divorce, but the alimony I'll get makes it worth the hassle. Daddy had a business trip planned, so I came along to celebrate my new freedom.' Another appreciative

173

glance at his body. 'What did you do to your thigh?'

'Slipped on a patch of oil. Gashed it. Damn nuisance. That pool is calling, and I love to swim.'

'That's tough.'

'You haven't ventured in yet?'

'I don't.' She lay back revealing a pulse-raising outline hugged by the expensive swimsuit. 'I tumbled in a pool as a kid. My analyst says my fear of water stems from that.'

More likely a reluctance to mess up the immaculate make-up and spoil the elaborate bouncy hair-do, Nick thought. He had a flash vision of Lara emerging from the depths, her hair a fiery tangle, eyelashes sparkling with crystal drops, face glowing with pleasure, water runnels glossing her gorgeous brown limbs.

'How long do you have?'

He thrust Lara away. 'Sorry?'

'Your turn-around time in Singapore.'

He fell into the trap. 'Oh, this injury will keep me grounded for some while.'

'Just dandy,' she murmured. 'Maybe we'll share more than tea.' She offered her hand. 'Louise Sheridan.'

'Nick Hawkwood. Where in the States do you live, Louise?'

'Detroit and Palm Beach.' He should have guessed there would be more than one address. 'You must come visit when you make the transatlantic route.'

'So what business is your father in?'

'Military hardware. He's here to demonstrate our updated weaponry to this little nation's army. Just a formality, really. Their defence funds don't cover the purchase of even one of our new rocket launchers, Daddy says.'

Interest stirred. 'So why does he bother?'

'Business happens all the time. You go after something small and sometimes hit the jackpot along the way. The Far East is important. Leave a gap in the market and your competitor steps in, Daddy says.'

'Does that apply all over the world?'

'I guess.'

'But there are sanctions, embargoes on dealing with some nations.'

She shrugged. 'You don't go in, someone else will.'

'Daddy says?'

Her smile was lazily seductive. 'You airline guys are too cute for your own good. Are you married, Nick?'

'Not at the moment.'

'So how about you and me going on the town tonight?'

'Sorry. Important meeting. Could go on late.'

'Rain check?'

'Why not?' he said, thinking that 'Daddy' might be worth knowing.

Nick took a taxi to the Golden Orchid. He was confident Vinnikov would not try anything on the club's premises. In any case, the outcome of last night's attack would tell him he was dealing with someone who knew all the tricks. He left the taxi further up the street, telling the driver to wait. His business with Muna would not take long.

Approaching the club, Nick noticed the blank space. The poster advertising Lapis Lazuli's performances had gone from the wall. Faint apprehension sharpened his manner with the girl in the booth who demanded temporary membership fees. A different girl today.

'Is Lapis Lazuli dancing tonight?'

'You go in. Plenty girl to see.'

'I came specifically to see Lapis Lazuli,' he insisted, keeping his wallet in his pocket.

'She not here.'

Damn! 'How about tomorrow?'

'You go in. Plenty girl to see. Whatever you like you find in Golden Orchid.'

'It's *her* I want. Will she be here tomorrow?'

Buttoned mouth.

'Why has her poster been taken down?'

The mouth remained tightly buttoned.

Nick tried another tack. 'I have a date with her. I've

175

already paid the old Malay woman in the back room. If something funny's going on I'll report Vinnikov to the authorities.'

Alarm lit her dark eyes. Her slim brown hand moved towards a button on the counter. 'Leave that alone,' he commanded, 'or I'll report the whole damn lot of you.'

'I only take money at door,' she wailed.

'OK, just tell me where Muna is.'

Reassured by his quieter tone, her gaze rested on his shirt pocket. 'Koz chew.'

'No, it bloody won't! I can have police here so fast you won't hear them coming,' he threatened.

'She go away. Not dance here no more. You go Sembawang.'

Nick hesitated, still apprehensive. Should he confront Vinnikov? No, only Muna could give him the information he sought, and he knew where to find her. He walked slowly back to his taxi weighing his options. Although Vinnikov was unlikely to send two more heavies after him it was too soon to wander through that estate. Someone was sure to recognize him. Blond hair, pale skin, built to last, carries a knife! Safer to telephone.

Back in his room Nick poured a whisky from the mini bar and flicked through the pages of the directory for the Sembawang area. He was still vaguely apprehensive about Muna. Surely that pair in her act had not blamed the girl for their thrashing last night. Had Vinnikov sacked his star performer who had contracted to pay him two thousand dollars before leaving? It seemed very unlikely.

There were hundreds of Chengs. Nick could not recall the exact address, and that piece of blue card had been in the pocket of the blood-stained, ripped trousers he had thrown out this morning. It had been soaked in salt water. Illegible now, anyway. After ten minutes of searching he was successful. He hoped. Ten or more Chengs were tailors, but the address beside one was familiar. He dialled. A voice shouted in Chinese.

'Is that Cheng Li, Charles, the tailor?'

A short pause for switch of languages. Cheng Li, yes. You want suit, best come to my shop. I measure you exact.'

'I want to speak to Muna. Lapis Lazuli. It's very important.'

'Who is that?'

'I came to see her last night. In the rooms above your shop.'

Cheng Li disconnected.

Nick slammed down the receiver in frustration. Useless to redial. He would have to go out there. In the morning, wearing a baseball cap, jeans; the whole tourist get-up.

How are you going to find out? Leave that to me. You out-macho even Phil Dunne. And Dunne was dead!

He gazed out at the illuminated ships lying at anchor, whisky in his hand, telling himself he was a fool. Better to take James's advice and fly home. To what? A basic, charmless flat, long days somehow to fill, sleep disturbed by nightmares, Pete Higham demanding to learn about the ultimate horror. Knowing he had chickened out when the going got hard!

He tossed back the rest of his drink, eyes narrowing. Way out there was Pulau Pelingi and a girl with red hair. If he had not gone to Andy's sister's engagement party they would not have met. No aborted wedding. He would have finished his tour with James's squadron and never have served with the SF Flight. Some other poor bugger would have crossed into Iraq that night. Some other poor bugger would have been introduced to Attard and his fiancée. *He* would have felt nothing when she turned to greet him. *He* would not now be plagued by a letter he had shredded without reading it.

An insistent tapping brought him from his thoughts. He walked to the door, thinking it was the girl wanting to turn down his bed. Louise Sheridan stood there dressed in a pale silk tunic and trousers. Hair bouncy as ever, lips highly glossed, eyes full of invitation.

'Hi, thought I'd check if you'd already left for your meeting. That rain check we talked about; care to take me to a party tomorrow night? Home of one of Daddy's important business contacts. Name of Vydecker. *She* is a De Witt.'

Nine

The phone was ringing. It kept ringing. Nick came from heavy sleep and groped with his right hand. It knocked over a glass of water. Not water. He could smell whisky. The damned phone was still ringing. He opened one eye. Recognized nothing. He was not in his Hereford flat. The cream-coloured instrument was on a small shelf across half a mile of bed. Only because it was getting on his nerves did he squirm free of a mangled sheet to roll across and silence it.

'Can't you read? I have *do not disturb* on my door,' he grunted.

'Have you seen the *Straits Times* yet?' asked James.

'I haven't seen anything and I have no wish to.' He squinted one-eyed at the clock. 'Cracker, it's barely six!'

'You're a soldier. Six is reveille.' A pause. 'You been on the piss again?'

Nick dragged himself to a sitting/sagging position. 'From the thudding in my skull I'd say it's quite probable.'

'An exotic nightclub dancer known as Lapis Lazuli has been murdered.'

James's words slowly registered. '*What?*'

'Her body was discovered beside the MRT track near Sembawang. A passenger spotted it just before dusk yesterday. She'd been strangled with a blue chiffon scarf.'

'Oh God!'

'Come to my office. Make it latest by nine. I've an Air Marshal and assorted hangers-on arriving an hour later for an escorted tour of Kranji war graves. And sober up!'

179

Nick replaced the receiver. That was James in squadron commander mode. Brooking no argument. He stared at the overturned glass, at the whisky dripping to the carpet. He had ordered a half bottle with a meal from room service last night. One thing had led to another. So what? He was no longer the Wellnuts' guest. He could do as he liked in a hotel room. Muna's murder was sobering news, however. As he read the report in the newspaper hanging on his doorknob he wondered if he was indirectly to blame for her death.

James was dressed in immaculate starched uniform, ready for his VIP guest. Euan Goss was with him. They both wore grim expressions.

'This is bloody serious,' said James without preamble. 'I want you to go through in greater detail what you told us two nights ago, so we can pick up on anything that might incriminate you.'

Nick resented his tone. Told him so as he sat in a visitor's chair. 'There's nothing to *pick up on*. As for yesterday, Joyce waved me off from your place at around ten thirty. I checked in at the Oriental just before eleven. Had to wait until midday for someone to vacate a harbour view room. I sat in the coffee bar reading the papers. They came there for me when the room was ready. The waiter and a receptionist can vouch for my presence during that period. I unpacked, bought a paperback, ate lunch beside the pool, then sat in full view of umpteen people while reading.' He turned to Euan. 'You phoned me at around fifteen hundred. I was there then.'

James took that up. 'What did you call Nick about?'

'That's irrelevant,' Nick said brusquely. 'I dropped off for a while and woke to find an American divorcée propositioning me. Her daddy deals in military hardware. Yes, I thought that would raise your eyebrows, and no, it wasn't a fiendish plot to pump me full of drugs to warn me off further probing. She's after some sex to celebrate her freedom from the poor bastard she's taken to the cleaners. She thinks I'm a BA pilot on a few days' stopover. I vaguely recall her leaving my room last night. Then zilch!'

'Since yesterday afternoon?' asked Euan incredulously.

Nick was greatly tempted to lie. 'There was a break of several hours early evening when I took a taxi to the Golden Orchid.'

'Oh, jeez!' exclaimed James.

'Muna's body had been found by then,' Nick pointed out. 'The newspaper report mentioned that she'd been dead for some hours. I have watertight alibis for the whole of yesterday.'

'What did you do at the Golden Orchid?' demanded Euan.

Nick bridled. 'Asked a few questions, turned round and went back to the Oriental. I'd told the taxi driver to wait for me.'

'So he knows where you're staying?'

'Euan, she was dead before I got in his bloody cab,' he said explosively. 'What is this? The third degree?'

'You don't know this country, how things work,' said James.

'You've only been here a few weeks. Does that make you an expert?' he fired back.

'If the police get one sniff of your involvement with that girl they'll worry away at your story until they get what they want,' warned Euan, who had been much longer in his post.

'You're concerned about my involvement with *you*, that's all,' Nick countered. 'The police can worry away to their hearts' content and they *won't* get what they want. I went nowhere near Muna or Sembawang yesterday. I've just given you proof of that.'

'You had a long session with her at Sembawang the night before.'

'So I did, James, but the *Straits Times* gave time of death six or eight hours before she was found. I was esconced at the Oriental then. Nothing to do with what happened the previous night.'

There was an impasse. Into the silence Nick asked if they

were registering a vote of no confidence. Both men treated the question with the contempt they felt it deserved, judging by their expressions. Then James leaned back with a sigh.

'You've been twice to the Golden Orchid.' He didn't know about the first time and the episode with Dr Rahman. 'You've had a face-to-face with a dodgy Russian who, for some unclear reason, decided you had to be bought off. You went to Sembawang asking damn dangerous questions of a prostitute. Shortly after leaving her you were chased by two thugs. You put them out of action, but not before one had managed to stab you. You were chased by a crowd of local residents who saw you with a knife in your hand. You swam, Christ knows how, to the terminal where Euan fortunately encountered you and got you to a doctor before you needed a blood transfusion. Then you returned to the Golden Orchid asking to see Lapis Lazuli around the time her body was discovered. Would you say all that was the behaviour of an innocent man?' James leaned forward to emphasize his point. 'Because no policeman anywhere in the bloody world would.'

'But no policeman anywhere in the bloody world could prove I was involved in the murder of that girl.' Anger drove Nick to his feet. Resting his hands on James's desk, he established sizzling eye contact. 'You showed me Dunne's file and suggested I ask questions at social functions that you would find difficult. Because of that I have been drugged and humiliated by an up-market Chinese bitch, bribed by an oily Russian, attacked by two bruisers who would have killed me if I hadn't known how to look after myself, and stabbed in the leg by one of them. Now I'm being interrogated by you two. Well, sorry old mate, I have nothing more to say to either of you. I'm no longer a guest of the Defence Adviser, so what an Army officer does during his long leave is entirely his own affair.'

'If he runs into trouble with the local authorities it will become ours,' James returned with matching heat. 'British service personnel taken into custody here come under our sphere of responsibility. We're expected to investigate and liaise on their behalf.'

Nick straightened with an impatient outflung hand. 'For Christ's sake! *I've done nothing to warrant arrest.*'

'GBH on two nationals. In possession of a knife in a local housing estate. Running away when challenged. Known to have been intimate with a murdered prostitute. What more do you want?'

'A name; an identity, for a start. Who is this guy? Where can he be found? At Sembawang I was no more than an anonymous shadowy Caucasian. To Vinnikov I gave the name John Smith. Every Brit who goes there doubtless uses the same alias. No big deal!'

'You took a taxi from my house to Sembawang. That driver could identify you. The tailor Cheng Li, and his customers, would recognize you. You asked a family for directions to the MRT. They saw you clearly; heard you speak. You took another taxi from my house to the Oriental. The doorman called one up for you yesterday; could have overheard you direct the driver to the Golden Orchid—'

Nick interrupted grittily. 'I've been working with SAS guys for a year and a half. I'm not an ingénue!'

'Neither are cab drivers,' snapped James. 'They notice things.'

'OK, let's put cards on the table. What are you really afraid of?'

James got to his feet. 'Want it on the chin? You've been through a tough time. The general public has no idea of the full demands service life can make on us. Those weeks of incarceration will have scarred you permanently. You emerged reasonably whole. And *sane*,' he added with emphasis. 'But you're impatient. Always have been. You're out to prove nothing has changed; that Nick Hawkwood can still conquer all things. You're getting dangerously involved in issues outside our justifiable concern.'

'Who started the whole thing off?'

'The same patsy who soon told you to leave well alone,'

James admitted quietly. 'I apologize again for insulting your intelligence and setting you up. As a former squadron colleague and friend I should have known better. I'm speaking as both now. Fly home, Hawk.'

Nick's mouth twisted. 'You sure it's not the Defence Adviser speaking?'

'Him, as well.'

It seemed the right moment to leave. He came up with a suitable exit line which he directed at Euan Goss. 'Better warn your Australian counterpart that the world's leading marine scientist also frequents the Golden Orchid. If the police discover that they could regard *him* as a murder suspect, even though he's been out on an offshore island. Maybe Alex Foyle should pack him off back to Wagga Wagga, just to be on the safe side.'

At the Oriental Nick found girls cleaning his room. He took up the paperback and descended to the poolside restaurant for coffee. The book lay unopened as he watched a young Chinese lapping the pool with expertise. Nick envied him his swim. If he, himself, could work off some of his aggression with hectic action he would not feel so depressed.

Had he set in motion the need to kill a lovely young girl? He could shift the onus to Philip Dunne and that damn file, of course. How close had the man got to Muna? What was the truth behind the vessels he had starred in red and blue on his list? There was now no hope of help from Euan. Dead end there. Dead end in every direction. Poor choice of phrase. Two bodies for sure. Maybe others he knew nothing about.

He was suddenly certain Dunne had not tracked Muna down. Too many repeats of *check on lapis lazuli*. He had used lower case letters, which surely indicated he had not known it was a name rather than a semi-precious stone. Yet he had somehow discovered its connection with shipping movements. What had set him off in that direction? Euan apparently jealously guarded his status as handler of all things nautical, so, although Dunne had clearly availed himself of Euan's meticulous records, something or someone must initially have driven him to investigate.

Yes, Dunne had surely gone deeper into the activities of Muna's cousin rather than those of the girl herself. Not surprising. Only by following Attard had Nick stumbled on the truth about Lapis Lazuli. Dunne had reputedly been uninterested in extramarital sex. Unlike his wife, who was having it away with a fellow officer. Not for the first time Nick felt sympathy for Philip Dunne who was 'great fun, especially when he'd had a few'. As Vicky had also said, it was a rotten way for a hero to end: eaten by fishes.

All at once, Nick knew how to combat his depression. Returning to his room, now spotless, he thumbed through the phone book and put in a call to Collins Air Charters. Fifteen minutes later he walked to the MRT station, introspection behind him. His air ticket had a return date on it. That was when he would use it. By then he would have put in enough independent flying hours to impress a military medical board.

Ferdy greeted Nick warmly; gave him a cup of tea and asked where he planned to go. 'I'd stay in Singapore air space. Fly up-country and restrictions start.'

'Oh boy, I've had a gutful of that! Just felt like getting up there away from it all. You know how it is.'

'Do I, and how!'

'Thought I might chase the coast. Take in the lie of this island. Maybe renew my acquaintance with that twenty-foot high merlion.'

'So long as you don't ditch in the hope of meeting a real one.'

'I'm leaving that for Attard to discover for the world.'

Ferdy laughed. 'Wouldn't he just love it!' His brow creased. 'But you've just given me an idea. Take a big swag off your hire charge if you'd run an errand for me.'

Nick put down his empty mug. 'Depends where and what it is. It also depends on how many dollars you deduct.'

'Make it worth your while.'

185

'Brief me.'

Ferdy absently scratched his hair-sprinkled chest where his shirt lay open, dropped another tea bag in each mug with the other hand and poured on to them water that had gone off the boil. 'Got a call day before yesterday to go out pick up Gray at first light. Seems some equipment had gone phut and needed coupla new components. He had to come over for them.'

'Don't they carry spares?' Nick asked, tingling with sudden awareness. Attard was on Singapore Island yesterday?

Ferdy nodded. 'Usual practice. Guy responsible slipped up. Bloody unfortunate for him; their stuff is checked at the start and normally runs without a hitch. Gray let off like a transvestite galah. Don't ever cross that guy, Nick. Take your life in your hands.'

'He was less than delighted with my aerobatics.'

'Never likes being upstaged. Thing is this. They couldn't let him have the parts; said it'd be a week. I flew Gray back late afternoon in a rare state. First Senoko gave the thumbs down, then the doc he saw told him to take it easy for the next coupla weeks. He ranted all the way back about having to deal with shonky professionals. I kept the rotor going and shoved him out the door. Prima bloody donna! Guess his team got it full blast. As for poor Lara—'

'It's her choice,' Nick interrupted curtly, his mind chasing the facts that Attard dealt with Senoko and had been advised to rest. A dose of clap? Hardly. Was it too much to hope he had a dicky heart? Senoko made components of all types. Perfectly natural to buy from them, but funny how that company kept cropping up. Attard had been in Singapore since early yesterday morning! That parting shot at Euan had been intended as no more than that. Could he have unwittingly hit on something?

Ferdy continued. 'Had a call from Senoko two hours ago. They had the parts. Must've worked through the night. Out here cut-throat business means what it says. Add to that the Chinese reluctance to lose face by admitting failure, even temporary, and a week becomes next day before you know it. I called Gray, agreed to do my best to get the stuff out there, but after your call had three more straight off. I'm weighed under today and tomorrow. Wouldn't care to jaunt out to Pelingi, would you?'

A long moment of hesitation. Nick berated himself. Until he was back to making snap decisions it was pointless to face a medical board. 'How big are the components?'

Ferdy pointed to two small boxes on a shelf. 'There's also some mail arrived today. Dozen or so letters.'

'OK, you're on.'

'Good on yer. Eases the pressure. Downside is I don't get to see the luscious Lara.' He pulled the appropriate chart from a drawer and spread it on the sloping table top. 'Gather you two met at a party in London a few years ago.'

'That's right.'

'You married, Nick?'

'No.'

Ferdy glanced keenly at him. 'Missed your chance there, mate. Good-looking guy like you and a stunner like her. Think what gorgeous kids you'd have had.'

Nick rested on his elbows, studying the chart closely. 'I'd like to get underway ... and you're under pressure, remember.'

A moment's pause before Ferdy said speculatively, 'Shall I tell you what I think?'

'No, just log my flight plan.'

Once airborne, Nick conceded that today he *was* seeking freedom from something. In that bubble cockpit he could pretend to be the man he was before walking into a room and setting eyes on a tanned redhead with a name from a classic Russian novel.

As he headed out to sea over the giant merlion, the sense of unity with blue infinity was overwhelming. He was ruler of his tiny kingdom until it was time to return to earth. As the coast gave way to endless sea below his feet, Nick thought of his conversation with Kim Collins. If the Chinese belief in affinity with the elements was right, Ferdy was wrong. A man whose affinity was with the air and a woman who communed with water would be incompatible partners. Lara had the right man now.

There was a mass of shipping plying to and fro this important harbour. As Nick overflew them his short sense of freedom fled. Was Muna's cousin aboard one of the vessels that looked like bathtime toys way below? Were that sailor's activities serious enough to prompt the murder of a simple young girl . . . and the attempted murder of an Englishman who paid for sex, then asked probing questions about her moonlighting activities?

His mind again worried at all the confusing information stored in it, adding the fact that Attard could be involved in more than sex sessions to boost his ego. Approaching Pelingi, Nick reflected that Chris Franklin's ploy had worked. There was more than enough to keep his brain occupied during this leave.

The north side of the island had undergone an amazing transformation. Beyond the clearing where they had landed before, tents had sprung up as if a mushroom had scattered spores overnight. The size of the camp surprised Nick. His knowledge of scientific investigations was, admittedly, close to nil. Attard's set-up was not much smaller than a military field headquarters. He was impressed. All this because of rogue seaweed of which most of the world's inhabitants were unaware!

Switching off all systems, Nick climbed out to the now familiar humidity that made a man breathe faster to fill his lungs sufficiently. Reaching into the cockpit for the boxes and letters, he noticed the top envelope was addressed to Lara from Renée and Maurice Scott. Letter from home! He immediately saw the couple's faces, smiling with warm approval as Lara introduced him.

A well-trodden path from the clearing led to the camp. Nick followed it with the boxes under his arm. Through open tent flaps he saw banks of equipment, water tanks and computers. A well-financed, highly professional operation, as far as he could see.

Twenty-five yards from the beach Nick was accosted by a young, bronzed, blond-bearded man who appeared to be expecting him.

'Oh, heard the chopper come in. Thought it would be Ferdy.'

'I'm the sub. Ferdy's up to his eyes.'

'As long as those are my spares under your arm you're welcome, whoever you are.'

'Name's Nick Hawkwood.'

'Craig Bentley. I'm the poor sod who's been ostracized for not checking the spares list.'

'You have my sympathy.' He handed over the two boxes. 'Emerge from Coventry.'

'Great! How about a beer?'

He declined with regret. 'Have to be orange juice or mineral water, I'm afraid.'

'The canteen's over here. We've a selection of soft drinks.'

Nick went with him to another long tent containing a cooker, two microwave ovens, a fridge-freezer, sink and several trestle tables with folding chairs. It reminded him of his stint in Bosnia.

'How's progress?' he asked the man bringing cans from the fridge.

'Too early to say. We're still gathering the stuff. Once we have enough we can bombard it with all types of potential killers.' He handed Nick a can. 'You're aware of what we're about?'

'I've met Attard. He left me in no doubt.'

Craig grinned. 'Brilliant marine scientist, but a terrible pain in the arse humanwise.'

'But he allows beer drinking during working hours?'

The grin broadened. 'He's presently forty fathoms deep.'

'Ah,' he said with understanding. 'You're not from Down Under, from the sound of that accent.'

'Cornwall. Played around with crabs and kelp from the

time I could walk. Studied in Edinburgh, Cape Town and Perth. Sat on Attard's doorstep until I was a mere wraith to secure a place in his team.'

Studying Craig's sturdy physique, Nick said, 'I suspect credentials from Edinburgh, Cape Town and Perth did the trick well before wraith stage.'

'Plus persuasion from a girl I'd met in Perth, who was a member of his permanent team. I thought I'd scored there, but my boss cut me out. Proposed to her on the flight from Oz.' He grimaced. 'A winter and spring alliance, but some women go for power rather than brawn and virility. She's forty fathoms deep with him.'

Nick heard that with relief.

'Our divers normally work in pairs. We've three, but Dennis has a bad attack of the squits. Gray went down with Lara instead. She tried to dissuade him, but he overruled her, of course. God spake from the high mountain.'

'Why didn't she want him with her?'

Craig crushed his empty can with his heel and tossed it in a large plastic bin. 'Gray had a check-up when he went across for the spares. Doc told him to rest.'

'What's wrong with him?' Nick asked as he disposed of his own can.

'Dunno. Been feeling off-colour for several days. It must be worrying him enough to see a medic.'

'Don't you have one on your team?'

'This isn't a polar expedition. We're only a short flight from medical help. A couple of our guys are trained in emergency first-aid. Guess they suggested he seek professional advice.'

'Not much point if he ignores it.'

The bearded head wagged. 'No one gives Gray *advice*. They offer facts: he decides how to treat them.'

'He's a fool.'

'He's too brainy to be a fool. He's what my granny used to call "a little Hitler". I should get to work with those parts you brought,' he added, moving to the entrance. 'He'll expect the coolers to be up and running when he surfaces. Senoko told him a week. Next thing, they're ready. I should make sure we've not been palmed off with duff components. Are you able to wait while I check them out?'

Indecision again. For God's sake sharpen up, Hawkwood! He was keen to get away before Lara could appear looking wet and wonderful, but there was no chance to ask Craig how long he might be. There she was, running across the beach towards them. She looked wet and frightened.

Craig started forward. 'What's wrong?'

'Gray's trapped. I can't bring him up.'

'How d'you mean, trapped?'

'No time to explain. I need Den down there right away.' She appeared not to notice Nick in her urgency.

'Den can't even stand. He can't go down.'

'He'll have to,' she cried. '*Come on*, I need help.'

Nick pulled off his shirt, saying to Craig, 'Get the sick guy's gear. I'm fully trained. *Move*,' he instructed, as Craig hesitated. Then he turned to Lara. 'Fill me in.'

She was completely professional. Nick was simply another diver to be briefed in an emergency. 'He's not been a hundred percent for the last two days. Shouldn't have gone down. His reactions were sluggish. Didn't seem fully aware of what he was doing. I signalled that we should go up. He ignored me and penetrated further than before to cut samples.'

She was growing calmer as she put the facts to someone she knew and trusted. But he was still only another diver. 'We've been working around the edge of a huge mass so close to the shore we don't need a back-up boat. For some insane reason he suddenly headed right into it, slashing wildly with his knife. It was obvious what would happen. It closed around him faster than he could cut it away. I can't free him; it needs two. He's caught in the vile stuff, hanging there like a fly in a spider's web.' Fear returned as she gazed at Nick. 'If we don't get him out soon, it'll be too late.'

Still undressing, Nick asked, 'Is this stuff poisonous?'

'Not to humans.'

'Maybe you got that wrong.'

'No.' It brooked no argument,

'OK, we'll get him,' he said reassuringly as Craig arrived with wetsuit, air cylinder, fins, mask and stab. jacket. Stripped to his underpants, Nick donned the familiar gear. Indecision had fled. He could deal unhesitatingly with another person's crisis!

The silent green world they entered soon darkened as they neared the fringe of rogue vegetation. It was then Nick's blood ran cold. Several yards within the floating mass a rubber-suited figure was held fast by thick strands that resembled the ropes of bondage. It could not struggle; just hung helplessly. Air bubbles rising from the mask proved Attard was alive. The familiar hovering terror lambasted Nick in an immobilizing rush. He fought to breathe. He was being crushed to death and unable to move. The ultimate horror!

A bizarre face appeared before his. It had enormous eyes. Hands waved at him, then pointed. They were not the hands of Death squeezing the life from him. And he could *see*! Lara drew him back from the edge of the abyss that was always waiting for him, and urged him forward.

Nick touched her arm, pointed at the gauge on her air cylinder then at Attard's. Did the fly in the web have the same amount of air left? She nodded. Just enough. If there was no hitch! But the hitch was the way the cut ends of the growth reached out for fresh anchorage. Them! Take too long over this rescue and there would be three flies in the web!

Also trapped in the hostile mass were fish and all manner of flotsam. It seized on anything within its reach: all embracing. It grew darker and colder as they penetrated the octopus weed. Time merged with the infinite ocean to deaden perception of its passing. There were only the sounds of his rhythmic intake of air and the bubbling exhalation. The thudding of his heart.

After an age of arduous hacking and tugging they reached the trapped man. Nick glanced swiftly at the gauge on Attard's cylinder. Approaching the red line! Leaving Lara to deal with the last few strands, Nick upended and began attacking the growth beneath them. Impossible to retrace their route. The severed ends had already re-embraced themselves. The only exit was underneath the evil stuff. There, where less light penetrated, the tentacles were frailer. Easier to cut, less inclined to cling, but greater depth used more oxygen and two cylinders were almost empty.

He rose again to meet Lara and take Attard's other arm. Together, they pushed back through a fast-closing exit route, seeking the line from the marker buoy. The dark blob now at the top of it was an inflated dinghy containing two men. They hauled Attard aboard and removed his mask and breathing tube. Lara scrambled in to bend over her man in concern as they took the boat shoreward, where a small group waited to take their boss to his tent.

Left alone, Nick swam the short stretch of deep water, then removed his fins and walked across the beach to the abandoned dinghy. He dropped them and his mask in it; added the air cylinder. His life jacket followed. In the act of lowering the heavy-duty zip of his wetsuit he began violently to convulse. Stumbling away from the boat, he vomited copiously.

His ears were ringing with their harsh voices as they came for him again: his eyes were covered. They knew he understood their language. It was part of their torment; speaking about him as if he were an animal.

They laid hands on him and he spun round with a cry to fling them off. He saw a girl; stared at her with terror still riding him. She was part of it; she had made him suffer. He saw his father standing behind her: heard his voice. *Now, now, Nicky, little men never cry. They have to be brave whatever happens.* He had had no notion of what awaited his son as punishment by proxy. He was too drunk to care!

When he grew aware of water lapping his feet, and Lara standing beside him, Nick had little idea how long she had been there. He felt exhausted, utterly drained.

193

'Is it over now?' she asked softly. 'Would you like to talk about it?'

He shook his head. No, it had not happened! He desperately needed a double whisky. Several. But he was flying. No, must not fly: risk of the bends. Not if he stayed low all the way. He felt too tired to attempt a return yet, but it would be dark if he waited. Would Ferdy prefer to be minus an aircraft overnight rather than have it reduced to scrap metal at the foot of a giant merlion? No contest!

'Nick, you look terrible. Come over to the first-aid tent and let Bingo check you over.'

'I need a stiff drink, that's all.' He forced himself to walk to where he had left his clothes. 'Do you run to hot showers here?'

'And a lot more besides. Are you staying for the night?'

'Have to.'

She picked up his shirt and trousers; held them out. 'Thanks for your help. We always made a good team, didn't we?'

He took his clothes and walked away to contact Ferdy, who took the news on the chin.

The team decided to finish early after the drama. Used to life under canvas, Nick felt at ease with the seven men and three women who gathered for a curious fry-up eaten at the trestle tables. The casual camaraderie, the sly baiting, the easy laughter, the professional back-chat reminded Nick so forcibly of similar times in his own world, restlessness drove him from the communal tent. The moon was huge; the sky a luminous silver canopy. Warm seductive breeze, shimmering argent sea. God, how bloody romantic!

He walked down the beach swamped with longing. Back there just now it came home to him how easily he might lose what he most valued. Unless he could banish his demons for good he had no hope in hell of being reinstated. An erotic bondage dance, a human fly caught and held immobile in a living mass – those were all it took to send him teetering on the edge of a black hole.

He had performed normally until left alone on the beach.

He remembered taking off the diving gear; remembered throwing up. Then nothing, until he found he was standing ankle deep in water and Lara was there asking if it was over. He swallowed painfully. Dear God, what if it was never over?

'Had enough of scientific mumbo-jumbo?' Lara was beside him again. 'Sea looks beautiful, doesn't it? You'd never guess that vile stuff was multiplying like crazy beneath that shimmering surface. People are too complacent. They have no idea how serious a threat it poses. The world will wake up when it's too late.' She registered his silence and sighed. 'Sorry. More scientific mumbo-jumbo.'

After more silent moments, she said, 'Walk?'

They moved off together. There was just the soft rush of waves breaking and the distant sound of the socializing they had left. Nick was glad of her company; anyone's company would be welcome so long as he stopped wondering how he would face being told his military career was over.

'That business this afternoon. It wasn't about us, was it.'

A statement rather than a question. 'A link with your other world?'

'Other world?'

'Bosnia, Oman, Northern Ireland. The stuff you'd never talk about. Why are you in Singapore, Nick?'

'Using up overdue leave.'

'When do you fly home?'

'The twenty-fourth.'

They walked on slowly. Too far from the camp to hear the others now. Just the soft rush of waves. Very seductive.

'Bring me up to date. You said you were posted from James's squadron. Still flying, though?'

Seduction over. 'How d'you think I got here today?'

She gave him a swift glance. 'Treading too near that other world?'

'Probably.'

'Sorry.' After a moment or two, she asked quietly, 'Have you found someone else?'

'Quite a few.'

'How are Jon and Lucy; your father?'

He stopped abruptly. 'You'll have read all that crap about the Hawkwoods they dragged out and printed recently. Doesn't that answer your bloody question?'

She looked shaken. 'I don't follow. Who printed crap about you?'

He had had enough and set off up the beach. 'It's been a heavy day and I'll be making an early start in the morning.'

'Nick,' she called after him. 'You're nowhere near to forgiving me, are you.'

'No,' he said under his breath. 'Nowhere near it.'

In the morning Gray Attard was the subject of concern for his team. Feverish and incoherent, with a mottled rash around his lower torso, there was no question of his shaking it off unaided. The two first aiders agreed he should be hospitalized.

Nick called Ferdy and asked his permission to fly the patient over right away. It was given. Nick then asked that an ambulance should be waiting at the airfield.

'No idea what's wrong, Ferdy, but he looks pretty sick. Needs attention asap.'

'No worries, he'll get it.'

Grabbing a bacon sandwich and a mug of tea from Craig, Nick walked to the helicopter and began his pre-flight checks. They brought Attard and settled him with a pillow and blanket on the narrow rear seat. Then Lara arrived with two overnight bags.

'He'll need some personal things,' she explained to an unsmiling pilot.

'You're one of them, are you?'

Her eyes flashed. 'He'll expect me to be there.'

'Same as he expected you to pull him out of that mess yesterday!'

Thirty minutes by the direct route. He would stay low. Visibility one hundred percent. Cloudless sky. Wind no more than a zephyr. Unlikely to be brought down in the sea to join Philip Dunne. Small wonder his body had never been found. The poor devil had probably been caught in that floating mass.

The great merlion, the Oriental Hotel, the tall business and housing blocks were all way over to his left when Nick approached Seletar low over the sea. He circled the airfield and came into the hover before gently setting the aircraft down. He had not said a word during the entire flight to the woman sitting beside him. She had made no attempt to speak to him. Two people who had once been set to spend the rest of their lives together!

An ambulance was parked beside Ferdy's office. Two white-clad attendants jumped from it, set up a collapsible stretcher and waited just clear of the downdraught from the rotor. Ferdy came over while Attard was being transferred. He spoke to Lara before she jumped in the ambulance with the two bags. Nick concentrated on winding down, and the ambulance had gone when he climbed from the cockpit.

'Gray looked pretty duff,' remarked the Australian as they walked to his office. 'Cold beer?'

'Spot on.' Nick put the flight chart and emergency pouch on the desk. 'Thanks for ordering the blood wagon. Sorry about the delayed return.'

Ferdy offered a chilled can. 'Lucky you were still there. He'd have had to wait for me to get over there for a pick-up.'

Nick then launched into a description of the tricky rescue, which widened Ferdy's eyes.

'Jeez, I wouldn't go within a hundred miles of that stuff! Sounds like something from a horror movie.'

'Better believe it!' Nick crushed the can with his heel and tossed it in the bin. 'What's the reckoning for the flight?'

'I'll work on it. Send a bill to the Wellnuts' place.'

'I've moved to the Oriental. Couldn't stay under their feet.'

'So come to dinner again. Kim enjoys your company.'

He turned in the doorway. 'My turn to play host. I'll be in touch, fix a date. Thanks for the flight.'

'Any time, sport.'

When Nick reached his room he saw the message light on his phone flashing. Louise Sheridan's voice came over loud, clear and bitchy.

'You missed a *great* party last night. I'll be having poolside tea today with a tycoon I met there. Don't bother to come over.'

Ten

Chapter two of the paperback made little sense. Nick had forgotten chapter one; if he had ever read it properly. He began again and found he vaguely remembered the gruesome murder on page three, and the sexy woman detective put in charge of a team of male chauvinist subordinates. She was in for a rough time, that was sure. He had had a large cooked breakfast and was now stretched out on a comfortable lounger beside the pool, but he was prevented from enjoying much of the sexist sniping by the jingle of his mobile beside him on his towel.

'Yeah, Hawkwood,' he murmured.

'Hallo, Nick. Vicky Goss here. You're due to see the doc today about your leg. Had you forgotten?'

He had. 'No. Just getting ready now.'

'I'll be along for you in twenty minutes.'

'No need to trouble you. Tell me where to find him. I'll take a taxi.'

'I want to talk to you. Twenty minutes!'

He swore under his breath. He was not favourite with Euan. Another meeting with the man's wife was the wrong move just now. Well, at any time, he supposed. With great reluctance he pulled on shorts and a shirt then went to his room. The gash in his thigh was bothering him somewhat. Yesterday's sub-aqua activities had not constituted the rest advocated by the doctor, but it could not be classed with Attard's pig-headedness. He had responded to an emergency; Attard had responded to vanity.

Nick was tying his tie when his doorbell chimed. Vicky

walked past him and crossed to the large window. 'What a super view!

'I was about to come down. Your twenty minutes are five short.'

She turned with a blithe smile. 'I've always wanted to see what these rooms are like. Are you going to offer me a drink from your mini-bar?

'No. Does Euan know about this?'

'I'll tell him tonight. Not even a teensy gin and tonic?' she persisted persuasively.

'If you're desperate for one I'll buy it downstairs in the bar.'

'I was told you're a man of great daring.'

'Not with other men's wives.' He scooped up his small change and pocketed it with his wallet.

They sat at a small black glass table. Nick ordered her drink and a small beer for himself. 'You said you want to talk to me.'

She leaned towards him, the fine blonde strands of her hair bright beneath the light from massive chandeliers. 'I'm furious. I think James and Euan are being quite unbelievable over this business.'

'What business is that?' he asked, signing the chit for the drinks.

'If I hadn't insisted that what looked like a paralytic seaman was a friend in dire straits, my stuffy husband would have left you on the docks. Joyce did her wifely duty by whipping me away from "boys' talk", but I think I deserved to know what had happened to you that night. I made Euan tell me everything.'

He drank lengthily. 'Really?'

'Oh, *yes*! James should be shot for giving you that file, then turning against you when you did as he asked.'

'Vicky, he asked me to talk to a few people at parties, that's all. I exceeded my brief. And he hasn't turned against me. I judged it politic to distance myself from him and his family. Not fair to risk exposing them to danger.'

'Fair enough, I understand that. But to refuse to help you find whoever tried to kill you is downright lily-livered.'

'You've been reading too many ripping yarns, Vicky. It's only in them that people are dubbed *lily-livered*. By buccaneers, usually.'

'Phil Dunne was after pirates.'

His hand stilled with the glass halfway to his mouth. 'Say again.'

'A couple of evenings after Alison flew home to her "dying" mother, I found Phil on the verandah during a drinks do for some Commonwealth VIPs. He'd had one or two too many and had sensibly removed himself from HOM's eagle eye. He and I always hit it off – he loosened up when Alison wasn't around – and he began bragging about how everyone would sit up when he had added two and two to make twenty bloody five. Those were his actual words. I asked him to explain, but he just tapped his nose and told me to wait and see. "I'm chasing pirates", he said. "And I've almost caught them."'

Nick leaned forward urgently. 'Did you tell Euan what Dunne said?'

She made a face. 'He got uptight if I talked about Phil, so I tended not to. Stupid, of course, because Phil was straight up. That's what made him good company. Never any fear of landing myself in a tricky situation. Bit like you – except you're far sexier than he was, poor dear.'

Nick hardly registered her last comment; his brain was racing. 'He actually said he was *chasing* pirates?'

'Yes, but he was slightly pissed, as I said.'

'That file of his; the ships he listed. We know two of them were boarded and robbed.' Nick spoke his thoughts eagerly. 'Euan was going to check out the others. But that's not on now.'

'Why?'

'High Commission staff can't get involved. I see their point.'

'Checking information in his office isn't *getting involved*,' she said in disgust. 'I'll go to work on him.'

201

'No point. I was supposed to get from Muna details of other vessels her cousin served on, but that's no longer possible.'

'Do you know the cousin's name?'

'Yes, why?'

'We're friendly with some of the local Navy guys.' She gave a cat-with-the-cream smile. 'One, in particular, is rather sweet on me. In a strictly honourable Singaporean way, you understand. If I ask him nicely I could get you any information you want. Will tomorrow be soon enough?'

The doctor was not happy with Nick's wound: feared it had become infected in spite of his prompt treatment. The surrounding area looked puffy and red. Nick admitted it was causing him some discomfort.

'Have you been resting it, as I advised?'

'Oh, yes.'

'Continue to do so. I'll give you a course of antibiotics. Come back when you've taken them all. I'd prefer not to give you strong painkillers right now, but if you find you really need them contact my receptionist. I'll send a prescription along to the High Comm.'

'I'm now staying at the Oriental.'

'There, then.'

Nick watched the man write a prescription for the antibiotics. 'I suppose you had to study tropical medicine for a practice out here. Different from what you'd encounter in Scotland.'

He glanced up. 'When I first qualified I dealt with female problems that are the same the world over. My male patients more often injured themselves in climbing accidents or on the oil rigs. We Scots are tough and healthy because the climate is so bracing, not because we eat haggis and porridge,' he added with a grin.

'So what prompted you to move to the tropics?'

'I married a Singaporean.' He handed Nick the prescription. 'Complete the course even if things improve in a couple

202

of days. And stay clear of brawls!' He waved his hand at Nick's leg. 'I know a knife wound when I see it. We Scots are not only healthy, we're proud and therefore rather quick-tempered in our cups. I've patched up many a Gordon Highlander on a Saturday night. But they were rank and file. Officers should rid themselves of aggression in more gentle-manly manner, on the squash courts. Goodbye, Captain Hawkwood.'

Vicky tried to persuade Nick to have lunch with herself and Euan. He declined. 'Not a good move under the circs. Euan's a fortunate man, Vicky. Make sure he stays that way. Thanks for getting me to Doc McIntosh, and for your help with the shipping list. Please don't do it if there's any chance of it coming between you two.'

'I can handle Euan. I'm not so sure about you. If I get this information you'll follow up on it, won't you?'

'Of course.'

She bit her lip. 'And it'll be dangerous.'

'I know how to deal with danger.' He kissed her cheek. 'You're getting as bad as your stuffy husband.'

'Don't end up like Phil,' she begged.

'I'm simply trying to find out why he did.'

At his request she dropped him at the top of Orchard Road. He was disinclined to return to poolside lazing, so he went for a drink and a sandwich in the Marriott. There, he pondered Dunne's tipsy statement about chasing pirates. A few veils were lifting from the enigma of that file. Nick was sure Vicky's call on the morrow would confirm that the vessels listed by Dunne had all been boarded at some time, and that Muna's cousin had served on each of them. The significance of the red and blue stars would then become clear.

The grid references probably indicated where the ships were boarded. The only aspect he had not yet deciphered was the meaning of the groups of initials, some of which James claimed matched with those of companies manufac-turing defence equipment not necessarily in line with inter-national rules.

Finishing his snack, Nick decided to pursue that line. An experienced private investigator would go better equipped, but he could lie his way through most situations, if pushed. So he took a taxi to the Senoko factory, which proved to be a white rectangle with large tinted windows built on ground level, apart from offices above the eastern end of the workshops. It had taken almost an hour to reach it, so Nick reasoned that the lunch break would be over, even if they had one. Attard's components had been produced ultra-swiftly. Maybe sweatshop conditions prevailed.

He mounted to office level unchallenged. There, he found a receptionist in a tailored dark-green suit. She was almost as stunning as Fleur Yang, but he was not taken in this time by the demure fragility of her appearance. She was certain to be a tough cookie beneath the outer submissiveness.

'Good afternoon. I'd like to meet Mr George Chow,' he said, recalling the name of one of the directors mentioned by James. 'I haven't an appointment, but I'm sure he'd be happy to see me. I'm the military consultant to Rees and Hardy. My great uncle, Sir Charles Fanshawe, is one of the directors. I've stopped off briefly in Singapore on my return flight to England and he asked me to make a courtesy call on Mr Chow, if I had the time.'

Her smile was pure Oriental charm. 'Mr Chow will certainly wish to see you, sir. If you give me your card I'll take it in to him.'

Nick pulled out his service identity and waved it in her direction. 'Major Hargreaves. I'm not a member of the company. I just advise them on military hardware.'

She looked impressed. 'One moment, sir.'

After the half minute it would take her to relay the information to her boss, she reappeared to invite him in. George Chow, thin, fortyish, smartly dressed in a dark suit, wore a broad smile as he offered his hand. 'Major Hargreaves, it is extremely good of you to spare the time to visit me.'

Nick gripped the hand very firmly. 'How do you do, Mr Chow. I'm afraid I can't arrange to entertain you to dinner, which is my normal practice – so many strategic defence meetings to fit in – but I have an hour or so free, and I promised Sir Charles I'd make contact with you, if possible.'

'Please sit down. Can I offer you tea?'

'Thank you, no. I'd prefer to use the short time at my disposal looking over your factory. I understand you've secured a contract with Rees and Hardy. I'd like to report back on the facilities you have here.'

Chow made no attempt to deny a contract had been secured. He was all too keen to give 'Major Hargreaves' every assistance, and led him down a rear stairway to the workshop floor, talking enthusiastically. Nick was impressed. No similarity to a sweatshop. The factory was cleverly designed, although somewhat cramped, and the equipment was well maintained. The workforce was young – quite a few were women – and Nick could not help comparing these neat, industrious people with the architypical British factory worker. He well understood how a week could become the next day overnight here.

While showing appropriate interest in Chow's commentary, Nick was searching for clues. To what he was unsure, but Vydecker had put money into Senoko, and Alison Dunne's grandfather had recently forged links with Rees and Hardy. There must be a clue to *something* here. When they had covered every aspect of the workshop and its output it seemed Nick was doomed to disappointment. Knowing he must maintain his cover story, he glanced at his watch.

'I really must push on now, Mr Chow. Another meeting. This has been most interesting. I'll be able to give Sir Charles and his fellow directors a clear assessment of your production capabilities.' He offered his hand. 'Thank you for your comprehensive tour.'

But George Chow was looking beyond him and smiling. 'How very fortunate you returned at this moment,' he said to someone who came alongside Nick. 'Major Hargreaves is the military adviser to Rees and Hardy. He has paid us a courtesy visit on his way back to London. Major, please let me introduce the other director of Senoko, Mr Jonah Lee.'

Nick shook hands with a younger, round-faced Chinese, dressed like Chow in dark grey. 'Glad of the opportunity to congratulate you, Mr Lee. Senoko may be small but your workforce is well trained and industrious. I foresee satisfactory growth.'

Saying goodbye, Nick walked out to high humidity and oppressive skies. A storm had blown up. Stair-rod rain would fall at any moment and there were no taxis in sight. He set off resignedly towards the main road on the far side of the factory complex. Then, as the first fat raindrops smacked on the tarmac, a cab swept up to a nearby building and disgorged three business-suited men. Nick broke into a fast sprint to secure it before it departed empty, and settled on the rear seat in double satisfaction. A dry return to his hotel, *and* the clue!

The last time he had seen Jonah Lee, co-director of Senoko, the Chinese had been dressed in a red dinner jacket at the Collinses' party, where he had interrupted Nick's initial meeting with Fleur to take her off for a business talk with Vydecker.

As Nick entered his room the phone rang. He took up the receiver. 'Hawkwood.'

'My God, never expected you to be in. Could you possibly be lying low and keeping out of trouble?'

'What do you want, Cracker?'

'Barbara Fielding contacted Joyce. We're invited to take you there to dinner tomorrow evening. Under the circs I think it would be politic to go.'

'Impossible! I've flown home, as per your instructions.'

A short silence. 'Do it for Joyce. Might melt the frost that settled after you left. She blames me.'

'She's so right.'

'Come for a sundowner. We'll go on to their place together.'

'To give the impression I'm still staying with you?'

'They'll take that for granted. There'll be other guests, so it shouldn't be too heavy going. Rendezvous eighteen hundred?'

'For Joyce.'

'Thanks.' A woman's voice spoke in the background, and James then said, 'Sorry, have to go. Air Marshal turned up unexpectedly. Attendance has to be danced. Tomorrow at sundown, right?'

After a shower Nick put on shorts and a loose shirt, intending to continue what Vicky had interrupted that morning. The storm had passed; the sun was blazing down again. A lounger, and tea with sandwiches were exactly what he needed. He left the paperback where it lay. Too much sleuth-thinking to do. The feisty woman detective could wait.

At the end of a drowsy hour in which he was able to link Fleur and Jimmy Yang to Vydecker, Vydecker to Senoko and Jonah Lee, Senoko to Sir Charles Fanshawe, Fanshawe to Philip Dunne, and Dunne to Jimmy Yang, Nick realized he had a circle that told him nothing. There was no missing link that gave him a lead to follow. He was just going round and round. As for Vinnikov, Muna, her matelot cousin, and possibly two heavies, they appeared to form a separate circle. All he had was a mysterious 'big boss' receiving letters from the sailor, and nameless wealthy men who gave stag parties. So far, no evidence that Vydecker was involved there.

Dunne had told Vicky he was chasing pirates. Another of his crazy stunts? What if that file of his had no real significance? The 'mystery' of Alison Dunne's sudden return to England had turned out to be no more than desperation to see her injured lover. Fanshawe's directorship of Rees and Hardy could be a normal transition from government office to semi-retirement perks. Happened all the time. Vydecker had shrewdly invested in an up and coming company producing popular merchandise. There were innocent explanations for it all.

That evening, he decided to dine in the hotel's elegant à la carte restaurant as if he really were a tourist on holiday. To

that end he dressed in a shirt starched as only Chinese laun-
derers can, dark trousers and his Army Air Corps tie – a
subconcious desire to be no more than a military pilot in
mufti enjoying his leave?

His doorbell rang as he was brushing his hair. He walked
over to admit the girl who changed towels and turned down
the bed. The girl was thirteen, English, dressed in a brief
cotton dress and flushed with nervous excitement.

'Emma! Whatever are you doing here?' he asked in
dismay.

'I *had* to speak to you,' she said in a breathy rush, walking
in before he could stop her.

He turned, leaving the door strategically open. 'Does your
mother know you're here?'

Her flush deepened. 'I don't have to inform her of everything I do. I'm not a child.'

No, by God, you're not, Nick thought, seeing her well-
formed breasts thrusting against a bodice that made little
allowance for them. He wanted her out of his room, and fast.

'I was on my way downstairs for a drink. I'll buy you a
Coke. We can talk then.'

She looked defiant, but scared as she stood her ground.
'What I want to say is *private.*'

'OK, we'll find a very quiet corner. Come on!' When
she refused to budge, he added, 'When you tire of being
alone here you'll find me in the cocktail bar.' She caught
up with him halfway along the corridor. 'Did you close the
door?'

'Naturally,' she said with offended dignity.

Nick groaned inwardly. Adolescent adoration was a new
one on him. He had little idea how to handle it short of
ringing James with a request to collect her. More immediate
in his mind was the way he could persuade a military medical
board to reinstate him as soon as possible.

Installing Emma on a semi-circular padded seat in a corner
well away from the bar, Nick ordered a small lager and a
Sprite. The girl had said *yuk* to Coke. She was still very pink

in the face, but her impetus of courage was seeping away in this rendezvous for smart, sophisticated adults.

'How are Gina and Robin?' he asked as they waited for their drinks.

'All right, I suppose, as children go,' she responded with a pitiful attempt at poise. 'Nick, I want you to come back to us. It's absolutely *deadly* without you. James is being as beastly as he can. I *hate* him when he's like that, and so does Mum. They're hardly speaking to each other and—'

'Hey, hey, calm down,' Nick urged as the waiter approached. He signed the chit and turned back to Emma, taking the line he thought would do the most good. 'Let's be grown up about this, shall we? James is not being beastly but lovingly protective of you all.'

Her round face registered immediate incredulity. 'Protecting us from *you*? That's ridiculous.'

'Not from me, from some undesirables I unwittingly upset. I made the decision to come here. James merely approved. And you know you don't hate him, Emma.'

'Was it the *undesirables* who stabbed you?' she asked, wide-eyed with hero worship.

Dear God, were James and Joyce still talking freely with window shutters open? He sidestepped the issue and told her he would be coming to the house for a drink tomorrow before going out to dinner with her parents.

'Come for the whole day. We're going to the swimming club. Teach me how to dive like you can.'

'Another time. I can't swim at the moment because of my leg,' he said without thinking, which brought them back to the subject he had tried to avoid. 'Drink up your Sprite.'

As an attempt to distract it was useless. The full glass was left where it stood. 'Is it absolute *agony*?' she asked in a near whisper.

'No! Emma, it's almost six thirty. Your mother'll be expecting you at the dinner table,' he said bracingly. 'I'm pretty sure no one at home knows where you are, so they'll worry. How did you come here?'

'James's official driver brought me. I told him I had to deliver something very important to you. He's waiting outside.'

He got to his feet. 'Then he can drive you back.'

She gripped the seat with each hand as if to prevent his physically plucking her from it. 'It's that damn list of Philip Dunne's that's causing all the trouble, isn't it? Nick, *please* don't go to Sembawang again. They might actually kill you next time.'

He took out his mobile. 'I'll tell Joyce you're on your way.' But the intention was foiled by sight of a redhead in a clinging black dress. She saw him, hesitated, then cautiously approached. Out of the frying pan!

'Nick, what are you doing here?'

'I could ask you the same,' he returned bluntly.

'I have to stay somewhere overnight.' Then she noticed Emma still gripping the seat firmly. Her eyes widened speculatively. 'Are you together?'

'This is Joyce Wellnut's daughter. She brought me a message and is just leaving,' Nick said, barely crediting the interpretation Lara seemed to be putting on the situation. Not *another* who thought he fancied schoolgirls!

'Won't you introduce me,' demanded Emma, rising and eyeing this rival from head to toe.

'Emma, meet Dr Lara Scott. She's a marine scientist working with a team trying to rid the sea around here of a particularly noxious growth.'

The girl's face flushed scarlet. Nick was shaken by the fury of her expression and was totally unprepared for what followed.

'You cold-hearted *bitch*! How *could* you leave him standing in the church in front of hundreds of people and all his squadron friends? Mum says it's too much to hope it was because you knew *he deserved someone better*.' She then rounded on Nick, tears sparkling her eyes. 'How can you bear to even *speak* to her after what she did? Hasn't she hurt you *enough*?'

210

As an exit line it was devastatingly effective. That corner of the cocktail lounge grew silent. Lara looked stunned. Nick wondered wildly how soon he could take a hatchet to James and Joyce as he watched Emma run down the broad staircase, past the ornamental fountains and out to the sweltering evening.

He turned back to a stony-faced Lara, put a hand under her elbow and led her away from curious eyes. He stopped at the head of the stairs. Constant human traffic flowing up and down made the spot suitable for private conversation. If only he had any idea what to say.

'Have you informed the whole of Singapore?' Lara demanded fiercely.

'I've told no one. Emma listens at keyholes.'

For several moments she struggled for control, gazing over his shoulder with unseeing eyes. Then she met his. 'I need a drink.'

'There's another, less public bar.' He made no attempt to touch her as they walked to the circular room overhanging the atrium's bubbling water features. His urge to lambast the Wellnuts remained as he ordered whisky, and vodka and lime. They watched the fountains in silence until their drinks arrived. Even then there was mutual wariness.

'So how's the patient?' Nick asked her, knowing the ice had to be broken.

'Not good. They're unsure what they're dealing with, which doesn't help.'

'A nuisance,' he agreed. 'Go to a doc with swollen cheeks and he gleefully says *mumps*. With spots, *measles*. Arm hanging loose, *dislocated shoulder*. Black eye, *drunken punch-up*. Mix symptoms and they're flummoxed.'

That appeared to conclude the subject, and silence returned. They finished their drinks. 'Would you like another?' he asked.

She shook her head. 'What are you doing here?'

'Not seducing schoolgirls.'

'Nick!'

211

'Like you, I need somewhere to sleep.'

'James and Joyce?'

'Are tied up with social commitments. They felt obliged to take me along; I felt I was cramping their style. I've never been overly keen on drinkies and chit-chat. Rather spend my time more actively, as you know.'

Awkwardness again. He had spoken without thinking. This intimacy was getting to him. He had ordered her usual vodka and lime without asking. The drink had relaxed her; put a sparkle in her eyes. The black dress had a deep vee that showed off her tanned cleavage. He tried to avoid looking at it, but it had a magnetic effect on his eyes. She was not wearing a bra; the dress fitted so closely it revealed no outline. Only her nipples were softly prominent. He remembered how they felt in his mouth, how—

'Have you had dinner?'

His gaze jerked up to meet hers. 'Uh . . . no.'

'You haven't arranged to meet anyone?'

'No.'

'So shall we find somewhere to eat?' Seeing his hesitation, she said, 'We can sit in opposite corners, if you'd rather.'

And deprive himself of her cleavage? He had been living dangerously for the past few days. Why stop now?

'The restaurants here are filled with business diners. Let's go somewhere quieter,' she suggested. 'Gray took me to an Indian place he knows well. It's—'

'I know a pseudo-Russian place,' he said swiftly. 'We'll go there.' No way would he eat with her in Attard's favourite curry restaurant and be told where they had sat, what they had ordered and how he had overawed her with his massive ego.

The Silver Troika was fairly crowded, but Mikhail found a table for two in a corner flanked by potted vegetation. He showed no sign of recognizing Nick; Nick adopted a similar act. He ordered wine, again without consulting Lara. It was what they always drank. She spent the first few minutes studying the 'Russian' murals and decorations. He spent them studying her. It could have been three years ago, except that so much had happened since then.

The waiter returned with the wine and poured. Nick nodded, still struggling with a time lapse. Their glasses were filled. Lara raised hers. 'Skol!'

'Skol!' Their usual toast almost defeated him. He studied the menu intently while a whirligig of memories frazzled his brain.

They ordered. What now? 'How hopeful are you of finding a solution to that weed?'

She seemed disconcerted by the deliberately neutral subject, but rose to it with only the barest hesitation. 'We refer to it as Medusa. It's difficult to predict a level of success until we've had a chance to study it in depth.'

'You're speaking figuratively?'

A faint smile. 'As you discovered, the least time spent with it in situ is advisable. We're learning as we go along. The first two batches we collected were useless. It doesn't survive in small clumps.'

'There's the solution. Break it into small clumps.'

'How?'

'Depth charges?'

She accepted his suggestion with another faint smile. 'Have you any idea of the size of the mass growths, how widespread they are? There are several means of killing Medusa, but each is highly active. Any living thing within a three-mile radius would also be poisoned. The sea itself would become noxious within an even wider radius. The tested toxins are notoriously waterborne.'

'So why bother with anthrax etcetera? Shove a mass of Medusa up your enemy's waterways.'

She drank more wine. 'Don't let's talk shop.'

It was the only safe subject. Their starters arrived and Nick could then discuss condiments. But there was only so much that could be said about salt, pepper and wine vinegar.

'Did you discover this curiously pleasant place with the Wellnuts?' she asked, eating stuffed mushrooms.

The perfect cue! 'No, I was introduced to it by a renowned jewellery designer. I brought her here a week ago.' God, was it only seven days since he was lured and drugged by Fleur? 'She's Chinese and as stunning to look at as the stuff she creates.'

Lara stopped eating. 'You can't mean Fleur Yang.'

'I can, and do.'

'How on earth . . . I mean, what brought that about?'

'She introduced herself at that party where you announced your engagement. The rest was natural progression of a delightful nature,' he said deliberately.

The mushrooms immediately received undivided attention.

'Is there a woman around who *doesn't* know of Fleur Yang?' he asked.

'I suppose she wouldn't have the same reputation in western Europe and the USA. Hard to vie with Dior, Gucci, Chanel, Michaela Frey, and so on, but she's known at home and throughout the East. I have a Yang necklace. Turquoises. Mum and Dad gave it to me for . . . a special occasion.'

He recalled the necklace she had worn at the Collinses' dinner party. 'Must have been very special. Her things cost a fortune.'

'Dad had the usual tight-fisted grumble. Said he could have bought diamonds for that amount. But I'm not the glittery type.'

He knew. She had chosen a pearl and opal engagement ring. Her father had returned it to him four days after the non-wedding. It and the gold band had gone back to the jeweller in the fullness of time. She was not wearing one now. The God of Marine Sciences had presumably been too busy being brilliant to buy one.

'What's she like?'

'Eh?'

'Fleur Yang.'

'Oh . . . as fabulous as her designs. And as expensive.'

'So it was a one-night stand?'

214

'Definitely. Those are the only stands I have these days. Too busy for anything else, and I get maximum pleasure without the hassle of female tantrums.'

'Isn't that what all men want?' she riposted sourly.

They were served with their main course and Nick ordered another bottle of wine. They had got through the first remarkably quickly. Cutting his steak, he said, 'How long are you planning to stay on the Island? Won't the project be held up if you have to wait for the doctors to come up with a diagnosis?'

'I hope they'll know tomorrow. They're doing tests. All the time Dennis is unfit to dive we can't progress far, anyway. He's still suffering. I called to tell them the situation here and to check that Dennis isn't now showing the same symptoms as Gray. The hospital wanted to know.'

'Is he?'

'No.' She rested her knife and fork on the plate and looked at him with faint appeal. 'We agreed no shop.'

'There was no agreement: you decreed.' He ate more steak. 'Right, do you know much about *feng shui*? No? Kim Collins explained in great detail.'

His monologue on the subject got them through that course, and they wisely declined dessert. Their coffee drinking was accompanied by Nick's dissertation on the merlion.

'Kim told me the first explorer to land here saw creatures he took to be lions – hence the name Lion City – but they were tigers.'

Lara pursed her lips. 'Could have been striped lions. Who knows.'

'A tiger was once seen strolling behind the famous Long Bar at Raffles.'

'A tall story designed as a tourist trap.'

'Not necessarily. I was told there could still be tigers deep in the Malaysian jungle. And elephants.'

She smiled. 'Pink ones, no doubt.'

He shook his head. 'My informant was stony sober.'

'But were you?'

Time to go. Things were getting too intimate. He signalled for the bill. Lara departed to the ladies' room, so Nick seized his chance to approach Mikhail.

'Excellent meal,' he said.

'Thank you, sir.' Still acting!

'No doubt you're glad I didn't offend your other diners with my alcoholic antics this time round. Summon a taxi for me, will you, but stipulate *not* the one whose driver swore he drove me from the Silver Troika too drunk to stand and not from Miss Yang's apartment drugged to the eyebrows. Such a terrible liar will charge me ten times the fare and swear his meter isn't rigged.'

Deeply disconcerted, Mikhail instructed a waiter to call a cab then beat a retreat to the kitchens. One score dealt with. The major one remained.

Lara emerged and asked what her half of the bill came to.

'Have it on me,' he said, leading her out to the taxi just arriving.

'How much, Nick?'

He told her. Maybe it eased her conscience over spending the evening with her former lover rather than at her current one's bedside. They sat at each end of the seat in the car. Understandable enough, but they couldn't make the entire journey in silence. Shop it would have to be.

'On the subject of the merlion, I'm hoping you might come across one down there with Medusa.'

She played along. 'You never know. The sea around these islands is chock-a-block with the most amazing things. Much of it has been grabbed by Medusa, of course. No merlions, so far, but some rare fish. Dead, naturally. Jetsam of every kind. Natural enough near a vital port. Curious what ships' crews abandon, though. Things you wouldn't consider rubbish in the normal way. Clothes, cooking pots, *armchairs*! The prevailing currents tend to sweep flotsam towards Pelingi, Gombak and neighbouring islands, so there's a lot of it along their shores. Partial wrecks, rotting crates.' She gave a rather forced laugh. 'Humanity uses the sea as a communal dumping ground unaware of the beautiful world beneath the surface. Small wonder Neptune takes his revenge now and again.'

'Is that your beloved speaking?'

She rounded on him. 'I have a mind of my own.'

'Indeed you have!' he said tersely.

That silenced them until the taxi swept into the circular drive of the Oriental and the doorman greeted them with the usual 'Welcome back'. They walked between bubbling pools to the glass lifts. Lara pushed button seventeen. Nick left things that way and got out when she did. They walked together until she stopped outside her door. She took out the plastic key and opened it.

'Emma Wellnut has an adolescent crush on you,' she said, showing him she had not forgotten the start of the evening.

'One of my reasons for moving out. When are you planning to marry your boss?'

Totally thrown, she floundered. 'I . . . we're on Pelingi until the end of summer. Lots of lab work to do when we get home. *Vital* work.'

'Ah, so you can happily put off that moment of commitment for an indefinite time.'

It hurt. Her door closed in his face.

Sleep was elusive. He lay staring out at the headlights of vehicles crossing the Nichol Highway and, further out, the lights of ships at anchor. It had been quite a day. The dawn flight with Attard, Vicky Goss with her urge to help, a visit to Senoko, Emma's hero-worship. Lara.

At some time during the early hours words jumped from the nocturnal jumble of recollection and sent the rest packing. *I'm chasing pirates and I've nearly caught them. Prevailing currents tend to sweep flotsam towards Pelingi, Gombak and the neighbouring islands. A lot of it all along their shores. Partial wrecks. Neptune takes his revenge now and again.*

Was the missing link to be found full fathom deep?

Eleven

After tossing and turning for most of the night Nick fell into a deep sleep, waking when the morning was well advanced – too advanced for breakfast in the special club room. He called room service, then showered and shaved. His meal arrived as he emerged from the bathroom in a towelling robe. He sat and poured from the big silver pot, and drank the welcome caffeine. Way out at sea a purple sky was shot through with frequent lightning. Another tropical storm over Pelingi, Gombak and points southwest of the islands.

As he gazed at the elemental violence it gave rise to dark thoughts; threatening images. All over the world there were people at this very moment suffering even more cruelly than he at the start of this year. Many would be tortured unto death; others would be thrown back into society as human vegetables. How many would later sit in indulgent luxury with a useful life ahead, as he was now doing?

Deep inner pain for all those victims beyond help, beyond rescue, merged with the heavy guilt of survival, whole in body and mind. The distant storm epitomized hostility, violence, inhumanity. Each slash of blinding lightning a pulse of remembered agony; every deep rumble of thunder was the tumult in his breast each time they dragged him towards further torment. For countless minutes he travelled in the realms of hell, until the defences he had resolutely built with the aid of Pete Higham pulled him back from the bottomless gulf.

Dry-mouthed, sweating, Nick stared at the breakfast

congealing on the plate. His breathing slowly calmed and
nausea retreated. He poured fresh coffee, opened a miniature from the minibar and laced it with whisky. The regres-
sive moment passed, but he could not face breakfast. He
stood by the window watching the storm retreat as his inner
one had, and slowly reached a decision. Chris Franklin and
the SAS boys had given him back his life. He must honour
the risks they took by living it to the fullest degree. Always!

Reaching for the telephone directory he looked up Senoko
Components and punched out the number. A company that
could make next week into next day overnight had to be
working on Sunday. It was.

'George Chow, please.' Several clicks. 'Ah, Mr Chow,
Major Hargreaves here. Good morning. I shall be meeting
Sir Charles tomorrow afternoon. It would be useful if you'd
let me have a list of all the companies you supply with
components, and what they manufacture. An impressive overseas market would certainly sway R and H in your favour,
in addition to my positive report. I'll be at the Oriental until
early evening. Perhaps you'd fax the list to me before I leave
for the airport.'

The Chinese was happy to comply; offered any further
help.

Dressing in off-white trousers and a tan shirt Nick went
down two floors and knocked on Lara's door. No response.
She must be at the hospital. He took a taxi; enquired at the
desk. The patient was in a private room on the fifth floor.
Yes, it was all right to go up. So far, so good! But Nick
halted in the corridor when he saw Lara coming from a room
several yards ahead. She looked shaken. Good God, was
Attard dead?

He stepped into her path. She glanced up, said nothing
and sidestepped. 'Lara, what is it?' She walked on as if he
had not spoken. On the point of following, Nick spotted a
white-coated Malay emerging from the same room. He looked
familiar.

'Dr Rahman?' Nick walked to him. 'You treated me for

heat exhaustion at your private clinic about a week ago.'

'Of course.' The man smiled recognition. 'Slight effects of hypnosis, too. You're not signing in as a patient, I hope.'

'No, I'm here to enquire about test results for Professor Attard. You've been treating him?'

Rahman frowned. 'You're a friend; a colleague?'

'I flew him over from Pelingi yesterday morning. How ill is he?'

Another frown. 'You are a member of his team?'

'He was trapped thirty feet under. Dr Scott and I went down to release him. He was clearly unwell then. By yesterday morning we realized he needed hospital treatment.' He glanced back along the corridor. 'Lara seemed too upset to speak just now. Why?'

'Perhaps because she is a woman,' came the curious reply. 'Dr Scott is merely the Professor's deputy?'

No mention of fiancée. Well, no ring on her finger. 'On the scientific side, yes. I'm the team's diver and pilot.'

A faint smile. 'A man of action rather than science, eh?'

'How ill is he?' he asked again.

Rahman turned back into the room. Nick followed. Attard was comatose. 'I did not question Dr Scott, but I have to disregard patient confidentiality to ask if you know anything of Professor Attard's sexual activity over the past ten days or so. He is too ill to tell us, and it is important that we trace his movements. Others will certainly be at risk.'

'He visited the Golden Orchid Club around a week ago. No idea if he's been back,' said Nick, understanding Lara's behaviour. Clap was far from romantic.

'We shall have that club checked out. This is a relatively new problem originating in West Africa. We know little about it yet, except that women are carriers and unaware of being so. They pass it to any sexual partner, who can then infect others.'

Disturbed, Nick asked, 'Do the patients recover fully?'

'Some are left impotent, but they otherwise return to normal health.'

'So how long will the Professor be unfit to work?'

'Some weeks. But he is superbly fit for his age and should make a satisfactory recovery.'

Nick guessed Lara would not let him in if he knocked, so, seeing the room maid's trolley in the corridor, he tackled her with a story about his girlfriend not answering her telephone. He was worried. Would she please knock and, if necessary, open the door with her key?

A knock brought no result. A second, along with the announcement that she was the room maid, brought the impatient occupant to the door. Surprisingly, Lara walked away, leaving Nick free to enter. The bed looked as rumpled as his own had been this morning. The scent of her talc and perfume hung in the air. A glass half filled with vodka and lime stood on the small table. It was all so familiar.

'Mind if I help myself to a drink?'

A vague handwave at the minibar gave permission. She picked up her own drink and finished it in a gulp. 'Pour me another.'

When he came up with the glasses, she asked, 'Why did you go to the hospital?'

He sipped his whisky. The sky over Pelingi was clear and bright. The storm had moved on. 'I came here earlier. Guessed where you'd gone. I went hoping to see you. Wanted to make you an offer.'

Her head turned; her lovely eyes had a bruised look. 'What are you talking about?'

'You'll be short of a diver for a bit. Until Dennis is back on his feet I'm happy to help out. Cut some Medusa for you.'

'Why would you do that?'

'I'm on leave, and the tourist trail palls after a while. It'll keep me in practice, too. How about it?' She said nothing. 'You'll be going back to Pelingi now, won't you?'

A heavy sigh. 'The doctor's talking about *weeks*. How can we continue with the programme?'

'By accepting my offer while arranging for replacement

221

divers to join the team asap. You must be fully briefed on what he's aiming to do, so go ahead and do it.'

Silence while the second vodka and lime went the way of the first.

Nick tried again. 'Last night you were so all-fired passionate about the beautiful world under the sea. Now you're considering letting Medusa swallow it up just because the Emperor of Marine Science has been a naughty boy.'

She rounded on him. 'How like you! Denigrate anything you're not personally involved in.'

'I'm bloody offering to *get* involved,' he flung back. 'Any denigration is aimed at his morals, not his professional standing.'

She sank on the bed, gazing distractedly through the window. 'God, what a mess!'

He sat on a chair facing her, choosing his moment and his words. 'Had you no idea he sought relaxation of that nature?'

Her response was a while coming. 'It may be my fault.'

He knew what she was saying and was relieved. Surprised, though. She had been highly passionate and inventive with him. Then he recalled how long it had initially taken him to get her into bed. Thank God, she had followed the same pattern with Attard.

'I'm not sure I can continue working with him.'

That was a woman speaking. The men in the team would shrug and think *chacun à son goût*. 'You won't be. Not for some weeks. By the time he takes over again your tests on Pelingi will almost be over, and you'll have come to terms with this.'

She shook her head slowly. 'It was a great professional partnership. Perfect understanding, identical aims. It worked, *really* worked. Why he wanted to turn it into . . . it was so ridiculous! On a seven four seven he suddenly tells the girl to bring champagne because he's going to propose marriage. He says it loud enough for everyone around to hear. There's excitement and laughter. He goes on one knee in the aisle with a dozen passengers watching. I thought . . . I thought he was joking. It was so *ridiculous*! "Say yes, say yes" they were all crying. He's like that. Sweeps aside opposition.'

Nick said nothing; thought of his own proposal. Walking over Dartmoor it began to rain heavily. They found a kind of grotto in a rock formation, too late to stop themselves being drenched to the skin. He had taken out his handkerchief to wipe her face and knew that this was the right moment.

'Would you consider becoming Mrs Hawkwood?'

'I'd *love* to become Mrs Hawkwood.'

They had celebrated with kisses, mineral water and pork pies while rain continued to thunder down.

But she had run from becoming Mrs Hawkwood.

'I never knew why his two marriages ended,' Lara mused, still on the same theme. 'The wives walked away; that much he told me. I guess I've found out why.'

'It's not such a terrible crime,' he murmured.

'Huh! Trust a man to take that line.' She looked fiercely across at him. 'If you discovered your wife found "relaxation" in a male brothel how would you feel about *that*?'

'I was saved at the eleventh hour from the possibility of facing that dilemma.'

Her eyes blazed. 'God, Nick, you know how to twist the knife!'

'Take a leaf from my book,' he invited levelly. 'Twist one in his guts. He thinks he's the kingpin. Abandoning this project will reinforce his ego. Go to Pelingi and prove you can do it without him. The team'll go along with that. I sensed that most of *them* weren't exactly worshippers at the Attard shrine.'

She made to speak but bit the words back.

'My offer to dive for you removes any valid reason for halting work already underway.'

'What are you hoping to get from this magnanimous gesture?' she asked caustically.

'No grateful thanks, apparently. I have time on my hands, I enjoy diving and it's a perfect opportunity for me to brush up my technique.' I also have my reasons, he added silently.

He saw her indecision. Attard's indiscriminate lust had knocked her for six, although she had allowed herself to be coerced into the prospect of being wife number three without too much resistance. Presumably, professional infatuation could not accept feet of clay.

'You told me in no uncertain terms last night that you had a mind of your own,' he said. 'Make it up here and now, then we can call Ferdy to fly us out.'

She got to her feet, stretching tall as if in defiance. 'What's your room number?' He told her. 'I'll get through to you as soon as I've fixed it.'

Nick packed a few things in a grip and arranged for the rest of his baggage to be held by the hotel until he returned. Then he called James at the swimming club, apparently waking him from an after-lunch snooze. He sounded irritable.

'Yes. Wellnut.'

'I guess Joyce will welcome the cessation of snores.'

'What are you so bloody chirpy about?'

'Found a way of keeping out of mischief. Attard's in hospital. Likely to remain for some weeks. Means they're short one diver. I've volunteered until they get a replacement. I'm flying out to Pelingi later today. Have to miss the Fieldings' dinner tonight.'

'That's been cancelled. He's under the weather. Touch of dengue. Joyce has planned something instead.'

'Give her my apologies. Still frosty?'

'Somewhat. I'll survive,' he said against the sound of children enjoying the pleasure of water. 'Is Pelingi a good idea? Far be it from me to say . . .'

'Then don't. No way can the High Comm be affected by what I do out there.'

'It's not the High Comm I'm concerned about.'

'I'll call you when I touch base again. I owe you and the Collinses dinner. By the way, be sure to tell Joyce I've gone to Pelingi when you go to bed tonight.'

There was a significant silence. 'May I ask why?'

224

'The info will reach the ears of your stepdaughter and stop her coming to the Oriental again.'

He left James to work on that.

The telephone rang as soon as he replaced it. Lara. 'Ferdy's tied up, but one of his pilots'll fly us out.'

'When?'

'Half past six. *Eighteen thirty* to you gung-ho service types.'

Some knife twisting of her own? 'OK. RV seventeen forty-five third bubbling pool from main access. Over and out!'

There were two and a half hours to fill. Poolside lounger, tea and a pile of sandwiches, the feisty woman detective! He began yet again on chapter one. The gruesome murder seemed less so the third time around. As for the female DI he soon tired of her and skipped a few pages to the 'tart with a heart'; the account of her exploits with a series of clients all of whom had a motive for killing the other prostitute run by the same vicious pimp. A second death was on the cards when his mobile played its tune from the table beside him.

'Hawkwood.'

'It's Vicky,' she whispered against the background of children enjoying the pleasures of water. 'I'm at the club. Got to be quick; Euan's gone to the Gents. Those ships weren't all boarded and robbed. Only those that sailor was on. My friend is now very interested in him. These are the names.'

Nick grabbed a pen and scribbled in the margins of the paperback as she listed them.

'All the others are on the regular run to and from West Africa. If you want anything more, let me know.'

'Vicky, you're brilliant!'

'Any time, so long as you promise you won't do anything risky now I've told you. Oh, must go. He's coming back with a suspicious look on his handsome face. Take care, Nick.' Then louder, 'Yes, Marie, Thursday will be fine. 'Bye.'

Nick switched off the mobile with mixed feelings. She had been so helpful, but he wished she'd be open with Euan.

The poor devil was only jealous because she provoked it. One day she might find the worm turning and her world would tip-tilt. On Euan's part, he should recognize his wife's hunger for excitement and try providing some himself.

The thriller suffered its usual fate as Nick lay back with eyes closed to consider this new information. By the time he returned to his room the notion that he had stumbled on two rings or operations had been strengthened.

An envelope lay on the floor. It contained the fax from George Chow which Nick had asked the desk to send to his room so he could pass it to Major Hargreaves when they met later that day. He put the list in his grip. Between dives he would consider all the facts and try to correlate them, hoping for a breakthrough. He very much wanted to solve the mystery of Dunne's file. A growing sense of identification with the man he had never met also prompted a desire to give the hero a known resting-place – a soldier's commitment to honour the dead!

Starting early on the first morning, Nick and Lara went down three times with large net sacks. Taking care not to let Medusa engulf him Nick still found the task unpleasant. The strands were tough and so prone to cling they used long-handled tongs to transfer the severed clumps to the bags. The growth had engulfed a large amount of flotsam; had embalmed a number of sea creatures. This second encounter with the subterranean menace had shown Nick the full extent of its threat.

The team members seemed little concerned by Attard's absence. The general mood was upbeat and relaxed. Dennis was on his feet and starting to eat. He would be fit to work in three days. A supplementary diver was on his way from Perth, ETA Singapore tomorrow night. Ferdy had been booked to fly him across early the following morning. Would Nick stay until then?

It was difficult to be alone on Pelingi. Nick had to resort to walking along the beach with Dunne's list, George Chow's list, and the paperback bearing details of vessels that Vicky had given him. Sitting with his back to a tree, Nick studied these with the aid of a torch and began to make some sense of Philip Dunne's notes. The ships served on by Muna's cousin were starred in blue. *Check on lapis lazuli.* Blue stars because of that link?

Red stars for ships on the West Africa run. No connection with Muna's cousin; yet robbery on the high seas. So what was the significance there? He puzzled over it for a while without light dawning and wished he could call on Euan for a mariner's inspiration.

He then turned to details of Senoko's customers. Most were in India, Hong Kong, Japan, Thailand, Indonesia. A couple in Sydney; one in Shanghai. These were regularly supplied with components. A good steady trade. He could understand their desire to expand into the western market. A contract with Rees and Hardy would be a real coup. Hence why Vydecker was investing and pushing for it?

He scanned the list of what these customers manufactured. Half a dozen were engaged in work for their country's armed services, either producing weapons or larger components for them – as did Rees and Hardy. The rest made anything from refrigerators to ultrascan equipment for hospitals. All perfectly straightforward.

Nick was about to put the paper back in the envelope when he felt a jolt of excitement. Three of the companies were listed as DBH Systems, LTD Spares and NBC Inc. Those initials were also on Dunne's list, he was certain. Putting the two sheets side by side he saw by the light of the torch that he was right. His excitement increased as he realized all the initials noted by Dunne matched up with Senoko customers, even though some were registered as full company names. Reduce them to initials and bingo!

He sat for some while gazing at the dull glint of water while the soft, warm night breeze played over him. *I'm getting there, Phil*, he said to the ocean. *You linked these companies, but made no mention of Senoko. I've uncovered their*

*involvement, but where do we go from here? What did you
know that I haven't yet discovered? You were chasing pirates,
so are the red and blue stars somehow connected?*

Finally, afraid he might not discover the truth before he
must fly back to England, he returned to the tent he shared
with Craig and two others and continued to beat his brain
for a flash of enlightenment. He woke to begin another diving
session none the wiser.

By lunchtime the amount of Medusa in the water tanks
was starting to please the team. It was fusing into large enough
clumps to stay alive for a useful length of time. More was
still needed and Nick prepared for another series of dives
with Lara. The sea had grown markedly choppy. They faced
the prospect of a storm heading their way, which would halt
underwater activity.

'I think we should move to beyond that jutting area. We'll
be better protected,' Lara said, pointing along the beach to
where Nick had done his thinking in the moonlight. 'It still
drops down sharply close inshore, but the current is deflected
away by the build-up of shingle.'

'OK, you're the boss.'

'Yes, very funny!'

'But you are,' Nick said forcefully. 'In Attard's absence
his deputy takes over. Everyone thinks you're making a hell
of a good job of being the leader.'

A caustic glance sufficed as she headed along the beach.
Nick was annoyed. Had she allowed that man to dominate
her to the extent of undermining her self-worth? If she had
it was not his concern. Just get on with the job, Hawkwood!

They had been down fifteen minutes when they came across
debris from a ship. Cooking pots, china basins, wooden
animals, fabric that had been clothing, all enmeshed in
Medusa. Lara touched Nick's arm. *Look, just what I described
to you!* He nodded.

They then moved further towards the long spur looking
for samples free of debris. The sea grew murkier. Shingle
from the ridge floated around in the current, settled, then

rose again as the circling water disturbed it anew. In the semi-obscurity it was not so easy to find exactly what Lara needed.

She soon signalled that they should turn back. They were simply wasting oxygen. But, on the point of following her, Nick felt a stab of anticipation over something he spotted ahead. It was indistinct but tantalizing enough to drive him on for a closer look.

It was not even a partial wreck; no more than a few feet of deck with the stub of a mast that was firmly lodged in the buttress of shingle. Nick approached, heart hammering, praying that it would be what he hoped for. He reached out to touch it; swam past to study it from the other side. Through the thick green filter of sea water it was just possible to make out the letters *Sea Ha* on the splintered fragment of hull.

Forgetting Lara, his purpose in diving, the low level of his oxygen, he swam the full length of the spur then back again. Unwilling to give up, he made a second survey of that underwater shingle deposit moving more slowly, peering more closely. When his watch told him he must return to the surface he spotted the human remains: his sole reason for being on Pelingi.

Twelve

The storm arrived mid-afternoon, the brunt of it hitting Pulau Gombak ten miles away. Nick watched as razor-edged lightning struck the dark blob almost continuously for half an hour. Wall to wall vegetation, the sound of screams, souls in torment! Small wonder violent elements bombarded it so relentlessly. His mood was in tune with the turbulence. He feared the huge, surging sea would dislodge what he had found.

On surfacing, he had contacted James. 'I've found Philip Dunne along with a chunk of *Sea Harrier*. You and Euan will know the correct authorities to inform. Tell 'em to make it snappy. A storm is bearing down on us.'

The authorities clearly did not attach an 'immediate' tag to the recovery of a body that had been in the sea long enough to have the flesh stripped from it.

The storm swept through, leaving a clear evening softened by moonlight. The drama had brought work to an early halt. Nick was unable to relax; he was listening for the sound of rotors. After the communal dinner he went out to the beach, pacing for a while then sitting against the same tree in a subconscious vigil.

Lara came to him there. 'Message from James Wellnut. Navy divers on their way.'

'At last!'

'He's been down there a long time. Another hour or two won't matter.' She sat beside him. 'Tell me about Philip Dunne.'

'Fearless jet pilot decorated for bravery. Happier in male

230

company and engaged in daring, active pursuits. Faithful husband; one daughter. Fun to be with when slightly pissed despite chauvinist attitude towards women. Died prematurely.'

'That's it?' she asked curiously.

'That's it.'

'So why, Nick?'

'Why what?'

'You didn't come here to help the project, it was to look for him, wasn't it?'

He looked out at the calm sea. 'You said prevailing currents swept everything towards these islands. I wondered, that's all.'

'But you didn't know him.'

'I was getting there.'

After a moment or two, she said, 'He's part of your other world, is he? Who recently printed crap about the Hawkwoods, Nick?'

He offered no reply. It was peaceful now; the water, the beach, even the palms were silvered by the enormous moon. Philip Dunne was part of something that was bridging the abyss between the past and a questionable future. Philip Dunne was immensely important to him right now.

They came not in a helicopter but a high-speed launch, bringing underwater arc-lights, a lifting cradle and a makeshift coffin. A Chinese police inspector concentrated on questioning Nick and made heavy weather of it. Not a man to accept facts without minute examination of the reasons why he should. Before long, Nick began to see the wisdom of James and Euan's reluctance to arouse police suspicions in any way. Inspector Choi seemed liable to pin Dunne's death on Nick, given half a chance.

Fortunately, the operation to rescue the skeleton and evidence of disaster at sea took the divers a shorter time than expected, and the launch's skipper was urging departure. Nick asked to return to Singapore with them, which led Choi to agree it was advisable that he should be accessible for further

231

questioning. Nick hastily packed his grip and shook hands with people he had lived and worked with for a short while.

'Your replacement diver will be coming over with Ferdy in the morning. I can't do anything useful here tonight, so I've cadged a lift with the Navy. Best of luck finding the answer to Medusa.'

'Watch this space,' laughed Craig.

Lara walked with him to the dinghy where a sailor was waiting to return to the launch. 'Thanks for the help, anyway.'

Nick glanced at her, glad he was making his getaway now. 'Brushed up my skills. Learned something, too. That growth should be taken *very* seriously. Be careful down there with it.'

'Is that real concern I hear in your voice?' She was not being caustic, and he chose to counter the gentle encouragement she was offering as he stepped in the dinghy.

'It is. The same goes for Dennis and the guy joining you tomorrow. You saw what it did to Attard. Be warned – all of you!'

Even so, he could not resist the urge to look shoreward in case she waved. She was walking away back to her friends and colleagues.

The Oriental could not give him the same room but he could have the one next to it. Fine! They brought the baggage he had stored with them, he took a long relaxing bath, ordered coffee and sandwiches from room service, then sat to eat propped against fat pillows in solitary splendour and missing the rough and ready camaraderie on Pelingi. For he had just been in an environment similar to one he knew well and felt easy with – echoes of the military life he badly wanted to resume. Luxury and pampering were OK if shared with a girl. Boring on his own.

He was too hyped-up to sleep. Too late to ring James, but the perfect time to put through a call to Cornwall. He dialled.

'Good afternoon. Hawkwood Books.'

'Hi, Lucy.'

A short silence. 'Where are you?'

'Singapore. Where else?'

'We never know with you.' There was evident relief in her voice. 'How's it all going, Nick?'

'Great. Has young Andrew stopped bawling night and day?'

'Yes. We got him a mobile covered in African animals that emits grunts, roars and squeals. Tinkling bells and flying angels got us nowhere, but he loves this. We reckon he's going to be a big game hunter when he grows up.'

Feeling immense relief that the boy was no longer constantly distressed, Nick said, 'Better make it clear to him they're armed with cameras these days. No killing allowed.'

'Except for poachers. Saw a TV documentary last week showing the extent of it. Elephant tusks, rhino horns, leopard skins, crocodile hide. And worse. They keep live animals in cages so small they can't even turn round. They're in captivity like that until they're sold on to be slaughtered. Made me sick to watch it.'

'Is Jon there?' he asked sharply.

Heavy breathing. 'God, I didn't think! *Sorry*, Nick.'

'Just get Jon.'

How long would it take her to treat him normally again? Answer: as soon as he could hear things like that and react normally; as soon as he could see a man helplessly bound by underwater growth and not struggle with demons; as soon as he was back with a squadron doing what he had always done superbly well!

His brother came on the line. 'My heart's sinking already. Phone call instead of e-mail equates to favours about to be asked. More snooping in Mousehole?'

'Not necessary . . . and phone call instead of e-mail means a sudden urge to hear a familiar voice. Have you concreted the back garden yet?'

'Decided to keep the lawn. Lucy says kids need grass to play on.'

Good-looking guy like you and a stunner like her. Think

what gorgeous kids you'd have. They would surely have had one by now; maybe another on the way. Was that what Lara had run from?

'You still there, Nick?

'I found Dunne's body – his remains – today. No rush to inform the widow. She's snugged up with lover boy.'

'Brief me.'

Nick gave an Army-style report centred on his activities at Pelingi; said nothing of Muna's murder and his own fate at the hands of armed thugs. The less Jon knew about that the better.

'I'm back at the Oriental, it's o-one hundred here, and I thought I'd touch base with the news.'

'Yeah, great! It's good you've been catching up on your diving skills. Never know when it'll come in useful, like freeing guys who're trapped. That stuff would make a super biological weapon. Fly over, drop five thousand tons of it in the enemy's rivers and reservoirs. Death by dehydration! Cheap, too. Just pull it up out of the sea.'

Nick nodded. 'Just what I thought. Together we could make a fortune selling it to aggressive regimes.'

'You're not getting tied up with Lara again, are you?' Jon asked carefully.

'I left her on Pelingi three hours ago heading happily back to her colleagues as I headed happily back to Singapore. Finito!'

'As finito as before you met up out there?'

'There is one thing you can do for me,' Nick said firmly. 'Find out all you can about Rees and Hardy. Fanshawe has recently become a director. I'd like a list of the other directors and of who else they supply besides the MoD. Particularly overseas customers.'

'What are you up to now?'

'Just interested. Asap, Jon.'

'Are you still flying back on the twenty-fourth?'

'Reason why I want that info fast.'

'You've found Dunne. Spend the rest of your leave drinking and wenching.'

234

'Something you tagged a bad idea two weeks ago. Check R and H, brother mine, and tell Lucy I'm bringing her a present she'll love.'

'Where d'you plan to stay when you get back?'

'My flat. I'll mail the gift . . . and things for the kids, too.'

'Watch yourself, Nick.'

'Unnecessary warning. You're speaking to a fully trained member of Her Majesty's armed forces.'

'Yeah . . . and we both know what can happen to them.'

Nick winced at the caustic words. 'Good to talk to you, Jon.'

'Likewise. Glad you did.'

'Over and out.'

Settling for sleep, he lay thinking of Jon's legacy of battle. Bitterness would probably remain for years. He had a devoted wife, and two children to teach and guide; a growing business that interested him. But when the children matured and departed, and Lucy found it increasingly difficult to care for him, the full cost of that one impulsive act in Bosnia would be felt.

Jon's injuries had brought them close together in brotherhood; his own mental one was keeping them apart. Lucy could not cope, so he would stay away until she could. She had been marvellous throughout the various crises of Jon's recovery; a truly loyal and loving wife. He was thankful Andrew was plaguing her less. Maybe all that wailing truly was normal for a kid his age. Nothing sinister in it at all.

He closed his eyes. That boy was a chip off the old block. No tinkling bells for young Hawkwood. Had to be elephants, lions and jungle noises. He would be off on safari before they knew it, taking pictures of powerful and beautiful beasts for the world to enjoy. Poachers just left pathetic carcasses with bloody holes where tusks or horns had been wrenched out.

It shafted into his brain like the lightning striking Gombak. Elephant tusks – ivory ornaments. Rhino horns – aphrodisiacs and ancient remedies. Crocodile teeth, monkey entrails! My God, he had been driven by mistake to an apothecary named Yang; had seen all manner of stuff stored in jars or hanging from hooks. The West Africa run! What if Dunne had been chasing not pirates but *smugglers*?

Soon after breakfast, feeling Judas-like, Nick dialled the Goss number knowing Euan should have left for the office. Vicky answered.

'Hi, it's Nick.'

'Good thing this isn't video phoning. I've just stepped from the shower. Euan said you'd found poor old Phil,' she said with a touch of sadness. 'I guess they'll fly what there is of him home. Alison can have her flag-draped coffin and volley of rifle shots after all.'

And shed not a tear, thought Nick. 'That'll be for him. He earned them, not her. And it's for him I'm bypassing Euan now – much as I dislike doing it. Do you happen also to have an admirer in Customs and Excise who would do a favour for you?'

'Wait a sec while I go through to the bedroom for pad and pen. I can find out *anything*, sweetie. My stodgy husband is respected by the locals. They look on him as the typical stiff upper-lip British officer.' She giggled. 'It might be because I once said he was a direct descendant of Nelson. I was joking, but you're never sure if the Chinese recognize it.'

Nick waited, visualizing the naked Vicky crossing a bedroom to pick up the extension and prepare to write. The Judas feeling did not extend to his imagination.

'OK, Nick, fire away.'

'Those ships on the West African run, have you still got the list?'

'Sure have.'

Can you get for me their ports of call and details of regular cargoes? What they bring here and take back. Customs must have copies of their manifests which would give the names of companies exporting and those receiving the merchandise. Ask if anything illegal has ever been found on those vessels, and how thoroughly they inspect the cargoes. It's my guess there's no more than random spot-checking.'

'Nick, wouldn't it be better if I took you to meet him?'

'Thanks, but no. He's unlikely to unburden this info to an Army officer on leave, but if he thinks it's for Nelson's descendant he'll be fully forthcoming. I also have some things I need to follow up and time is growing short. I have seven days to solve the puzzles in that list of Dunne's. Appreciate your help no end, but please don't do it if it'll make things awkward between you and Euan. Oh, give me your mobile number. Might need it.'

He next dialled the Collinses' number. George said Mrs Collins had already driven to the university. Captain Hawkwood could reach her there on extension twenty-nine. He did reach her and she sounded pleased that he had made contact.

'I hear you have been having some adventures. I was not aware you counted deep-sea diving among your skills. This explains many things to me.'

'It does?' he asked cautiously.

'A soldier who flies has affinity with both earth and metal. If he also spends much time beneath the ocean he has affinity with water, too. A complex character! What can I do for you, Nick?'

'You enlightened me on *feng shui* and the merlion. I'm keen to learn something about Chinese medicine. Do you know someone who would spare a little time to talk to me?'

'You wish to have a consultation with a practitioner?'

'Not for myself,' he said hastily. 'To gain some knowledge on the subject. I'd pay the usual consultation fee, of course.'

'I must advise you that no practitioner will be prepared to reveal the secrets of his remedies. There are many charlatans who dispense supposed cures that are concoctions of their own devising. They can be dangerous. Genuine healers practise under strict regulations, but each has his own range of remedies, jealously guarded. If you are not in need of medical help I suggest you go to the library, where there are books on Eastern medicines and cures.' Humour crept into her precise voice. 'An active man like yourself will tire of reading within an hour or so. It is a hugely involved subject.'

'Oh,' he said flatly. 'Well, thanks.'

'Ferdy says you fly home next week. Why not follow it up there?'

'Yes. I'll be in touch with a dinner invitation before I go.'

'That will be very nice.'

Frustrated in that direction, Nick was hesitating on how best to spend the morning when the telephone rang.

'Have you seen the *Straits Times* yet?' asked James.

'Been too busy.'

'Page eight, centre column. My counterpart from KL is here for a conference on bilateral defence regs due to start in fifteen. Catch you later. Better still, come to lunch. Joyce might melt a little, and I need to talk to you.'

'I'll be there.'

Nick immediately removed the newspaper from the bag that had been hanging on his door. The relevant column was headed 'MURDERED DANCER SOURCE OF NEW MYSTERY ILLNESS'. He read with growing astonishment of the arrest of Stanislav Ivanovich Vinnikov and two Afro-Asians charged with the murder of the dancer known as Lapis Lazuli. There was a list of other charges that would ensure the Russian was locked away for good.

The gist of the report was that Vinnikov had employed a girl without insisting on medical clearance. Muna Zainal, half Filipino-half Balinese, had contracted a disease known to be rife in West Africa. When club members began to fall ill they demanded money from Vinnikov to compensate for his carelessness. Unwilling to publicize their immoral activities – several were respected local businessmen – rather than inform the authorities, they circulated letters to members advising them to find relaxation elsewhere. Many did.

Vinnikov had grown alarmed and traced the source of the illness to his star performer, who, unknown to him, had been selling her body for personal gain. He then sent two employees to collect the girl so that he could arrange medical treatment for her.

The men maintained that she refused to go with them and, during a struggle, one of her scarves became wound around her throat. They panicked and ran. They could not say how her body came to be beside the MRT track. During questioning they suggested that she was later killed in vengeance by a club member.

There was a long account of the police crackdown on the Golden Orchid, which the accused manager insisted was no more than a club offering drinks and select entertainment. He denied all knowledge of prostitution; said what his dancers did when they left the premises was not his responsibility.

There was a footnote. Several residents of the estate in Sembawang claimed that two men of Afro-Asian appearance had been found semi-conscious the evening before the girl's body was discovered. Police did not attach much significance to the reports, saying the men had probably been inebriated.

Also given little credence was another story concerning a blond foreigner seen standing over one of these men with a knife, who was chased by residents until he plunged in the sea. Inspector Lim said it was common for all manner of information to be offered in cases of violent crime. People sometimes imagined suspicious incidents, and more often turned normal events into dramatic developments. He hastened to add that the police always welcomed help from the general public. Things that might appear unimportant frequently led to solving a case.

Nick lowered the newspaper feeling he might laugh if it were not for the violent death of young Muna. The report certainly put paid to some of his theories, at the same time explaining a great deal. For instance, Vinnikov's suspicions of his motive for visiting the club; the bribe to silence him. The Russian really had taken him for a snooping official, or even the legal representative of the members demanding compensation.

At what precise moment the Russian had made the connection between Muna and the infected men Nick would never know. Nor whether the two thugs had been set to follow him to check on his movements on leaving with the bribe in his pocket, or whether they were in Sembawang to grab Muna, saw him leave that flat, and decided to get rid of him before he also fell ill and made trouble. Thank God he had not taken up Muna's invitation for sex. It then occurred to him that Attard clearly had. Well, he was in good company with several respected Singaporean businessmen!

The room maid arrived to clean, so Nick took the newspaper down to the coffee bar and read the column again. It gave him some answers, but not all. There was still the business of the merlion letters to be delivered to the 'big boss'. Maybe they were simply invitations to parties where girls like Muna would perform. If so, where did a sailor who happened to have served on a series of ships that had been boarded and robbed fit in? Any wealthy high-flyer with a penchant for stag parties could easily organize them himself. John Vydecker, for instance.

Nick sighed. James maintained he was flogging a dead horse there. Maybe he was. There was no concrete evidence of criminal activity by him. Yet he had connections with a Chinese girl who drugged men for no apparent reason; with that girl's brother, who dealt with his personal affairs; with Senoko, a company supplying others on an arms black list. Anyone in Singapore who ran a business wisely kept in with Vydecker. Such a man had to be dealing deep. Nick just *knew* it. Same as he knew the answer to Dunne's list would concern the American.

On that thought he quit the hotel and took a taxi to Vydecker's bank. The premises were hushed and highly suggestive of prosperity. Marble mosaic floor, potted palms, geometric pendulous lighting, leather-topped writing-desks, black hide chairs. He crossed to a discreet corner occupied by a Fleur Yang clone and sat in the upright chair before her desk.

Miss Lily Chan – her name was on a brass plate on her desk – glanced up to give a beguiling, submissive smile. 'Good morning, sir. How can I be of assistance?'

'I'd like to talk to someone about investments,' he said. 'My uncle back in Australia has left me a very large sum of money and I was told this is the best place to come for advice on how to make it work for me.'

'Are you thinking of long-term investment, or buying into the stocks and bonds market, sir?'

He feigned innocence. 'There's a difference?'

She reached for her telephone. 'I'll see if Mr Cheng is free. He'll explain all the options to you.'

While she spoke briefly in her own language Nick studied her ivory features, ivory blouse and tailored black suit with a jade dragon on the lapel. There was a jade ring on her right hand. Manicured nails were tinted pink like her lips. Black hair was drawn into a plaited chignon. Her voice was soft; her eyes hid her private thoughts. These Chinese girls appealed strongly to his new desire for gentleness, but their demure manner was deceptive. He no longer trusted it.

Mr Cheng would apparently be glad to offer advice. Could she ask the gentleman's name? Would Mr Hargreaves please follow her? Could she arrange for tea or coffee to be brought?

Harold Cheng, expensively suited, fortyish, had prominent cheek bones, yellow teeth and impeccable manners. But as soon as the formalities were over and delicate cups of tea had been brought, Cheng got down to business. Nick had to admire the exquisite tact with which the question of how much money was involved was approached. After inventing a yarn about inheriting his uncle's cattle station, which he had now sold on, he quoted a sum he knew would change Cheng's interest from polite to avid.

'I'm here on holiday – first time I've come to Singapore – and from what I've seen of it I reckon my money could work well for me here. Fleur Yang suggested I should discuss investments with you.'

Cheng's neat ears pricked. 'Miss Yang?'

Nick leaned back in his chair. 'Funny how things turn out, isn't it? I walked into a shop that sells brooches and rings, looking for something to take home for my girl. I said rather light-heartedly that at their prices maybe I should invest my recent inheritance in Yang jewellery. The young woman who was helping me fetched Miss Yang herself. She said anyone wanting to make investments of any kind should come here for the very best guidance in financial matters.'

Harold Cheng apparently believed his Australian client to be genuine. Within twenty-five minutes he had put forward for Nick's consideration a short list of companies he would recommend as rock-solid investments, and a shorter list of up and coming businesses with every promise of giving rich returns in perhaps five years. Did Mr Hargreaves require immediate dividends or was he able to wait for companies to become fully established?

'Rock-solid sounds about right,' he said. 'I'm not much into gambling. Like to be certain of what I'm getting for my money.'

Cheng produced his first smile. 'Then you could, indeed, safely invest in Yang, Mr Hargreaves. Miss Yang sells world-wide and members of several European royal families are among her clients. But a gentleman like yourself would probably be more interested in buying shares in Senoko Components. Fine engineering with an expanding market. The directors are about to secure a contract to supply Rees and Hardy, a major British defence manufacturer. Or you could do equally well with the Cordova Line, a long-established maritime corporation nearing maximum potential. A very secure investment, sir. Operating between Dakar and Singapore the line is all set to gain the monopoly in container business between the two ports. Their latest vessel is nearing completion. It will be the largest in their fleet.'

A fleet marked with red stars on Dunne's list! Nick got up to leave. He picked up the two sheets of paper and offered his hand.

'Thanks for your advice, Mr Cheng. I'll look over these

recommendations. If I've any questions I'll ring you. As I said, it seems to me Singapore is pretty smart businesswise.'

Cheng walked round his desk to open the door, still impeccably polite as he asked how long Mr Hargreaves planned to stay in the country. It would be possible for him to look over the premises of some of the companies, if he had the time.

'My plans are liquid,' he said. 'I might take you up on that when I've had time to consider these options.'

Harold Cheng said he would be glad to offer any help Mr Hargreaves needed, and added that Vydecker International would provide unrivalled service to ensure his money reaped the richest returns.

Nick walked the short distance through pre-lunch crowds to the Marriott and ordered a beer. His brain was teeming with speculations. Cheng had discreetly pushed Senoko and the shipping line Dunne had been interested in. Substitute smugglers for pirates and the man's tipsy confession to Vicky Goss might tie in better with those red-starred vessels. Container ships. One only had to travel along the coast road here to see miles of the huge metal boxes piled high upon each other. It would be easy enough to spirit away contraband goods. Impossible to mount a twenty-four-hour watch on such a vast area.

Someone with a legitimate reason to be around the docks could check on them after dark. A sailor – like Muna's cousin! When the stuff arrived he sent a letter with a merlion stamped on it to the 'big boss'. Nick sighed. It was all too high-flown. An Edwardian ripping yarn. Why send notes in this age of mobile phones and text messages?

He studied the lists Cheng had given him. Among the rock solids was Yang Jewellery. Mmm. He knew Vydecker had large investments in Fleur's artistic flair. Also in Senoko. So had the man financial interests also in Cordova ships, Bee-Yin Furniture Company, Marina Pharmaceuticals. KY Investments, Sentosa Ceramics and Tanglin Optics? A visit to the library to study the directory of companies after lunch should wise him up on that. The companies listed as slightly more uncertain ventures were possibly in line for Vydecker's interest after gamblers had set them up . . . or knocked them down. Once the risk element was settled he would buy the company.

Nick stared into his empty glass. *Was* Vydecker Muna's big boss? She could not tell him, nor could Philip Dunne say if the American had featured in his investigations. Each had left him with a puzzle and damn-all means of solving them.

His mobile jingled. 'Hawkwood.'

'You were coming to lunch,' said James.

Nick glanced at the time. Twelve thirty! 'Be there in ten,' he said calmly. 'This taxi queue's a mile long.'

It was twelve fifty when he walked into the familiar room and instantly regretted having lost the freedom and pleasure of a house open to the elements. He had enjoyed living here.

Joyce greeted him warmly. 'You've acquired a tan at last! No longer resemble a newly arrived pinkie.' She kissed his cheek. 'How are you?'

'All the better for seeing you. Can't say the same for your husband. There's a distinct glaze of disapproval in his eye.'

'There speaks the blond foreigner holding a knife said to have been chased into the sea by a pack of residents! An unlikely yarn, say the police. You're bloody lucky they took that view, Hawk.'

He shrugged. 'Let's face it, it does sound highly improbable. You and Euan can now relax . . . until Inspector Choi arrests me for the murder of Philip Dunne. He seemed set on the idea last night.'

James scowled. 'The sooner you fly home the better. Let's eat. We've been waiting half an hour for you.'

The first part of the meal was enlivened by Joyce's questions about how Nick came to discover part of the *Sea Harrier* and the skeleton amid all that ocean. She was fascinated by his description of Medusa's inexorable advance, and how he and Lara had had to cut Attard free of its deadly grip.

'Thought you said he's in hospital,' murmured James.

'So he is, *now*. Between you and me he's got this African disease Muna's been spreading around. Told you I spotted him at the Golden Orchid, didn't I? He was already suffering from it when he made that dive – against all advice – and apparently headed straight in the stuff. If I hadn't been on hand Lara would never have got him out. Most likely have been trapped by it herself. She was full of solicitousness until she discovered what was ailing him,' he added, tucking in to the cold chicken and tropical fruits salad. 'It ended that Winter and Spring relationship at a stroke.'

'How is Lara?' Joyce asked casually.

'Apart from badly dented hero-worship, much the same.' He faced her across the table. 'If you're really asking if she's been infected, no. They didn't, apparently.'

'She must be relieved,' commented Joyce, who was rarely disconcerted.

'I wouldn't know. I was there simply to help out until the relief diver arrived.'

'So now that's over how are you planning to fill your time?' demanded James.

'I've been trying to read a murder mystery for the past week. Maybe I can get down to it now. Can't swim because of the leg, but I'll take you on at squash . . . if you're up to it.'

'Cheeky bastard!'

'And I want to fix up a couple of flights with Ferdy. The more hours I put in before I go in front of a board the greater my chances of being reinstated.'

James regarded him thoughtfully. 'It's early days yet.'

'And?' he countered aggressively.

'And they're not likely to rush into sending you up after what you experienced earlier this year.'

'You mean I can fly my arse off successfully at my own expense, but no way will the Army risk letting me loose with one of their valuable helicopters again.'

'I'm saying they'll err on the side of caution. There are

eager lads lining up to become pilots. Human replacements are cheaper than aircraft. And you know as well as I those are spread too thinly to maintain all the commitments our precious PM forces on us.' He attempted a lighter note. 'You'll get your wings back – pride of the AAC, weren't you – but you'll have to curb that damned impatience while they bumble their way through to a positive decision.' He smiled encouragingly. 'Good idea to have a trip or two in Ferdy's helos while you're here.'

'So long as you stop landing on islands and going to the rescue under the ocean,' put in Joyce with a smile that was not in the least encouraging. 'Can't resist playing Action Man, can you? Given half a chance, you'd dare all to deliver Milk Tray to damsels in totally inaccessible places!'

Nick accepted the change of mood. 'Not that much of a fool. Today's damsels are capable of shooting rapids or swinging over chasms to get their own chocs.'

Joyce suggested the two men had their coffee on the verandah while she changed her clothes for a parents' meeting at the younger children's school. 'Running a bit late, Nick, so forgive me for shooting off. Come to the club on Sunday. We'd all love it. James can stir himself and let you beat him at squash. Do him good.'

Her husband made an expression of disgust. 'Get yourself off to parental duty, woman!'

Nick sank on a cushioned chair with a sigh of pleasure. This open-air house was very much to his liking. How good it would be to sit here for an hour or so getting to grips with all the clues, while enjoying the song of orioles and few other sounds. But James had invited him because he needed to talk, so conversation it must be. The maid brought coffee, poured it, then left.

Nick took several sips then set his cup back on the table. 'So what do you want to talk about?'

James frowned. 'You and Vicky Goss.'

'In what context?'

'In the context that Euan has found out you're using his

wife to continue your sleuthing. He's gunning for you.'

Nick was untroubled. 'How did he find out?'

'A Singapore Navy friend of the Gosses rang him with "additional information". Euan's livid. He's forbidden Vicky to contact you.'

'Idiot! You can't *forbid* wives in this day and age.'

'I agree. He should instead give her a good hiding.'

'She'd love it!'

James grinned. 'I told him she would. He left my office, face like a thundercloud. Thought I should warn you to expect a challenge for pistols at dawn.'

'He'll lose her before long. She's the kind of woman who doesn't want to get her own chocolates; she wants the guy who'll dare all to bring them. Can't he see that?'

'All he sees is some other guy bringing them. You.'

'She flirts because he won't. But she's wise enough to do it with men who won't take up the challenge. If one ever does, she'll run like hell. It's Euan she wants, but too much unwarranted jealousy will kill the relationship.'

'So why are you fanning the jealousy?'

Nick drank more coffee while controlling his resentment. James was merely being diplomatic, not pulling rank. 'Vicky called me offering her help. She was fond of Philip Dunne in the way I guess she's fond of me. She's furious that you and Euan pulled out of the game; she wants to solve the riddle of Dunne's file. Oh yes, she knows about it. Twisted Euan's arm – or something of his – until he told all. She knows people who can supply information I couldn't get. I told her to go ahead provided it didn't cause marital strife.' He countered his friend's gaze. 'We've been over this already. You obeyed orders to keep my mind occupied, I took it further than expected, you're obliged to pull out – diplomatic immunity in another guise – I'm no longer your guest. That makes me a free agent and I guess I *am* like the guy who brings the chocs. I can't give up halfway up the mountain; I have to deliver the goods. I've found Dunne and given him the dignity of a defined resting place; I'm near to understanding those notes of his. I have a week in which to get the remaining answers. If Vicky can speed up the process, I'll let her. Time Euan dragged himself into the twenty-first century or he'll lose his diplomatic posting as well as his wife. Fielding has already sent in one adverse report. Any hint of pistols at dawn and the Gosses will be sent home.'

James poured more coffee. 'Have you finished?'

'Not quite. I'm no more rapaciously interested in Vicky Goss than I am in your Emma.'

'I never suggested you were – in either case. You misread my words. Joyce has moved Emma's room, by the way. She's now on this side of the house.' He gave a faint smile. 'Have to have bloody big ears to eavesdrop.'

The telephone rang briefly, then Joyce called through from the hall that James was wanted. Nick gazed at the trees giving shade and peacefulness to that airy verandah. At the end of seven days he would have to leave this tropical atmosphere for the gentle summertime of England, to battle for his future. Maybe he would come back one day under better circumstances. And stay in a house with no glass in the windows.

James returned and sat heavily. 'That was Inspector Choi. DNA tests show the skeleton isn't Dunne. It's Jimmy Yang. Sorry, Hawk.'

Thirteen

Nick defied Dr McIntosh and swam in the hotel pool that afternoon. Thanks to the antibiotics the wound in his leg was no longer inflamed, and he was so restless only physical activity would get him through the rest of the day. That he had not, after all, offered Philip Dunne a hallowed resting place in his homeland was a curious blow. Determination and defiance faded, leaving a sense of anti-climax; failure even. He abandoned his intention to study the directory of companies. To hell with Vydecker. Men like him invariably survived and prospered, leaving behind a trail of victims.

Needing to work off his pessimistic mood, Nick bent his mind to completing a hundred lengths. When he emerged to lie on a towel-covered lounger he found the exercise had not helped. He still felt depressed, almost taking pleasure in the throbbing wound. The penalty for ignoring James's advice to leave things well alone. What a bloody fool he had been!

That pantomime at Senoko . . . and the one at Vydecker's bank this morning! What the hell did he think he would achieve? He had bent his strict rules regarding other men's wives to pursue some wild idea of piracy; the smuggling of animal parts for Chinese medicines. And God knew what else. Then there was the fiasco with Fleur Yang. All to what purpose? To prove the Hawk was indestructible. Action man personified!

If he was honest he knew he had been the kind of lover who wanted to brave all to bring chocolates. Had he failed to accept that Lara needed to fetch her own? Was that what had driven her away? It remained a mystery because he had binned her letter. Been a bloody fool even then!

The mental scourging continued until he reached the bottom line. James had put it in plain language. Human replacements are cheaper than aircraft. For every washed-up pilot there were twenty boys eager to supplant him. Nick was nearing thirty. He had had plum postings; had served in several war zones. The approval of military chiefs as well as the sun had shone on the AAC's golden boy as he met every challenge with natural skill. But he had been so good at his job he had been given a top-secret mission. And failed!

Dear Christ, the failure had been *spectacular*. Mission aborted. A costly aircraft destroyed; two friends burned with it. Falling into terrorist hands. His present attempt to prove he was equal to any challenge was pathetic. The ragheads *had* destroyed the Hawk: broken his wings. He had once flown as high as the hunters whose name he had been given, but even hawks had eventually to drop to earth.

The familiar demons drove him back to his room and the minibar. *When you're ready to talk about it contact me.* He would never be ready; it had not happened. He opened and drank a second miniature whisky immediately after the first. The demons insisted it *had* happened. He had to silence them; drive them out of his head. He screwed the top from the third bottle. He would start on the gin next. As he swallowed the liquid anaesthetic he stared across the harbour in the direction of Pulau Gombak. Maybe he should go there and live with the evil spirits. *They* would willingly employ him.

He jumped nervously when the phone rang right beside him. For a moment or two he was transfixed by this normality in the midst of horror, then he picked up the receiver with an unsteady hand.

'Hawkwood.'

'Good evening, sir,' said a melodious female voice. 'This is Reception. There is a gentleman here wishing very much to speak to you on a most important matter. He asks if you would do him the honour of coming to the fifth-floor lounge. Captain Hawkwood?' she prompted after a short silence.

'Yes. I'll come,' he agreed jerkily.

In the bathroom he splashed his face with cold water and ran a comb through his hair. Then he changed into shirt, tie and trousers. Only a Chinese would request 'the honour' of a meeting. Inspector Choi to arrest him for the murder of Jimmy Yang, perhaps. Whatever, the call had brought him back from the edge of the abyss quicker than any cocktail of spirits.

He did not immediately see the humourless policeman when he entered the lounge where several groups of chairs were still occupied by businessmen completing afternoon meetings. As he stood wondering if the girl had given him the wrong RV a voice to his right spoke his name. He turned to see a handsome middle-aged Chinese in a dark suit; a stranger. Beside him a striking woman of similar age wearing a smart dress of white-spotted navy silk. Beside her, Fleur Yang.

'I am Henry Yang.' The man gave a hint of a bow before turning to the woman. 'My wife Francoise; my daughter Fleur. How do you do, sir.'

Nick shook his hand, then spoke a brief formal acknowledgement of Mrs and Miss Yang. Fleur merely copied her mother's sober-faced quarter bow with linked hands. No hint that she had ever set him up.

'Will you please sit with us for a short while, Captain?'

Yang waved a hand at a low table half-circled by a curved settee. The Yangs settled on this, leaving a large armchair facing it free for Nick. He sat, trying to push away the memory of that night with the girl who today looked as stunning as ever in a black sheath.

'We wish to express our gratitude to you for recovering the remains of our son; my daughter's brother. The news was given to us late this morning. I immediately informed the members of our extensive family. We felt you would not wish thirty-three people to come, so I am speaking on behalf of them all.'

As Nick was about to embark on a suitable rejoinder, Henry Yang continued. 'Jimmy was a good son; hardworking. He did not wish to join our silk-exporting business as I had hoped, but he studied law and made us very proud when he qualified. He was a little wild, but no more than most young men, and Group Captain Dunne channelled his energy in acceptable directions. That was good. Jimmy was ambitious for a boat of his own. He enjoyed very much to go to sea. We have consoled ourselves that his life ended while he was feeling great happiness. But you have given us back his bones to put with those of his ancestors. We are greatly in your debt, sir.'

Nick was beginning to feel uncomfortable, but he knew he must not dismiss the speech lightly. 'My sincere condolences to all members of your family. A very tragic accident.'

'It was written.'

This stark evidence of mixed cultures took Nick by surprise, as it had during his meeting with Fleur. The French strain in the family that was also echoed in Mrs Yang's first name tended to make one forget their inbred Oriental beliefs.

Henry Yang picked two parcels from beside him on the seat and placed them on the table. 'These represent the gratitude of Jimmy's parents and sister, Captain Hawkwood.' He stood in unison with his wife and daughter. 'You will be welcome in our home whenever you wish to come. Our doors are permanently open for you.'

Nick hastened to rise and shake the man's hand in farewell. The two women silently nodded again, and all three moved off with quiet dignity, leaving him nonplussed. Tempted to seek the bar for a decent-sized drink, he decided to take the packages to his room, shower, and dress for dinner in a top-class restaurant where he could indulge in French cuisine and a bottle of good wine. That should indicate 'bugger off' to any lingering demons.

While he was shaving, the room phone rang again. Maybe this time it was Inspector Choi wanting to arrest him. It was Vicky Goss. Nick was nonplussed anew.

'Euan is listening on the extension so that he can hear what we say to each other,' she said after greeting him. 'This is the first thing. Because he's so mean-spirited about helping you with Phil's file I've been doing it instead. This had led him to believe you and I are having a mad, passionate affair. He's wrong, of course, but I wondered if you'd like to start one as from now.'

'Like a shot, if you weren't married and I wasn't in love with someone else,' he said off the cuff. 'Sorry, Vicky.'

'Just a thought. Well now, would you like the information I got?'

'Yes, please.'

'Customs checks are supposed to be thorough, but so much cargo passes through this port it's reasonably easy for stuff to be brought in illegally. It's impossible to check the contents of every container, and even when they have been checked it's possible for things to be added or extracted before it's shipped on. Our friend admitted that it's not exactly unusual for members of their staff to accept bribes. They try to stamp it out, but it's a fact of life. With me so far?'

'Sure.'

'Now, the Cordova Line running between here and West Africa that you're interested in. A few years ago there were several instances of contraband goods being found – he said there were probably more that missed the checks – but ownership of the line changed hands and it has stopped. At least, they haven't discovered any. It's now owned by an international consortium. Guess the name of one of the directors.'

'John Vydecker.'

'Clever boy!'

'I went to his bank this morning; pretended I had a large sum to invest. They gave me a list of reliable companies. Cordova was one. It's my guess Vydecker is a director of each one on that list. I already know he's influential in Yang Jewellery and Senoko Components.'

Vicky let out a muted squeal. 'That's one of the companies receiving regular shipments through Cordova!'

'Is it, by God?' he breathed. 'So there *is* a link between them. I wonder if Dunne knew what it was.'

'I was so upset that it was Jimmy you found, not Phil,' she said with a sigh. 'Alison won't get her flags and rifle shots over the grave.'

'Maybe next time I look,' he murmured, still struck by this evidence of his suspicions. 'Vicky, did you manage to find out what was delivered to Senoko?'

'Didn't know you wanted that. I could get the answer for you tomorrow.'

Nick dodged that issue. 'Any idea of the regular ports of call for the Cordova ships?'

'Yes. Got a pen?' She read out a list that did not surprise him.

'Just as I thought. All the African ports where dodgy stuff could be picked up. Great!'

'Anything else you need?'

'No. Thanks all the same. I stipulated all along that I didn't want to cause a problem between you and Euan. I'm truly grateful, Vicky. You're an angel.'

'I'd rather be a devil,' she said irrepressibly. 'Take care, Nick.'

'I will. Euan, did you get all that?'

'Sod you, Hawkwood,' came the explosive comment before the line went dead.

In his underpants and with only half his chin shaven, Nick sat pondering all Vicky had told him. An hour ago he had mentally thrown in the towel. Now he was a big step forward along the road to elucidation. Six days left. He hadn't brought Dunne's bones from the sea so they could lie with those of his ancestors, but he could surely catch the poor devil's pirates for him.

The plan to dine in gourmet style no longer appealed. That needed a girl with glowing eyes and soft words sharing his table and making promises with every glance, every gesture. Sighing, he contacted room service and ordered a substantial meal with a bottle of wine.

His glance then fell on the plain-wrapped parcels. Might as well open them. The contents of the larger one astonished him. Heavy jade silk splashed with pink chrysanthemums spilled from it. Even his inexperienced eyes told him this was top-quality fabric.

The smaller package contained a black box with *Yang* engraved on it in white lettering. A jade rhomboid on a fine gold chain lay on white satin inside. He gazed at it with mixed feelings. That girl was surely up to something illicit along with her sponsor, yet she could design jewellery as striking and unusual as this pendant.

The two gifts added up to a very expensive gesture. Did it mean so much to the Yang family to be able to put Jimmy's bones where they should be? Was it usual to give so generously? Singaporean Chinese were intriguing. Highly westernized, contact with them was easy and comfortable until it was shafted by inborn Oriental beliefs. *It was written.*

Had some intangible will sent Jimmy Yang out to sea that day specifically to drown? And had that same force preserved Philip Dunne's life in the air over the Falklands so that he could die with the young Chinese lawyer he had befriended?

Had that SIS agent lost last-minute control of the defector, and had he, himself, been sent out to fall into the hands of merciless fanatics because it had been written? Was this a realistic creed, or was it merely a way of dealing with disappointment, grief, disaster? Laying responsibility at the door of the Fates maybe dispensed with the anguish of thinking *if only.*

He ate his meal pondering this concept. Perhaps it had not been mere unlucky chance that Jon had passed that house in Bosnia and heard children screaming. Back in the depths of timelessness, the mystical powers of good and evil had tossed a coin and decided that outcome as they decided everything.

He finished off the wine as he gazed out at the night, sensing a curious peace descending on him. He could not have prevented his father from descending into an alcoholic hell, nor his mother from leaving them without a backward glance. Lara had not run from *him* that terrible day. She had simply done what had been planned long, long ago. Not her decision; not his fault!

He fell asleep, realizing his future was not such an unknown quantity. What was written would happen. It was out of his hands.

Dressing for breakfast, Nick noticed an envelope lying inside his door. It must have been delivered while he was in the shower. Jon had faxed the answers regarding Rees and Hardy. The exercise had been facilitated by contacting one of their father's former colleagues, whom they had known well from boyhood. Matt Coolidge could get information about almost anything from friends and acquaintances, who expected favours in return. The names of Rees and Hardy directors were pretty run of the mill. A couple of retired politicians, several entrepreneurs, a peer or two and a brace of women. Lady Felicia Graves, former nubile actress who had married a microchip tycoon and inherited his millions six months later, had been fully 'exposed' by *Hello!* magazine. Lady Blanche Fielding was unknown to Nick. Never having mixed with the aristocracy, all he knew about the breed was from frequent scandals in the press.

He scanned the list of regular overseas customers; those that Matt could trace. The armed forces of a number of small nations. Civilian bodies such as coastguards, marine police, air ambulance services, who all used R and H tracking systems. Builders of hydrofoils or ocean-going ferries. At the bottom, several shipping lines. The name Cordova jumped up from the page to set Nick breathing in triumph, *'Yes!'* Those West African ships surely held the solution to Dunne's file. It was within his grasp. No way would he give up.

While eating breakfast he studied the grid references Dunne had noted, and plotted them on the chart James had given him. As before, they appeared haphazard with no link between them. Dammit, there had to be one. Then, as yet another Fleur Yang clone glided across to pour more coffee for him,

256

Nick realized it had been staring him in the face. And what a link it was! The common factor to them all was their proximity to Pulau Gombak.

The coffee grew cold as he stared at the chart, deep in thought. Vicky's Customs friend said the contraband activity had stopped when a new international consortium took over the Cordova Line.

Men with brains and know-how. Men with wealth and loyal manpower behind them. Men with connections in all the right places. Men with few principles and governed by greed. Men like John Vydecker!

The girl brought a clean cup and saucer, poured hot coffee, removed the other. Nick was unaware of her. His pulse was racing with excitement. What if there were pirates *and* smugglers in the scenario; if Cordova ships carried contraband goods unknown to their crews? Unknown save to one, who passed information to a contact in Singapore. Then, at a prearranged RV the vessel was boarded and robbed at sea. A common enough occurrence, except that these pirates steal things the captain isn't aware of carrying. Reports on the incident would record the theft of normal cargo, and the contraband was landed secretly at some point along the coast under cover of darkness.

Absently drinking the coffee, Nick gazed at the blob on the chart that was Pulau Gombak, three-quarters surrounded by a reef. A place haunted by evil spirits. An island neither seafarers nor fishermen would approach. A dot in the ocean with so fearsome a reputation even shipping kept well clear. The perfect area for a highly organized enterprise.

Walking back to his room along the balconies around the impressive atrium, Nick was drawn from his deep thoughts by a resonant female voice announcing his name. Louise Sheridan in tight blue linen trousers, tight white cotton shirt and blue mesh baseball cap was watching his approach with prurient interest.

'Thought you'd gone back to l'il old England,' she said as they closed. 'Haven't seen you around.'

'Been scuba-diving off one of the islands.'

She made round eyes at him. 'Aren't we the big macho male! Daddy's going out to Sudong Island with some military guys to watch them firing on their gunnery range. Mom and I are invited by their wives to a coffee meeting at some club of theirs. Dullsville, but it helps Daddy's business deals along.' Her sexy smile washed over him. 'Keeps him sweet so's we can shop with no upper limit. Bought a real neat swimsuit held together by tiny gold chains. I'll be wearing it for tea beside the pool at four this afternoon. Maybe you'll see it.'

'Your dishy tycoon headed west again?' he asked dryly.

Her eyes flashed. 'His technique hadn't advanced beyond college boy tumbles.'

'Disappointing for you.' He made to pass her. 'I'll have to miss the gold chains. Appointment with the airline doc. Make the most of Dullsville . . . for Daddy's sake.'

He was in his room before a train of thought prompted fresh speculation. American 'Daddy' who was off to watch the Army firing was ruled by the business maxim: If *I* don't deal in this, or with them, someone else will. Scruples were swept aside in the quest for gain. He went in where others feared to tread if there was a chance of making dollars.

Nick swiftly unfolded the chart once more and studied the crosses with which he had marked Dunne's grid references. All within easy reach of Gombak. An international consortium would consist of men from varying nations, most of which probably lay in the West. Would these shrewd, unscrupulous moguls believe in *feng shui*? Would ruthless, hardheaded entrepreneurs be influenced by ancient Oriental beliefs and myths? They might regularly ship prohibited ingredients for Eastern remedies and potions, but would scorn to use them.

He took a deep breath. What if the pirates took their plunder to Gombak, not to Singapore? After the vessel's captain reported the theft, customs officials would be patrolling the coast watching for the movement of stolen cargo. How simple to dump it where no one would dare to set foot, until the pressure eased. Then it could be moved to its true destination.

Bouncing theories around in his mind, Nick tried to recall all he had heard about Gombak. Shipping came to grief on the rocks: a narrow channel through the reef. The Japanese used Gombak for obscene purposes. Fast boats were heard going back and forth. If they were able to breach the reef, so could others.

He had flown over the island. Wall to wall vegetation. Yet the Japanese had reputedly built a lookout tower and manned it for several years. It must therefore be possible to store plundered cargo for a mere several weeks.

Lara had spoken of currents sweeping flotsam towards Pelingi and Gombak; mentioned the surprising items thrown overboard. Pots and pans, clothing – even an armchair. Discarded cargo from crates also containing smuggled goods that earned the real bonanza?

It added up; made sense. Why else would Dunne and Jimmy Yang have taken *Sea Harrier* way out into shipping lanes? The old, familiar sense of adventure flowed through him; the desire to dare and win. The date of his return flight threatened. Act now!

Ferdy was as cheery as ever when he answered Nick's call. 'So how's Jacques Cousteau today? I'm trying to guess whether you're aiming to topple Gray from his pedestal, or you've taken my advice and moved in on the luscious Lara in his absence. You'd have gorgeous kids, you two.'

'Ferdy, do you have an aircraft with floats?'

'Would any self-respecting hire company at a former seaplane base *not* have one?'

'I'll be with you by ten thirty. I've only landed on water twice, and then in a helo, so I'll want a package that includes a pilot. You, preferably.'

'To go where?'

'Gombak.'

'What the bloody hell—'

'Ten thirty. Fuel her up so's she's ready to go.'

It was a beautiful blue and white float plane; graceful lines, compact cockpit and fat, oversized feet. The sight of the dainty aircraft rocking gently beside a slipway on gleaming water beneath clear blue heavens aroused no aesthetic appreciation in Nick. He saw merely the means to an end.

Ferdy would fly it; said she was his prize baby who needed specialist handling. While he did the prelims he curbed his curiosity but gave it full rein once they had skimmed over the water, sending up sun-sparkled spray, and lifted from one element to another.

'So what's this all about, Nick? I've postponed two bookings for this. Shall have to smooth feathers when I get back.'

'I owe you one, pal.'

Ferdy grinned. 'Tell the truth, fancied something with more of a kick in it, though can't think what you plan to do at that spooky place.'

Knowing the Australian deserved the whole story Nick embarked on it, omitting only his visit to Sembawang. 'If I'm right there'll be stuff stored there, or strong evidence of regular traffic.'

'Jeez, how the hell did you figure all that from a list made by a guy who can't explain it himself?'

'I've been trained to make sense of things; put two and two together to make an understandable sum.'

'You really believe in all this?'

'Until I'm proved wrong. Can you land near the gap in the reef? I'll swim ashore and take a look around. Might take a while. That OK?'

Ferdy nodded. 'No way I'm leaving without you. Waiting time bumps up the bill and that can't be bad.' A few minutes later he asked, 'What if you come up against a coupla guys camped there with this supposed booty?'

Nick was watching Pelingi growing larger as they approached. 'They won't know I've been and gone.'

'Ha, stupid question to ask a soldier, I guess. If you get your proof, what then?'

'I'll present my case to the relevant authorities and hope to God they take it seriously. I'm leaving on the twenty-fourth. No choice. I *am* still in the Army.'

'Any reason you wouldn't be?'

Hearing curiosity in his companion's voice, Nick realized he had spoken defensively. He shrugged it off. 'Leave suggests you're a free agent. You tend to forget they can call you back at any time. Your life belongs to them during your term of service. They order; you obey. Military law has to be severe. Prevents men calling a strike, like civilians. No such thing as a go-slow or work to rule.' He sighed, momentarily back in the life he was describing. 'The lads try it on, mind you. Have to watch them, although the wise commander knows when to turn a blind eye.'

He was returned to the present by Ferdy saying, 'You love it, don't you?'

'There's Attard's camp,' he said neutrally.

Always ready for some aerial fun, Ferdy swooped down to roar over the clustered tents in noisy salute. Then, in case they had not recognized who was flying the float plane, he did it again and got several shaken fists from the team members.

He laughed boisterously. 'We'll drop in on the buggers on the way back.'

'Only if you deduct that time from my account.'

'Skinflint!'

They banked and headed for the further island; a dark-green shape edged with a frill of spume marking the reef. Nick began to tense. He recognized the overture to any military exercise, the preparation for action. Not exactly fear, although there was a healthy dash of it in there with excitement and heightened adrenalin. If anyone should be on the island they would not miss the approach of an aircraft. Unless they were camped right on the water's edge, the time it would take them to draw near enough to see it riding the water would be long enough for Nick to slip into the sea and sink beneath the surface.

He had no qualms about swimming to Gombak. Staying underwater most of the time, he would surely approach unseen. Then he would judge the right moment to emerge and slip under cover. He had not lightly been dubbed the Hawk. His ability to take others unawares was renowned. However, as he watched their approach to this knot of land said to be inhabited by evil, he felt certain no one would be guarding the stores. Gombak's fearsome reputation was protection enough.

Ferdy circled. It was easy to spot the gap in the reef from the air. No boat drawn up on the shore. That ruled out the unlucky coincidence of clashing with the collection of stored plunder. Good. It reduced the risks.

Ferdy cut his speed and banked prior to landing. 'Can't get too close in. Bloody swell around the rocks would have her arse up in no time.'

Nick nodded. 'Put down wherever you can.'

'Reckon you can swim through that?'

'No probs.'

'Watch yourself, mate. Current's very strong.'

'I'll go with it. Should be all right on the way in. Coming back could be a problem. You might have to throw me a line. Can do?'

'You've got it, but you're mad crazy, you know that?'

Nick watched with a pilot's interest and admiration as Ferdy brought the elegant aircraft from the clear air to a shifting, gleaming, transparent surface. While he stripped to swim trunks Nick resolved to extend his own experience with float planes. This one bumped along sending spray flying past the windows until she sank almost with a sigh on her sturdy floats, and slowed to a halt. Ferdy had no need to swing the aircraft round so that Nick could enter the water unseen from the island; the current did the job for them. It also showed Nick it was flowing in his favour. He would have to fight it to save being swept past the gap in the reef, but he was prepared for that.

He turned to Ferdy. 'I'll signal from the shore when I'm about to swim back. Taxi down as far as that spur. The current will take hold as soon as I come through the gap in the reef. Keep your eye on me and throw the line in good time. If I miss it we'll have another go further along. I can keep going until we bring it off. After white water rapids this should be a doddle.'

'If Kim knew I was here she'd be offering up prayers to the gods. In her opinion this place is fully bedevilled.'

'If I don't reappear you'll know she's right,' grunted Nick, lowering himself on to the float and pulling goggles over his eyes.

'How long do I wait?'

'If I haven't signalled from the beach in forty-five minutes radio for a high-speed launch . . . and you'll know *I'm* right. Smugglers are using Gombak.'

He dropped into the sea and felt the chill strike his body. With more time at his disposal he would have bought a wetsuit, but he was not sub-diving and the swim to the island should not take more than twenty minutes. Beyond the reef the quieter water would be warmer.

Free of the floats, he took a deep breath and sank below the surface. The pull was stronger than he expected and his first worry arose. If he missed the gap would Ferdy spot his head in the spume and put into action the pick-up plan? Going up for air, he saw he had travelled much too fast parallel with the break where the sea rolled without sending up spray. Sod it! He should have started out further east.

Backing his hunch that there was nobody presently on Gombak, he abandoned underwater swimming for the advantage of knowing where to head. Even then he almost missed the gap. Near to the reef the sea grew wilder, but the backward flow of waves hitting the rocks overrode the steady pull of the current. This made it easier for Nick to take advantage of the stronger tug of swell around the irregular ridge.

Nearing this, he submerged to take a look at what he was

being drawn towards. The gap was clearly visible as a much lighter area in the foaming depths; easier to identify below the surface than above it. He began porpoising at regular intervals, and adjusting his direction.

In no time he was snatched up in the crashing turbulence around the rocks, fighting for survival in a situation he had badly underestimated. More than once he was dashed against rock then dragged back with a ferocity that tore at his flesh. Gasping, flailing, he drew breath into his lungs and dived to where the surface turmoil was reduced to a mere subtle, insidious commotion.

Riding the reef swell was too dangerous, so Nick propelled himself through the cascading miasma towards the paler area praying he would get through it before he was forced to seek air.

The roaring in his ears matched that of the element around him by the time he broke surface. The pain in his chest was so great he felt it must burst open. But he was beyond the reef. Just. The sea's demand for a sacrifice had been foiled. He floated gently, glancing at his watch. Twenty minutes had passed. Better get ashore fast. Ferdy had to be reassured, and the only way back to the float plane was through that same perilous gap.

Nick struck out for the shore. Easy swimming. Until he grew aware of a dark shadow in the water ahead. Not an inner bank of rock! He dived, then surfaced swiftly. This island *was* bedevilled! Between himself and the meagre shore-line was a floating mass of Medusa.

Treading water, he reasoned that his theory must after all be wrong. No launch could come here with that weed ready to wrap itself around propellers and keel. Was there any point in searching for a way past the growth so that he could set foot on the cursed Gombak? The rebel in him, the trait that had driven him to succeed so often, urged him to do now what he had come for. He owed Dunne that much.

Diving again, he swam alongside the weed in the hope that it had not yet formed a complete stranglehold of the island. He was forced to surface twice before reaching a gap

that would give him access to the shore. He swam to it
thinking there would probably be no way through in a month's
time.

His feet touched shingle. He walked on to Gombak,
pushing up the goggles to survey the wall of trees lining the
shore. No sign of life. Now he had battled his way through
he had not expected any. A small boat could possibly come
and go, but who would consider it necessary to remain on
guard?

Blood was running from several gashes on his left arm.
A glance at his thigh showed that the close encounter with
rocks had reopened an inch of the stab wound, also oozing
blood. Nothing he could do about it. Get on with the job!
Pulling from the back of his swim trunks the plastic pool
sandals he had tucked there, he slid his feet in them and
turned to signal his arrival to Ferdy. His means of escape
looked a long way off.

The sandals protected his feet from spiny or poisonous
creatures to be found in places like this, but he still trod with
caution. The tales of evil spirits, of screams being heard,
seemed entirely feasible now he was about to enter the gloomy
interior. The hairs on the back of his neck rose as trees closed
in around him, bringing an eerie silence. The ghost of Wu
surely hovered here.

He had been in jungle many times, dressed in a cam suit
and tough boots, smeared with insect repellent and armed
with an SA 80. So what in God's name was an Army captain
doing here practically naked and minus a weapon of any
kind? It was worse than irresponsible. He had surrendered
to impulse, in haste to find the answers before he must fly
home. No planning. No preparation. No bloody *brains* behind
his actions!

At that point he realized he was treading a rough track
formed of chipped rock that ran ahead as far as he could see.
His pulse quickened. No evil spirits were responsible for this
piece of basic engineering. It was man made!

Smartening his pace, he was soon sweating heavily and

bombarded by mosquitoes savouring his blood, yet he pushed on eagerly. The track could accommodate a small wagon or trolley. It must lead to a store of some kind.

The atmosphere grew dimmer, even more stifling. The trees now formed a dark-green canopy blocking air and sunlight. There were noises in the undergrowth; rustlings and slitherings. He glanced at his watch. If he had not reappeared within forty-five minutes Ferdy would radio the Navy boys. So he could continue for another eighteen before turning back.

The way narrowed as vegetation began invading that corridor of access. Vegetation that was unbroken, untrampled. Nick frowned. Slowed. This section of the track had not been used for some while. Anticipation died as reason told him no one would bother to transport plunder this far when it would be well out of sight just yards from the beach. On the brink of turning back, Nick saw it rising up between the trees. The Japanese watch tower! It had to be. Excitement flared. Bugger the passing time! He *had* to investigate.

Ten yards further on, a figure silently materialized from the dimness, setting Nick's heart pumping with adrenalin rush. Automatically tightening his hold on a weapon he was not carrying, he swiftly scanned the immediate area, every nerve tensed, knowing he was dangerously vulnerable. No sign, no sound, no hint of others in the vicinity. Poised to dive for cover, Nick then registered that the other held no weapon. Indeed, there was nothing threatening about this gaunt, staring man with straggly hair and beard, dressed in ragged shirt and shorts.

'Who are you?' Nick asked quietly. But he already knew he had found Philip Dunne. *It was written.*

Fourteen

E arly evening. They sat on the Wellnuts' wide verandah with pre-dinner drinks: James, Joyce, Euan and Vicky Goss, and Nick. James was so disconcerted he failed to comment on his friend's dangerously casual solo invasion of Gombak. Joyce had muttered about the guy who delivers chocolates; Vicky was highly emotional. Euan was impossible to read. Nick himself was lethargic to the point of dreaminess. It had been quite a day.

As neither Nick nor James had met Philip Dunne, Euan had had to make a positive identification to Inspector Choi at the hospital two hours ago. Diplomatic immunity prevented further police involvement, although the High Commission would later produce a report that would enable Singapore Police to close their file on Jimmy Yang's death. Choi did not hide his dissatisfaction and made heavy remarks about Captain Hawkwood's amazing ability to find men lost at sea. James smoothly engineered his departure before the question of Nick's immunity could be raised.

As Cranford Fielding was still laid low by dengue fever and his deputy was attending a conference in Kuala Lumpur, James was handling everything. A fortunate circumstance for those most closely concerned.

In response to Ferdy's mayday call a crew of sailors, armed to the teeth in expectation of confronting pirates caught red-handed with their contraband, had been less than happy with a Robinson Crusoe situation instead. The captain of the high-speed launch had declared that it was not his job to rescue crazy Englishmen stranded on a haunted island, but he seemed impressed by Dunne's ability to survive there for so long.

James had sent an ambulance to collect the pair and take them to the private hospital used by British diplomatic staff. Robert McIntosh had examined the man returned from the dead and declared him to be in need of little more than rest and nourishment. The pilot who made a hobby of jungle jaunts had known every means of staying alive in deprived situations.

The Scottish doctor had also treated the cuts on Nick's body and given him another course of antibiotics, while offering his opinion of tourists with a penchant for gung-ho adventures. Yet his parting handshake had been firm and accompanied by a smile. 'Well done, man.'

Knowing what Jon had discovered about Alison Dunne's lover, James had suggested he contact Sir Charles Fanshawe when Philip declined personally to inform his wife of his rescue.

'It'd be too much of a shock for her to pick up the phone and hear my voice after wreaths cast on water and a memorial service. She and Charles are close. He'll break the staggering news gently. He can also tell the FO, the RAF . . . and anyone else who might be interested in my survival.'

It had been said with great weariness, but Nick had detected bitterness in the man's tone. Poor devil, knowing his reappearance would prove an unwelcome shock for the wife who believed she was a widow. So James had completed the necessary formalities back at his house. The younger children were in bed – Emma was fortuitously on a two-day school trip to a rubber plantation – and the time had come for Nick to fill in the remaining gaps concerning his discovery of the former Defence Adviser.

In truth, he longed to sit quietly in that house open to the evening air and think his own thoughts until sleep descended. No hope of that. He owed these people an explanation, because his headstrong decision this morning had now made Philip Dunne's catastrophic voyage very much their concern.

Vicky could hold back her curiosity no longer. 'I still don't understand how Phil came to be on Gombak.'

'He's terribly confused, but he managed to give me some details in fits and starts,' Nick said.

'Did you tell him you found Jimmy Yang's bones?'

'That can wait. He knew Jimmy was dead.' Nick's brow furrowed in concentration as he relayed his interpretation of the garbled story Philip had given him. 'They were apparently making for Pelingi to anchor for the night. Sun was low and blinding by the time they reckoned they'd soon make a landfall. They then heard a great roar and turned away from the sun to see a fast launch shoot out from behind Gombak. *Wham!* Phil was flung into the water. Couldn't see much with the glare on the surface, but he soon came across bits of wreckage. He and Jimmy were wearing lifejackets yet the Chinese was nowhere in sight. Phil thought the launch's propeller must have caught the lad.

'By then Phil was aware that the current was sweeping him towards Gombak.' He looked around at his friends. 'It's too strong to fight. I discovered that this morning. Phil was vague about the lapse of time between the collision and finding himself on a patch of rough beach. He must have been dragged through the gap I found.'

'Devil's own luck,' murmured Euan.

Nick was unsure whether he referred to him or Philip Dunne. 'His watch gave him the time, the date, the magnetic north and other info useful to a castaway. He's an expert on survival, so he survived.'

'But *how*?' demanded Vicky, eyes huge with excitement.

'By catching fish, birds, even snakes; by eating fruits and boiled roots. Anything that provided nourishment.' He nodded at James and Euan. 'We've all done survival jaunts. When you're hungry you'll eat anything.' He pushed away thoughts of food bowls that rattled on stone floors, but were not really there. 'Water was no problem. He collected rain from the frequent storms. And here's where he *did* have the Devil's own luck, Euan. He discovered the old Jap watchtower. It's little more than a rotting skeleton, but there's a subterranean chamber evidently used by the soldiers on duty. Four iron bedsteads, cooking pots and earthenware bowls – all left there when we took Singapore back. He showed me some basic tools he'd discovered; thick with rust but a few were usable.'

'For what?' asked Vicky, still incredulous.

'Making a raft. I deduced from Phil's rambling monologue that the first he made was smashed up by a storm before it was completed. His second attempt has got as far as a grid of branches bound by creepers. He'd initially written *HELP* with bits of rock on the beach, but they were also washed away during a storm. Bit of a longshot, that. I would never have spotted it from the air, so passing jets certainly wouldn't.'

'But he *tried*. He tried *everything*,' cried Vicky fervently. 'I think he's terrific.'

Euan visibly resented her admiration and attempted to dampen it. 'It wasn't too clever to get himself in that predicament in the first place. What the hell was he doing in a small boat way out around those islands?'

'I imagine it was for the same reason Nick went there today,' James said dryly, turning to Nick. 'Are you going to explain?'

Nick fixed him with a look. 'Is that file to become general knowledge now?'

'Are Joyce and Vicky to hear your interpretation of it? I imagine so. They know half already. As to *general* knowledge, I'll reserve judgement until Philip is lucid enough to explain his notes to us. There's a chance we're wrong.'

'You mean *I'm* wrong, don't you? If you recall, you washed your hands of any involvement. High Comm staff couldn't be mixed up in local affairs; had to be careful not to adopt colonial attitudes.'

'Just answer Euan's question,' James said, with a hint of exasperation. 'We *are* mixed up in it now.'

Nick would have liked another whisky, but he felt too tired to get up and pour it. James had stopped playing host; wanted

270

to firm up on the present situation in case of official questions on the subject. The cuts and mosquito bites on Nick's body were bothering him; his limbs ached from the strenuous battle against the sea that morning. It was difficult to hold his wayward thoughts together. He addressed Euan initially.

'Briefly, I reached the conclusion that illegal substances were being brought from West Africa on the Cordova Line ships, which were intercepted by men on fast launches who removed them before the vessels docked. These attacks were recorded as piracy with details of cargo lifted each time. But I guessed the captains were unaware they were carrying the real prize. It was never listed, so the traffic continued undiscovered.'

'Traffic in what?' asked Euan stonily.

'Rhino horn, monkey glands, animal skins – all the banned items Africa has that earn big money in Far Eastern markets.'

'Pretty wild guesswork,' Euan said derisively.

'Not when you study Dunne's notes,' Nick countered, growing irritated.

'Go on,' urged Vicky.

He sighed. 'I had another look at the list of grid references and realized they were all in the vicinity of Gombak. That's when I suspected the island of being the place where the contraband was stored until it could be delivered to the black marketeers. I was wrong about that, but the fact that a launch smashed into *Sea Harrier* close to Gombak must confirm my reasoning that the stuff is being lifted from ships in that area every time. Must be a connection somewhere. In a day or two we can check with Phil; see if it's wild guesswork, Euan.'

'So you got Ferdy to fly you out to Gombak thinking you'd find all that African stuff,' said Vicky.

'I think I did it to find a man who clearly isn't meant to die yet,' Nick said slowly. 'How else would he have left that island?'

There was a curious silence, until Joyce said, 'You look

271

all in, Nick. Why don't you stay overnight? The room you used before. I'll get Cora to bring you a tray. You can eat dinner in peace.'

He gave a sleepy nod. 'Sounds like a great idea. Thanks.'

The meal was still on the tray when Cora took Nick a morning cup of tea. He had slept the sleep of exhaustion for eleven hours.

Alison Dunne had been persuaded not to fly out to be with her husband because he would be returning to England in a day or two. That was the reason given to everyone who rang the High Commission or the Gosses' home after reading the *Straits Times*. Flowers and baskets of fruit arrived at the hospital along with cards and letters from friends the Dunnes had made during their time in Singapore. No visitors were allowed. Radio, TV and news reporters were specifically denied access.

In fact, a sailor on the rescue launch sold the story to a local reporter. It was picked up by international agencies, and by evening the double sensation was in print worldwide.

British fighter ace turned diplomat, believed lost at sea, has been found alive after eight weeks on reputed torture island by British Army pilot recently snatched from terrorists by SAS. What a story!

Philip Dunne's career and private life were given in detail; the colourful history of Miles Hawkwood and his sons lost no drama in the retelling. Nick's swim to an island believed to have evil connections was given prominence, and he was said to be living up to the nickname *Hawk* given by military colleagues familiar with his courage and daring.

British TV correspondents with cameramen were desperate for pictures and interviews. The Wellnuts' house became a refuge for Nick. One of James's male clerks collected his things from the Oriental and settled his account. Not unhappy to be back in the house he loved, Nick nevertheless fretted over the restriction on his movements. Four days left in which to link Vydecker with the smuggling racket and to get even with Fleur Yang. Philip could provide vital facts, but McIntosh would not yet allow visitors.

The phone rang almost non-stop during that first day. Joyce always answered, efficiently silencing persistent reporters and bare acquaintances seeking reflected glory with invitations that included their military guest. Any calls she was uncertain about Joyce put on hold, until she discovered whether or not Nick wanted to take them. One he immediately declined was from Louise Sheridan, who claimed Nick had become a close friend and would surely want to accept Daddy's invitation to dinner. He told Joyce to say he was studying top-secret orders that would mean an immediate return to the War Office in London.

Towards late afternoon she came to the verandah where Nick was enjoying the breeze that usually presaged a downpour. 'Do you want to speak to Lara?'

Did he? After all the publicity, did he? He hedged. 'Where is she?'

'On Pelingi, I imagine.' She regarded him shrewdly. 'I can say you're sleeping, or pissed out of your skull. It's up to you.'

He would be flying home in four days. End of story. He nodded and walked to where the receiver lay on a table. Joyce took the chair he had vacated, too far away to overhear.

'Hallo, Lara.'

'Hi, Nick.' She sounded very calm.

'How's Medusa?'

'Still propagating.'

'There's a mass of it circling Gombak. Intended to let you know before I left.'

'On the twenty-fourth, still?'

'Yes.'

A short silence. 'I just wanted to say I'm glad you found Philip Dunne. Especially not as a skeleton. You can get to know him now.'

'That's right.' He could see her so clearly; see the tents

and the rest of the team beavering away; see the beach, small waves lapping it, trees stilled now the stormwind had died – all of it silvered by the moon. And he wanted to be there.

'Nick, I'm sorry about all that crap on your family history in the papers.'

'Yes.'

'And I didn't know anything about your ordeal in Iraq. I truly didn't.'

'You wouldn't. Wouldn't make the headlines in Oz.'

'Your other world.'

'Yes.'

Another short silence. 'Well, safe flight home.'

'Thanks.'

'Bye, then.'

'Bye.'

'*Nick*!' It was swift and sharp before he could replace the receiver.

'Yes?'

'I've written another letter. Please don't bin it unread.'

She disconnected, and he returned to the verandah deep in thought. Joyce glanced up. 'OK?'

'She wanted to say goodbye.'

She handed him a double whisky topped up with water. 'Thought we both deserve one after recent events. Cheers.'

A surge of unexpected emotion roughened his voice as he gripped the cut crystal without drinking. 'I'll miss you when I get home.'

She shook her head. 'You'll be too busy sorting things out, getting back to work.'

'I don't know,' he murmured, studying the clear liquid as he battled with the dread he was forever thrusting away. 'I just don't know.'

She leaned forward, kissed him lightly on the cheek. 'I do. You'll be fine, Nick.'

The sound of running feet broke the moment. Emma hurtled along the verandah and stopped a few feet from them, her face working, her eyes wild and shimmery as they focused on her hero.

'The others told us as soon as we got back from the trip. *Everyone* knew about it but me. *Why* was I away when you ... you ... oh, Nick, you're ... you're ...' She broke down and began to sob as only distressed adolescents can.

Joyce cast Nick an apologetic glance, then went to her distraught daughter to lead her gently away. 'It's *your* house Nick's staying in, *your* family he regards as his friends. When you go to school on Monday you can remind everyone of that and crow over *them*.'

Nick swallowed the whisky in two gulps, then went to his room before further drama could be enacted. He sat for untold minutes lost in another world. *Your other world.*

The storm veered away to break over Jahore on the mainland of Malaysia, close enough to be reached over a causeway. The breeze dropped, leaving the familiar humidity as the sun sank in a purple shadow cast by retreating storm clouds. The tropical suddenness of day into night spurred Nick into action.

After scribbling an explanatory note he slipped from his room and down the back staircase to the kitchen, where he asked Cora to give the envelope to Mrs Wellnut. He then crossed the grounds at the rear of the house, absently nodded to the bemused security guard, climbed a tree overhanging the wall and dropped to the ground outside. He began walking.

Quiet tree-lined streets soon gave way to flashing headlights, shop windows, laughing and chattering, motor horns, fairy lights, neon signs. Chinese faces, Indian faces, Malay faces, some revealing cross-cultures, Western faces, all surged past him. Nick saw only one. Bearded, gaunt, incredulous. Philip Dunne. For seventeen days that man had given him a purpose; a goal. There had been motivation for each day. That had been snatched from him. Dunne had now become everyone's concern.

Nick lost count of the number of bars he entered, of how long he wandered aimlessly feeling a stark sense of loss and isolation. He saw water. Clear, crystal water dancing and sparkling with pinpoints of light. Young men and girls were sitting on a low wall surrounding the fountain, laughing and flirting together. They moved to make space for him. He palmed some water, splashed it over his face.

Nick sat there for a long time. He felt too tired to move on, and it was pleasant with the fine spray dampening his skin and listening to the cascade splashing into the pool. When he finally emerged from his thoughts he found he was alone and the fountain no longer played behind him. The ring of small lights had gone out; there was just a dark gleam of water within the circular wall. The lovers had gone home. Shops had finally closed. Those few people left in the street walked purposefully towards nearby apartment blocks.

A clock somewhere struck three. Nick's watch gave him the same information. Time for bed. He hailed a cruising taxi and gave directions. A short time later the driver drew up before a hotel and quoted the fare. Too exhausted to argue, Nick paid him and entered the dim foyer. A turbaned Sikh asked him to sign in then gave him a room key. The corridor was empty and hushed as he searched for room 28. Stripping off, Nick slid thankfully between the sheets.

In the morning he found he was in Hotel Pelingi.

A 6 a.m. call to James met with his advice to return at once. 'Today's shift of newshounds hasn't arrived yet. Get here before they do. We'll almost certainly be able to talk to Phil later this morning. I want you and Euan there. He can make his own way; we'll go in my official car with Mahadzir driving. Means we can hop out quick at the clinic and call him up when we plan to leave. Bloody media!'

Nothing was said, no questions were asked about last night when Nick reached the house. Normal good mornings were exchanged as if he had been there all the time. It being Saturday, the children were not going off to school, but Joyce must have set some rules. Gina and Robin were exaggeratedly subdued while Emma gazed in silence at her hero and refused everything but a cup of tea. Nick ate heartily, having missed dinner last night, then took the *Straits Times* and another cup of coffee to the settee on the verandah. James came to him there.

'We're off. I've contacted Euan. He's on his way. Mahadzir's bringing the car round now.'

A few reporters with flash cameras chased them fifty yards along the road. All they would get were fuzzy images of two men on the back seat. A bit pointless when they had already printed clear squadron pictures of both James and Nick in flying suits near their aicraft, looking suitably heroic.

Despite having had only three hours' sleep Nick was hyped-up Last night's depression had evaporated. He could not wait to compare notes on that file, and spring the surprise about the real Lapis Lazuli.

The patient was delighted to see them. 'God preserve me from nurses. I daresay when you're in terrible pain they're a blessing, but they can be a bore when there's nothing wrong. They keep saying I need fattening up. I'm not a bloody Christmas turkey. Hi, Euan, how's your chirpy girl Vicky?'

'Fine. She sends her . . . best wishes,' Euan said, very obviously toning down the message.

Philip nodded at James. 'You're the lucky blighter who took over my job. How did Charles Fanshawe take the news?'

'With understandable emotion. He thinks highly of you.'

'It's mutual. He's a great guy. One of the old school of diplomats. Devoted to Queen and country; defends both with great energy.' Without reference to his wife and daughter, he then turned to Nick and grinned.

'You look more the part with clothes on. Those plastic shoes were hysterical.' He swiftly sobered. 'If you hadn't arrived when you did I could well have been a goner by midsummer. Did I thank you?'

'No need.'

'I've been reading about you in the *Telegraph*. Quite a guy! Found young Jimmy during a diving session amid voracious weed.'

'I thought it was you until the experts found otherwise.'

Philip looked puzzled. 'They could have been anyone's remains. Why think they were mine?'

James and Euan had taken chairs along the rear wall so the focus was on Nick. He saw his opening and went for it.

'I had a hunch *Sea Harrier* had gone down somewhere near Pelingi. For the past two weeks I've been slowly making sense of those notes in a blue folder James found in your desk.'

Philip's expression underwent a slow change as memory returned. 'My God, that file! The damning evidence with no proof.'

'I've deciphered a lot,' Nick told him eagerly. 'And added to it. Jimmy Yang's bones indicated that I was on the right track, so I investigated Gombak expecting to find contraband stored there. You were a gratifying bonus.'

'*I* considered that possibility, which was why I took *Sea Harrier* out there for a looksee,' returned Philip with increasing vivacity. 'Unfortunately, they got me first. Have to disappoint you, Nick. No one came near that island while I was there.'

'It was merely a theory. But we're right about interceptions taking place in that area around Pelingi and Gombak – hence the launch that hit you.' He leaned forward in his urgency to consolidate his interpretation of Philip's red-starred vessels.

'Cordova Line ships are carrying banned goods from West African ports, at a guess without the knowledge of their captains. A local syndicate sends a launch to stop and board the vessels, lifting cargo in which the true prize is hidden. The official report of piracy lists only the loss of mundane merchandise. Much of it is then dumped from the launch before it arrives at an RV with some inconspicuous vessel, which transports the smuggled goods without difficulty to a spot where trucks – whatever – are waiting.' He frowned. 'Gombak as a temporary store was an attractive idea. I don't know the Singapore coastline well enough to guess the true offloading point. Euan could probably make a stab at it, if he had a mind to.'

Euan responded sharply. 'If Phil had worked with me on it at the time, I could probably have cracked it without much trouble. Going off half-cock on *Sea Harrier* wouldn't have been necessary . . . and he wouldn't have spent eight deprived weeks on Gombak.'

Philip got to his feet and walked around the bed to perch on it facing the angry Navy man. 'You have to understand it was all circumstantial, based on hearsay. It was also bloody difficult to believe. One false move and I could have created a hell of a stink. I felt the least number of people involved the better. Until I had undeniable proof, that is. I also had a personal desire to pull it off single-handed.' He gave a bitter laugh. 'Made a right Charlie of myself instead.'

'No!' said Nick forcefully. 'Those notes showed you were almost there. I've uncovered a lot more. If we collate our intelligence I reckon we'll come up with the final piece in the scenario. The proof you're after.'

'And *you're* after,' accused Euan hotly.

Nick ignored him. 'It's my opinion this is a highly organized criminal operation conducted beneath the cover of legit business. There are limitless markets in this part of the world. I've no idea of the going rate for rhino horn, ivory, animal parts, leopard and croc skins, but it's high enough to warrant the risk of exposure and prosecution for some of Singapore's most influential tycoons. John Vydecker, for one. I'm bloody certain he's in it up to his neck, although you didn't mention him in those notes.'

Philip's eyes were sparkling with life when he turned back to Nick. 'Too risky to name names on paper at that stage. You're right. Vydecker is a principal player. But you apparently haven't worked out who heads the consortium.'

'And you have?'

'Yes, early on.'

'So who?' Nick demanded urgently.

'Our Head of Mission, Cranford Fielding. And it isn't rhino horn and skins they're dealing in, it's *diamonds*.'

Fifteen

They drank coffee at the Wellnut house in varying stages of disbelief, confusion and frustration. Philip had grown excited and lost the thread of the case he was presenting just prior to being interrupted by Barbara Fielding's arrival at the clinic. Dr McIntosh no longer had grounds on which to deny her access to the patient, so the three men had to vacate the room. After waiting for her to leave they were told Group Captain Dunne was now exhausted and needed to rest. They could visit again in the early evening if the patient was willing to see them.

So they had the germ of an explosive story that James and Euan found difficult to believe, but Nick did not. He was restless and impatient. In three days he would fly home. It was imperative that he saw the whole thing through. His last mission had been a tragic failure. This one *had* to succeed. He had to prove he was back on top.

James was deeply perturbed. Said so for the third time. 'We can't make accusations of such magnitude without iron-clad proof. The repercussions would shake the foundations of the Diplomatic Service and the FCO. Fielding has a long career behind him. If not particularly distinguished, it at least appears to have been dedicated and steady. Is he likely to throw it all away when he's on the brink of the golden hand-shake and pensioned retirement?'

'The ideal time to take risks,' Nick said forcefully. 'Retirement can be a living death to men who've been in the public eye all their lives. Arthritis and incontinence beckon.' He turned to Euan. 'Vicky swears he's the type to keep porno

280

books in a locked drawer and have secret meetings with other pervs. A cottage in the country with true blue Barbara would put an end to any hope of stimulation. Smuggling diamonds provides excitement and the kind of money that will fund a secret erotic life back home.'

Euan glared at him. 'Vicky talks a lot of nonsense sometimes, and Phil's yarn is just that.'

'But it ties in with *my* findings. It makes sense,' Nick insisted.

'He's been in severe isolation for two months living off snakes and berries. It makes men fantasize,' said Euan coldly. 'It's a fable dreamed up on Gombak.'

'That's not what I'm saying,' insisted James. 'The file Nick worked on was compiled before Phil was stranded on that island. I'm merely pointing out that this is a highly damaging concept based on information supplied by a Chinese lawyer who can't now substantiate it because he's dead. We can't act on supposition.'

'Then we'll get proof,' said Nick.

'How? Not by any more Lone Ranger stuff by you. This has to be handled with finesse.'

'Balls! It has to be handled with speedy action. Phil's reappearance will alert those involved in this set-up to any danger he might present. They'll cover their tracks and we'll never get them.'

'It's not *our* responsibility to get them,' argued Euan heatedly. 'Smuggling diamonds from Sierra Leone to Singapore on West African ships doesn't come under our jurisdiction.'

Nick got up from the settee in disgust. 'You're always whingeing about nautical affairs being primarily *your* concern. This is a sodding nautical affair. When are you ever going to take responsibility for anything? No wonder Vicky rates you a wimp!'

'OK, calm down,' cried James, also getting to his feet. 'Euan's right. This doesn't come under the High Commission's jurisdiction.'

281

'Even when the Head of Mission himself is up to his super-cilious eyebrows in it?' Nick raged.

'We don't know that for certain.'

'Then find out!'

James was furious. 'On what basis? Phil isn't yet fit enough to discuss his cryptic notes, and you've been involved with murdered prostitutes and getting yourself stabbed on forays that have proved only that you're as reckless as ever you were. Even more so.'

Breathing heavily, Nick said, 'I found Philip Dunne for you, you bastard.'

'Only by a fluke,' put in Euan. 'You were expecting to find men with wooden legs and parrots on their shoulders, then tackle them single-handed to prove what a super-macho guy you are.'

James sighed. 'Insults are getting us nowhere.'

'Which is exactly where you're happiest to be,' accused Nick. 'I never had you down as an on-the-fence man, Cracker, but you've become one. Claim diplomatic immunity and leave well alone! OK, play safe and let the boss man run a lucra-tive criminal trade. But I'm just a soldier on leave. No restric-tions, no qualms. I'll do my damnedest to shop him. *And* Vydecker. *And* that two-faced Yang woman. When I've got them all banged up behind bars there'll be no dirt on your hands. Or *yours*,' he added to Euan. 'You can both blame Chris Franklin for leaning on you to set me up when I arrived, because I'll bloody finish what you made me begin.'

He walked away to his room, slammed the door and locked it. He was shaking with anger. Those two were trying to stop him from regaining control; suggesting he had lost the ability to reason. Forcing the ever-present demons from his mind, he lay on the bed, shutters open to glorious daylight, and went through all Dunne had revealed.

Jimmy Yang was not the villain Nick had been led to believe. Wild, certainly, but he had drawn the line at abet-ting criminal activity. His desire for the expensive things most young men yearn for was indulged by Vydecker until the gullible young law student was in hock for an alarming amount. When Jimmy qualified, Vydecker offered him employment with the inducement of reducing his huge debt with monthly deductions from his salary. At his wits' end, and having alienated himself from his father, the young Chinese saw a way out of his predicament.

At that stage he had had no indication that his benefactor was engaged in any but legal business dealings. Vydecker was avuncular in manner, and Fleur thought highly of him, so he gratefully took the job of personal legal eagle to the banker. By the time he discovered the true nature of his work he was well and truly caught in the net. Vydecker made it clear arrest and imprisonment for debt was but a phone call away, and Fleur emphasized his ethnic duty and loyalty to their parents. Jimmy's disgrace would be borne by the whole family; they would be dishonoured if he was imprisoned. Did her brother wish to kill his father who would lose face and respectability through reflected humiliation? All very Chinese!

Jimmy's association with Philip had begun with an offer to crew on *Sea Harrier*. It became a regular occurrence and friendship sprang up between them. Philip confessed this morning that he had always wanted a son to share his adventures, and Jimmy had answered that need. It seemed Philip had also answered a need in the young lawyer. Jimmy began to confide his fears and suspicions. It was from these that Philip had compiled the notes in the file James had found.

After a period of six months or more Jimmy made the astonishing discovery that what was being stolen from the Cordova Line ships concealed the true prize. He had overheard a conversation between Vydecker and another man, who were unaware that he was working late sifting through box files in a nearby storeroom. The pair were deciding to scrap the Dili operation because the rubies, sapphires and pearls could only be brought in in meagre quantities and Customs were catching on to the frequency of the piracy.

Dumbfounded, Jimmy heard them discuss the success of

the Sierra Leone diamond run and the need for additional companies for onward transportation of the stones. They had run through the list of Far Eastern small manufacturers in which they already had agents, then had spoken of their intention of breaking into the Hatton Garden market. Vydecker had stated that he now held majority shares in Senoko Components and was backing the bid for a contract with Rees and Hardy. The other man agreed to activate an agent there. When the meeting ended, Jimmy had watched through a gap in the storeroom doorway and recognized Fielding as the other man.

Philip then realized he had stumbled on a widespread smuggling organization. It added up. Fielding had held the post in Sierra Leone before moving to Singapore. He would have contacts there: contacts in the diamond industry, men in government offices, wealthy entrepreneurs. All he had needed was a partner with business wizardry and enough funds to set the traffic in motion. Once it was up and running, profits would swiftly offset the outlay. John Vydecker was the big man in Singapore; a rich merchant banker with influence throughout the Far East and avaricious enough to go for the idea. The two men moved in the same social circles making it easy to drop a word in a receptive ear.

As Nick lay reviewing all Philip said this morning he had to allow that James was right. Without Jimmy Yang they had no firm evidence, no reliable witness. They could not prove their suspicions. As things stood, any lawyer Vydecker hired could successfully file a counter charge of slander. Against whom? One Nicholas Gareth Hawkwood. The others could claim diplomatic immunity. How Philip now stood in that respect Nick was unsure, but he, himself, would have no such protection. He would blow all hopes of resuming his career.

Further brain searching increased the urgency to act; act *now*. Dressing swiftly, Nick went down the rear stairs and climbed the tree to drop on the far side of the wall. One or two hopeful newsmen lingered by the front entrance.

They did not see him as he walked away towards the centre of town. A cruising taxi got him to Raffles Mall within minutes. It was crowded. Saturday, and women were seriously shopping.

There were two well-dressed Asian men in the Yang showroom, each looking at top-of-the-range jewellery. Nick dawdled by the display cases set in the walls until one man left with a trinket worth half an Army captain's annual salary. Nick then crossed to the elegantly dressed girl.

'I'd like a private discussion with Miss Yang,' he said with a tight smile.

The assistant locked the showcase to safeguard the pieces on display. 'Please follow me, sir. I will call Miss Yang from her design studio.'

He was shown into the small room with a promise that Miss Yang would be with him almost immediately. The startling photograph on the wall today merely suggested to Nick the many faces of Fleur Yang. He stood behind the door so that she was well into the room when he closed and stood with his back to it. He knew sharp pleasure to see her serenity shaken when she swung round.

'Captain Hawkwood!'

'It was Nick the evening we had dinner at the Silver Troika.'

She looked as striking as ever in a black sheath with a huge white silk rose on one shoulder. There were diamond triangles in her ears; a matching ring on her finger. The sight of them fanned his anger.

'What are you doing here?' There was only the barest suggestion of apprehension in her lilting voice.

'I went back to the Silver Troika,' he said, remaining solidly blocking the door. 'Mikhail didn't appear to remember me. Surprising, as I apparently got so drunk when I was with you I annoyed and upset other diners. Had to be put in a taxi and sent home. A humiliating experience for the renowned Fleur Yang . . . yet Mikhail didn't remember that, either. You'd think something so terribly embarrassing would be imprinted on his mind, wouldn't you? And on yours.'

'What are you doing here?' she demanded again.

'Of course, my own recollections of that evening are somewhat different. Taxi to your apartment. The ultra-sophistication of the black and white decor of your reception lounge, the unusual blue and sharp yellow of the seduction couch. You see, I have a good eye for colour. The satin thong you removed with such confidence was pale gold to match your dress.'

He gave a savage grin. 'Whatever you doctored my drink with made me very woozy and sick, but failed to drive out a single memory of our time together. I've been over and over all we said and did, tried to understand what scared you so much. This morning I finally knew the answer.'

She took a step towards him. 'Please stand away from the door. I have work to do.'

He stayed where he was. 'You were at great pains to tell me how headstrong your brother was. Crazy. Easily persuaded by others. Then, to divert my probing of your debt to Vydecker and his bank, you let slip the fact that Jimmy was financed personally and professionally by him, also. It didn't take much to conclude that your American friend had deliberately cultivated your brother's extravagance in order to gain a hold over him. Vydecker needed Jimmy to handle legal work he couldn't place with the bank's team of lawyers. When I asked you how long Jimmy had been in charge of your backer's private affairs you answered automatically. Then you realized you'd been indiscreet and grew alarmed.'

Nick looked her over through narrowed eyes. 'You'd already discovered I don't have a sister, which made me a person to be wary of. Who was Nick Hawkwood? Did I pose a threat? You decided to warn me off; fix it so that no one would take me seriously if I tried to make trouble. Once I was under the influence of whatever you put in that whisky, you phoned Mikhail. I'm only guessing, but I reckon he collected me from your place and drove me back to the restaurant, where he called a taxi and spun the driver a yarn about loutish behaviour among the diners. The poor guy

286

believed it when I chucked up all over his cab. James Wellnut believed it when I did the same in his house.' He took a deep steadying breath. 'But James is an old friend. He later accepted the truth, and he also began to wonder why you would take such drastic action after a normal, friendly meal. I now have proof of my suspicions regarding the work Jimmy did for Vydecker.'

'My brother is dead,' she said coldly. 'You found his bones.'

'And made your parents happy to be able to put them with his ancestors.'

'We showed our gratitude with gifts.'

'Particularly the pendant you offered.'

'It was not necessary to come here to remark on it,' she said, again moving towards the door he still blocked.

'That's not why I came, Fleur. I wanted to look at your diamonds. Your *Sierra Leone* diamonds.'

Shock stripped away the poise that had seemed inbred. Her serene features hardened into an expressionless mask as she stared back speechlessly.

Nick applied more pressure. 'I might prefer something made from sapphires or rubies lifted from ships on the Dili run. Or have you run out of them now that outlet has become too risky? Customs officials were growing too suspicious. Is that who you thought I might be, Miss Yang?'

She sank on to one of the black armchairs. Her hands were shaking. Nick moved away from the door. She was not going anywhere for a while. 'At the Silver Troika you spoke of your brother with contempt. Jimmy was no different from most of us at his age; dazzled by the good things in life but not so much that he would resort to crime to get them. Unfortunately, he crossed the path of someone who played on the desire for status symbols, luring Jimmy into amassing a horrendous debt that would ensure he did as he was told to escape exposure.'

He perched on the arm of a chair close enough to her to add force to his words. 'Young Jimmy was prepared to face the music and died in the process. He doesn't deserve anyone's contempt. When the truth comes out, *you* will be the one who'll bring shame and humiliation on your family. It will be all the greater because you're known internationally, thanks to John Vydecker and his cronies. The Yang silk company will suffer through your disgrace. Your father will lose face in the business community, and with his family and friends.' He added the ultimate blow. 'He could die of shame when your sins are made public.'

She gave a moan and covered her face with her hands. Nick gave the poster of the 'face of everywoman' a final glance as he moved to the door. Jewels had been the downfall of many women throughout history. He felt no sympathy for this one.

'You were right to be suspicious of me, but you made a grave mistake that night. I have an aversion to being humiliated, particularly in front of valued friends. It gives rise to an undeniable need to strike back.'

Lost in thought, Nick walked to Raffles and ordered a light lunch with half a bottle of red wine. Dwelling on what he, himself, had discovered, and what Philip Dunne had revealed, he suddenly found an exciting connection. He had concentrated on Vydecker, who had been the obvious link with everything and everyone, but there was now another surprising main player. Jimmy Yang had apparently overheard the two top men discussing the Far Eastern companies in which they had agents operating, and their intention to activate one in England. The American had shares in Senoko Components, Senoko was negotiating a deal with Rees and Hardy, who counted among their directors *Lady Blanche Fielding*! The name that had meant little to Nick when he read Jon's e-mail now made nerve-tingling sense. If he added the fact that one, at least, of Senoko's directors was a friend of Vydecker and Fleur Yang, it kick-started an amazing theory.

Diamonds meant big money, but Fielding and Vydecker had to maintain their cover as High Commissioner and merchant banker. No way they could vend the stones themselves. They had agents to do that. *Agents in companies!* So what was there in Singapore that provided the means of sending small, valuable stones to many destinations? Senoko Components! It would be easy enough for Jonah Lee to insert small packets inside engineering components, then mark the boxes so that agents at the receiving end could extract them on arrival.

His heartbeat accelerated painfully. What if the boxes were stamped with a merlion? What if the letters of Muna's sailor cousin had been padded envelopes containing diamonds? The most unsuspected means of moving them from pirate vessel to source! History was full of instances when valuable gems had been transported by penny post, in barrels of grain, within a human or animal body, and so on. Armed guards and secure vans issued invitations to thieves. In this case, the thieves were not offering opportunities to others of their kind.

What of the 'big boss'? He had to be Vydecker. Fielding was too tied down by official duties to operate freely. His input would be the direct dealing with his supplier in Sierra Leone; something he could continue to do when he occupied a retirement cottage in England and linked up with his titled relative on the board of Rees and Hardy.

He pushed aside his plate. This morning he had accused James and Euan of sitting on the fence; claimed *he* would act even if they felt bound by limitations of their jobs. So *act*, Hawk!

The turbanned Indian doorman whistled up a taxi. Nick told the driver to take him to Senoko Components. Where better to start than in the merlion's den?

The same willowy girl was at her desk on the first floor. She glanced up; stiffened at the sight of him. No Oriental charm today!

He wasted no time on preliminaries. 'Major Hargreaves to see Mr Chow on important business.'

She got to her feet wordlessly, entered the office Nick had

been in just a week ago, and closed the door. Several minutes ticked past before she reappeared to wave him in. Two men were on their feet waiting for him. Matching dark, tailored suits; unmistakably hostile. It did not deter Nick. He saw the presence of Jonah Lee as a bonus. Two birds with one stone!

'Glad you're both here,' he began. 'Saves time and gets right to the core of the matter.'

'Which is?' demanded Lee harshly.

'The way you run your business. Your more lucrative business. The one you plan to extend by exporting your components to Rees and Hardy in England. I'm here to assure you that a contract with them will never be signed.'

George Chow blinked nervously. 'You have no authority with that company, Captain Hawkwood. I recognized your picture in the *Straits Times*, and read your real name. Then I could not understand why you came here telling lies and wanting details of our customers. I checked with Rees and Hardy. They know nothing of a Major Hargreaves.'

'They also know nothing of what you conceal in certain batches of your components. I aim to tell them.'

'But you are a consummate liar,' said Lee. 'After your visit here I remembered that I had seen you before. At a party a week earlier. So you could not have arrived in Singapore that day, as you told my partner.'

Chow nodded several times. 'Now you come again saying you are Major Hargreaves. It is very suspicious.'

'Perhaps I should summon the police,' suggested Lee.

'Perhaps you should,' countered Nick, sitting in one of the visitors' chairs with every suggestion of confidence. 'When they arrive we can all go downstairs and examine the crates or boxes standing ready for export to . . . let me see . . . to companies like DBH Systems, LTD spares or NBC Incorporated.' He quoted some names he recalled seeing on Philip Dunne's and George Chow's lists.

Chow was looking totally bewildered. 'Who are you? Was it more lies in the newspaper?' He glanced at Jonah Lee. 'Do you understand this man?'

Nick pressed on, addressing Lee because of his growing belief that George Chow was genuinely unaware of the significance of the conversation. 'I'm sure the police will be as interested as I am to discover how you mark the relevant boxes for easy identification by your agents at the receiving end. Is it a merlion?'

'What is this about a merlion?' demanded Chow, snapping his head back and forth to confront both Nick and Jonah Lee several times.

Lee responded by activating the intercom on his desk to speak rapidly in Chinese to the girl outside. Nick guessed the cavalry would soon arrive, so he swiftly embellished his guesswork to enlighten George Chow on how his company was being used.

'Senoko Components has been distributing packets of diamonds smuggled in from Sierra Leone. I have a list of your customers who are involved in this illicit trade. Mr Lee is working for John Vydecker, who has bought up large numbers of shares in your company and is pushing for the contract with Rees and Hardy so he can extend the operation to Britain. If you're as innocent of this as you appear to be, I advise you to engage a top-flight lawyer as soon as possible. This diamond network is about to collapse. You will be trawled in along with the big and numerous little fish connected with it.'

The Chinese was dumbstruck, continued to switch his gaze from one man to the other like a sideways nodding mandarin. His partner walked around the desk to face him, smiling urbanely. The reassurance this was meant to give was ruined by the satanic illusion created by stripes of gleaming yellow and dark shadow cast over his face by sunlight through the half-open window blinds. Lee's smile looked evil, in consequence.

'George, Englishmen are known to be eccentric. It is the tropical sun. They cannot stand it. It affects their minds. They have discarded use of the sola topi and suffer from periods of madness as a result.'

291

Nick shot to his feet, boiling with anger. 'We'll soon discover whose sanity is in question when the rats start scuttling from the sinking ship, leaving you the only one on it.'

At that moment the door was opened by a large, turbanned Sikh wearing a dark-green uniform and a gun belt. The cavalry, in the form of a security guard.

Jonah Lee snapped an order. 'Escort this man from the building and down to the main road. Put him in a taxi and tell the driver not to let him out until he reaches the Oriental Hotel.'

As the Indian put out a hand to seize his arm, Nick said aggressively, *'Don't even try!'*

The guard looked for guidance from Lee, who nodded. 'Just escort him.'

'And tell the driver it's not the Oriental but the British High Commission. I've moved back there . . . under the diplomatic protection of your fellow conspirator, Cranford Fielding. Somewhat picaresque, isn't it?' He walked to the door, then turned back to George Chow. 'Don't forget that lawyer. You're going to need him!'

'What the *hell* d'you think you're doing?' roared James. 'Have you gone stark, staring mad?'

Nick was equally furious. 'How many more times will you suggest they bent my mind, then use it to excuse your failure to deal with things?'

Colour suffused James's face. 'I'll deal with this when I have proof. At the moment there *is* none.'

'Exactly! We'll only get it by undermining them. Setting alarm bells ringing. Forcing them to attempt to cover their tracks. They'll now be running scared. That's when thieves fall out, make mistakes, give themselves away.' He wandered restlessly back and forth the Wellnuts' verandah beneath his friend's stormy gaze. 'I gave the impression we were about to inform the authorities.'

'*We!*'

'*I*, then. I offered enough relevant facts about their

operation to suggest police, Customs and Interpol were on the point of swooping.'

'And when they don't?'

'They will,' he insisted. 'As soon as one of them panics enough to dump the rest of them in it, we'll have our proof.'

'Stop saying *we*. You're in this alone, chum.'

Nick halted and put him right. 'Oh no, your boss has used his diplomatic status to engage in criminal activity. Is continuing it here and now. As an employee of Her Majesty's Diplomatic Service, albeit on temporary attachment, it's your *duty* to put a stop to it.' He walked up to James and faced him out. 'Don't hide behind the argument that you're here to deal with defence matters, and diamonds don't fall into that category. The representative of the British government in this country is a bloody dyed-in-the-wool villain. You are an officer and a gentleman, who has pledged willingness to lay down your life for your country – almost did on several occasions. I'm not asking you to die over this, just to help me put him behind bars.'

James gave a deep steadying sigh. 'That's a lost cause. Fielding has immunity out here and it would never come to a prosecution at home. There'd be a whitewash: you know there would. The PM wouldn't allow the country's international image to be bruised, much less deeply scarred, by a scandal of this kind.'

Still highly aroused, this truth merely exacerbated Nick's aggression. 'Then help me put Vydecker behind bars.'

'He's an American civilian. My duty doesn't cover sorting *him* out.'

'*Oh, for Christ's sake!*' cried Nick explosively. He resumed his pacing; the only means of easing his unbearable frustration. 'There was a time when you'd be up for anything. What's happened to you?'

'I've matured,' came the quiet reply. 'I also have a wife and children I love and want to protect. I'm still bound by the promise to offer my life for my country, but I'd willingly give it for them in or out of the Queen's service. Don't push me on this, Hawk. I can't take the path you're set on following.'

The driving force slowly weakened; his heightened heart-beat began to reduce to a normal rhythm. Energy drained away, leaving him inexpressibly weary. He leaned on the verandah rail, staring out at trees forming a filigree pattern against the pink dusk sky. The trees hid whatever lay beyond. There could be a wilderness out there.

He was climbing a wall that shifted and softened as he dug his fingers into it. He was escaping from heat and life-threatening danger. Fear drove him, yet his desperate scramble set the wall crumbling further. He was sobbing with effort, sobbing with pain, sobbing for two men he had killed, who were burning. Then he was at the top of the wall, crouching like an ape. Ahead lay darkness. He had to enter it because it was safer than the inferno behind him. But this darkness hid an even blacker darkness, and there was no safety in it.

'Sundowner. Drink up!'

Nick stared at the chunky glass containing pale liquid that appeared in front of him. He stared at the man standing beside him holding the glass. It was important to make him understand.

'I can't let them win.'

'They won't,' was the reassuring reply.

Yet, as Nick drank the stiff whisky, he was unsure who 'they' actually were.

Euan arrived with Vicky. They all planned to go out for a meal when the men returned from visiting Philip. But there was a strained atmosphere between them. Nothing was said to Euan about Nick's visits to Senoko and Fleur Yang, but it was clear James was not relishing the coming meeting with his predecessor. Nick knew his friend would prefer him not to go. Yet he surely had the right to speak to a man he had saved from probable death.

The sundowners – he had drunk several – had steadied Nick. He was eager for more revelations from Philip. But he now knew he was on a lone crusade; one he determined to see through to the end. Three days in which to get a result. Surely Philip would tonight offer facts he could use to bring Vydecker and Co. to justice. At least set their downfall in motion. That would be satisfactory enough. No way could he fly back to England with the situation unresolved.

They heard a car draw up. 'That sounds like Mahadzir, right on time as usual,' said James. 'We'll get him to do the business as per this morning. There'll still be some persistent newshounds haunting the clinic.'

They were moving towards the door when someone came through it. James had been mistaken about the advent of his driver. This visitor caused collective consternation. No one moved; no one spoke. Books on etiquette offer nothing on the correct way to greet the head of a diamond smuggling operation who arose from his sickbed to arrive unexpectedly . . . and bloody inconveniently!

Cranford Fielding's complexion looked yellowish; his linen jacket hung on him. The fever had sapped his strength. He glanced around the room; gave a taut smile. 'Have I crashed an intimate party? Sorry, Joyce.'

She rose to the occasion, as always. 'No, not a party. We're all going out to eat when the men get back from the hospital.'

'Thought you were still confined to bed,' put in James, recovering from this most unwelcome development. 'Should you be out so soon?'

'Hard luck that this should happen when I was laid low and Clive's tied up in KL. Put a heavy load on your shoulders, James, having to do our job as well as yours. A relative new boy. But I'm sure you coped as well as could be expected.'

'Euan handled liaison with the police. Had to confirm identity. I'd never met Dunne.'

'No. Well, you can both relax. I'm back at the helm.'

'You don't look fit enough,' James said stiffly. 'Give yourself another day or two at home.'

'Not necessary. I'm an old hand at tropical fevers.' He

gave a short cough of a laugh. 'Been at this game since you were in nappies. I don't mean to keep you from your dinner. Just called in to tell you I've been on the phone to Alison. Assured her Barbara and I will do everything possible for Philip. As soon as he's fit to leave the clinic I'll move him to the Residence, where he'll recuperate in privacy and comfort until it's judged expedient to fly him home.'

Another short barking laugh. 'He can't take up the reins out here, naturally. You're well and truly in his shoes, James. No, he'll be interviewed by the FO, then returned to the RAF for a decision on how his career should progress. At forty-six the decision will be crucial to his future. I shall submit a report on his work here, with a character reference. It's expected of me. What I say will carry considerable weight, of course. He'll be relying on that. He'll also have the backing of Sir Charles Fanshawe, which will go a long way to restoring faith in Philip's worth.'

He raised his eyebrows in significant manner. 'He'll need all the support he can get to tide him over this rash episode. If he were twenty years younger a bout of wildness might more easily be overlooked, but in a mature man . . . Well, I will do what I can for him. I'm sure he'll appreciate the need to tread most carefully from now on.'

'It's not Phil who needs to do that,' Nick said, delighted by this undisguised threat of professional blackmail. Evidence of satisfying cracks appearing in the upper levels of the organization.

Slight tightening of his mouth was the only evidence that Fielding had heard. He continued his blithe performance as Head of Mission. 'Go off and enjoy your evening, children. Everything is well in hand.'

James visibly struggled with himself before nodding. 'If you say so. We'll call in on Philip before heading for the restaurant.'

Fielding's mouth tightened further. 'I've just explained that Philip is now *my* responsibility.'

'I have grapes and a couple of paperbacks for him,' James

persisted doggedly. 'As I've taken the poor devil's job I'd like to wish him well.'

'Same here,' said Euan in the same vein. 'Phil and I were good friends. It's really something when a man you've mourned returns from the dead.'

'And I want to hear more about his amazing survival after being run down by a pirate vessel,' said Nick with deliberate emphasis. 'As the man who found him, I think I'm entitled to hear the full story of his adventures.'

Fielding gave Nick a cold glare. 'You'll hear it in good time. Philip is exhausted and confused; can't think straight. Barbara said he was rambling; jumping from one half-sentence to another. Privation makes men hallucinate.'

'He was perfectly rational with us this morning,' Nick countered.

Fielding began turning away. 'I think *you* are hardly the best judge of that.'

Nick was after him like a shot, standing in the doorway to prevent his leaving. 'What exactly are you suggesting?'

The older man stiffened, pure venom in his expression. 'Stand aside! You reek of whisky. Men become alcoholically aggressive very swiftly in this oppressive climate.'

'As swiftly as they turn to crime?' Nick demanded with savage glee. 'Which of them sent the message that set you up from your sickbed like a bloody jack-in-the-box? Was it Fleur, Jonah Lee, or your bosom pal Vydecker?' He glanced beyond Fielding to grin at James who was signalling urgently to Euan. 'I told you panic would set in. Didn't take chummy here long to attempt to put Phil out of bounds, did it?'

He concentrated on Fielding again. 'It's a case of horse and stable. We already know how you ship the diamonds from Sierra Leone and how they're then distributed throughout the East. We also have the names of the main players. I worked out most of it from Phil's notes. He filled in the gaps this morning. We'd marked Vydecker as the boss man. You came as a very nasty surprise.'

The High Commissioner spun round to face James. 'Does

he have medication to deal with these crazed outbursts? Tranquillizers; some means of sedation?'

Both James and Euan appeared at a loss how to handle this dismayingly developing drama; said nothing.

Vicky broke the silence. 'You're the one in need of medication. Dengue makes men behave irrationally. You're still suffering. Euan and James will help you to your car and instruct the driver to get you home as fast as he can.'

Even as Euan turned to her, Fielding rasped, 'Your husband has hung on to his post by the skin of his teeth. My next report will advise that he return to the Navy immediately.'

She stepped forward indomitably. 'What makes you think you'll be here long enough to send another report? When the truth comes out you'll be *finished.* No good hushing Phil up – not that he'll let you – because Nick knows everything and has the guts to act on it.' She shook off Euan's restraining hand, glaring at him. 'Not like some people.'

'If you can't control your foolish wife, Goss, take her home,' Fielding said heatedly. 'Has she been at the whisky bottle, too?'

Joyce joined the fray, but in her usual controlled manner. 'I think everyone is simply upset by your ruling regarding Philip. As Euan said, it's rather overwhelming when someone returns from suspected death. Our husbands, and Nick who rescued Philip, naturally wish to visit him. They are all servicemen, unlike yourself. They share a bond civilians rarely understand.'

'Out of the question,' snapped Fielding. 'Dunne needs to be kept quiet. The medical staff have been instructed to turn away visitors. Which is just as well, Joyce. Servicemen or not, they appear to be unwisely under the influence. Or crazy,' he added, turning to Nick once more. 'Everyone present knows your recent history. We were prepared to assist a man we believed to be in the final stages of recovery. That's clearly not the case. You're dangerously unstable. Wild accusations, threatening behaviour, drunkenness. I've seen it before. They broke your mind,

Hawkwood. You're washed up. Finished! You need to be kept under restraint.'

Hot blood rushed through Nick's body; his head pounded with sudden pain. *Mad creatures must be put to death. They are a plague on mankind. Should his throat be slit to let the blood slowly ooze out, or should he be confined in a dark place until the devils claim him?*

The face before him was white, not brown, but he had never seen them so this could be one of them. He lunged forward, grabbed at the throat, pressed the carotid with both thumbs. He was yelling curses, reciting the foulest invective known to military men, choking the terrifying threats from his tormentor.

A chorus of voices rose. Strong hands were pulling him away. He released the throat so he could fight off the others who were going to carry out the threats. No! No! Dear God, *no*! He fought even more desperately until soft words penetrated the horror.

'It's all right. Nick, it's *all right!*'

Through a haze he saw a pale face. Pretty. Blonde hair, cornflower-blue eyes. She would not harm him. Vicky was on his side. He ceased to resist the firm grip on his arms. Stood limply, gradually returning to the present.

'The man's a lunatic,' cried the first voice, hoarse now and ranting. 'You assured me he was in the last phase of convalescence or I'd never have given permission for you to have him here. I want him under constant supervision until he's put on tonight's flight to London. I hold you responsible, James. Don't let him out of your sight. I'll secure a seat and arrange for a security guard to escort him to the airport to board at the last minute. Can't risk having him run amok at Changi.' A spate of painful coughing. 'This will seriously damage your standing here. *Seriously* damage it. And your future career. That goes for you, too, Goss. You should both be *very* careful what you say and do from now on.'

The sound of footsteps growing fainter. A car engine

starting; revving up. The crunch of tyres on gravel. Silence. Nick drew in a long shuddering breath. Everything shifted back into focus as the hands on his arms fell away. Tension fairly crackled across that silent room as Nick surveyed the immobile figures around him. Friendship appeared to have flown on the four winds.

'That's us well and truly deposited in the shit!' Euan's face was flushed; his features grim. 'You should have put this maniac on a flight to London long ago. Under escort!'

'Whose side are you on?' cried Vicky. 'And how self-centred can you get? Can't you see that bastard's trying to bluff his way through this with over-the-top tactics. You stand there whingeing instead of asking Nick how best to call HOM's bluff. *He's* got the guts to do it.'

Euan rounded on her in uncontrolled fury. 'For once in your life *shut up*! I've kept this job despite your immature determination to wreck it. I've worked bloody hard to maintain confidence in my ability. I might ask whose side *you're* on. A few minutes ago you opened your big mouth and helped your lover-boy put paid to my career. Yes, I'm whingeing, Vicky. I followed my father and his father into the Navy. It's the life I love. You've just helped to put it in limbo, if not kill it stone dead.' He took a deep breath. 'And if you say one more word tonight our marriage will end the same way.'

Vicky gaped at her husband in astonishment. Before she could misjudge his mood and speak, James directed his fire at Nick.

'I don't believe today is happening. You've gone too bloody far this time. You take some wild theory cooked up by Dunne to ease the humiliation of his wife's affair, and latch on to it in a bid to prove you can still hack it. Christ, anyone who suddenly loses it and tries to throttle a man still needs help. Specialist help!'

He pushed a hand through his hair in frustration. 'Diamond smuggling! Pirates! It's the stuff of bloody fiction. I've said it before: it's possible to shuffle info around to fit any scenario

300

you want. The entire concept's ridiculous! All we have are the vengeful outpourings of a young Chinese deeply in debt. Through his own idiocy. And he's now dead. There's no *proof* of any of it.'

'Yes, there is,' argued Joyce with spirit. 'Nothing that could be used in a court of law, but Cranford's running scared. Why else would he deny you access to Philip Dunne – an astonishing move for an innocent man – and why get rid of Nick so summarily?'

'Because he tried to choke the bloody life out of him,' James countered heatedly.

'That merely gave him the perfect excuse. It's my guess some means of shutting Nick up would have been found. These men have a great deal at stake, James. Nick's right. After giving Cranford proof just now that the operation has been blown, they'll either be forced to close it down or collective greed will lead them to infighting and eventual betrayal. It's only a matter of time before proof presents itself.'

'Really?' he asked with heavy scepticism. 'And what do Euan and I do in the meantime? As he says, we're well and truly in the shit.' As Nick began to cross the room he said sharply, 'Where are you going?'

'I'm about to throw up.' He halted in the middle of the room. 'You're welcome to come and watch. Or I can do it here. Take your pick.'

The friends and former squadron colleagues held each other's gaze for a long moment. Eventually, the fellowship hovering in James's eyes sent Nick along the corridor to his room alone. Once there, he pocketed his passport, gulped some water from the flask beside his bed, then scrambled over the verandah rail and dropped to the ground. No one was going to put him on a flight home tonight!

Sixteen

The evening was oppressively humid; Nick was super-charged with adrenalin. Fielding would pay. Vydecker would pay. Fleur Yang would pay. And Jonah Lee. He wanted them all on their knees begging for mercy. He knew about that.

He pushed through the crowds, oblivious of everything around him. James claimed he needed help. Sure he did. Help in finding the proof that would nail them all. It had to be there. Think. *Think!* Go over it all again. Everything he had uncovered and all that Philip Dunne had told them this morning. God, was it only this morning? It seemed a life-time ago.

Facts swam around in his head. They mixed with images that seemed unconnected, but he was sure they were not. Rees and Hardy . . . Senoko Components . . . Daddy says you don't do business with them someone else will . . . taken from ships by pirates . . . delivered to Vydecker for safe-keeping . . . son of my uncle, a sailor. Bingo!

The taxi driver asked which area of the docks his passenger wanted. Cordova Line, of course. But it was a ghost area. Empty basins, deserted jetties. He wandered beside towering metal walls stretching as far as he could see. The air reeked of floating garbage, oiled ropes, rusting metal and the many substances packed in the containers stacked almost to the sky.

A uniformed man with a German Shepherd on a lead stopped him. Identification, please. Why was a British Army officer walking here in the darkness? Muna's cousin? Many,

many thousands of seamen came and went through this port. Go home now. Come back in the morning.

A taxi back to the city. *Have* to get proof. So where the hell to now? Take the MRT to Sembawang. They would have forgotten him now. Forgotten the bicycles. Forgotten the girl with a blue scarf tight around her throat.

Cheng Li (Charles) had shut up shop. He hammered on the door. Hammered again. Cheng Li (Charles) did not appear. Sod it! He went down the alleyway to the rear. Windows all open; residents cheerfully yelling at each other. Up the steps to the peeling blue door. Hammered on it. A woman came; spat out a harsh question in Chinese. Where would he find Muna's sailor cousin? Narrowed speculative eyes. Koz chew. How bloody much? A man pushed her aside. Never heard of Muna. The Asian equivalent of bugger off. Slammed door.

Back to the MRT station. *Have* to get proof, but only three days left. On the train, but to where?

There was dim lighting and a hushed atmosphere at the clinic. The big Sikh at reception resembled the Senoko security guard. No, sir, absolutely no visitors permitted at this hour. Well past midnight. In the morning? No, Group Captain Dunne far too ill to see anyone. Doctor's orders.

The Yang showroom was closed and dark. The mall well nigh deserted. Taxi to the Silver Troika. Closed and dark. Senoko Components who could turn next week into tomorrow overnight must have a late shift. At the gate another large uniformed Sikh with a German Shepherd on a lead and a gun in his belt. Mr Jonah Lee, sir? Away on a business trip.

Ha! The rats were starting to desert the ship!

No taxis way out here. Walking, walking back to the city. *Have* to get proof. Only three days left! Go through it all again. Unsure about what he must go through. Diamonds? Yes, diamonds. Caught up in a floating mass beneath the sea. No, that could not be it. Lapis Lazuli . . . koz chew . . . it's your other world . . . only three days left.

A voice floating on the air. English. 'Do you need a lift into town?' Aircrew en route to Changi. Went on one knee in a 747! He sat in the back with a uniformed girl. No, she did not know Muna's cousin. Sorry.

They dropped him right outside and drove off fast. He went up to his room and fell on the bed. Christ, he was exhausted, but there was no time to sleep. *Have* to get proof. Only three days left. Hands suddenly seized him and he awoke riding the familiar steed of terror.

James dismissed the timid room maid who had let him in with her pass key. 'I checked the airport and Immigration at the causeway. Then I had a hunch you'd come to Hotel Pelingi.'

Nick was now fully alert. He had seen James looking this way before: when two of their pilots were killed in a collision, and when they had ferried UN investigators to a mass grave in Bosnia. But he was unprepared for what came next.

'Emma's been snatched. They'll exchange her for you.'

James had come in his own car. He drove as fast as possible in the morning traffic, but it took more than half an hour to reach the house. During that time he briefed Nick.

Mahadzir had been driving Emma to spend the day with school friends when he had been stopped by a police car. Two uniformed men had approached. While one bent to the window to engage the Malay's attention, Emma had been lured from the rear seat by the news that her mother had had an accident and needed her. It was slick, over before Mahadzir could reason that there had not been time enough for such a development. He was now distraught.

'The demand note was delivered an hour later. By a seven-year-old boy who had been given money to hand it in,' said James.

'And they'll do a straight swap?'

'That's right. No cash. Just you.'

'So you can't any longer doubt that Fielding is up to his neck in this dirty business.'

'He certainly wants you out of the way, but surely he wouldn't sponsor this. Putting Emma through hell. He has children and grandchildren. Euan's seen him with them when they come out here. Says he's very fond of kids.'

'Yeah, and men like that have been known to murder them. No one would link him with major crime, but he's in there running it. You let me slip through the net last night. This is his way of getting back at you. And a sure way of guaranteeing you produce the rabbit from the hat.'

Silence until they arrived at the house. It was unusually quiet. The servants were nowhere to be seen. Joyce was standing on the verandah, gripping the rail. She looked pale but composed.

Nick halted several yards from her. 'Sorry, Joyce. I didn't dream they'd resort to this.'

'Just give me back my daughter.'

He nodded. 'What do they want me to do?'

James took a folded page from the table and held it out. It bore the merlion stamp. The instructions were precise. No police involvement. No tricks. No back-up team. Captain Hawkwood and Mrs Wellnut must go to Sentosa and present themselves at the giant merlion at exactly four o'clock. The girl will be there with a Chinese woman dressed as an official guide. They must go to her as if they are parents collecting a lost child. The mother will be allowed to take the girl to the cable car station. She will be followed all the way. If she makes any sign to hidden observers both she and the girl will be taken hostage before they can leave the island. Captain Hawkwood will follow further instructions. Any attempt by him to disobey will endanger Mrs Wellnut and her daughter. Many eyes will be watching. No harm is wished on them. They will return safely so long as Captain Hawkwood does exactly as instructed.

'Sounds simple enough,' murmured Nick.

'Too simple,' claimed Joyce. 'How can we be certain they'll have Emma, much less let me take her?'

He glanced up. 'It's me they want. Emma's simply the lure. Once I turn up at the merlion and go quietly, she'll just be an encumbrance. They'll let you take her, Joyce.' He turned back to James. 'Nothing cloak and dagger about this lot; prefer to work in daylight amongst a milling crowd. Suggests great confidence and vast resources.'

'There has to be in an organization of this kind. High stakes and big money. Worth playing dirty for.' James glanced at his watch. Long uneasy hours ahead for them all. 'Joyce, d'you think Cora could rustle up coffee and scrambled eggs for Nick? He hasn't had breakfast.'

Her expression asked how he could think of food in this situation, but she nodded and headed for the kitchen. When she had gone Nick challenged James.

'Not thinking of staging any heroics, I hope. You've two more kids at risk.'

'I'm all too aware of that.' He exhaled heavily. 'I'm also aware that I basically started this ball rolling. All that guff I gave you about being targeted as Dunne's replacement, and having a family to protect. God, how our words rebound on us!' A pause. 'I've checked. Our nearest Special Forces team is unlikely to get here in time, so we'll have to use the resources available to us. There's a British warship in, at the moment. Euan was there at the crack of dawn doing his stuff. I called him on my way to collect you. He said a couple of the officers on board were at Dartmouth with him. He's pretty sure they'll be up for whatever we need. Now, Sentosa is a small island. Three ways to leave it: ferry, road bridge and cable car. The most likely—'

'Cracker!'

'Shut up and listen! Would *you* sit back and do nothing under the circs?'

'I've no wife and kids at risk.'

'So you're prepared to walk out there this afternoon and face endex? Without putting up a fight? Without regrets?'

Nick gazed into space as images again flashed before him. There had been times when he longed for death; a *swift* death. No more pain. No more whispered threats from people who came and went so silently he was never sure if they were there. No more tricks with food and water bowls. No more water constantly dripping until each plop on the stone floor reverberated in his head like a drum. No more sitting in his own filth. No more denial of sight. No more . . .

James's voice came to him as if from a far place. 'Hawk, your friends brought you back from Iraq. We'll get you back from this.'

It had been raining, but the sun was out again. Heat rose from the paths like a shimmering haze. Nick walked with Joyce towards the rearing merlion at the top of several flights of steps edged with flower-beds, and separated by level areas where fountains cascaded into ornamental pools. He heard nothing of the merry chatter around him, saw only the great leonine head atop the curled scaly body of a fish. Joyce held his hand. She had been holding it since they left the house, gripping it tightly in her fear.

He felt none. The Hawk had soared high. Higher than most. But he had flown heedlessly too near the sun and burned his wings. Destroyed the means to fly. He saw the fire clearly. They were in it; trapped there. Andy and Tim. They were screaming. He knew all about screaming; about agony. But he had been alone with his. They had not been watching helplessly. Had not heard him. They did not know what had happened. Nobody knew. Thank God, it would soon no longer matter. *It was written.*

At the base of the merlion a sturdy, middle-aged Chinese woman waited with a white girl dressed in tennis clothes. Joyce gave a muffled moan; started forward. At the same time, the sobbing girl rushed at her.

A voice spoke behind Nick. A male voice. 'Go back down the first flight of steps. Look straight ahead. Don't hesitate. Keep walking, and do exactly as I say. The girl and her mother will be followed all the way to the cable car. If you do anything foolish, if you have brought anyone with you, they will be taken and never seen again. Now, move!'

At the foot of the steps Mikhail of the Silver Troika walked to him with a smile of greeting. As they shook hands like

307

friends coming upon each other unexpectedly, Nick felt something prick his palm. Two more men converged on them, calling out their pleasure at the chance encounter. One slapped Nick on the back; kept a firm hand on his arm. They walked in a small group down a side path leading away from the main attractions. There were fewer people meandering there.

The bordering shrubs and trees soon began to blur. Nick's shoes now had lead soles. His head was rising from his body. There was a loud roaring in his ears. The merlion saying farewell, of course!

Lieutenant Commander 'Flip' Driscoll hugged his Eurasian cousin close to his side, kissed her ear, then spoke softly into his mobile phone,

'There are still three men with him, but I think they've somehow slipped him something. He's all over the show and they're having to support him. If it was a lethal dose he's already a goner, Euan.'

Euan swore like a true seafaring man. 'Are they still heading for point X on the plan of the island?'

'Affirmative. Exactly as we guessed.'

'Sure they haven't sussed you?'

'Binnie and I are making like hot lovers. They haven't given us a second glance.'

Sitting in his car parked by the cable car station on Singapore island, James spoke into his mobile to Commander Ryan Meader, who was strolling with his Indian friends and their children.

'Where are they, Ryan?'

'In sight of the cable car station. They're still hugging each other and hurrying. No sign of a tail.'

'No one's trying to intercept them, or crowd in on them?'

'Plenty of people around. Couple of lone males who could be suspect, but Joyce and Emma are moving quite freely. We're about to split up so that I can board the same gondola.'

Leaving that line open, James spoke to Euan on a sat

phone. 'They're nearing the cable station. All well so far. How about your sector?'

'Problem. We think Nick's been doped. Enough to subdue him; make it impossible for him to break away. They could have outgunned us, James. He might already have a lethal dose in his bloodstream.'

'Bloody hell!'

'*Hold!* Flip's coming through again.'

James waited, deeply disturbed. He had unwittingly started Nick on this path. If they had already made his end irrevocable, he would live with guilt for the rest of his days. Yet, since reading their demand, Nick had seemed resigned to the final solution. He had spoken intelligently, acted the same way. Yet he appeared to have retreated to another world where he was the sole occupant, detached from the emotion and drama of this moment.

Euan's voice in his ear: 'They've almost reached point X, where the sea wall runs for a short distance around the curve in the path. There is a boat riding there. We were right. They *are* planning to get away by sea. Flip says there's no one else on that path now, so it'll look too suspicious if he follows any further. He's having a hectic cuddle on a seat while maintaining observation. We need to start up.'

'No! It's too bloody soon! You mustn't make a move until Joyce and Emma are safely here with me.'

'Leave it too long and we'll lose them,' Euan argued. 'Where's Joyce now?'

James snatched up his mobile. 'Ryan, they're putting Nick aboard. How long before they can move to follow?'

'Problem,' came the terse reply. 'Bloody cable car's stopped. Mechanical failure. There's gondolas hanging over a sheer drop; screaming people inside. Your wife looks scared. I think she's about to go back down the steps.'

James's hand holding the phone was slippery with sweat. 'Stop her! She mustn't change the plan.'

'Tricky. There's several single guys up here on the

platform. Could be watching for any back-up moves.'

'Look, Joyce knows the plan, although she doesn't know you by sight. It's vital that she sticks to their instructions or she'll put herself and Emma in danger. You *must* make contact somehow and ensure she stays put.'

'Will do, but nothing's moving here. Delay is inevitable.'

'Listening out.' James was trembling as he took up the sat phone again. 'Euan, the cable car's stopped. Mechanical failure. Indefinite delay. Joyce is still on Sentosa. Hold off until she gets over here.'

'Not an option. Flip reports they've fired the engine. We *have* to go now.'

'*No!* They're not safe yet.'

A brief silence, a curt acknowledgement to someone. Euan came back on the line. 'They're away. We'll lose them unless we move now, James. Not my decision, it's Frank's. He's the captain of the vessel.' There was the background sound of an engine roar. 'Look, now Nick's aboard, Joyce and Emma are no further use to them. I'll send Flip over to join Ryan at the cable station. That duo can handle anything and anyone. They'll make sure Joyce and Emma are OK. Believe me. Now, make your call, then clear the airwaves. The Navy is now in command.'

Even in the given tense circumstances James could not miss the faint note of triumph from a man who felt he had played second fiddle throughout this affair. Euan was boss man at last!

James worriedly explained the situation to Ryan, then disconnected and dialled another number. 'Ferdy, all systems go!'

'Righto,' came the laid-back rejoinder. 'I've had the blades ticking over, so I'll be in the air in five.'

James left his car, taking the phone with him, and strolled over to the cable station where mild panic was underway as mechanics worked to get the system moving again. He told himself Euan was probably right. Joyce and Emma were safe enough now Nick was in their hands. The rabbit had been produced from the hat. James hoped with all his heart the rabbit was not already in the grips of the Grim Reaper.

Nick recognized the shimmering grey stuff. The sea. There was a vague shape before him. Ought to know what it was, but not sure. He was lifted high in the air, then he plunged again.

'Going down to seventy-five, Andy. Should be a light flashing the letter G three times. See anything? They must be down there.'

There was the reek of fuel, the low throbbing of engines.

'ECL to ground idle.'

'Confirm ECL to ground idle.'

They were on fire. The aircraft was yawing, undulating. He knew they must land immediately. Bloody shitty place to be stranded in!

Get out fast! But he couldn't remember where the door was; couldn't make the effort to move.

A deafening roar. The extra fuel tank had blown! Tim had been crushed by it. There was a soft crumbling wall leading to safety. He ought to be climbing it. Hands seized him and he remembered it was not safe anywhere. The roar turned into an explosion. The ground rocketed forward beneath him. He was falling. No, they were pushing him down, down; binding his arms to his sides with ropes.

Suddenly, the black abyss was there gaping wide before him. He knew this time he would go in. *They* were thrusting him in. As his head entered he began to scream.

His shoulders and torso entered. *Mad creatures must be destroyed. They are a curse on society.*

Now his legs and feet entered. He was totally entombed. Terror possessed him, uncheckable. His screams echoed fainter and fainter as he plunged ever further into hell; ever further into insanity. Yet a faint pulsebeat managed to protest: *This must not be written!*

Euan felt a charge of excitement as the Navy launch surged away from the jetty. He and James had correctly guessed that by choosing the theme island of Sentosa for the RV, Nick's abductors would make their getaway by sea. He had prematurely presented this as fact to Franklin Chen, the Naval friend who had chased up for Vicky the information on Cordova Line. Now Frank was chasing pirates at Euan's behest. What he did not know was that an Australian free-lance pilot was about to join the pursuit in a helicopter. Ferdy was James's idea. He had insisted. Before long, Euan would be glad of it.

They soon reached the southernmost point of Sentosa from where there were unbroken views both east and west of Singapore's coastline.

'Here's a puzzle, Euan,' said Frank, binoculars to his eyes. 'I see no sign of them. There has been no time for them to seek a haven from our sight. I do not understand this.'

Euan frowned. Flip had seen them cast off and put to sea. They must be out there somewhere.

Knowing all vessels had to follow the marked channels through this crowded strait, Frank again studied the coast in both directions. No launch fitting the description they had been given. Then he gave a satisfied grunt. 'Aha, I think they do not mean to bring your friend ashore in Singapore after all. I see them now. They are heading out past Belakangpadang. Maybe they will transfer him to another vessel in the outer reaches. Here, take a look.'

While Frank gave orders to his helmsman, Euan caught the other boat in the powerful lenses. He was thrown off balance as a surge in power had them leaping forward, bumping and thumping against the strong tidal flow between massive tankers at anchor awaiting permission to enter the basins.

Gripping the brass rail, Euan spread his feet wide as he continued to mark the distant speck they were tardily following. This was a second unexpected move on their part. Neither he nor James had considered a dash out to sea with Nick. They thought he would be taken around the island to the place where the diamonds were normally landed, and dealt with there. The intended plan was that Frank's armed launch would intercept them before they went ashore, saving Nick and catching the pirates at the same time. The outcome was now uncertain.

The radio crackled, then Ferdy came through loud and clear, asking for their position. Euan gave it and explained the unexpected change in plan.

'Have a look from up there for an obvious RV. Could be a Cordova vessel, at anchor or moving very slowly.'

'Will do.'

Euan then had to tell Frank about Ferdy. He took the news with the usual Chinese acceptance of the unavoidable. He was anyway more occupied with getting his boat around shoals and the many hazards of that ultra-busy waterway with as much speed as he dare risk. The British were a curious breed, he knew. He had long ago ceased to wonder at what they did. But he really wanted to catch those pirates.

Ferdy over the airwaves: 'I see you and the other launch. No obvious RV vessel that I can see. Those buggers look to be heading for Gombak. You don't think they mean to dump Nick there. Crude justice for rescuing Phil Dunne? I don't much care for that notion. Can you head them off from the island?'

Euan consulted with Frank. They were only slowly gaining on their quarry, who had made a very fast getaway. After working out how long it would take them to reach the other boat, Frank looked doubtful. 'I think we cannot catch them before they are level with Pulau Gombak. Soon afterwards we could fire across their bow and stop them. Dangerous waters around that island, Euan.'

He nodded. 'I know it. Daren't risk driving them on the shoal, and endanger Nick.'

Frank's dark eyes questioned him. 'You do not care about the safety of the others?'

'They're your concern, not mine.'

It was true enough. Frank dropped the subject,

concentrating on their thrusting, juddering pursuit that sent spray flying high past the windows. Gombak was no more than a dark blob on the horizon. Euan pondered Ferdy's idea as he stood with feet well astride, riding the vessel's motion. *Did* those bastards plan to maroon Nick on Gombak to die slowly? He sighed. This op was going pear-shaped. Once the crew ahead realized they were being chased, they would dump Nick overboard. Swift death, instead. And the evidence gone. Just four guys out on a nautical spree, they would say when stopped and boarded by Frank.

Ferdy again: 'Can't you get a move on, Euan?'

He ignored the jibe. Pilots had no idea of the sea's demands. Next minute there was a roar overhead and a shadow fell across the cabin. It moved on to reveal a blue and white helicopter around fifty feet above them. Euan's mouth tightened. This launch was powerful, but it was fighting a notoriously strong current which reduced its performance. He watched through the forward windows as Ferdy flew on towards Gombak. The aircraft was not armed, as they were. What did he hope to do?

Within ten minutes the helicopter had reached the other boat. Euan watched in disbelief as it matched the vessel's speed, losing height until it appeared to be flying alongside it at wavetop level. Ground zero!

'That pilot is crazy out of his brain,' cried Frank. 'Is he wanting to cause them to die? Your friend also to die?'

'I think he's trying to save him from that,' Euan murmured slowly, fighting rising envy. 'He's always wanted to be a hero.'

Ferdy on the airwaves: 'That's scared 'em. I'm going to try turning them. Might not work. If it does, you come up on their port beam and we'll have them in a pincer movement. Then, between us, we can surely force them to head straight for Pelingi, where they'll have no option but to stop. If they won't do it voluntarily, that bloody underwater growth will sort them out.' He actually chuckled, as if he was not mere feet from a watery grave. 'Are you guys with me on that?'

Euan raised his eyebrows at Frank, who met the query with uncharacteristic inscrutability. Euan took it as his only possible response to a ludicrous proposal. But what if it came off?

'*If* you turn them, Ferdy. But until we see it happen we're keeping up our present course.'

Another chuckle. 'Fair enough. Watch this space!'

Euan's heart moved up to his mouth as he watched the blue and white shape edge forward until it was flying a short distance from the nose of the launch, ahead of it and slightly to starboard. The man at the helm would be very worried and unsettled by this madness. He would automatically veer to port to gain a clear run. He did. But the helicopter also veered, maintaining its position and forcing the boat further to port.

'My God, he's doing it,' breathed Euan. 'I've never seen anything so sodding risky in my life . . . but he's *doing* it.'

At his side, Frank gave his command to alter course. The Naval launch raced in a curve, almost on its side in the grey-green swell. Clutching at the brass handrail to stay on his feet, Euan experienced an alien surge of recklessness prompted by the thrill of what they were attempting to do. Mad; crazy! But he had never felt so alive and triumphant before. Correct procedure, the subconscious desire to command went by the board as he saw the improbable becoming the possible as the helicopter continued to 'nudge' the boat away from Gombak and on course for Pelingi.

The buzz of excitement now invaded Frank. Invaded his crewmen. Their great sweeping curve brought them parallel with their quarry in a matter of minutes. They began to close in on it menacingly as Pelingi hove into view.

Through the binoculars Euan could now see there was another man in the helicopter. He was leaning from the left hand seat holding what looked like a revolver, but was surely the means of firing distress flares. It looked threatening enough for his purpose. More so was the bow-mounted gun on the Navy launch, now being manned by a grinning Malay.

Frank switched on his speaker system and barked a

315

command for the other boat to stop. It did not. Yet there was nowhere for it to go save to the island fast looming ahead. In a futile bid to get away it attempted to cross the bows of the offical launch. Frank nodded to the Malay, and a burst of fire had their quarry back on course. Frank then barked a second warning over the megaphone.

Euan detected signs of panic aboard. Four men. No sign of a fifth: Nick. The buzz, the adrenalin-charged elation began to die. For a short while he had lost sight of the reason for what they were doing.

A second burst of gunfire settled the issue. The other vessel began to slow. Frank nudged their own boat in close, commanding them to approach the island and anchor half a mile offshore.

Ferdy on the airwaves. 'Thanks, guys. We make a good team. Can't see hair or hide of Nick on board. Guess he's down below. I'm gonna land on the island. The scientific team here has basic medical facilities, if needed. See you ashore.'

The sun was starting its downward path as they dropped anchor alongside the other boat, in water well clear of the Medusa mass. With the gun trained on them the four men sat on deck, heads bowed. They did not look so tough. Frank boarded with three crewmen to apprehend the suspected pirates. They were his main concern.

Euan swung across and hurried aft to take the steps down to the cabin. Eyes dazzled by sunlight on water had to adjust to the dimness below as he scanned the bench seats expecting to see Nick's inert body. Nothing. The cabin was empty!

He stared from the porthole towards the distant mass of Gombak. Had they dropped him in the sea over there? Before Ferdy caught up with them? Certainly not after that. One of the two pilots would have seen it happen. Had they all along been aware of being chased and got rid of Nick early on? If so, this long pursuit had merely been distracting tactics.

Frank joined him. 'So where is your friend they drugged and carried off?'

Euan detected a hint of accusation. This man had only the word of several Englishmen that it had happened. He had not seen it for himself. Frank needed a body, dead or alive, to justify seizure of the four on deck. Euan needed one to justify coercing Frank into this chase. And he needed one in the hope that he would not shortly be arranging for Jon Hawkwood to cast wreaths on water somewhere near Gombak.

He heard a faint sound from beneath one of the bench seats. A sound resembling an echo coming days after the original cry. It was eerie. He sank to his knees and crawled beneath the table between the seats to peer at the dim space below. There was no space. It was filled with what looked like one of the cigar-shaped heavy wicker baskets used to take pigs to market in outlying areas. Another eerie sound from it. Hollow, plaintive, but now recognizable as human. His heart began to thud; his mind closed to the possibility.

He backed out, looked up at Frank. 'Help me pull this out, will you?'

It was heavy. Still Euan's mind refused to accept it. But he had to when the basket was in the open well of the cabin, and he saw Nick's green eyes staring wildly at him through the wicker weave. He was making this curious whimpering sound. This man he had been so jealous of had been thrust inside the basket, filling it so tightly he could not move a muscle, probably could scarcely breathe. Had they intended to dump him on Gombak like *this*?

The pathetic whimpering came again; terror-darkened eyes stared at him. Euan drew breath quickly to ease a stifling sensation in his breast.

'For God's sake help me get him out, Frank,' he said urgently. 'Here's your evidence . . . trussed up like a pig.'

Lara and Dennis had showered, changed into shorts and T-shirts, and were drinking tea after their final dive of the day, when they were drawn from the tent by shouts from their colleagues. They walked the short distance to the beach as a helicopter began to descend to the clearing used as a pad by Ferdy and his pilots. But more attention was focused on two sleek launches anchored just beyond the team's marker buoy. Lara thought one looked similar to the boat that had arrived to collect Jimmy Yang's bones.

'What's going on, Perry?' she asked of the lanky scientist who doubled as their radio operator.

'Bit of excitement for a change,' he told her with a grin. 'That's Ferdy coming in. Told me the Navy has been chasing pirates. He happened to be airborne and offered to help. Seems one guy might have been hurt. Ferdy's standing by to fly him back.'

Lara welcomed this interruption to the daily routine. This Medusa project that had initially been so vital and interesting had lately lost its appeal. She was glad of this brief contact with the outside world; glad of the chance to see and speak to someone other than the people she lived and worked with.

Bingo murmured, 'I'll do what I can before they load him in the chopper. Painkillers, bandages, dressings.' He chuckled. 'We're all so bloody healthy here I haven't had much chance to use my medical expertise, so this guy may be treated to the whole shebang once I lay hands on him.'

A dinghy was being lowered beside the Navy launch. Lara could see someone being helped into it by white-suited sailors, then an outboard motor coughed before the dinghy began to approach the beach. Behind her, the loud *chook-chook* of helicopter rotors had quietened to a swish as they idled ready to depart. She regretted that; wished they would stay for a while. The aircraft would rise up and disappear behind the trees; the boats would head for Singapore. Half an hour from now it would be as if nothing had happened. They would sit around drinking and yarning in the mess tent, then she would go to bed after crossing off another day on her calendar. Another day nearer Nick's departure.

Ferdy came up beside her, touched her arm, said quietly, 'You'd better brace yourself. This guy they're bringing ashore may be on his way out.'

318

She frowned at him. 'I've seen bodies before.'

'Not Nick Hawkwood's.'

Her heart suddenly thumped like a punch in the chest. 'What're you talking about?'

'It's him they're bringing in. I heard he's in a real bad state.'

'Oh, my God!' She sat down suddenly on the shingle as her legs folded.

Ferdy squatted beside her. 'Sorry, girl. I suspected all along there's more between you and him than meets the eye.'

'But how . . . ?'

'It's a long story. Maybe you should come in the helo with him.'

She had turned cold. Her brain had ceased to function. The dinghy was no more than thirty yards away now. Dennis, Bingo and Craig were wading out to it. Why had they come here? Why not to some other island? Then she would never have known about this.

Ferdy moved forward. She stayed where she was, growing colder still. There was a civilian in the dinghy. A white man dressed in pale trousers and a yellow shirt. And there was Nick sitting beside him. Well, *slumped*. But he could not be dying, could he? Lara's legs gained enough strength to get her upright. Her brain clicked on again.

They helped Nick from the small boat on to the beach. He stood there swaying, gazing at Bingo and Craig like a rabbit blinded by a car's headlights. The civilian was shaking his head, holding his hands up in a 'back off' gesture. The two scientists looked puzzled: even more so when Ferdy crossed to grip Nick's shoulder in friendship, prompting an astonishing reaction.

Nick shrank away from the contact. 'No! No! I can't take any more of it. I *can't*. For God's sake just put me out of this misery.'

As startled as the rest, Ferdy said, 'Relax, Nick, we're going to take you home.'

'Lies, *lies*,' he yelled staring wildly. 'I know where we're going. I'll do anything you want. *Anything.* Just don't put me there again.' His voice rose hysterically. 'It won't hurt *him.* He's crazy. Doesn't remember you; what he wrote. Tormenting me won't punish him. He won't know about it; won't care.' He backed further. 'It isn't justice, it's sadism. I'll go mad if you put me there. I'll go out of my mind. I'll be like him. Is that what you want?'

The civilian beside Ferdy spoke in firm tones. 'We're your friends, Nick. You're safe with us.'

Nick rounded on him viciously. 'Nowhere's safe! Climb a wall away from a fire. Not safe! Run into the desert. *Not bloody safe!* Don't tell me you're my friends. Friends don't do what you're doing. I keep telling you, I never knew who they were. Told to pick up two people, that's all. Whatever you do to me, I can't give you names. I don't *know* any names.' His voice began to break, grow laboured. His head drooped; his body sagged. 'Christ's sake, it's the *truth.* Would I go through this agony if I knew? I'd bloody tell you *anything* to make you stop.'

Lara was immensely disturbed and shaken by what was happening here on this small, isolated island shore. A number of men and women were grouped uncertainly around someone who appeared to be hallucinating. She had never seen Nick this way. Whatever had happened on those boats this afternoon? He looked frighteningly unfamiliar, but he was surely not dying. More likely to be high on something. She had seen druggies on the streets of Sydney, stoned out of their minds. Nick was certainly not fully in his right now, and it was tearing at her old wound. She moved towards him, full of compassion.

'Nick, we all want to help you.'

His head jerked up. He stepped back, holding his hands up in a ward-off gesture. 'Keep away! You began it. You're the one,' he shouted accusingly. 'They're sitting there whispering. *Staring* at me. They're all laughing. What a fool! What an idiot! He thinks he's brave in that uniform with a sword, but he's really naked. He's not a man. Just look at him. He's *nothing.* No wonder she ran away.'

His shoulders drooped again. He looked down at himself, muttering, 'Naked . . . and filthy. Stinking. Terrified of the devils.' He sank suddenly to his knees and curled up with his arms over his head, wrists pressed tightly together.

There was a silence no one knew how to break. A ring of eyes stared down, appalled at the sturdy man in pale trousers and blue shirt, doubled over so abjectly. The same man who had flown a helicopter out here, then undertaken an emergency dive to rescue Gray Attard from Medusa.

Lara was shaking; her cheeks were wet. Whatever was ruling Nick had led him to return to that church in Cornwall on the day she would never forget. And now she knew the depths of humiliation he had suffered at her hands.

Through her tears she saw the man in the yellow shirt make a move forward to say in commanding manner, 'Captain Hawkwood, we're ready for take-off, sir.'

Nick uncurled and got to his feet with unexpected vigour. 'Then let's roll!' he said in a normal voice. He began walking beside the man who had seen how to break into his delusive state and persuade Nick on to the aircraft. Yet he was still under the impression that he was elsewhere, with other men.

Ferdy spoke over his shoulder to the grouped scientists. 'I'll radio in later, OK?' He glanced at Lara. 'You coming?'

She said through her tight throat, 'I'm not sure it's a good idea.'

'I am. Kim's the best person for him right now, but he'll need you later on. Take my word, girl.'

So she went. Just as she was and without a word of explanation to her team. She was unaware of the dinghy returning to the launch, or of her colleagues' expressions as they watched their redoubtable leader turn one hundred percent woman.

The Chinese co-pilot looked apprehensive when Nick insisted he must occupy that seat in the cockpit, but Ferdy settled the matter by saying the lad was under instruction. Nick seemed satisfied and settled on the rear seat. The other man sat beside him, then pulled Lara in.

His smile was strained. 'I'm Euan Goss, assistant to James Wellnut. You must be Dr Scott. I'll give the you full lowdown at a suitable time.'

Lara sat numbly throughout the brief journey, trying to make sense of what was happening while Nick instructed someone called Tim to test his guns, and talked crisply to another man named Andy about camels and a rocket launcher.

Euan murmured, 'Nick's apparently been given a shot of something. That's why he's acting this way.'

'No,' she said hollowly, 'it's his other world.'

Seventeen

James snatched up the mobile phone after just two rings. 'Wellnut!'

Euan said: 'Mission accomplished. How about you?'

'Both safe here at home. Cable started up shortly after you broke contact. How's Nick?'

'We've got him here at Ferdy's place.'

'Have you called McIntosh?'

'Kim's confident he was injected with no more than a mild sedative to reduce his resistance and make him woozy. Anything worse would have produced violent symptoms by now.'

James gave a sigh of relief. 'If Ferdy agrees, it might be as well for him to stay there until I sort out a flight home. I want Joyce and the kids to go with him, but I'm meeting with resistance. Things are likely to happen fast now. They could target any one of us. Vicky's here, by the way. I thought she was too vulnerable at your place alone. And I've sent one of our security guys to watch over Phil. When you've fixed for Nick to stay the night, get over here fast. I've already had a guarded conversation with Clive in KL. He'll leave on the early morning flight. We have to make a decision about what to do about Fielding, and Clive's the only one who can put any action into effect. Euan, we're in one hell of a fix.'

'Nick's in a worse one.'

James frowned. 'I thought you said he's OK.'

'Physically, yes.' A short hesitation. 'We were wrong on one count. Instead of heading round the island, the bastards shot out to sea on course for Gombak.'

323

'They intended to dump Nick *there*?'

'Seems likely. There was a refinement. When we forced them to divert to Pelingi, and boarded, we found Nick crammed into one of those baskets used to take pigs to market.'

'Dear God! D'you think they meant to leave him on Gombak like that?'

'We got him out, took him ashore where he began hallucinating. We thought it was due to the drug he'd been given, but Kim believes the experience has caused him to retrograde to those days in terrorist hands.' James heard Euan's deep sigh. 'He's in a world of his own. This has finally driven him over the edge.'

'Dear God!' he said again, deeply upset.

'Kim's going to attempt to bring him back from wherever he thinks he is. Now I know Vicky's with you, I'd like to stay here until there's some indication of how things are going.'

'Good man. Keep me posted, and pray he responds to Kim's professional help.'

Euan disconnected, leaving James staring at the small phone in his hand. A cavalcade of memories dashed through his mind. Joyce had spoken the truth to Fielding last night. Servicemen shared a bond civilians rarely understood. It had something to do with putting their lives in each other's hands. Maybe it was too late, but he owed Nick whatever was in his power to do.

'James, what is it?'

He only half-heard Joyce's concerned question as he crossed to the two Naval men, who had accepted James's offer of a sundowner.

'Are you both willing to take on another little job?'

Flip frowned. 'Problem with the rescue?'

'No, they pulled that off perfectly. As I'm loath to leave my family right now, would you be prepared to locate public telephones and make a couple of anonymous calls for me?'

The pair exchanged glances, then nodded.

'Thanks. I'll give you a list of names and companies you'll suggest Police and Customs check out. Tell them you have evidence they're involved in smuggling diamonds from Sierra Leone. Advise them to move quickly before the evidence can be destroyed, or the perpetrators leave the country.'

'Is this on the up and up?' asked Ryan, startled.

'Absolutely. I want the whole lot put behind bars, but the info can't come from the High Commission. Are you on for it?'

They got to their feet. 'Write the lists.'

James took up a pen. Cordova Line, Senoko Components, Yang Jewellery: Jonah Lee, Fleur Yang, John Vydecker. His pen hovered for a moment then, grim-faced, he added the name Cranford Fielding.

Nick remembered this house. And the woman standing in the lofty hallway. He had something to tell her. 'Your bloody merlion's a phoney. It doesn't protect anything. Or any*body*.'

'But *I* do,' she said quietly. 'Anyone who comes to my home is perfectly safe.'

'Nowhere's safe.'

'If that is so, you might just as well be here as anywhere else. I was about to have some tea. Will you join me?'

'Water. *Clean* water.' He craved it.

'George will bring you some,' she said.

He liked this woman. Had liked her the last time he had been here. She was small. And serene. That was why he liked her. She posed no threat.

'Come through to the verandah, Nick. You shall have your water, and I my tea, where it is cool.'

He followed her; saw again the carved chairs with red cushions. Remembered. 'There'll be a storm.'

'Quite probably. But it is calm and quiet afterwards. Violence of the elements is always followed by peace.'

'There's no such thing as peace.'

She sat. She even did that serenely. He walked about, wondering why he was there. She said nothing; gave him no verbal clue. Just sat quietly, unafraid. The manservant came with a tray. Put it on a low table, then offered him a tall glass. He drank the water greedily; in one draught. There was a jug on the tray. Ice cubes clinked against its sides. He refilled the glass; emptied it. Wonderful clean, pure water!

His heart was racing; his head ached. Yet she looked so calm. 'What you said about freedom. When I fly. Freedom from what? We know now, don't we!'

'What do we know, Nick?'

'There's no freedom anywhere. It's all written.'

She sipped the pale, clear tea; replaced the cup in the saucer. 'When things are written it is necessary for us to read what is written. Freedom comes from understanding what it means.'

'I know what it means,' he told her forcefully. 'I *know* what it bloody means.'

'Then perhaps you will tell me.'

He swung to confront her. 'You're clever. Work it out yourself.'

'But *I* do not know what it is that was written.'

Her voice was soft, unchallenging. Unlike theirs. A gentle voice. He stared out at the night. Beyond the trees lay the black unknown. They were out there waiting for him.

'They'd spotted the fire, of course. You can see for miles in the desert. Nothing to block the view. That's always the danger. Bloody shitty place to be stranded in. We're taught how to survive until the rescue flight gets to us.' He frowned, remembering. 'But they got there first.'

'Who got there first, Nick?' It was like a voice in a dream; light, disconnected.

'I never saw them. From first to last. Never! The guys said they took out three when they lifted me. I think there were more. Different voices. I knew them so well.' He clutched the verandah rail. 'I still hear them. In the darkness, I hear them.'

'How do you feel when that happens?'

'I send them packing. They always say *they* won. I won't listen.'

'Because they lie?'

He fought one last battle. And lost it. 'It's terrible to be blind. Living in constant darkness. You hear more clearly. You *smell* everything. They thought I didn't know they were there, but I could smell them.' He remembered hearing the bowl that wasn't there. He remembered finding it but not hearing it arrive. His sense of smell had misled him then. And he had been further injected with fear. They *could* come without his knowing.

'There's no day, no night. No rain, no sun,' he told the darkness beyond the trees. 'It's cold without clothes, without any cover. Trying to sleep on a stone floor. It's damp. That bloody water dripping, dripping. Never stops. Drives you crazy.' His heart leaped wildly. '*No!* Not that! I rattle my chains so I don't hear it. They didn't think of that. Chains being useful. It felt good to put one over on them.'

'And how did it feel when they did it to you?'

He had forgotten the woman drinking tea. Turned back to her. She knew. He believed she already knew. Soon, everyone would know.

'They did the usual, at first. What we're trained to expect. If they strip and blindfold you first, it makes it more stressful. You can't see what's coming. Can't prepare for it. After a while there's so much pain your brain numbs. Can't concentrate on what they're demanding. If you pass out, they chuck icy water over you.'

His body was now aching so badly he sank on to one of the carved chairs, gripped his hands tightly between his spread knees, tried to regulate his breathing.

'Did you meet their demands?'

He glanced up. Small, neat face. Black eyes full of liveliness and intelligence. Modest, long-sleeved tunic. Pretty. He liked pink on women. It was a soft colour.

'The electric shocks finally made them accept that I *couldn't* tell them. I sodding didn't *know*.'

'You were thankful when they accepted your ignorance?'

He frowned, finding an answer difficult. 'I wanted the torture to stop, but I thought they'd then finish me off. They stayed away so long I began to think they'd gone off and left me there to rot.'

'That was a worse thought than the prospect of being killed by them?'

He was back on his feet, breathing hard. 'I didn't want to die; swiftly or slowly drawn out! There's still so much to do. The Apache conversion. Real hellfire flying! Leading a squadron of my own! So much still to do.' He told the darkness his guilty thoughts. 'I'd watched Andy and Tim die in an instant. Gone at twentysomething. Endex! And I thanked God it was them, not me!' He exhaled painfully. 'Even during the worst of the agony, I wanted to survive.'

'And you have. You can do all those things that are still to do.'

The words floated to him through the listening silence, but he scarcely heard them. There was now an unstoppable surge rising within him, an undeniable impulse propelling him head-long into the chasm he had fought so hard not to enter. It had happened. It *had* happened. Useless any longer to refute it.

His cheeks grew wet. His shoulders began to heave. His breathing grew even more laboured to ease the pressure in his chest. He grew smaller, weaker. Insignificant. Worthless. He could no longer hide it.

'They eventually came back: told me I must bear my father's punishment. I must kneel, not sit. I must bow my head, never look up. There were noises. Loud noises. Whistling. Hissing. Sudden silences. Then I would hear them whispering about what should be done to mad creatures. They said Miles Hawkwood was mad. He had written lies and infamy. He had blasphemed. His son was also mad. The world should be rid of such creatures. How should it be done?'

He was somehow back in the chair, and she was listening,

her face calm, her hands resting in her lap. 'This made you very afraid?'

'It made me angry. I kept telling them it would be no punishment for him; he was past knowing what happened to his son. I said they were crazy to do this. They said I was the crazy one. I told them they'd never break my mind. They'd never win.'

'You fought them?'

'Oh, yes! I sang all the songs I knew. Recited nursery rhymes. I talked to my brother about the things we'd done as boys. I ran through pre-flight checks, emergency drills, combat strategy. I told myself the plots of books I'd read. I did everything I could,' he assured her earnestly. '*Everything.*'

She nodded her understanding. 'Yet it was not enough?'

He looked away; stared at the floor for long moments. 'They whispered that I was raving like a lunatic; talking to myself. They said I was filthy and disgusting, unable to live like a normal person. They should slit my throat to release the mad blood, or they should leave me in a dark place for the devils to possess.'

The abyss seemed almost welcoming now. The fight was over. He was exhausted. 'They laid me in what seemed to be a metal cage so narrow they had to push hard to force me in it. They closed the lid. It pressed against my nose. I couldn't move. Every part of my body was touching the metal. I could hardly breathe. They went away.'

'So you sang songs? Talked to your brother?'

'I was desperate; terrified. I've hated small spaces since I was a boy. It was worse than any fear I'd had before. I thought they'd left me there to die like that.'

A quiet moment. 'But you survived, Nick.'

He felt immeasurably weary, but had to descend to the depths now he had come this far. 'They then saw what they had to do. When they came for me, I didn't know how long I'd be in the cage. Once, they pushed me in, then pulled me straight out. Tormenting me! Next time, they left me until I was screaming to be released.'

'They then took you out?'

He nodded. 'But I knew there'd be a next time. Out of the darkness hands would seize me.' The pressure in his chest was now almost as great as when that cage had enclosed him. 'The horror stayed even when I was back in the cell. I knew they were winning. Knew I couldn't go in that thing again. I *would* go crazy; lose my mind. When they came I begged them not to put me there. I . . . I *grovelled*. Said I'd do anything they wanted.' He swallowed hard, forcing words through his tight throat. 'And I did.'

His heartbeat was thudding through his body; his head ached so badly he felt sick. But the avalanche was impossible to halt. 'I said I was Miles Hawkwood. Said I was evil and blasphemous. Rabid like the savage curs that roamed the streets. Said I should be put to death. Said a curse should be put on my sons and their progeny forevermore.' He could barely say the next words. 'I put a curse on my brother and his kids. I said it.'

After a while, from a long way off, came a gentle voice. 'Nick, a curse has no strength when made under duress. So you were not put in the cage again?'

'No need. They'd won.'

'You felt they *had* broken your mind?'

He shook his head slowly. 'Worse. They'd proved I was a coward.'

Silence, then more quiet words. 'But you had defied the pain and constant darkness. The lack of warm covering. The whistling and hissing. The constant kneeling. The chains. Most men could not have done that.'

'Most men aren't soldiers.' He studied the little Chinese woman through tired eyes. 'I'd been working with the SAS. Some of the toughest guys in the world. If they knew what I'd done they'd say I wasn't worth risking their lives to pull me out of that place.'

'You believe you were not worth saving?'

'I failed to complete my mission. I watched my brave crewmen die and burn. I allowed myself to be captured by the enemy. I cracked and played into their hands. Does that answer your question?'

She nodded. 'Very fully. But you condemn a soldier. Does it not occur to you that you withstood those things a soldier is trained to expect, until they realized you could not give them the information they wanted? What they did after that was not to a soldier, but to a man who must take the punishment his father merited. The rules were then different. Yet you still withstood all they did. Only when they discovered a fear that is quite unconnected with military bravery did you find courage impossible. There is no one person alive who does not have one fear that cannot be faced.' She gave a faint smile. 'Even those tough guys who rescued you will have a weakness they hide . . . until circumstance reveals it.'

They gazed at each other silently for some time. 'Nick, you must understand that you are two people. A soldier and a man. Each has an ethos. Do not burden one with the mistaken guilt of the other and say he was not worth saving. I know the man, and I say he was.'

'So do I.' Lara came from the dimness of the room on to the verandah and stood looking at him through red-rimmed eyes. 'I remember the time we were stuck in one of those capsule lifts. Only ten minutes, but you were starting to find it difficult. And those underwater caves, where the rock ceiling suddenly dropped to form a narrow passage through. You went, but the look on your face said it all.'

He remembered.

She sat heavily in one of the carved chairs, still holding his attention. 'If you want to know what cowardice really is, listen to this. A girl once loved a man and wanted to be his wife. But she also wanted to make a name for herself as a marine scientist. For twelve months she pestered the top man to give her a place in his team. No go. So her wedding was planned. A swanky affair. Friends and relatives flown over from Australia. Military uniforms; bridesmaids in crinolines – the whole shebang!

'The night before the wedding she gets a call offering her

the chance she's dreamed of. The chance of a lifetime! But the project is in New Zealand and it's a three-year contract. Immediate acceptance or someone else gets the job. What must she do? Mother is overexcited and emotional. Aunts and cousins are comparing wedding finery. Father and uncles are tanking up in the village pub. Bridesmaids are urging a hen night. Lover is indulging in the hair of the dog with his lusty pals.

'She wants him, but she also wants this fantastic opportunity. The obvious solution is to postpone the marriage, but the wedding snowball is rolling inexorably onward; unstoppable! So she must go through with it and tell her lover afterwards. Tell him that after their week's honeymoon in Barbados ends, and he goes to Kosovo for several months, she'll fly to New Zealand and see him three years later. Because she's already accepted the job.

'The following morning she lets the arrangements go ahead. Even gets as far as putting on the bridal gown and being photographed. Know what the bitch does then? She runs away when backs are turned because her father says, "Nick's a very lucky man. With a lovely wife like you, he'll be a general in no time."

'Two hours later she calms down and realizes what she's done. Even considers going back to put things right. Then knows things *can't* be put right. She knows she's going to New Zealand come what may. Knows it'll be better for her lover if she doesn't leave him after one week as his wife. But she hasn't the courage to face him and explain. In fact, she's so craven she lets three months pass before contacting the people she's hurt and humiliated. People she claimed to love, would you believe?

'She wasn't tortured, degraded, brutalized beyond endurance. She was being offered a choice between two wonderful things she wanted and hadn't the courage to make it with dignity. *That's* a true coward, Nick. *That's* the one who's not worth saving.'

Eighteen

The minor headline in the *Straits Times* was cagey.
PIRATE SYNDICATE MAY INVOLVE TOP NAMES.

Flip Driscoll and Ryan Meader had made a joint decision to extend their anonymous tip-offs to the Press. In line with James's directions they had suggested to the police a search of Senoko Components' Dispatch Department, and the vault at Yang Jewellery, in addition to an investigation into John Vydecker's involvement with Cordova Line.

Their calls to Customs recommended thorough checks on details of thefts from Cordova Line vessels, a search of their godowns, and the wisdom of alerting the captains of any ships already en route from Sierra Leone. When they mentioned the name of Muna's cousin they were told he was already under observation for another matter.

'Pull him in on this one,' Ryan had advised.

Nothing was said about Cranford Fielding apart from the giving of his name with others. Retribution had been enough for James. Let the fates decide the follow-up!

But there had been another leak to the *Straits Times*, this one for a rake-off. It prompted a major headline.

BRITISH ARMY OFFICER SNATCHED AT SENTOSA IN EXCHANGE FOR DIPLOMAT'S ABDUCTED DAUGHTER.

Somehow, news of the Naval launch and helicopter chase had reached the ears of a junior reporter, who wrote up the story with great panache. After receiving guarded confirmation from the Navy, the editor gave it three columns on the front page. It made exciting copy, particularly when linked

333

to the earlier reports of this same Englishman discovering first the bones of a drowned Chinese lawyer, followed by the astonishing rescue of a second mariner who had survived eight weeks on Pulau Gombak. Captain Nicholas Hawkwood was highly newsworthy.

He was aware of this once more when Ferdy drove to the Wellnuts' house. The car was mobbed by waiting newshounds. Cameras flashed blindingly, avid faces peered through the windows, questions were shouted against the closed car. The security guard cleared a way through, and Ferdy edged the vehicle in to roll to a halt at the door.

Nick's brain was teeming with questions. He had read the papers this morning and could not figure out how so much information had reached the *Straits Times*. He had telephoned James and been advised to join him as soon as he felt up to it. A lot had happened overnight.

James did not know the half of what had happened! After a bath in which he had metaphorically cleansed himself, Nick had crawled between cool, crisp sheets and slept immediately. During the early hours, he had semi-roused to find Lara asleep beside him with a tanned arm lying across his stomach, strands of hair soft against his chest. It had been immensely reassuring.

This morning it had been a different story. Her gorgeous naked body had been warm against his, there for the taking. And, saints be praised, he had taken her! No half measures, either. Even set against their past sessions, this had to rate as one of the best. Maybe because his taboo had been broken, but certainly because they knew so well how to please and excite each other. No tentative experimentation. Straight into full-blooded ravishment.

It was not only physical release that had brought Nick's new lightness of spirits. That hovering darkness had slipped away during the night; the demons had crept back defeated to their black chasm. The supercharged restlessness that had been ruling him had thankfully quietened to leave a sense of peace and confidence. He had rediscovered Nick Hawkwood.

Perhaps not exactly the same man he had known before, but this one would do very well.

In the bright, airy room leading to the Wellnuts' verandah, Nick halted sighing with pleasure. 'When I get home I'm going to buy myself a house with no glass in the windows.'

'You'll bloody freeze to death,' said James. 'Anyway, you'll be charging around, as usual, and never have time to live in the place.'

Nick offered his hand. 'Thanks for yesterday, Cracker.'

James shook it. 'The thanks are mutual.'

'*Very* mutual,' said Joyce softly. She kissed his cheek. 'That's from the whole family.'

The quiet moment was broken by a rushing figure who hurled herself against Nick and clung to him, sobbing. Joyce eyed an apology, taking gentle hold of Emma's shoulders.

'I promised you the chance to speak to Nick later, darling. He has a lot to discuss with James right now.'

A tear-streaked face gazed up at Nick. 'You were willing to sacrifice your life for me. If they'd killed you, I'd have killed myself.'

'Then I'm glad they didn't, and you didn't,' he murmured, finding this adolescent melodrama more than he could handle.

Pulling free of her mother, she reached up and kissed her super-hero on the mouth. 'Thank you, thank you, thank you.' In stepping away from him she caught sight of Lara. 'What's *she* doing here? You didn't save *her* life.'

Joyce hurried the girl away as Cora entered with coffee and biscuits for everyone. James sighed. 'It's like a bloody circus in this house sometimes. Were you as dramatic as Emma at her age, Lara?'

She gave him a frank look. 'Can't remember that far back. I seem to have aged rapidly over the past couple of weeks.'

'Haven't we all!'

Cora dispensed the coffee and left. James then brought them up to date, accepting Ferdy, Kim and Lara as fellow participants in the developing drama.

'The Gosses are on their way over. Euan's been with Frank

335

Chen since breakfast. It appears the four guys who took you yesterday, Nick, are talking their heads off blaming everyone so's to ease the pressure on themselves. Chief spokeman is Mikhail Zukov, a Singaporean of vague Russian ancestry. You've met him before.'

'The manager of the Silver Troika. He wore a vindictive smile as he pressed that stuff into my palm.' Nick recalled that quite clearly. It was what came after that he had no memory of.

'He's not smiling now. He's a frightened man. And frightened men name names. He claims he was told to grab you by Harold Cheng. Guess who that bastard works for.'

'I know. I hoodwinked him into giving me advice on investing an inheritance from my uncle. He obliged with a list of companies Vydecker either owns or holds majority shares in. They're all linked to this diamond cartel, you bet.'

James frowned. 'You didn't tell me about that.'

'It was around the time you suggested I drop the investigation and fly home.'

'Hmm, wasted advice, as usual! Mikhail Zukov appears to be a heavy used by both Cheng and Jonah Lee. He claims the Vydecker bank owns the Silver Troika and he'd lose his job, and a hell of a sight more, if he refused to do what they ordered. The other three with him yesterday were the normal crew of that boat. In their eagerness to clear themselves of any association with abduction and attempted murder, they're well into a description of their normal job. And that is to take masked men out to an RV near Gombak, stooge around while their passengers board a container ship, then take them and some boxes back to a point along the coast near Gedong. They don't understand why the masked men throw the contents of the boxes overboard sometimes, but they're well paid and it did not do to be too curious.'

'Christ, that applied to yesterday, did it?' demanded Ferdy harshly. 'They didn't want to be *too curious* about stuffing a helpless guy in a basket to dump him on a deserted island

336

to die very slowly. Just so long as they were paid well for the job.'

Nick's heartbeat accelerated as vague images arose, but he thrust them down. No time for that. He needed to hear all James had to tell.

'So are the police bringing in Cheng and Jonah Lee?'

James gave him a straight look. 'You won't be surprised to learn neither man can be traced, at the moment, But they've got George Chow.'

'*He's* not involved,' said Nick in disgust. 'I'm sure he had no idea what his partner was doing.'

'But he'll know Lee's haunts and contacts. They'll get him, and the rest, once they have evidence of piracy apart from what these characters who snatched you are saying. Men are blabbing, but until they find some solid proof it's all hearsay.'

Nick scowled. 'Men of professional standing like Cheng and Lee don't skedaddle overnight for no reason. What about the Yang woman?'

'Ah, you're going to enjoy this,' said James with a broad smile. 'Your co-conspirator took exception to being held incommunicado by a man he had cast as a prime villain. Last evening, when he was feeling a great deal better, he coaxed a nurse into lending him her mobile phone. He rang this number – it used to be his a few months ago – and asked to speak to you. I gave him the latest sitrep, and he damn near exploded. Got back to me an hour later. He'd been in contact with a chap he regularly played squash with and knew well. A police inspector. Outcome: Yang workshop was raided, some employees were rounded up, including the foreman. They're being questioned. Gems have been seized. There's a police presence at the showroom. They're waiting for a rep from the company that installed the safe to arrive and open it. Fleur's the only one who knows the combination.'

'And she can't be found,' supplied Nick heavily.

'Spot on!'

'Any news on Vydecker?'

'Phil's working on that. He made a lot of useful contacts when he was doing this job.'

'What's the betting on the Yank's sudden disappearance?'

'No takers.' James registered Nick's expression. 'This will take weeks, months to unravel. Even Phil acknowledges that. The most either of you could do was set the ball in motion, and you did.'

'But someone has helped it along the way. The person who leaked facts early enough yesterday evening to make the first editions of the *Straits Times*.'

James smiled. 'I finally came off the fence.'

'Nice to have you back.'

They heard a car arriving; muted Press commotion heralding it.

'That'll be Clive,' said James. 'I briefed him at the airport this morning. He went direct to Fielding's house to size up the situation; find out what the man had to say, if anything. The *Straits Times* have merely mentioned "top names" in their cautious column about the piracy, so Fielding could pretend ignorance. Yet he'd have to discuss Emma's abduction and terms of release with Clive. There's been no call from the Residency this morning, not even from Barbara, although I know they both read the morning papers during breakfast.'

Clive then entered, every inch the diplomat in a tailored cream suit and Old Etonian tie. He was unhappy at finding the room full of people. He frowned. 'James, I'd like a private word.'

'No need for that. My friends are fully aware of the situation; even participated in it. You can speak freely.'

Clive played safe and used official language. 'Cranford's health deteriorated following a severe dose of dengue. He took the late night flight home, on doctor's orders. Essential that he seeks a cooler, healthier climate soonest . . . or else! Barbara has begun packing ready to follow. As of now, I'm acting head of Mission.'

*   *   *

The young diplomat set on going onward and upward fast filled Fielding's shoes to overflowing. He deftly handled police enquiries and persistent newsmen. He also changed Nick's airline booking, upgrading it to first class in accordance with diplomatic status. This was because Robert McIntosh said both Nick and Philip would be fit to fly home by the end of the week and it made sense for the two men to travel together.

Nick was glad to be given two extra days in Singapore. He had finally confronted and defied his demons, with the support of Kim and Lara. The last barrier had gone leaving him free to move forward. He had telephoned Pete Higham; made an early appointment to discuss the future. Relaxed and revitalized, he was in no hurry to leave.

The *Straits Times* reported little more of the case over the next few days, but much news was relayed by Philip, who had friends in useful places. Muna's cousin added a piece to the jigsaw. He claimed he had been paid anonymously to sign up for voyages in specific ships on the Dili run. He had had instructions to ensure any crates bearing a merlion stamp were stacked at the top of a piled cargo, easy to reach when the vessel was boarded. Before going ashore and signing off he was always given a small padded envelope also bearing a merlion stamp, to take to the Golden Orchid and give to Muna for collection. These envelopes were invariably given to him by another crew member. He might know some of them again; could not swear to it. He had no idea what the envelopes held. He was paid well and it did not do to be too curious. He had not been approached recently. He missed that extra money. He knew nothing about his cousin's murder.

Nick, Philip and James agreed the envelopes had almost certainly contained stolen gems which, delivered in this manner, were unlikely to be traced. The Yang safe had contained a bag of unpolished diamonds for which there was no paperwork in the files. All the girls who worked in the showroom could offer was that men with briefcases sometimes talked privately with Miss Yang in the client room but, as far as they were aware, Miss Yang visited suppliers to select her stones. She knew precisely what she wanted for her famous pieces. She was a superb artist!

The superb artist still had not been traced. Neither had Jonah Lee and Harold Cheng. The Vydecker family were known to have been called urgently to the USA because Mrs Vydecker senior was thought to be dying.

'Heard that one before,' Philip said with some bitterness.

Euan was able to offer news from the nautical front. There was not much. The Cordova godowns contained nothing to further the piracy case, but the search had uncovered a stash of drugs and an investigation was underway to trace the source. It was an ill wind!

Frank Chen had taken his launch around to Gedong and discovered the jetty alongside a rough boathouse where the pirates had taken their plunder ashore. Police questioning of mariners plying those waters, and of residents in the area, had led to the identification of three men. They had fled overnight.

The authorities in Sierra Leone had been alerted: two Cordova ships had been detained in ports and searched. The captains of those vessels that had been robbed were being interrogated. Companies regularly supplied by Senoko Components were all under investigation. As James predicted, it would take months to unravel. Curiously, Nick discovered his urgency to resolve the affair lost a lot of its fire during the final five days of his leave.

Now the moment of departure was near. They all gathered for an early dinner hosted by Kim and Ferdy. It was a lively meal due, perhaps, to an air of relief; a sense of getting back to normality. Nick felt it strongly; knew an urge to motivate his future that had been in hiatus since Christmas.

When the others went inside after drinking coffee, Nick and Lara remained on the verandah where the smell of imminent rain was on the rising breeze.

'There'll be a storm,' he said. 'I apparently chose the wrong month to come here.'

'Come back during the right month.'

'Mmm, something for the future.'

She smiled. 'Yours promises to be so jampacked I doubt you'll fit it in.'

'How about yours?'

After a moment, she said quietly, 'I was hoping you might have some ideas on that.'

So here it was. Crunch time! He had known it must come. He leaned on the rail, staring out at the darkness that no longer seemed fearsome, and put into perspective the past five days they had spent in each other's company.

'My only ideas at the moment concern those things you say will jampack my next few years. I have to pass a medical board, take a flight refresher, get posted to a squadron, put in a minimum of six months flying with them, then apply for the Apache course. All that will just get me back to where I was before. Only then can I start considering my future.'

'That's the soldier talking. What about the man?'

He considered that. 'A soldier is pledged to obey orders. The man might shrink from what he is told to do, but the soldier prevails. *Must* prevail. Other lives are on the line.'

'Your other world.'

'My other world, yes.'

Into the brief silence she said, 'I'm still in love with you. I knew as soon as I saw you again here in this house a month ago.'

He turned back to her; thought her unbearably desirable in ice-blue silk with the breeze stirring tendrils of bright hair around her face. Time to go!

'What's happened out here – these last few days especially – it's all been larger than life. Don't be fooled into making impulsive decisions you'll regret when everything cools down. There are seas and oceans still to be explored. Go and explore them, Lara.'

She looked upset. Came closer. 'I thought you'd forgiven me. I thought we now had—'

'We have,' he intervened swiftly. 'If you feel the same in a year or so, get in touch.'

Her indrawn breath absorbed the blow, but she persevered. 'In a year or so I may be too late.'

'No,' he said with conviction. 'The only lady I'll be passionate about for a long time to come will have rotors and two powerful engines.'

The travellers took a taxi to the airport. The others stayed at the house to enjoy the rest of the evening. The leavetaking had its moments, but servicemen and their wives were familiar with frequent farewells. More often than not they would meet up again somewhere, and take up where they had left off. Their lives were like that. Goodbyes were rarely final.

Nineteen

Seven months later

The masked pirates who boarded Cordova vessels have been caught and charged, their evidence leading to the arrest of two packers in the dispatch department of Senoko Components.

George Chow, cleared of any charge, has a new co-director and has just won the coveted contract with Rees and Hardy. Lady Blanche Fielding has resigned from the board of directors.

Jonah Lee was apprehended in Thailand a month after he left Singapore.

Harold Cheng was arrested in Hong Kong at the home of a distant cousin who knew nothing of the smuggling of diamonds.

John Vydecker greased many palms, in addition to employing forceful blackmail on a number of leading businessmen and officials. Did they really want details of those private parties splashed over the pages of the *Straits Times*? Together with much hasty shredding this ensured the token investigation found no case against either Vydecker Banking or its president.

The Golden Orchid Club, along with several others of its kind, has been closed down during a purge of establishments offering male members drinks and entertainment.

The Yang Silk Company is now run by two nephews. Harold Yang will never recover from the shock of his daughter's involvement with stolen gems. His wife watches him sitting for hour after hour, just staring. She knows he

343

has taken the weight of her dishonour on his shoulders.

In Manila, a beautiful Franco-Chinese calling herself Peony is making a bid to conquer the fashion world with designer evening bags and shoes encrusted with semi-precious stones. Her wealthy American backer plans to introduce these to his exclusive boutiques in all major US cities. Peony is set to climb to the very top of the fashion tree. It was written.

Cranford Fielding lives quietly in his retirement home in a Berkshire village. His pension and golden handshake allow him and Barbara to have whatever they want. They would be content but for the ever-present fear that a rap at the door will one day bring an unwelcome caller. A retired government servant is no longer protected by diplomatic immunity, and Interpol keeps case files open for a long time.

Inquiries in Sierra Leone have been unproductive due to rampant corruption and the constant changes in positions of authority. The Cordova Line has been fined for carrying illegal diamonds, but cleared of known complicity. No one has yet been charged with smuggling the stones aboard. Investigations are ongoing.

The Wellnuts are making many friends and enjoying their settled life. James has taken to aerial joyriding with Ferdy. He now unhesitatingly shreds any mysterious notes or files he comes across!

Vicky Goss is four months pregnant and blissfully happy. Euan finally delivered the chocolates!

Philip Dunne's divorce is going ahead even though his wife's affair has ended. He is Station Commander of a joint forces Harrier base, and gives frequent lectures on personal survival. The money paid by a national newspaper for an exclusive on his eight weeks on the bedevilled island of Gombak he has spent on a half-share in a small executive jet.

The team on Pelingi failed to find an easy means of killing Medusa. Research is continuing in laboratories worldwide. Lara has left Attard's team and is working with a small Anglo-French group in the Seychelles. The serenity of these islands and the absence of Attard's drive to be the best have given her a breathing space to assess her priorities. To aid this she is going to England for Christmas. She has not mentioned this in her e-mails to Nick. It is to be a complete surprise.

Miles Hawkwood died a month ago. Both his sons were at his bedside. He had no idea who they were.

Nick passed his medical board and a flight refresher course. He is presently an instructor at the Army School of Aviation, teaching young men and women the intricacies of the Lynx helicopter. It is not what he hoped for, but he frequently reminds himself that, but for a rendezvous with a merlion, he could still be grounded and fighting demons. He has applied for selection to the Apache conversion course, but competition is fierce.

He has become a high-profile member of the Corps over events in Singapore. These were reinforced by Philip Dunne's series of articles in the *Daily Telegraph*. Both he and Nick appeared on BBC TV back in the summer. They are seen by their respective superiors as splendid advertisements for military excellence. All this appears to have put an end to media obsession with Miles Hawkwood's bleak history. Maybe the punishment inflicted in his name has freed the son from the burden of his father's culpability.

There is no woman in Nick's life right now, although two of his female student pilots are dropping heavy hints about the squadron Christmas party. He has not yet told them he is going on leave before the party. Philip Dunne has invited him to fly to Norway for a ten-day mountain trek defying the elements. It is the perfect answer to clearing from his mind the darkness of last Christmas.

Louise Sheridan's 'Daddy' is looking into the prospects of bringing diamonds out of Sierra Leone 'unofficially'. As he has always said, 'In business, if you don't deal with them someone else will.'